LONE ARROW'S PRIDE

Karen Kay

Lone Arrow's Pride

AVON BOOKS
An Imprint of HarperCollinsPublishers

AVON BOOKS
An Imprint of HarperCollins*Publishers*
10 East 53rd Street
New York, New York 10022-5299

Copyright © 2002 by Karen Kay Elstner-Bailey
Map courtesy of Trina C. Elstner
ISBN: 0-7394-2656-7

This book is dedicated with love to my sister,
Vicki Gene Isley.

And to her family:
her husband, Wayne Lenz
Kurt and Angie Isley
Melissa Isley
Greg Isley

Acknowledgments

Because one never writes a book alone,
I would like to thank
the following people who helped:

Jeff Rides-the-bear and his wife, Trivian.
Thank you for your assistance and for sharing
some of your thoughts and history with me.

Paul and Robert Bailey,
who catered to me,
listened to me, did all the chores
while I was under deadline,
and who allowed me to share in
their unique sense of humor.

Frank Benjamin,
my inspiration and friend of thirty-five years,
who, by the way, makes a practice of rescuing people,
including yours truly some thirty-five years ago.

And Karen Krebsbach and her daughter, Keesha.
Not only were you both inspirations,
always will we be friends.

LONE ARROW'S
PRIDE

THE BOZEMAN TRAIL

BOZEMAN
FORT ELLIS
FORT C.F.
VIRGINIA CITY
MO
MEDICI
FO
BIG HORN MTNS
WYOMING
IDAHO

F. SMITH

MONTANA
MEDICINE WHEEL
FORT PHIL KEARNEY

NORTH DAKOTA

FORT RENO

MISSOURI R.

BOZEMAN TRAIL

NEBRASKA   SOUTH DAKOTA

FORT McPHERSON

COLORADO

Prologue

Somewhere in the Bighorn Mountains
Autumn, 1866

The two men stumbled through the pine-covered forest, clutching their ill-gotten treasure in their arms. Something in these woods, something on this mountain had been watching them. That same something now chased them.

Only they could not see it. And the rain pounded at them.

Trembling in fear, half-running, half-turning back to see who or what followed, the two men staggered ever higher into the mountains. Rivulets of water, mud-colored from the filth which clung to their scalps, streamed down their faces, catching in their beards.

The men's clothes, wet and reeking of sweat, stuck to their bodies. Overhead, black, swollen clouds grumbled, as though they, too, threatened bodily injury.

"*Leave this place,*" whispered the wind.

The two men froze midstride; they straightened up, and wide-eyed, turned to stare at one another.

Although neither man adhered to a firm religious belief—nor was either one given to flights of fancy—there was something about this place . . .

The Indians told of gods who lived and roamed in these mountains.

"Let's cache this gold and get outa here," said the smaller man.

"Yep," replied the other fellow, a man whose beard was thick and black. "Have ya been keepin' the map ah told ya ta keep, Jordan?"

"You dinna tell me to keep 'un, Dixon."

"What are you? Some sort of idiot?" It was no question, and Dixon, the bigger of the two men fairly roared the words as he poked his companion with a hard jab to his ribs. "How're we supposed ta find this place again?"

Jordan cringed. Sidling away from Dixon, if only by a few feet, he said, "We could leave some sign, somethin' to mark where we've hid it. Like this." He bent down to push together a couple of sticks, forming a cross.

"You numbskull!" said Dixon. "Think!" He gestured to the ground in a crude fashion. "Don't ja know that them sticks'll be washed away by mornin'."

A streak of lightning bolted from the sky, hitting the ground so near the two men that the earth shook. Instantly, both men fell to the ground, landing in swollen puddles of mud and slime.

Said Jordan, the sandy-haired man, "Don't matter what ja think. We gotta stash this loot and get outa here, 'afore whatever it is that's out there gets closer."

"Hmmm," said Dixon, scratching his dirty beard and

lifting his gaze up toward the rock face of the cliff. "Well, would ja look at that!"

"What? Ah can't see nothin'."

"Up ahead of us." Dixon pointed. "D'ya see? Thar's a cliff. We can dig a hole in it 'n' cache the gold there. C'mon. Hurry," he added, although it took little incentive to persuade his companion to move quickly. Another flash of lightning had both vagrants crouching on hands and knees, scampering toward the cliff.

Peering over the cliff, Dixon laughed. "Look at these caves. This'll suit our needs real comfortable, like. We can stash the loot in one of these here caverns, then we'll cover the whole thing up with dirt, an' then you can mark the spot with some sort of carvin', right here in the rock. The same sort of carvin' that you're good at, d'ya hear?"

Jordan grinned. "That's a right good idea."

"O' course it is." Dixon slapped the back of the littler man, making the poor fellow stumble forward. "Now get yerself ta work."

As another streak of lightning blazed from the sky, Jordan propelled himself forward, and sliding down to a ledge below them, fell into one of the caves.

He worked quickly, on hands and knees, while Dixon, the darker, burlier man, stood guard.

"Hurry!"

"Ah'm hurryin'. Ah'm hurryin'."

Finished, Jordan stepped out onto the ledge.

"Here," Dixon handed down a knife to his companion. "Get yerself ta carvin'."

Quickly, spurred on by his fear of the mountain and the gods he was certain watched them, he did as he was asked and etched a carving into the face of the stone.

Finished, he stepped back, as though to admire his

handiwork, but at that same moment, another bolt of lightning hit the earth, causing the ground to tremble. And without another word, both men scrambled to their feet, neither of them wise enough to stop to get their bearings.

Or perhaps they both felt certain that, even if they did not remember the exact spot where the cave was hidden, the symbol <<<<>>>> would lead them to their treasure once more.

Oh, foolish, foolish men.

Chapter 1

The Bighorn Mountains
1866

Having been led to this spot by a strange sort of whirlwind, eleven-year-old Carolyn White huddled under the ledge of an overhanging rock. It was her only protection against the rain. Her long, brown hair, greasy and unkept, lay matted against her head; while huge, fear-stricken eyes looked out on the midnight scene before her. Nervously, she fingered the silver locket around her neck; this piece of jewelry, and the clothes she wore, her only worldly possessions.

She shivered, her thread-bare shawl no longer able to protect her from the elements. Luckily for her the center of the storm focused upon one mountain in particular, not her own. She watched the crashing of lightning in the distance, listened to the roar of the thunder, little aware that it was this, the heavenly spectacle, that was more than responsible for the atmosphere of terror and doom surrounding her.

And Carolyn *was* frightened. But if she were to be truthful, she would admit that fear was becoming her constant companion—ever since she had been left in the middle of this huge country, alone.

Alone, except for that curious whirlwind.

What was to happen to her now?

Although Carolyn felt instinctively that it was wrong to do so, she could not help wishing that she, too, had been taken by the illness that had stolen away her loved ones.

But such a thing was not to be. Disaster had come swiftly, in the form of a cholera epidemic, which had swept through her family's caravan. The disease had hit in force mere hours after their wagon train had departed Fort Phil Kearny, following a three nights' stay.

At first, Carolyn had thought nothing of the setback, not even when her parents had been too sick to continue on and her family's gig had been one of the few left behind the main caravan. After all, what had there been to fear? The wagon master had said he would keep to a slower pace so that when the sickened families had recovered, their part of the entourage might rejoin the rest.

But when her parents had become worse, the actuality of her situation had taken a firm grip over her. Their deaths marked the beginning of what was to become a daily reality.

In the end, only Carolyn had survived, for even the few remaining people, who had at first seemed immune to the disease, had perished. Even the oxen were gone.

Now, when Carolyn thought back to it, those days

had been lost in a mental haze. It all seemed unreal. All those people she had known, dead.

It had been a very long time—several days in fact—before Carolyn had been able to move away from the protection of the wagons. For no matter how horrible her loss, it had been there, surrounded by the remains of her parents' possessions, where she had felt close to something familiar. In the end, it had been hunger which had caused her to leave.

Uttering a final farewell to those she loved most, Carolyn had moved off, a single, solitary figure, alone upon the Bozeman trail.

Now she had only herself to care for, since her mother and father were gone. . . .

As she had trekked northward, the sun, heat and wind caused her to look with longing toward the mountains which sprang up in the west. But she knew she had to keep to the trail. Fort C.F. Smith lay ahead of her . . . if she could but get there.

Carolyn could no longer remember when the trail had become indistinct; forgotten, too, was the moment when she had realized she was lost.

But although Carolyn might be young, she was not incapable. Using the sun and mountains to get her bearings, Carolyn had followed a river which she thought might be the Tongue River.

And surely, if she were at the Tongue River, she knew Fort C.F. Smith could not be far away. And Carolyn, aware that trails often followed natural waterways, had kept to the river.

The fact that the path climbed higher and higher into the mountains hadn't concerned her, for Carolyn had realized that she would need to cross the mountains in order to get to the fort. However, perhaps she should have been more attentive; for too soon, she had realized that she was lost; totally, utterly.

As the trail markings evaded her, she had begun to roam through the mountains, using the sun as her only guide by day, the stars by night.

Not so gradually, hunger had become a daily way of life and Carolyn watched with resignation as her body grew thinner and thinner. Unable to hunt for food, she had found herself living on grasshoppers, and these, not even cooked.

Something growled, and Carolyn's eyes popped open. Had she not been so hungry, she might have laughed, for her fear was entirely misplaced. It had been her stomach making the sound, another reminder of her sorry fate.

She sighed. Had she been dreaming? Carolyn glanced around her, noting that grey streaks of light now dotted an otherwise midnight sky. She held out her hand to the air. When she pulled it back, and it came away dry, she knew she would have to move on.

Where was the whirlwind?

It was odd that Carolyn had begun to characterize the inanimate objects that she saw, giving them personality. Since becoming lost, she had even begun to talk to trees.

But the whirlwind was different; different because it had seemed to rescue her.

She had first come into contact with the thing a few days earlier. It had happened on a mountaintop, where such a view was spread that even an eleven-year-old could appreciate it. However, the place had also been a site of constant wind, and Carolyn, while trying to keep the gales from blowing her hair into her eyes, stumbled face forward over an unusual set of stones.

"Oooph!" The breath had been knocked out of her as she fell onto her hands.

Although not hurt, she had cried out, stunned momentarily by the sound of her own voice. And for an instant, she had wondered why she should even try; why bother going on?

Because she was no quitter, that's why, answered another sturdier, more rational thought.

Pulling a face, Carolyn had lifted herself up onto her elbows. It was then that she noticed them, the stones.

"I wonder who put these here?" Carolyn had asked herself, getting to her feet and gazing at the large and unusual circle. Why a circle, high atop a mountain plain? "Are there people here?" she asked herself. "And if there are people who live here, what kind of people are they?"

"Indians?"

The word had barely escaped her lips when fear shot through her. She had heard about the Indians who attacked pioneers along this trail. Hadn't the campfire tales abounded with these stories? Stories, detailing the brutal tortures, the maimings and worse?

Well, if there were Indians here, she had better leave this place quickly.

No sooner had she formed the idea than she came face-to-face with the whirlwind. It had seemed to appear out of nowhere. Not only that, it had come right up to her, stopping directly in front of her, and spinning, always spinning, as though it watched her.

"Well, hello," she had said to it at last. But what else did you say to a whirlwind?

"Fancy seeing you here," she had gone on to say, trying to speak to it as though such things were an everyday occurrence. She went further. Reaching out toward it, as though she might shake hands with it, she had said, "Well, I must move along. It's been awfully nice meeting you, master wind. But if you will excuse me." And she made to skirt around the thing.

But no matter in which direction she stepped, the wind had changed position, too.

As though it were alive.

The idea scared her, but only a little. It was not that she held no fear of it, it was only that she could see no harm in a slight bit of whirling wind that stood barely taller than she. Alas, if the truth were to be known, it was somewhat reassuring to find something else that seemed alive.

And so she said to it, "You don't happen to know the way to Fort C.F. Smith, do you?"

There was no answer.

"Pity," she said. "My parents and all the others from my wagon trail are gone. Only I remain alive, but for how much longer, I do not know. My only chance is to find Fort C.F. Smith as quickly as I can. Do you know the way?"

But when no immediate answer came from the wind, she made a move to step around it, half afraid that the thing would again block her path. But this time, it did not. Truth to tell, the spinning wind moved away from her, where it practically ran down a trail of rocks.

Pity, she thought. It would have been nice to have some company.

"Good-bye, master wind," she had called out to it. She had even waved at it before she had turned her back to it, ready to move off in the opposite direction.

But the thing had returned to her, once more blocking her path. Then it had moved away from her, returning to repeat the entire process a second time. And Carolyn could think of nothing else except that this little tuft of wind wanted her to follow it.

Why not? Perhaps it did know the way to Fort C.F. Smith.

That had been a few days ago. Since then, the wind had led her to this spot, beneath this cliff. And then it had disappeared.

Sniffling and pulling her flimsy shawl around her shoulders, Carolyn stared out into the darkness. Would the wind return?

Or perhaps a more important question was, could she afford the time to wait for it?

Unfortunately, thought Carolyn, she could not, if for no other reason than the simple fact that she was hungry.

Exhaling, she stepped out from her cover, and no sooner had she done so, than the little clump of wind appeared before her. *Thank goodness.*

While Carolyn paused to say a quick prayer, it hesitated also. But only for a moment before it moved away from her, tripping its way, once more, downhill.

Carolyn followed it, trying to keep pace with it, yet she needed it to go slowly enough that she could get her footing. But regardless of how carefully she tried to negotiate the path, she could not help but run; the ground was simply too steep. She only wished it weren't so hard to see, as well.

Alas, she had gone no more than a few hundred yards when she fell over something which lay directly in her path.

And though a mat of grass cushioned her fall, the coldness of the ground and the wetness which clung to every blade there seeped through her clothes to her delicate skin, the chill of the icy droplets cutting straight to her bones. Carolyn trembled, and her teeth chattered.

Regaining her balance and sitting up, she came face to face with the one sight she had hoped she would never have to confront.

Involuntarily, she screamed, for as she glanced up, she looked into the darkest set of eyes she had ever witnessed. *Indians!*

Instantly a naked, masculine arm came around her, and a hand clapped over her mouth as foreign lips uttered, *"Oo-chia!"*

Looking into her captor's eyes, panic washed over her. She darted a look all around her. Her friend, the whirling wind, had disappeared.

Meanwhile, a strange scent, perhaps of pure sage and some other herb, assailed her. Had the Indian been burning herbs? The scent was so strong that the sweet-smelling odor clung to the man's skin.

Wide-eyed, Carolyn gazed around her. And though it was too dark to see well, Carolyn could make out no other figures. Was the Indian alone?

"Sáape? Sapée?" came a deep voice.

Dear Lord, what was the Indian going to do to her?

"He-lin-sa-ap-de-lah." The strange words came at her in a baritone—although, oddly enough, a pleasant voice. *"Bia!"* This last word was spat at her, and there was no denying the frustration behind it.

Carolyn tried to move but could not do so. The man held her firmly.

"Ha-wat-kaa-te?"

Obviously this last had been a question, but Carolyn could not understand it. She shook her head, or at least she tried to. Under the man's grip, she could barely breathe, let alone move.

The man shifted, placing her body between his legs, and at the same time, while keeping his hand over her mouth, the man bent and reached for a stick, its tip having been lit by the tiny fire.

How come she hadn't smelled that fire?

Carolyn wiggled to get loose, but she could not do it. The Indian was too strong.

He brought the hot end of the stick toward her face, and Carolyn gasped, partly from fright, but mostly because, in the stick's dim light, she could see the Indian's face a little more clearly.

Why, this was no man; this was a boy, probably no more than five or six years older than she.

She struggled against him, but she did so in vain, earning herself a roughly spoken, *"Oo-chia!"* for her efforts.

The boy pressed the burning ember closer and closer to her until Carolyn panicked. She was certain he meant to burn her with it. After all, wasn't that what Indians did?

No! This would not be her fate. She had not survived all this way to be subjected to torture, or worse. By goodness, she would fight.

Mustering up every ounce of strength that she had, Carolyn bit the fingers clamped over her mouth, gaining a brief moment of freedom.

And in that instant, she screamed.

"Ho! A-luu-te Itt-áchkáat, or Lone Arrow uttered the expression mildly, as though he were in the habit of being bitten by strange females as a matter of course. But after his initial shock, he brought his palm back to cover his captive's mouth.

He would have to be more careful with the girl, at least until he could tell her in a language that she understood to be quiet.

What was she doing here, anyway, disturbing his dreams?

He gave her a more thorough glance, his curiosity at once caught. What was a white youngster doing in these mountains?

At first he had thought that she might be a part of his vision, but he had soon disabused himself of that notion. The figure that he held in his arms was real, not the product of a helper—an animal or a person who would be a warrior's protector all his life.

Plus, she was white.

"Oo-chia," he tried to tell her in his native tongue to stop her struggling, but she did not understand; she kept fighting him, and Lone Arrow sent a frustrated glance toward her.

For two long weeks, A-luu-te Itt-áchkáat had prepared for his vision. He had cleansed himself in a sweat lodge; he had bathed himself in herb-scented smoke and had gone without food and water for four days. All this he had done so that he might communicate with his Maker—via his dreams.

During these four days of fasting, Lone Arrow had walked naked through these mountains, seeking a helper, asking the animals to speak to him, to assist him in having a vision. Several times he had seen bears, wolves, even buffalo, but none had spoken to him. None had been his special helper.

But this night was different; this night, he had at last realized the culmination of his hopes, for the spirit of the mountains had come to him. Taking the form of a whirlwind, it had been speaking to him of the future, had been imparting its own special wisdom and knowledge to A-luu-te Itt-áchkáat . . . only to have the girl trip over him.

In the confusion, the little tuft of wind had fled. And Lone Arrow was no closer to discovering the fate of a planned raid than he had been before beginning his vision quest. Would the wind come again?

Aa-laah, perhaps.

Frustration, which could rightfully be directed at this girl, filled Lone Arrow's soul, and had he been a lesser being, he might have vented his anger on her. But such was not his way, nor the custom of his people.

First he needed to determine what the girl was doing here, so far from the white man's posts.

"*Dé sapée?* Who are you?" he asked.

He gazed down at her, observing that her eye color held much in common with the hue of a beaver pelt; a brown color, but a lighter brown than that of his own people. He also noted that there was no look of comprehension reflected there in the depths of her eyes. In truth, all he could see, all he could sense about her, was fear; not only in her facial features, but also in the way her body trembled.

Would she know the language of sign? he wondered— if he ever dared to release her in order to use it?

He groaned.

"*Híi-laa,* young lady," he began, "*xapiiwaak,* are you lost?"

But it was useless. Even if she were capable of understanding, the girl would not be still.

Should he let her go?

He examined her more closely. Her clothing was

torn, her cheeks hollow, her hair dirty, and her bones visible beneath her skin. Not only was this girl lost, he determined, she was starving.

But her plight was not his affair. After all, what was she to him? She had interrupted him during a most important time in his life. And if she wanted to leave, as she was struggling to do, why should he convince her to stay?

Staring into her eyes one more time, he released his hold over her.

He would let her decide. If she were dull-witted enough to flee from him, a possible provider of food, far be it for him to change the course of her life. He had enough problems of his own . . . thanks to her.

Chapter 2

The Indian dropped his arms from around her, and Carolyn took a moment to stare back at the boy. She could determine nothing from his dark eyes, however. The only thing she knew about him with certainty was that he was Indian, and that, alone, made him a savage, deadly enemy.

Like a javelin, this last thought found its mark.

Carolyn's stomach turned over, as though to strengthen her fear, and without further incident, she jumped to her feet and ran away from him; ran, with every ounce of her strength. Down the hill, past trees and bushes.

Thorns caught on the material of her skirt and tore it, along with her skin.

But she barely noticed.

Carolyn checked her pace when a pain in her side demanded it, but only to a fast walk. Still, she hurried onward, alternating her walk with a few running steps.

Down the mountain she fled, following a stream that rushed along her path. Crossing it, she hoped to throw the Indian off her trail, if he were following.

As she jumped up onto the shoreline of the creek, she threw a look over her shoulder, not thinking to slow her passage. She took a step forward, a few more, and without realizing what she was doing, she slammed into something solid and furry—and screamed.

A bear; a big, black and *angry* bear stared back at her.

Involuntarily, she let out another scream, took a few paces backward as quickly as she could, and turned to run. But it was useless. Even she knew it was so. Going back the way she had come meant climbing uphill. The animal would have the advantage.

The bear reared onto its hind legs and roared. Like one hypnotized, she watched as the animal, claws bared, approached.

In less time than it takes to consider her choices, Carolyn burst into action, falling onto hands and knees and scrambling back the way she had come, wondering all the while what the pain of being mauled to death would feel like. Flashes of untold horror, and the realization that she might be eaten alive, swam before her eyes. Once more she screamed.

Something grabbed her hand, pulled her up and tugged her forward along with it, skirting around the bear and forcing her downhill.

"*Xaálusshée,*" a voice shouted at her. The Indian boy! And it wasn't the words so much as his intention which communicated to her: *Run!*

He dragged her with him only a little way until she came to her senses and began to match his stride. It wasn't easy, and she stumbled more times than she cared to think about, but the boy did not slow down, nor did he desert her.

How long it took them to career down that mountain, she might never realize. It seemed to take forever and yet, it was over quickly.

Looking behind her, Carolyn realized that they had left the bear some distance behind, the animal hindered by the rough footing. But the creature kept stumbling toward them, nevertheless.

The boy must have looked behind him, too, for he paused a moment. And then, he was pulling her after him again, only this time, the way was uphill and not very easily done.

The bear shortened their lead.

Coming upon a tree, the boy hesitated for a fraction of a second, pulled her forward, and, turning toward her, pushed her up that tree, motioning to her to climb high. Carolyn did not hesitate to do as he asked.

Then the boy scrambled up the tree after her, prodding her even higher.

The bear was upon them at once, huge paws shaking the tree's trunk. Carolyn held on for dear life, for the branches swayed as though they, too, wished to lighten their load.

"We're going to fall!"

The boy sent her a heated glance. Did he understand her words? Perhaps he had, for he put an arm around her and drew her to him, as though to say, "No matter your fate, I will stay by you."

The bear roared and prowled around the tree, swiping the trunk with great claws. Bark shattered under the assault, and Carolyn wondered if the bear, which she now recognized as a black bear, might be able to cut the tree down with those claws.

But although the bear kept slicing bits out of the tree, the animal did not climb it. Instead, it shook the tree trunk several more times. And when that still produced no immediate result, the huge animal grabbed hold of the tree's lower branches, pulling them as close to the ground as it could. It caused the boy to shift, to let her go and to scramble up to the other side of the tree.

Clearly, they needed to get farther away.

Rocks and a high ledge stood as a backdrop against the tree, and the boy jumped up onto that ledge. The instant he did so, he paused and knelt, reaching down to grab her hand. In one gigantic pull, he raised her up onto the ledge as well.

But even that wasn't enough. The bear started climbing the rocks after them. Did the animal never give up?

Carolyn cast a quick glance down, noting the animal's progress, but when she gazed back, the boy was gone.

"Dih-chi-puah!" a low voice demanded. Carolyn gave her surroundings a quick scan, but she could not find him. Where had he gone?

"Dih-chi-puah!" again came the demand, and this time Carolyn gazed down to find a small hole in the ledge, big enough to fit one slender body—just. But she could see nothing in the hole, nothing but blackness.

She hesitated.

"Dih-chi-puah!" And this time Carolyn knew without asking what the boy wanted. She cast a look over her shoulder, marking that the bear was only a few hundred yards away. That convinced her, and closing her eyes, praying that this was no trick, Carolyn jumped down into that hole. Youthful, masculine arms encircled her at once.

For a moment she breathed in a sigh of relief, snuggling toward the contours of the boy's chest. And, the good Lord help her, Carolyn could not remember a time when she had ever felt anything more wonderful than the texture of another person's warm skin.

In the meantime, however, the bear pawed at the hole in the ledge, and a shower of rocks brought her back to the present. Without thinking, Carolyn threw herself against the boy, almost knocking him down. But if he minded, he did not show it. Grabbing her around the waist, the boy scooted back, away from the opening, pulling her down to her knees until they were both crouching. Then, touching her shoulder—for she could not see him, or anything else, for that matter—he gave her to understand that she was to crawl forward, following him.

Carolyn had never cared for tight places—and particularly enclosed spaces where she could not see. The cool moisture of the rocks closed in on her, adding to her anxiety. But despite the tightness in her stomach, she kept one hand touching the boy and followed him.

Ouch! A jagged edge from one of the rocks sliced the skin of her arm and she cried out, more in shock than in pain. The Indian lad hesitated, saying, "*Di-chi-láa-che,*" and it took no genius to know that he warned her that the way was dangerous.

Soon the small cavern widened. The boy paused, rising up into a sitting position. Carolyn followed his lead and sat back against her feet, her hand still touching her hero, for she could see nothing.

She heard a strange sound—like the striking of a match. It must have been a match, she decided—one obtained from white man's trade most likely—for there was suddenly light. The boy had lit a torch.

And, gazing around her, Carolyn gasped.

Where were they?

The cavern had opened up into a more expansive section of a cold, moist cave. Cool rocks met her feet and above her more rocks formed a low ceiling, making the cavity appear much like a room, probably about forty by sixty feet. Moreover, the cave was crammed full of treasure the likes of which Carolyn had never seen.

She gasped. There were golden artifacts everywhere, as though they were merely being stored here. Statues, crosses, emblems of all sorts glistened and sparkled under the torchlight.

"What is this place?" she asked in a whisper, the sound of her voice reverberating off the cave's walls, giving her words volume. But the boy did not answer.

She stood, her head coming up to a mere few feet from the ceiling. Glancing down, she bent to pick up one of the crosses, pressing her fingers against its smoothness and noting the quality of workmanship that had gone into making it, such a beautiful piece. Where had this come from?

"Who did this?" she asked, but again, though her words were clear, there was no answer, only the touch of the boy's hand against her own.

He shook his head at her. *"Baa-lee-táa,"* he said, but she did not understand—well, at least she had not until he took the golden piece out of her hand. Putting it back onto the cave's floor, he shook his head at her, a clear-cut sign for the negative. In addition, he frowned, as though to say this was bad.

Of course, she understood. She was to take nothing.

But why not? she wondered. "This treasure is not doing anything here," she argued, "and I could use it when I return to my people. Couldn't I have just a little of it?"

The Indian shook his head, saying, *"Aan-nu-ttuua, xa-wíia."*

She touched his arm. "I—I don't understand."

The lad turned toward her, a look of confusion on his face before he said, "Cu-urse," and pointed to the cross.

Curse?

"You mean this?" She picked up the cross once more, pointing to it.

A quick nod from him sealed her doubts. Or did it?

Did the lad even know what he was saying? Or was he only parroting words he had heard? It was obvious that he did not speak English—at least not very well.

Besides, she didn't believe in curses . . . well, not much, anyway. Perhaps he meant that only this one piece of the treasure was jinxed—it was awfully big.

Replacing the object on the floor, Carolyn started to wander about the room, her hand reaching out to touch the golden pieces. Her graze was so gentle, one would have thought she stroked a child.

But the boy would not let her alone, and taking her hand, he led her through to the other side of the cavity; through probably the most glowing, dazzling display of wealth that Carolyn had ever seen.

At last, gaining the other side of the cave, the boy indicated another small passageway that led out, perhaps to another part of the mountain. Without pausing, he gave her to understand that they were to enter it. But Carolyn was not ready to leave this place . . . yet.

She was given little choice in the matter, however. The boy pulled her along with him, forcing her to bend down so that together, they could crawl out, using the tunnel. He extinguished the torch, but before he did so, Carolyn grabbed a small, golden cross that lay glittering at her feet.

True, Carolyn was no thief. But the past few weeks had been the most grueling experience of her life. And there was so much treasure here. Who would miss a simple, little cross?

Besides, Carolyn was not so young that she did not realize what this golden piece could mean to her. With it, she could buy the things needed to get herself back to civilization, perhaps to the gold fields of Virginia City. Maybe she could even go on toward Oregon, as her family had intended to do.

It was this thought which lay like a heavy inducement upon her. And for a frightened child, whose very life might depend on having such a trinket, the urge to take it was overpowering.

She slid the piece into the length of her pocket only moments before the boy led her out of the cavern. She followed him steadily, even up the constant incline.

As they emerged out of the cave and into the light, Carolyn heard a cry, far off in the distance, the sound much like the wail of a child. It took several minutes for her eyes to adjust to the light, but at last, when she was able, she saw that she and the boy stood at an impossible angle above the bear; she noticed, too, that the bear was looking away from them, its gaze going to the side of the other mountain, back from where it had come.

Carolyn stared off at the spot which took the bear's attention, and there she espied two cubs. And despite herself, Carolyn could not help thinking how cute they appeared, both sitting on a rock, both pawing the air at nothing in particular.

Carolyn smiled, but lost her balance, shooting rocks down the side of the mountain. She would have fallen off the cliff, too, had the boy not grabbed at her and pulled her into his arms.

However, once she stood firmly on the ledge, Carolyn saw that the bear glanced up at them, a wild look directed toward them, and Carolyn was more than a little glad for the smooth edge of the mountain that lay between them and it. The bear stood on her hind legs, and, with her head pointed directly at the two of them, she roared, but she did not approach.

Instead, as though making a final decision, the black bear came down onto all fours, and turning around, easily traversed back to her cubs. Herding her young together, she ambled back up the mountain, her youngsters following.

Carolyn paused to catch her breath, then sighed. The Indian boy's arms were still encircling her, and Carolyn let her head fall onto the youth's chest. A sense of being safe and secure washed over her. It was an emotion she had not experienced . . . well, since the cholera epidemic had struck her family. And, truth be told, Carolyn was loathe to leave the comfort the boy offered.

But too soon, as though he had also become aware of their proximity, he drew his arms back and took a few steps away from her; his action clearly deliberate.

Regardless, Carolyn could not let him withdraw from her so easily. "Thank you," she said, and, as a smile began to curve her lips, she gazed up as brightly as she could at the boy.

Then she decided: before she lost her nerve, before she thought of reasons not to, she would show him her appreciation. Reaching up, she kissed her hero on the cheek, the boy's fragrant scent making her feel a little dizzy, causing her to want to move in closer to him.

In reaction to her, however, as though she had embarrassed him, the boy took one pace backward. Worse, he brought a hand up to swipe at his cheek.

His action checked her movements, but only for a moment. After all, this youth had saved her life.

Throwing caution to the wind, Carolyn stepped forward once again, this time encircling her arms around him. It was only then that she became aware, for the first time, that, except for a brief bit of cloth covering his privates, this youth was naked.

And this thought had no more than materialized when the two of them snapped apart, as though by some natural force. Nonetheless, Carolyn could not help observing—perhaps for the first time—that the boy's chest was wide, well-developed, and . . . he was handsome. His midnight black hair—so very, very long—fluttered in the slight breeze around his shoulders and waist, framing his silhouette as though he were made of shadow and light.

And despite herself, despite, too, his obvious reluctance to hold her close, Carolyn grew enchanted.

Gazing up into his dark eyes, she smiled at him. But again, the boy did not return the gesture. Instead, he spun away from her, as though she were a particular piece of bad luck. He trod off swiftly, up the steep incline of the mountain. But he had taken no more than a few steps when he turned around, motioned her to follow, and turned back to his task: blazing a trail up the mountain.

Hmmmm. Despite his lack of manners, despite what Carolyn felt certain was discourtesy, she would not leave it at that; she could not leave it at that. After all, this boy had saved her life.

Lost in thought, she followed him. How was she ever to repay this boy? she wondered. Absentmindedly, she fingered the chain around her neck, until all at once she stared down at what she was doing.

This was it. Her necklace. She would give him her necklace.

Removing the silver locket from around her neck, she ran after the boy, and, tapping him on the shoulder, she threw her arms around him.

She said, "This is for you," and taking a step back, held her locket out to him.

This time, the boy did not move away. He stared down at her, then at the locket. However, he made no attempt to take the thing from her.

It would have to be up to her.

Scooting forward one pace, she drew the necklace over his head, at the same time saying, "From now, until the day I cease to exist on this earth, we are friends."

Then, with as charming a smile as she could muster, she patted the jewelry into place on him, her small hand pausing for a brief moment on his chest.

He stepped back, out of her reach, and nodded at her, signaling with his right hand that their exchange was over. And Carolyn was happy to observe that, though he fingered the locket, looking down at it with a strange expression, he did not remove it.

Instead, he turned away from her and motioned her to follow.

This was Carolyn's first exchange with an American Indian, and she could not help feeling a little uncertain, for she could not ascertain if the boy was happy with her and her gift or not. But perhaps it little mattered.

With a light shrug, Carolyn did as he asked and moved forward to follow him, although as she did so, she tripped and almost fell off the ledge, causing the boy once more to act the part of a hero.

Chapter 3

Virginia City, Montana Territory
Eight and a half years later

"Why us?" As soon as chestnut-haired Carolyn White asked the question, it hung in the air, unanswered. But, as though unaware of the reaction her inquiry triggered, she went on to say, "Why is it that we're the ones having the bad luck? Why doesn't it happen to the rest of them? We all came here at the same time, as part of the same caravan. Most of our neighbors are doing all right. Why aren't we?"

"Now, now," said Margaret Simon as she reached out to pat her adoptive daughter's hand. "It's not our place to question the ways of the Lord. We must make do with what we have."

"Yes, I know," said Carolyn, "but I still can't help wondering why we're not getting rich off this land. It's what was promised us when we purchased this stake.

And heaven knows, we paid dearly for it."

"Now, now, not to worry," said her mother as she deposited a basket of wash onto the floor. Turning, she opened a closet door which held an ironing board, and grasping hold of the board, she pulled it down. As she did so, she commented, "We'll make do."

Carolyn heard the words and tried to feel mollified by her mother's attitude, but she could not help wondering if they would. Or was her mother being overly optimistic?

For eight and a half years, eight and a half long, hard years, Carolyn's new family had been doing their best to eke out a living on this land. Of course it hadn't helped when, only a few months after arriving in the mining fields of Virginia City, Carolyn's father—a man who had adopted her without question—had fallen from a ladder.

He had broken both hips, and injured his spine, which left him semi-crippled. With aid, he could walk, but he could not do heavy work.

In the end, it had been up to Carolyn and her mother to take on the majority of the work—work that her father would have done, had he been able. Early on, however, the two women had discovered that there were some physical exertions a woman could not do as well as a man. It was this realization that had forced them to hire help.

In order to obtain the finance needed, however, they had borrowed money against their stake. And now they could not pay either of their debts. In truth, their expenses were already six months overdue.

"How much time did the banker say we had before they would be forced to take our property away from us?" asked Carolyn.

"Three or four months," answered her mother. "Maybe we have till the end of the year, if we're lucky."

Carolyn sighed. "I wish you and Father would let me hire out for other work. I could take in laundry, too, like you do."

"It's enough that you help me."

"Is it? If I were to bring in my own business, we could make double the money."

"And who would do your other work in the mining fields? Who would handle your chores? Besides, a young girl like you shouldn't be wasting her time cleaning another woman's clothes."

"Hmmmm. I wouldn't have to drop any of my routine chores, Mother," said Carolyn. "I'd just have to work faster with a few longer hours. I could manage."

"No, Carolyn," said her mother, firmly. "We've been through this before. As it is, you work too hard and don't go out enough with people your own age. It was never my or your father's intention to deprive you of what should rightfully be yours. You should have a husband."

Carolyn sighed. "But you know that I don't want to get married. At least not now. There must be something else I could do to help you and Father." She paused. "Although I suppose I could always marry Nathan Thompson . . ."

"No!"

"He proposed to me."

"He didn't. When?"

"A few days ago."

Her mother snickered. "We're not that bad off yet. I wish that man would leave you alone. Why he's older than your father and uglier than a rotten bull."

Both women gazed at one another, as though disbelieving the words had been said. Disbelief, however, grew into laughter.

Carolyn was the first one to speak. "But—"

"No, Carolyn, be patient," her mother cut in, although she did so with a smile. "We'll find a way to keep our stake. You must learn to put your trust in the Lord."

Carolyn fell silent. She did put her trust in the Lord. She always did. Although, Carolyn thought, sometimes it didn't hurt to help the Lord . . . just a little.

"What's this?" Margaret's voice interrupted Carolyn's thoughts, causing her to look up toward the older lady. Her mother was straightening away from her task, and she was holding up a dress—one of Carolyn's.

Carolyn gasped. Where had that come from?

She narrowed her brow, as her mother stretched out her hand, displaying something she had taken from the pocket of Carolyn's dress: a small, grayish-white object. One Carolyn recognized only too well.

It was a stone arrowhead. One she kept hidden away, along with other valuables . . . as a reminder of another time, another place . . . a boy she had known.

Carolyn arose, crossing the room toward her mother. It should have taken her three easy steps. But in the process of moving, she knocked over two chairs that weren't even directly in her path.

Amazingly enough, neither woman made a comment, except for the grimace on her mother's face.

Carolyn said simply, "It's an arrowhead," before she stooped down to pick up the chairs.

"Yes, I can see that," replied her mother. "What I mean is, why haven't I ever seen this before?"

Why hadn't she? Because, Carolyn thought as she set the chairs back upright, she kept it hidden, that's why. Also because she tried to forget anything and everything connected with that period of her life. And because, if she were truthful, she would admit that the arrowhead, as well as one other object, reminded her that she had done something—something that, when she thought of it now, made her feel ashamed.

Her mother, examining the arrowhead, said, "It looks ancient."

"I think that it is," replied Carolyn. "I picked it up on the ground in the Bighorn Mountains when I was only eleven . . . before your caravan arrived at Fort C.F. Smith. These arrowheads are scattered all over those mountains. Do you remember me telling you that I'd been lost in those mountains and that an Indian boy led me to the fort? I found it then."

"Is it an arrowhead that he used?"

"No, I don't think so," said Carolyn. "I got the impression that some other group of people—little people or some other kind of people—used these long ago. He told me in signs—at least I think it's what he said—that his people only use arrowheads made from bone, although of course, now, with the coming of the white man, they use steel ones . . . or bullets."

Carolyn's mother handed the arrowhead to her, and Carolyn closed her fingers over it. She would have to put it away, back into her private stash of things, later, when no one was looking. There it would keep company with another, more valuable object—the one she never handled or looked at—the one she had taken without permission.

"In the mountains, eh?" muttered her mother under her breath. Then, "It's funny that, as long as you've been with us, we've never really talked about what happened to you there." The older woman waved her hand when Carolyn might have spoken, going on to say, "Oh, I know about the Indian boy who found you, and who led you to the outpost. And I know that he saved you from a bear. But that's all you've ever told us." She paused, and then, hesitantly, she asked, "Is there more?"

Carolyn stiffened. *Of course there was more.* But Carolyn had never been able to bring herself to voice aloud what had happened there. It had been a harsh time in her life; one of great loss, one of starvation, one also marked by the stirrings of an infatuation with that same boy who had saved her, though he had never reciprocated her feelings.

"I know you've not wanted to talk about it, Carolyn, and so I've waited for you to open up to me on the subject," said her mother. "But you never have. Don't you think it best if we talk about it?"

"Perhaps." Carolyn nodded, remaining otherwise silent.

A moment, perhaps two, dragged by. Resolutely, her mother sighed. "Ted Hawkins came around looking for you yesterday."

"Did he?"

"He did. Such a fine-looking young man he is, too. Now, there's a boy, who, if he proposed—"

"I couldn't accept, Mother."

"Why not?"

"Because," Carolyn straightened her shoulders, "if I married him, I'd have to leave our home. His parents have their own property, and they're struggling with it, too. And if I left you for any length of time, you and Father would not be able to manage for very long. No, if I were to marry, I'd have to choose someone else, someone who would be able—and willing—to pay off your debt to the bank."

"Carolyn!"

"Now, Mother, I know it sounds hard-hearted, but it's not as if I'm in love with anyone. In fact, I've been wondering lately if it might be better, after all, if I looked upon marriage as an investment rather than a matter of the heart."

"Heavens!" Carolyn's mother crossed herself. She said, "Carolyn, I don't know where you come up with these ideas. We definitely would make do if you were to leave us. Do not worry about us. Besides, maybe having an extra pair of hands might help us, too."

"Then I definitely could not marry Ted Hawkins, could I?" Carolyn grinned at her mother before raising her hand to hold the arrowhead up to the light.

"Now Carolyn, be reasonable."

"I am."

"No, you're not. Your father and I want only your happiness. Most women desire a husband and a family, as well as love. Most wouldn't be happy without each of these things."

"I'm perfectly happy, Mother."

"Are you?"

Carolyn shrugged. "I worry about our stake here a little."

"A little?"

Carolyn nodded. "Yes, a little."

"Tell me, Carolyn, I've often wondered. You didn't, by any chance, fall a little bit in love with that Indian boy—the one who saved you?"

Carolyn gasped, the intake of breath making a tiny hiss.

But her mother must not have heard it, for she went on to say, "Because if you did, I wouldn't blame you. It would only be natural."

Carolyn paused to collect her thoughts. After a short time, however, she shrugged her shoulders and said, "Maybe I fell a little in love with the Indian boy, but if I did, it was probably no more than infatuation. We were chased by a bear. I wouldn't be here today if it weren't for him."

"Yes, I know," her mother replied, "but it's odd. You've never told us anything else about what happened there, and I've always wondered about it."

How true, thought Carolyn. It was strange. Strange, that she had lived with these, her adoptive parents for these past eight years, yet never had she told them the truth . . . at least the truth about her adventure in the mountains. It wasn't as if she weren't devoted to her new parents; she was.

They had taken her in, had made her a part of their family when she'd had nothing. She loved them, was devoted to them, would do most anything for them. But there were some things a person did not say; some things too private to share, even with those you loved most.

Carolyn let out a sigh. Maybe she should have another thought about that last idea. Perhaps it would do her some good to open up on the subject.

Dropping the arrowhead into her pocket, she sat on the closest kitchen chair, which, unfortunately for her, appeared to have a cracked leg, for it fell over as soon as she sat down. As though this sort of thing were commonplace, Carolyn rose easily enough and plopped down in another, sturdier chair. She said, "It happened so long ago and, to be honest, I've tried to forget about it."

Carolyn did not look up to regard her mother, did not see the woman move closer to the kitchen table.

"Forget what?" asked her mother, sweeping the broken pieces of the chair into a corner, perhaps to remain there until it could be fixed. The elder of the two women took a seat across from Carolyn.

The caves, Carolyn thought, she wished she could forget about the caves. But she could not so much as utter a single word about them. She had promised *him* that she would never do so . . . not to anybody . . . ever. She said, "When I think of that time in the mountains, I remember it as a happy experience; at least it was happier than that which preceded it. Following the tragedy that took away my parents, and then all the others . . .

"I know it's wrong, so very, very wrong," Carolyn continued, "but after watching my friends pass away, one by one, I wanted to die, too."

Her mother gasped. "I'm *so* sorry, dear," the older woman took Carolyn's hand into her own. "But after all, it's only natural that you would feel that way. You shouldn't torture yourself about that."

"I try not to. In truth, I do my best not to think of that experience at all. And as for the boy, I have to admit that when he found me and saved me from that bear, it was as though I were being given a new life. And yes, maybe I was a tiny bit infatuated with him . . . but, as you say, who wouldn't have been? There's one thing I can tell you true, however."

"What's that, dear?"

"There was never a chance of me losing my heart to

him." Carolyn looked up to catch her mother's gaze. "The truth is, he could hardly stand me."

"Oh, Carolyn, I'm sure that's not true."

"Yes, *I'm* certain it is. I practically threw myself at him. But I might as well have been poison ivy, the way he acted. He couldn't wait to get me to Fort C.F. Smith. As soon as we came in sight of it, he slipped away—without even saying good-bye." Carolyn swallowed the rush of emotion that arose all too easily in her throat, making it difficult for her to finish speaking. At length, however, she said, "And I never saw him again."

Tiny flickerings of grief threatened to undo her composure, but she swore she would not give in to the feeling. She knew from experience that it would abate soon enough.

Darn. Why did these old hurts never go away? Wasn't time supposed to heal all wounds?

But if Margaret Simon noticed anything unusual about her daughter, she said nothing. Instead, she went on to observe, "It's just as well that you didn't ever see the boy again, Carolyn. After all, he's Indian and you're white, and never the two shall meet—"

"Hmmm . . ." interrupted Carolyn. She did not want to hear more. Though she realized that the people in these Montana territories harbored a good deal of prejudice, for the most part—and this included her parents—it was not something Carolyn wished to discuss. Chiefly because she disagreed.

To her it was all such silliness.

No, after her experience in the mountains—with her life hanging upon the goodwill of one Indian boy—she would never be able to think of the Indians with any degree of hostility. In truth, when she thought of the boy now, she experienced only a feeling of affinity . . . and a slight nagging sense of guilt. . . .

Reaching into her pocket, Carolyn took out the arrowhead and set it down on the table. As she did so, the table—its entire structure—collapsed beneath her fingertips. Both mother and daughter shot up from their chairs, each attempting a rescue. Carolyn had noticed the table's weak leg. Now she grabbed hold of it and quickly replaced it. She made a hand motion toward it, too, as if to say, "There's the cause of the problem."

Her mother nodded, and with the table back together and upright, both women reseated themselves. However, neither of them made mention of the incident.

Carolyn gazed back at the arrowhead, and an idea struck her at once. "Maybe I could sell this—it is, after all, very old," she said. "Maybe this could be a sort of means out of our financial dilemma." Carolyn leaned back in her chair. With her attention centered inward, she said, "Yes, I think that's it. I don't know why I didn't think of it long ago. I'm going to sell it."

"There are so many of them in the country, dear, that I don't think you need bother. I hardly think they are valuable." Carolyn's mother patted her hand again and stood. "But you do as you think best."

Carolyn smiled. "You don't mind if I slip into town today, do you?"

Margaret Simon smiled lovingly back at her daughter. "Go on. Maybe you can pick something up for me at the general store while you're there."

"I'd be happy to," agreed Carolyn, arising. However, she was not to exit so easily. Her foot caught in the hem of her skirt, causing her to trip as she came up onto her feet. It sent her off balance, and she fell into the table.

That the table fell again to the floor, this time with a crash loud enough to be heard into the next room, should have been cause for comment.

Not in this household.

Without so much as a single remark between them, both Carolyn and her mother lifted up the table, and Carolyn, settling her chair next to it, said, "Although perhaps I should stay. You could probably use a hand with the ironing, couldn't you? Here let me—"

"No!" Her mother almost shouted the word, while Carolyn's chair took another plunge toward the floor. "I'll be fine, child, just fine. Why don't you go change your clothes and hurry on into town if that's what you think is the best thing to do."

Carolyn nodded. "All right, Mother, I will," she said and, spinning around, walked to the door which separated the kitchen from the living room.

She opened the door, grimacing as the doorknob fell off into her hand. Turning back toward her mother, she said, "I'm sorry. Sometimes, I don't know my own strength. I'll fix it tomorrow."

"It's fine, child, it's fine. Just set it down on the floor, and I'll have one of the hired hands look at it."

"But, Mother, I could fix it if I—"

"Not to worry, Carolyn. It's no problem. You have your own things to attend to."

Carolyn smiled. "All right. I'll see you at supper-time, then."

"Yes," agreed her mother, and it wasn't until Carolyn had left the kitchen completely that Margaret Simon, casting a quick glance upward—as though to the heavens—was able to breathe deeply.

That she crossed herself as well, might not even bear repeating.

Chapter 4

Carolyn stepped a slippered foot down from the buckboard and, coming around to the front of her rig, threw her horse's reins over the stable's hitching post.

Drat! Pulling on her short, black gloves, she noticed that her hands were shaking. Sliding her palms down her sides, as though to straighten her dress, she took several deep breaths in an effort to calm herself. But, the good Lord help her, even that no longer gave her peace of mind.

She knew the reason for her nervousness, of course. Though necessity might dictate that she do this thing, it was a little like consorting with the enemy, wasn't it?

Briefly, she wondered if she might be required to confront one of the two First National Bank's presidents, Nate Stormy or Leonard Blacken. It would be a test of congeniality, if she were, for she neither admired nor respected either of the two gentlemen.

In truth, they irritated her. Though the two made great shows at boasting of their integrity and honesty, it was a well known fact that they had obtained their "fortunes" by cleverly cheating the government and the Indians out of treaty provisions.

Nevertheless, whether a result of bribery or outright fraud, both men had gained positions of power within the territory. As a matter of record, Leonard Blacken, calling himself a "prince," was often seen parading about town in a Concord coach, which was drawn by white horses, complete with a gold harness.

And she wondered, why did men such as these need her parents' small stake to line their coffers?

Carolyn had no ready answer for this, and deciding to stop dwelling on it, she resigned herself to the necessary action. If helping her parents meant enlisting the aid of these scoundrels, then this once, she would do it.

That was why Carolyn had donned her Sunday best for this occasion. A black, silk dress, which felt like heaven next to her skin, Carolyn's "best" was adorned with black beading on the polonaise and pleated flounces, which fell to the floor. A small, black silk bonnet and a black, paisley shawl completed the outfit.

Lifting her skirt, she turned and came face-to-face with the livery man.

"Will you be long, miss?" he asked as he approached, reaching out to take the leather reins from her.

"No," said Carolyn. "No more than an hour or so."

The man nodded and, unhitching the horse from the buggy, led the animal toward the stable. But he must not have been terribly observant, for he banged into the stable's entrance and slammed backward, landing on his rump.

"Are you all right?" Carolyn asked, hurrying over to him and, lending him a hand, helped him to his feet.

"I'm fine, miss. You go on about your duties."

"All right," she said, "if you're sure."

The young man nodded, and turning away, Carolyn glanced down the street, at the storefronts that bordered either side. The one with the words, "First National Bank," held her attention.

Without realizing it, she jutted her chin in the air, as though to give maximum effect to her five-foot, three-inch stature. True, her hands still shook and her knees still wobbled, but she assured herself that she could do this thing. She would simply walk into the bank, show the president her treasure, get her money—hopefully—and leave.

Carolyn reached into her pocket and touched the smooth emblem she carried. She traced the outline of the small, golden cross with her forefinger. As she fingered the object, she was amazed that it should feel so warm. Gold was usually cold, wasn't it?

She took the cross out of her pocket but found she could not hold on to it. She dropped it to the ground.

Ouch! What was wrong with the thing? It was burning up. She stuck her fingers in her mouth.

Bending down, she reached out tentatively and placed one finger on it. No, it was cool now.

How very, very odd. It had been as hot as an ember only a moment ago.

Picking up the cross once more, she glanced at it curiously. How could it have become so hot so quickly?

It was puzzling. And so engrossed was she in attempting to make sense of it, she barely noticed the man to her right, standing on a ladder. Nor did she see that he had lost his balance and had fallen headlong into a puddle of water.

She did hear the crash, however. With a quick glance over her shoulder, Carolyn registered the commotion but not the cause. Her mind was on other things.

With the cross held firmly in her palm, she stared dazedly at it. What was it about this thing? Just to look at it made her uncomfortable.

Maybe that was why she so rarely took it out of its hiding place—and why the last time she had uncovered it had been when Betsy Smith had come to stay overnight. Carolyn had intended to show it to Betsy but had not been able to do it.

No sooner had Carolyn removed the cross from its hiding place, than Betsy had tripped over a rug. The simple slip would have meant nothing except that the stumble had caused Betsy to fall into the fireplace. The next thing Carolyn knew, Betsy's dress had caught fire. And in less time than it takes to think about it, Betsy had howled and run around in circles, causing the fire to grow. Truth be told, it had taken Carolyn and her parents several heart-stopping minutes to bring the situation under control.

Betsy had been saved, but there was nothing Carolyn could do to avert Betsy's indignation—perhaps rightly so. Despite the fact that it had been the middle of the night, Betsy had left Carolyn's home at once, and Carolyn had never seen her again except, of course, in passing.

Indeed, Carolyn had never glanced at the cross again either. Until now, there had been no reason.

It couldn't be that the cross itself had anything to do with all these accidents, could it?

No, of course not.

And though a little voice inside her kept repeating the word "cursed," Carolyn ignored it. It was too fantastic to be real.

Glancing up and down the street, Carolyn stepped into the road. But despite the precaution, she was so lost in thought, she did not notice the buggy heading straight toward her. The driver of the rig, however, stood up to shout at her, except he did not manage to utter a word. His rig ran under a low sign, knocking the poor gentleman senseless.

It was interesting, Carolyn thought. Was there a pattern at work here? If so, what was it?

She thought back to another time; one other instance when she had decided to show the cross to someone— her father.

She had taken the object out of its hiding place, had sought him out, intending to tell him about it. In truth, she had been no more than a few feet from him when the ladder he had been climbing tipped off balance. The ladder fell, taking her father with it, and both ladder and man crashed to the earth.

Odd, how her family's ill luck had seemed to start right there. Carolyn fingered the ties of her bonnet, her concentration lost in the past. It was strange, she thought. So many accidents.

"Cu-ursed." The boy's word echoed once more in her mind.

Nonsense. Such things were nothing but silly superstitions.

Carolyn took a few more steps across the road and, glancing up, noticed that she was standing right outside The First National Bank. Tipping her head to read the sign, she sighed, resigning herself to the task at hand.

It will all be over in a few minutes, she told herself. Climbing the few steps that led into the bank, she concentrated on her pure, stouthearted purpose.

Carolyn reached out a gloved hand to open the door leading into the bank, and pulled. It would not open.

She tugged a little harder. Still, nothing happened. She pulled on it once more, again, then three more times. But it was useless. The door simply would not open.

"Excuse me." She stopped a man who was walking by her. "Would you be so kind as to open this door for me?" she asked. "I think it's stuck."

The man tipped his hat and stepped forward. "My pleasure, miss."

Turning the doorknob, he tugged—to no avail. He pulled a little harder—still nothing. Next, he strained, he twisted, then he lent himself leverage by putting a boot to the side of the building, and he pulled once again—hard. Carolyn, seeing this, thought to help him by stepping in back of him, and, taking a hold of his waist, yanked on him. One pull, another.

Of course, someone on the other side of the door opened it, and the door swung open—too easily. And given the amount of effort both she and the gentleman were putting into their venture, there was little wonder that the two of them fell backward, off the sidewalk, and into a pile of hay, which had luckily been tossed next to the hitching post.

The gentleman, God bless his soul, did his best to avoid landing on her. But it put him into an awkward position.

However, he righted himself quickly enough and was the first to rise to his feet; then he bent slightly to lend her a hand. Dusting himself off, he gave her a slight bow, tipped his hat to her, and said, as though nothing out of the ordinary had occurred, "Happy to be of service."

"Thank you," was all Carolyn could think to utter, giving herself a good dusting. She was polite enough, however, to give the man her most winning smile.

"Oh, please!" Carolyn called to the other gentleman, the one on the other side of the door, the one who had opened it only a few moments before. "Please don't close that door."

"As you say, miss," the unidentified man responded, and he held the entryway open.

However, a smart wind whipped up, and Carolyn, sensing that the door was about to slam closed, stepped quickly through the opening.

"Thank you," she said, and took the few necessary steps to bring her to a teller.

"I wish to see the president of the bank, please," she said.

"Certainly," replied the man behind the cage. "Might I tell him who is calling and what this is regarding?"

"Yes," said Carolyn. "My name is Carolyn White. My parents are the Simons, who own a stake on the west side of town. I am adopted," she added when the man looked confused. "If you please, sir, I wish to ask the man in charge to appraise a piece of jewelry that I have."

"Jewelry?" asked the teller.

"Yes," said Carolyn. "Gold."

"I see," said the small man, pulling a dark blue curtain over his cage. "One moment, please."

Carolyn inclined her head. "Thank you."

It took no more than a few minutes before she was ushered into a room near the back of the bank.

"Mister Waters, sir," said the teller. "This is the young lady I was telling you about. A Miss White."

The banker stood. "Yes. Yes. Hello, miss," the banker said. "Won't you have a seat?"

Charmed that she would not have to confront either Mr. Stormy or Mr. Blacken, Carolyn swept forward and offered the man her gloved hand. "Carolyn," she said, smiling and taking the proffered seat.

"Now," said the banker, "what can I do for you?"

Carolyn cleared her throat. Darn, she thought. Sunlight filtered in from a window directly behind the man, making it difficult for her to see the banker's face.

This was not agreeable to her, however, since she wanted to get a good look at this man, if only to assure herself that he was the sort of gentleman who would keep his word. But there was little she could do.

She could not very well ask the man to stand and endure her inspection. "Sir," she began, "I have come here for an appraisal of a particular piece of jewelry in my possession. It is rare and old and is made of solid gold, I believe."

"Ah," said the man. "And do you have the object with you?" he asked.

"Yes, indeed, I do," Carolyn replied, reaching into her pocket to take out the cross. Only she could not do it. Once more, the metal glowed too hot to touch. "A moment, please."

"Certainly."

Carolyn tried again to take hold of it. Drat, she could not put so much as a finger on the thing without it burning her. Ever resourceful, Carolyn took a hanky out of her purse and, using it like a potholder, pulled the object from her pocket. Proudly, she held it out to the banker.

As she did so, and as he caught sight of it, she heard the man draw in a breath, as well he should, she thought.

The cross sparkled from the light overhead. To her delight, Carolyn witnessed that the banker's eyes glowed—almost more than the cross itself.

This was good. Surely he would purchase it from her.

With hope rising ever higher within her, she watched as, greedily, the banker reached across his desk for the treasure. But alas, he never did grasp it. Without warning, as soon as the man's fingers made contact with the metal, a gale of wind whipped in from the window behind him.

Unfortunately, there was glass and an encasement holding both objects in place. Both flew wide, flying into the room, and before Carolyn could react, an edge of the encasement hit the banker in the head.

He slumped over in his chair.

"Mister Waters? Sir?" Shocked, Carolyn stood up and bent over the desk. "He's out cold," she said to herself, glancing up to stare at the window.

And there, out of the corner of her eye, she caught sight of it, a small tuft of wind, spinning furiously, making a path toward the open prairie.

A whirlwind? Here?

And that's when it happened. *Cursed* . . . The young Indian lad's word came back to haunt her.

So many accidents, so much damage. *You don't suppose* . . .

Holding the cross in her hand and staring down at it, Carolyn at last came face-to-face with a stark reality.

First, her father; then Betsy Smith, and now the

banker. The Indian boy had been right. The cross was cursed.

Not only that, she thought as, like a domino effect, piece after piece of the puzzle suddenly fit together. *She* was cursed; *her family* was cursed. Anyone or anything connected with the cross was cursed.

Why had she not realized it before?

She was the reason her family was having so much bad luck. . . .

Chapter 5

The wind howled around a corner of the mountains, creating miniature tornados. Tornados which, as soon as they set down upon the land, became bearded, grubby white men. These men carried upon them not weapons but instruments, which A-luu-te Ittáchkáat did not recognize. Were these the tools of farming . . . or of gold mining?

The sun caught his eye, almost blinding him. But only for a moment. Quickly it changed, turning into another substance . . . that of gold. Bright, shiny gold.

And the white men's eyes rolled in their heads, while his people, his proud Absarokee people, cowered in fear.

But wait. The wind was changing again, becoming once more a simple tuft of spinning wind. It sped closer and closer to him, growing bigger and bigger, until at last only it filled his vision.

And then came the words, "Dáauk, they must leave.

They bring harm . . . to me . . . to the people. You must protect . . . you must protect . . ."

And then it was gone.

No, there was more.

There before him was the white man's fort, Fort Ellis. He saw it as clearly as if he stood next to it. And there she was, stepping down from one of the white man's carriages, her brown hair protected by an odd-looking hat that almost hid the simple, yet luxurious color of her locks. And he recognized her. He would always recognize her.

She turned; she stared at him. She reached out to touch him, and . . .

The vision went blank.

A-luu-te Itt-áchkáat, or Lone Arrow, awoke with a start.

And while sweat poured down his face, he stared out into the glory of a pink-stained sunrise. The fresh fragrance of a newborn day teased at his nostrils, helping to bring him back into the present moment. He inhaled the pine- and wood-scented air slowly, savoring each breath that he took, letting the wind whisk the ends of his waist-length hair around his otherwise naked body.

Still caught up in the passion of the vision, he remained oblivious to the coolness of the air, though he savored its bracing caress upon his exposed skin.

She came.

He let out his breath as his eyes surveyed the land around him, his view taking in the gentle rise and fall of the terrain surrounding him. It was as though he needed to do this in order to reassure himself that the land he loved most still remained as he knew it, untouched.

Ah, and such wondrous land it was, he thought. It was here where he felt close to the spirits; here where he could commune with nature; here where his heart could reach out to touch the essence of He, who made these things.

Yes, the Maker had surely smiled down upon Lone Arrow's people, the Absarokee, that He would give them this beautiful country in which to live. In truth, so fine was it that with its rolling, grassy hills, its bountiful game, and its sharp-edged mountains, many of the other tribes were beginning to covet this same country for their own.

It was not too hard to understand. Pushed westward by the advancing whites, a large number of Indian tribes were already pressing their way into Absarokee country.

The Crow welcomed these people, for the Absarokee territory abounded in richness. All were welcome to come here and to hunt, so long as they returned to their own homes when finished.

But not always did the other tribes go home; not always did they have homes to go back to.

Still, things in this part of the country might have been peaceful if the other tribes had abided by Absarokee decree. It was simple: leave their people alone.

But perhaps it was too much to ask. Always, it seemed that Absarokee women or Absarokee horses were at risk.

However, the old ones predicted even more change, even greater challenges would come to pass. It was now being said that the Absarokee people, though they had laid claim to this land for thousands of years, were soon to be defending their country against an even greater foe, the white man.

But though this might all be true, none of it mattered at the moment to Lone Arrow.

After eight and a half long years of absence, the Maker had at last smiled upon Lone Arrow, giving him a vision. Even the spinning wind, Lone Arrow's protector, had returned to him.

It was good; so very, very good. Yet, the vision had clearly shown him that there were problems.

Was *she* one of them?

Why did the white girl stumble so often into his thoughts? And why had he seen her coming here again?

In the dream, she had been separate from the white men. It was this fact which was leading him to believe that she might not be the problem.

But what if he were wrong?

He grimaced, for the thought worried him. Worried him because the white girl was mixed up with him in spirit, entangled with him in some way that he did not fully comprehend. Somehow—and Lone Arrow did not like to think this way—but somehow, she made him feel whole, as though she completed him.

He snorted at the thought.

Yet he could not deny what he had dreamed or the signs which were telling him what the future held. For with this vision, the Spirit of the Mountains, he who made the rain to fall and the wind to blow, spoke to him . . . something that had not happened in eight and a half years . . . not since she had left.

Had he been granted the vision because she was returning?

Lone Arrow scowled. The mere thought of her made him feel as though he were pulled in two directions. A part of him—that portion which felt motivated to defend his people—did not want her here. She would most likely cause him annoyance or, at the least, inconvenience.

Yet—and this is what he did not understand—there was another element in his nature, a very masculine part of him, which rejoiced at her homecoming.

Alas, Lone Arrow was no fool. Though he had always found her to be an aggravating little thing, he had also discovered her to be . . . bewitching.

And try though he might to keep from reacting to this little bit of knowledge, it was this very thought that irritated him the most.

"Do you mean to tell me that Fort Phil Kearny and Fort C.F. Smith are no longer in existence?" Carolyn asked, wondering if her distress was evident in her voice.

"Yes, ma'am, I do," answered the soldier who was probably no more than a youngster of fifteen. He was also the only other person to share her coach.

"What happened to them?" she asked.

"Well, ma'am," the young man began, leaning forward, "it seems that them Sioux, Red Cloud and Crazy Horse, won their war, so to speak. The army abandoned them posts a few years back . . . had to."

Carolyn frowned. "Oh, I see," she uttered.

But did she?

She opened her mouth to ask another question, but an unusually deep rut in the road jostled her in her seat, and she threw her hands out to her sides to steady herself.

The moment passed, and as she sat back in her seat, she said, "Then there is no fort in the Bighorn Mountains anymore? What happened to the Carters, the family that ran that post? Do you know where they went?"

The young man shook his head. "The Carters? I

don't rightly know, ma'am. Can't say as I've heard of them, let alone where they went. All I know is that there ain't no fort there no more."

"Oh," said Carolyn, though she would have liked to have voiced a good deal more.

Tipping his head toward her, the young soldier asked, "Then I take it you've been here b'fore, ma'am?"

Carolyn nodded, but did not volunteer anymore information, nor would she; not ever. That time period in her life was not something she wished to talk about to family and friends, let alone share her thoughts with a stranger.

The young soldier, thank goodness, as though taking the hint, gazed out the window, leaving Carolyn to try to piece together her thoughts.

Well, this was another fine mess she was in. What was she to do now? And why hadn't she inquired about Fort C.F. Smith before beginning this journey?

Frankly, it hadn't occurred to her that the fort would no longer be in existence.

Would it have made a difference if she'd known?

Carolyn pouted. She knew it would not have mattered one little bit. She was here because she had to do what she had to do. Her life, her family's very future, depended upon her success here.

It was why she had spent every last penny she had to get this far away from Virginia City. But time seemed to be running out; that and money.

And she could not, under any circumstances, go back home without her purpose accomplished. Nothing would go right until she fulfilled her duty. Nothing at all. She knew that now.

Which left her with a problem. How was she to find

him? And in a timely manner? It seemed almost impossible, yet, she had to make it happen.

Clearing her throat, she asked, "So is Fort Ellis the only fort, then, between here and the Bighorn Mountains?"

" 'Fraid so, ma'am."

At that news, Carolyn sat farther back in her seat.

"We'll be there in a matter of minutes," volunteered the young man.

Carolyn raised a brow. "Will we?"

"Yes ma'am. If you look out your window there, you'll see Fort Ellis just ahead."

Carolyn looked, more out of courtesy than curiosity, and what she saw was pleasing enough, she supposed.

Up ahead, a fort, looking very much like a series of logs which had been spread out upon the prairie, loomed off to her left. And behind the fort, to the east, sat a range of snow-capped mountains, their peaks looking tall and forbidding.

"What mountain range is that?" she asked of the boy, pointing to their crests with a white-gloved hand.

"Them are the Crazy Mountains, ma'am," the youngster replied. "Heard tell that Indians go there to seek their visions."

"Hmmmm," she said. Then, almost absentmindedly, she uttered, "Thank you," before turning away.

Darn! She pressed her face against the hard wood of the coach until a bump had her leaning away. How was she ever going to get over those mountains? Or perhaps more importantly, how was she going to find *him* without traversing those peaks?

Carolyn groaned. Even if she did manage to locate him here at Fort Ellis, would it do her any good? She had little idea of how to gain his cooperation.

Yes, she had a plan. Yes, she had gone over and over what she would do, if she were forced into it. But somehow it had all seemed so much simpler when, as she'd first hatched the idea, she had been safely nestled within her home in Virginia City.

Yet, she was resolved not to fail. After all, she was not here for herself.

Drawing in a deep breath, she gave the mountains one more quick scan, ignoring the sinking sensation in her heart. Somehow the task, which had not initially seemed so great, now loomed before her, and she began to doubt her ability to accomplish what she must.

How could she ever do it?

Because he would come to her.

Glancing once again toward the young man who sat opposite her, she asked, "Do the soldiers at Fort Ellis ever go into the Bighorn Mountains?"

"Yes, ma'am, though not very often," replied the soldier.

"I see," she said. Then, as though with inspiration, "Do you know if there is any plan afoot to go there soon?"

The young man shook his head. "I wouldn't know, miss. You could speak to the captain, though, as soon as you're settled in. He would know."

Carolyn nodded. "Thank you. I think that I will."

Of course she would speak to the captain. At the earliest possible moment, too.

Her mission was simple, if desperate. Find the cave, return the cross, go home.

Return the cross.

That, in essence, was the purpose of this trip. She must return that cross to that cave, and she must do it soon—for herself, for her family and their prosperity. Hadn't she dreamed as much?

She saw the cave again, moved through it, once more witnessing the glistening of the golden objects.

And always he was there beside her.

Together, they held the cross. Together, they set the cross back to its rightful place. Together, they embraced.

And all was right with her world. Her family's property had reverted back into their own control. Her mother smiled at her. Even her father walked again.

But most importantly, she and her love had embraced . . .

Carolyn sighed. It had been the dream which had led her back here; that, plus the knowledge that until she returned what she had irresponsibly taken, nothing would be right.

Of course, she hadn't believed the message in her dream. Not at first.

There were, after all, other ways of ridding herself of the object, the simplest of which was to throw the thing away. But it had not been as easy as it might seem.

Thinking back on it, it appeared as if the item had been granted a life of its own. Whenever she would reach for it, intent on getting rid of it, the cross would somehow elude her.

And the one time she had managed to throw it away, she had felt compelled to return to the place and retrieve it. It was as though she were connected to the object in a manner she did not understand. It was either that or, like a bad omen, her sense of guilt would not allow her to let it go.

Still, it all added up to one thing: she must get herself back to that mountain and to that cave.

However, she had little time in which to accomplish this task. In six short months, the bank would begin its threat to foreclose on her parents' property.

And though to another this might not seem the end of the world, to Carolyn it was like the kiss of death. Without that property, her mother and father would have nothing. Nothing for all their hard work and devotion. Nothing, for all the kindness that they had shown her.

No, her mission was clear. She must work quickly, steadily and, she must find *him*. For he was her only link to those caves.

"Ma'am?"

Carolyn glanced up to discover that her young traveling companion no longer sat in front of her. The door of their coach stood open, and he hovered in the opening there, his hand outstretched toward her.

"We're here," the lad said, unnecessarily. "Welcome to Fort Ellis, ma'am."

Carolyn smiled at him, and bending, she accepted that hand. With some trepidation, she alighted from the coach, one slim foot at a time. A feeling of déjà vu stole over her as she felt the sun beat down upon the top of her head. It reminded her of another time she had been in this same vicinity. Another time. Another place.

She had come home.

Home? Where had that thought come from?

Shaking her head, Carolyn stole a glance forward, espying the Crazy Mountains jutting up behind the fort. She would have to cross those mountains—and soon.

Still, it was not something she had to do today. Today, she would start her search for *him*. Today, she would speak to the captain about taking that trip into the Bighorn Mountains. Today, she would begin plans for what she must.

Grinning up at the young soldier in front of her, she said a quick "Thank you" and felt in her pocket to touch for the cross which she kept, of late, never out of reach.

Running her fingers over the smooth texture of its handiwork, she stiffened her resolve, making a promise to herself. She would find her Indian friend . . . somehow . . . and in a timely manner, too. And she would return this cross if it were the last thing she did.

Turning away from the spectacular sight of the Crazy Mountains, Carolyn took a step forward and tripping, fell over her trunk.

"Do you know where I could reach the one I seek, A-luu-te Itt-áchkáat?" Carolyn asked the young, pretty Indian woman, whose name she had come to learn was Pretty Moon.

"Him . . . not . . . here." Many hand motions accompanied the Indian maid's attempt at English.

Carolyn glanced at the sky, then fretted. It was getting on toward evening, and there was yet no sign of *him*. Having marched here on her own, she was reluctant to leave so soon and return to the fort. Still she could not afford to be caught here in the Indian encampment after dark. She had one further question to ask, and with words as well as the hand signs, which she had studied with care these past eight and a half years, she began, "Do you know of any way to get a message to him?"

The maid made a negative sign, saying again, "Him . . . not . . . here."

"I know that," Carolyn voiced aloud, not signing the

meaning of the words. Absentmindedly Carolyn fingered the silver locket around her neck, the gesture comforting. It was, after all, her one prize possession, for the necklace had been given to Carolyn by her birth mother, shortly before her death. It was also the same locket that Carolyn had once presented to *him,* although he had given it back to her once he had led her to the safety of Fort C.F. Smith, some eight and a half years ago.

Carolyn watched as Pretty Moon's gaze fixed onto the locket. Goodness, but that stare practically oozed envy. Did she like it?

Carolyn held the locket out toward the other woman, saying, with words and with signs, "Would you like to see this?"

The Indian maid nodded.

Carolyn beckoned her forward, and at the same time pressed a small button on it. The locket fell open at once, revealing a small likeness of a man and woman. Carolyn said, "It is a picture of my mother and father."

Pretty Moon clasped her hand over her mouth, obviously stunned by such a magnificent sight, one she had evidently never seen before. And with big eyes, the maid gazed up at Carolyn.

"White . . . woman . . . trade?"

Carolyn shook her head, and closed the locket's clasp. "No, I couldn't"—she added signs to her words—"It is the only treasure that I possess. Although once I offered it to . . ." Her voice fell off, but if the other woman noticed, she did not comment on it.

Instead Pretty Moon nodded at Carolyn and smiled. "It pretty. If . . . white woman . . . trade"—she held up a beautifully tanned skin—"Have many . . . things . . . you like . . . trade?"

"You most certainly do have many beautiful things, but, no," said Carolyn, as she glanced around her, noticing distinctly that none of the other Indians were inclined to talk to her. But then, it was not something she should take personally. Why should they be anxious to communicate? Especially at this hour.

This was the time of day when families would be serving the evening meal, although, Carolyn admitted, Pretty Moon did not seem to be in any hurry to leave. Carolyn said again, with words and with signs, "It is getting late. I will come here tomorrow. Perhaps there is something else I could give you if you could get a message to the man that I seek."

The young Indian woman made a negative motion with her head, and Carolyn gave up trying, at least for the time being.

"I will see you tomorrow," Carolyn reiterated, and with a smile and a quick sign indicating their talk was done, Carolyn turned to trod back toward the fort.

So little time, she thought; so much to accomplish. She had to find him.

Chapter 6

Darkness had fallen, and Carolyn decided that there was at least one delightful thing about being stuck in the wilderness, the only white female within a hundred-mile radius. And that was the joy of being able to bathe. At home, baths were rarely possible, unless one counted the swims in the creeks and streams. Real baths, with hot water and soap, were simply too much work.

But here at the Fort, Carolyn had been given no problem. More than seven young men had volunteered to do the back-breaking task of hauling water from fire-place to tub. However, the work had fallen to only five of the volunteers since two of the men had tripped over themselves and spilled scalding, hot water upon their persons. Alas, they had ended up in the infirmary.

Settling herself into the sudsy water, Carolyn frowned at the memory. Had her own bad luck caused the accident? And if so, would her mere presence some-where cause more?

She fretted. Time was, indeed, of the essence.

Where was he?

A-luu-te Itt-áchkáat. This was what he had called himself and it was only since arriving here that she had learned that those words meant Lone Arrow in the Crow language.

So, she thought, he was Crow Indian.

She had always wondered. Not knowing the tribes very well, he could have been anything, from Sioux to Blackfeet to Cheyenne or even Arapaho.

Nonetheless, even this bit of information, once gleaned, hadn't accomplished much. She still had not found him.

In the short time that she had been here, she had approached as many Indians as she could find, most of them Crow. Using the language of sign, she had asked about him, repeating his name; did anyone know him?

But the Indian men would not speak to her, and it had taken her many such tries with several of the Crow women to find one who was willing to talk to her.

So far only Pretty Moon had responded to her inquiry; most seemed afraid to approach her. And Pretty Moon had been helpful. For one thing, the Indian woman was one of few Crow women who spoke some English, even if it was a very crude form of it. Also, Pretty Moon had been willing to talk, woman to woman, about a few other things. Carolyn had learned much.

For instance, Lone Arrow was a Mountain Crow. And there were two divisions of the tribe: the Mountain Crow and the River Crow.

She had also discovered that Lone Arrow's clan was

one of the most revered clans within the tribe, but the reason for this Carolyn had not been able to determine, though she had asked.

Still, despite all this, she did not know that which was most important. Had she had been successful in soliciting someone to carry a message to him? Truth be told, Carolyn feared that, though she had spent several days inquiring about him, she had no more to show for her efforts than when she had first arrived.

In truth, so desperate was she becoming that Carolyn had toyed with the idea of entrusting one of the soldiers or traders with her secret. But she had thrown the idea aside almost at once.

For one thing she had given an oath to Lone Arrow to never breathe a word about that cave to anyone. Also, she feared that if she were to share that information with the wrong person, not only the treasure but perhaps her life could be at risk.

Gold could make men do terrible things.

Besides, she thought, it would be useless to solicit the help of a white man. Not only were there no expeditions planned for the Bighorn Mountains, it was doubtful if any of these soldiers would know the terrain well enough to lead her to the one particular peak she needed to reach, let alone find the cave.

Truthfully, the situation left her with only one option. She must find Lone Arrow . . . now.

Tomorrow, she thought, trying to calm herself. Tomorrow, she would rise early, would again go into the Crow village where she would try to question even more Indians.

There was nothing more she could do tonight. She might as well relax. So thinking, she sighed, and sank deeper into the warm, scented water of her bath. And even the reminder that she had best finish her toiletry quickly, so that she could get herself off to bed, did not detract from its pleasure.

Lazily, she raised an arm out of the bubbly water, following the motion with a soapy cloth.

The whisper of a slight wind met the coolness of her arm, creating goose bumps on it. Darn, she should have shut that window. Perhaps she should go do it now.

No, she rejected the idea immediately. She was not yet ready to leave the fragrant warmth of her bath. She would close the window when she was done.

With a low moan of delight, she lowered her arm and scooted down a little deeper into the perfumed water, if only to enjoy its delight a little longer.

Ah, heavenly. She closed her eyes.

A finger touched her cheek, stroked her delicate skin. She smiled. The silken graze was like a caress, and unknowingly, she leaned in closer to that massage. She was dreaming . . . had to be dreaming.

"The white woman has been asking for me?" The words had been whispered in a masculine voice, close to her ear.

She recognized that voice.

Carolyn's lashes flew up. She jerked her head to her right, in the direction of the utterance, letting out a gasp as her gaze met the deep, dark depths of midnight-colored eyes.

"Lone Arrow?" she uttered.

A quick, unsmiling nod was her answer, as the man came up onto his feet and, spinning away from her, trod toward the far side of the room.

Pleasure radiated through her, and her gaze followed him. Well, well, what do you know? Success. He was here, his presence seeming to scream at her that it had been much too long since she had last seen him.

She sighed, while her gaze scrutinized every small detail about him. She had forgotten, she realized; forgotten how exotic he was, forgotten how handsome was his countenance; forgotten how quickly her heart beat, simply at his mere proximity.

Truly, she could not help but stare. At this moment he looked larger than life, standing there with his back to her, his figure encompassed within the folds of a red, green and yellow trade blanket.

Her gaze followed him as he crossed the room, and then spun around toward her. His glance caught hold of hers, locked with hers.

She found herself barely able to meet his stare as she took in the changes that had come over him in these past years. His cheekbones were high, as she had remembered; although his nose was a little more aquiline than it had been when he was younger.

Lone Arrow had grown into a very handsome man.

His hair was still long, the ends of it now falling well past where his waist would be, there beneath that blanket. And under the room's candlelight, the mane of his hair gleamed brightly with the sheen of pure health. Funny, but she had forgotten how his skin looked, too—as though he wore a permanent tan—and how full were his lips, which were currently pulled down in a frown. Pulling her gaze up to meet his, she found him staring intently back at her.

She gulped. He looked formidable—foreign— standing before her. The shell earrings he wore, which hung from both of his earlobes, and the eagle feather, which dangled from a front lock of his hair, did much to heighten the unfamiliar image, she realized. In truth, he looked more intimidating at this moment than her memory recalled him being, and for a moment she felt ill at ease.

But, she reminded herself, these things did not matter. He was here. *Dear Lord, thank you,* she prayed.

However, he had certainly chosen the wrong moment in which to find her. Instinctively, Carolyn glanced down at the water and the suds still left in her bath. Were the bubbles enough to cover her body's most private places? She groaned as she brought her arms up to cover her bosom. Not quite enough, she answered the question; not enough by far.

She shot her glance back up at him.

He had not moved, and by the look in his eyes, she could see that he was annoyed with her.

Why? Why, each time she was in his presence, did this man seem to be irritated with her? It was this attitude she remembered most about him. Yes, he had helped her; yes, he had saved her life all those years ago, but as it had been then, and as it appeared to be now, he seemed anxious to be rid of her.

She said, "Hello."

He nodded, a brief unfriendly movement of his head.

She swallowed the lump in her throat. "I—I had not expected you tonight . . . as you can see."

He did not utter a single word in reply; simply crossed his arms inside that blanket so that the material of it pulled around his body.

"Please," she went on to say, "this is not exactly a good time to talk. If you would give me a moment to get out of the bath and dress, I would be able to receive you a little more properly."

Still, he said nothing; nor did he budge an inch.

"Please, A-luu-te Itt-áchkáat, if you would come a

little closer and hand me that towel on the chair in front of you, I can get out of my bath, dress, and then we can talk."

The man, however, did not even glance at the chair. Nor did he relent in his perusal of her.

He said simply, "We . . . talk . . . here . . . now."

Carolyn sighed. Did the man, like Pretty Moon, only speak pigeon English? She said, "Why, I couldn't possibly talk to you now, here," she motioned toward herself. "Look at me."

Not a single emotion showed on his face, nor did he allow his gaze to roam lower than her eyes. "There is no other place where we can speak in private," he said in perfect English.

Carolyn, however, despite her fretting, barely noticed the change in his speech. Perhaps she was too intent on other things, and she asked, "And why is there no other place where we can talk?"

Again, with a complete deadpan expression, he said, "The white man will not allow a woman such as yourself to talk to me in public, nor do you want to be seen doing so."

"That's silly," she said.

He shrugged. It was the first expression of emotion she had glimpsed on this man since he had arrived, and whether it was right to do so or not, she rejoiced to see it. Perhaps he was not as emotionless as he would like her to believe.

He said, "Even a few words spoken with me in public could taint your reputation. The white man has one standard of conduct for himself, another for the Indian. And most of my people do not wish to antagonize this person. At least not at this time."

"I see," Carolyn said, although did she really? What

did that mean? That she would have to sneak private conversations with the man? Drat! If that were true, it meant that she would have a much harder task trying to solicit this man's help. It would also add time to her quest; time she did not have. Barely daring to think, she continued, "Then, if you would turn your back for a moment, I will arise, and we can talk. I have come here seeking your help."

He nodded, as though he understood her perfectly, but he did not make a single movement.

She gestured for him to turn around.

But instead of doing her bidding, he asked, "Why has the white woman returned to my country? And why does she seek me out?"

Darn the man. She was not yet prepared to have this conversation. Not here; not like this.

She said, "How can I possibly speak to you about these matters, when I sit here with nothing between us but . . . but water? You must know that it puts me at a certain disadvantage."

He was quick to note, "Does the white woman need advantage?"

She moaned. "You might at least give me some privacy."

He nodded. "I might." But he did not stir so much as an inch. "As soon as I learn the white woman's reason in asking for me, I will go away from here and leave her alone. I give the white woman my word."

Drat! She had forgotten how truly obstinate this man could be. She wanted to scream at him, wanted to rant at him; for this and perhaps other transgressions that she remembered from their past. But she knew she dare not do it. Unfortunately, she needed his cooperation.

But she *did* glare at him, and she said, "You certainly time your visits well, don't you?"

He simply shrugged.

"You must realize that a woman is never prepared to begin a conversation with a man in such a state of . . . of undress."

He frowned at her; opened his mouth as though he might say something, but another thought must have crossed his mind, for instead of speaking, he shrugged yet again.

She grimaced, beginning to resign herself to the task at hand, but she could not help observing, "Perhaps another woman—of easier virtue—might feel comfortable in entertaining you in this manner. I, however, would prefer to be dressed."

She watched as a slight grin softened the features of his face. He said, "You say these words as if I have never seen you in the manner in which you came into this earth."

She drew in her breath, shutting her eyes, hoping against hope that by doing so, she could shut out the memory, also. It did not work, unfortunately, and she said, "I was eleven at the time, and if you will remember correctly, you were the one who ordered me to bathe." She did not add that she had well needed that bath, too.

But Lone Arrow did not mention it; he did no more than shake his head, smiling. At last, however, he shifted his position around until he had turned his back to her completely. Still, he remarked, "Ah, I recollect it well."

She could hear his soft laughter, and though she did not share what he found humorous about their situation, either then or now, she felt some relief in these, his last few words. At least they had been more personal.

In truth, the slight reference to their past seemed to have done much to bridge whatever barrier might have been erected between them. She could sense it. It was as if, for a moment, his guard had been lifted, at least a little.

What was it that he had said? That she could not afford to be caught talking to him? If that were true—and she had no reason to doubt it—she would have to be careful in her dealings with him. If she sought him out, would she make trouble for him? Was that why the Crow men had thus far refused to talk to her?

She would have liked to ask these questions and more, but Carolyn knew that now was not the right time or place to do so, and so she stepped out of the tub. The chair was only a short distance away, and with one foot out, one foot still within the bath, she made a grab for it. She hit the chair instead of the cloth, and lost her balance.

Darn! With a slight shriek, she fell over.

He turned around and was at her side immediately.

And Carolyn was more than a little mortified. She was naked. Naked, for goodness sake. And she was no longer eleven years old.

He was grinning at her, however, and as he placed the terry cloth into her hands, he observed, "Within my memory are times when you had many similar falls. Perhaps the white woman should take walking lessons."

He smirked, but she found nothing humorous in their situation, and she retorted, "Perhaps the red man should keep his observations to himself." She grabbed the towel away from him.

But he was not finished, and he went on to observe,

"You are right. The white girl I once knew is no longer eleven. In truth, I fear that she has grown into a beautiful woman."

Given another time, another place, Carolyn might have rejoiced to hear these words. But not now.

Now she stood before him in no more than a threadbare towel. And though the length of it was long and only her feet peeped out beneath it, she felt exposed, vulnerable.

With one eyebrow cocked, and a note of teasing in his voice, he said, "It is too bad that the white woman is not this other kind of woman—the kind you spoke of earlier—for if she were, I would tell her many things about herself, about myself, too. Many things, indeed."

It took a moment for that comment to register. And when it did, all Carolyn could do was gape at him. She said, "You mean a woman of easy virtue? Is that what you're talking about?"

He did not answer; merely leered at her. And a wicked, crooked smile it was, too.

Carolyn didn't think. She reacted instead, and slapped out at him, stating, "How dare you!"

Her hand whacked at a corner of his blanket, and though no serious damage had been intended, nor done, she managed to knock a portion of that blanket right off his shoulder.

He did nothing, however. Nothing except to continue to beam at her. Although after a time, he did observe, "It is good to know that The-girl-who-runs-with-bears is still full of fire."

"The-girl-who-runs-with-bears?"

"That is your name. The name that I gave you."

She fell silent. She hadn't known that he had called her anything. All she remembered from their past was how he had ignored her. Somehow, the idea that he had given her a name mollified her—at least a little.

However, she was in no mood to give quarter, and she said, "As you can see, I am fine. Please return to your corner over there"—she fluttered her hand in the general direction of the far wall— "and allow me to dress."

Perhaps it was the order; perhaps it was her tone of voice, or maybe it was something else that did it.

Whatever the reason, Carolyn grimaced as she watched the light of battle enter into his eyes. His gaze raked her up and down once, again, before he observed, "The white woman is dressed well enough. We will have that talk now, I think. Prepare yourself. . . ."

Chapter 7

Carolyn stiffened. "Very well," she said. "But in order to prepare myself, I still must insist that you turn your back."

Lone Arrow frowned, yet he met her request nonetheless and turned his back to her.

Carolyn fled to where she had placed the modesty screen, stationing herself behind the flimsy structure. She said, "I think that you do me a disservice, Lone Arrow. When we were little, you barely spoke to me. Now that we're older, you make suggestions. I fear that I must remind you that although I am a woman, I am a person who does not take well to innuendos or insults."

"*Ho,*" he said, and with some relief, she heard the note of humor creep back into his voice. "I agree," he continued, "you are more than a girl."

Quickly she drew on a nightdress before she commented, "You are deliberately misunderstanding me."

"Am I?" he countered. "My people tell me that a

white woman has been asking about me. They tell me that she wants to see me. It is a strange thing: a white woman asking after an Indian man, particularly here at a white man's fort. My people are very curious. I think that I am, too. What is it that you want with me?"

Carolyn peeped around the screen, and gave his back a sharp glance, trying to ignore the broad design of his stately pose. She fretted briefly. She was not quite prepared to broach this subject most dear to heart. Not yet anyway. And so she countered, "How is it that your people would be curious? Surely they would understand that I am the same girl that you saved eight and a half years ago."

"How would they know that?"

She drew her arms through the sleeves of a dressing coat and tied it around her waist before stepping around the screen. She said, "You must have told them about the incident."

Turning again to face her, he shrugged slightly. His gaze took in her clothed form, but she could not determine what he was thinking, for his expression revealed no emotion. "There was no point in doing so," he said.

Wasn't there? Hadn't she heard from soldiers, or perhaps from her former wagon master, that Indians bragged about their escapades?

Well, no matter. She said, "I disagree. There was good reason to speak up about it. After all, you saved my life and went out of your way to bring me to a white man's post. You were, you are, a hero. Surely your people would like to know that."

He turned aside, as though to make light of her words, but he offered no reply. Nor did she have any idea what to say next, particularly when she was not yet willing to lay bare her most urgent request.

After a while, she offered, "You speak English."

"I learned."

She gave him what she hoped was a sweet smile and swept forward, toward him. She said, "And I have learned to speak with sign language. I used to seek out the old trappers who often traveled through Virginia City, and I'm afraid I hounded them about teaching me the sign language until I had mastered it."

He nodded. "It is good."

He waited, his gaze roaming over her, from her face, down to the tip of her slippered feet. But he said no more.

She sulked, realizing that there was nothing for it. If this was to be the confrontation he wanted, she was going to have to make do with it. And although this was not exactly the sort of meeting she had envisioned having with him, for she would have presented him with her best face, she had to be thankful for one thing: he was here.

She proffered, "Won't you be seated?"

She took the chair nearest the tub, the place where the towel had previously been tossed, while Lone Arrow slid gracefully to the floor, sitting cross-legged.

She asked, looking down upon him, "How have you been these past few years?"

He placed his arms over his chest, and said, "I live well."

She inclined her head. "And your family? Are they well?"

"They are good."

"I have learned from other Indians here at the fort

that your name, A-luu-te Itt-áchkáat, means Lone Arrow."

He nodded. "That is good."

With these words her expression stilled, and she tried to sort out how to begin, finally deciding that her best tactic was to be blunt. Rising up from the chair, she sat beside him on the floor before she said, "I need your help."

He did not move a muscle, nor did he respond in any way to her, and she wondered if his lack of reaction meant he would not assist her.

Stiffening her spine, she began. "Lone Arrow, please forgive me for asking this of you. Believe me, if it weren't important, I would not have come here seeking you."

He inclined his head several times, showing his understanding, and he said, "I am glad that you have come."

"You are?"

He gave her a quick look of approval.

And she sent him a speculative glance in return. Did that mean that eight and a half years ago, he might have liked her . . . a little?

She inwardly grimaced. He might not be so happy about her return to this place, once she tells him *why* she has come. Nonetheless, she knew she had to come to the point, and she blurted out, "Lone Arrow, I need you to lead me back to the cave."

"The cave?"

"Yes," she said, "the one where the treasure is hidden."

She felt, more than witnessed, the barely perceivable difference in him; beheld that he withdrew from her.

All he did outwardly, however, was narrow his eyes. He asked, "Why do you want to go there?"

The truth, she cautioned herself. She must speak only the truth. This was a delicate point she remembered about this man so very, very well. He would know if she lied.

And so she began, "My family has come into some bad times. Things in the gold fields have not been so profitable for us, and we stand to lose everything we hold dear if we can't come up with the finance to pay our creditors."

As a look of confusion came over Lone Arrow's countenance, she reached a hand out to him, touching him and covering his fingers with her own. She explained, "In our world, the white man needs this golden rock, the same kind of rock that I saw in that cave. It is this golden rock that purchases food and housing for us, since we do not live off the land as you do."

She watched as he glanced down at her hand; watched as he flipped his hand over; observed him as his large fingers encircled hers. He said, "There is so much difference in the colors of our skin. Do you see this?"

She frowned. "Yours is only a few shades darker than mine. Lone Arrow, you leave the—"

"And yet those few shades make much difference, do they not?"

Carolyn drew her hand back from him at once. She asked, "What do you mean?"

He looked away from her, saying, "The golden rock means nothing to the Indian. You must know this. Yet it has great appeal to the white man. Very much, indeed. It is hard for the red man to understand. I have seen what the golden rock does to the whites. I have seen it drive white men crazy. Do you, too, have this fever?"

Carolyn cleared her throat and glanced at those fingers of his. Again she reached out to place her hand over his, as though to give comfort. She said, "Though I cannot deny that I would like to have much gold, in order to help my family, I do not believe I have the fever. That is not why I am here."

"Is it not?"

"No," she shook her head, and withdrew her hand as though his graze had somehow burned her. Dear Lord, what was happening to her?

Carolyn felt odd, as though a slow fire were being lit inside her. His touch, the feel of his skin upon her own gave her a curious feeling, as though she were all warm and fuzzy inside, and . . . she paused to take stock of herself. She felt *naughty*.

The thought came out of nowhere. Still, Carolyn wondered what it might be like if Lone Arrow were to take her hand in his, to pull her against him, to dip his head toward her, to touch his lips to hers, to caress her in all those places on her body which so suddenly yearned to be touched . . .

But he did not do it, thank goodness. In truth, he did the opposite and pulled back from her, saying, "If the memory of the gold rock has not driven you crazy, why have you returned?"

There it was; the direct question. She should answer, yet she did not feel it appropriate to tell him everything.

Or was she merely being cowardly? What would he think of her when he learned that she had been a thief?

But as though her pause had somehow offered evidence of her guilt, he stood and, turning away from her, paced once more to the corner of the room. From there, he swung back around toward her, saying, "You are here, then, to take the things that are in that cave?"

"No!" she denied at once.

"Why are you not?" he countered. "If what you are saying is true, that kind of treasure could help your family. Many people would do it, and no one would really blame you."

"That's true, but—"

"But those things in that cave are cursed," he cut in. "Much bad luck. Better to leave them alone."

She knew that . . . now. She said, "Please believe me. I'll not be wanting to take anything from there."

He frowned, looking as though he recognized her words as being true, but he also realized that there were certain conflicting facts in her story. He said, "Then why must you go there?"

"Because," she said, hesitating, "I—I . . . please don't think badly of me, Lone Arrow."

"How could I think any worse of you than I do at this moment? That cave—those things you saw there—were never something you were supposed to see. I only took you there because I had no choice. If I am to protect that mountain, the spirit that lives there and its treasure, why would I take you there?"

She swallowed. "Because I have not come here to steal anything."

He gave her a doubtful look.

She should tell him, she realized; she should simply muster up the courage and confess her misdeed. Perhaps he would understand. After all, she had been no more than eleven years of age, and she had been desperate.

She opened her mouth to tell him all; she took a deep breath, held it—

"The white man," Lone Arrow said, "has many habits that my people do not understand."

"Yes, but—"

"He takes without asking," he continued, "he makes promises he cannot keep, he has even taken our women as wives, only to throw them away and deny his own children."

Carolyn gulped. She said, "It is not good to generalize about an entire group of people. There are many differences person to person. Why, I could be very different from the image you might have of a . . . a white person."

Lone Arrow gave her a curious look, before saying, "Are you?"

"A—am I what?"

"Are you different? Are you unlike many of the white people of my acquaintance?"

"Of course I am," Carolyn answered at once.

"Are you telling me that you are a person of honor?"

"Of course I am a person of honor," she said, realizing as she did so, that she had sealed her own fate. Never, not ever, could she tell him her crime. Not now.

She said, "Lone Arrow, you simply must believe me when I say I do not intend to steal any more treasure."

He gave her a long look. His attention, however, seemed to catch on one thing, and he asked, "Any more?"

She stared away from him. Dear Lord, she was making mistakes . . . and she could afford none. She said, "I—I can't tell you any more. That's—that's what I meant."

She chanced a peep up at him, and winced. He looked stern, even more formidable than ever. As she watched, he brought up his arms to fold over his chest, although the blanket hid the full effect of his body from her. He said, "You have stolen before?"

This was yet another chance to come clean with him. She should take it now and tell him all. Surely he would understand, especially since all she wanted to do now was return the cross to its rightful place.

Or would he understand? If she had stolen something once, might he think that she would do so again?

She hesitated. "I—I—"

He tread forward. "Did you take something?"

"I—I . . ." Words failed her.

"Show me."

"Show you what?"

"What you stole."

"No," she said. "It's—it's only a little . . . wait. You are putting words in my mouth. I did not say I stole anything."

He ignored her. "What was it?"

"Nothing," she said. "Nothing . . . much. It is only that I picked something up there on that mountain, something of little or no value and I wish to return it."

"Humph! Might I see it?"

"It's nothing much, I tell you. Nothing to see, really. Besides, if I show it to you, you might take it from me."

"As well I should if what I think you have done is true. Tell me, did you take this thing that is 'not much' from that cave, or from the mountain itself?"

She opened her mouth to speak, found her voice caught somewhere between her throat and her tongue. She tried to get a word out, but could not do it. Nor could she incline her head. She sat on the floor, surrounded by the warmth of her nightgown and coat, herself frozen.

"Give me the item," Lone Arrow said, "for it is only then that I will decide if I will help you or not."

Should she? She sat mute, perfectly still. Finally she was able to utter, "No."

"No?"

"No," she said more emphatically.

"No, you do not want my help?"

"Not exactly. I need your help. It is why I am here."

"Then, what?"

"No, I won't show you what I have."

"Why not?" he asked. "If it is truly no more than a small thing . . ."

"Because—because . . . ?" Why? Oh, why hadn't she practiced what she was going to say to him before having to confront him?

While she paused, he paced back to her side, and Carolyn could feel the heat of his regard. He said, "If you give it to me, I will return it to the treasure mountain for you. If your intentions are honorable and you truly do not wish to take anything else from there, this you will do."

Carolyn hesitated. That sounded logical. Too logical.

Yet, why not do it? It would be so much easier to give the cross to him. Easier for her and faster.

But he would then know that she had been no more than a common thief.

Well, he was going to find that out about her anyway . . . in truth, if what he said was true, he already did think this of her. Plus, if she gave it to him, she could return home at once.

Except that she did not want him to know that she

had stolen an actual artifact. If it had been something small, of little use, like a stick or a stone, perhaps an arrowhead, then that would be less condemning.

There was another aspect to be considered, also. What if she did give him the cross, and he did not take it back to the cave in a timely manner? Or worse yet, what if he lost it?

And what if she gave him the cross, and he left her without so much as a by your leave? She would never see him again.

That thought struck her hard. Surely she did not still harbor a young girl's fantasy about him, did she?

No. She could not possibly. Well, even if she did—she thought, a little more honestly—she had to remember that she was not here for herself.

There was also one other possibility that she must consider. If she did not, herself, return the cross to the cave, would the curse still be broken?

Could another make restitution for her, given that she had been the one who had committed the crime in the first place?

Taking a deep breath, Carolyn came to a decision and, gathering her wits about her, said, "I'm sorry. As much as I would like to simply give the thing to you, and have you return it for me, I cannot do it that way. You will have to take my word for it that it is a *small* item, and ah, as I said, nothing much. Besides, I must be certain this thing is done . . . and quickly."

He pulled a frown. "What do you mean? Why do you hurry?"

"Because," she said, "my family is on the brink of disaster. I have come to realize that until this object is returned, I have no chance of helping them. In truth, I am a hindrance to them. Believe me, I have come to understand that this thing that I have—even though it is nothing much really—is, indeed, cursed."

Lone Arrow stared down at her, his gaze skimming over the full measure of her white night coat.

He did not believe her. She knew it, but she would not tell him more.

He narrowed his eyes at her, and asked, "What do you have to give me in trade if I do this thing for you?"

Carolyn fretted. So here it was at last. She had known it would come to this, had sensed that he would not donate his undivided time and attention to her . . . for nothing. This she had feared.

But at least in this thing, she was prepared. She knew what to do.

She said, "I have very little to offer you."

He let his gaze travel over the length of her scantily clad body as she sat before him; once, a second time, again, but he remained otherwise silent.

She followed that glance upon her own person. Did he know what she was thinking? If he did . . .

Of its own accord, embarrassment consumed her. Truth to tell, she felt her face tingle.

She sighed. No matter how often she had rehearsed this thing she knew she must say, she was uncertain she could go through with it. After all, it was quite one thing to resolve to make the offer she knew she was going to have to make; another thing to actually do it.

Carolyn gulped in a breath of air, preparing for the explosion which she knew would follow—that is, if she revealed all. *Courage,* she heartened herself. Aloud, she said, "I—I . . . could give you . . . m-my . . ."

He looked at her expectantly.

"M-my," she gulped. "My-s-e-l-f," she finished. This last word had been spoken in no more than a whisper.

But he had heard it, for he became suddenly very quiet. He squatted down beside her, but she would not acknowledge him, would not look into his face.

It would appear, however, that he would be having none of her shyness, for with a single finger under her chin, he lifted her face up until he could look her in the eyes, even though she refused to make that contact.

Alas, she was doing her best to glance down at the floor when she heard him ask, "Then, The-girl-who-runs-with-bears is not married? That she could give me this?"

She shook her head.

"And she would willingly give me this?"

She nodded.

"Then it must be more than a simple trinket that you took, Carolyn."

It was the first time Lone Arrow had ever spoken her English name, and the effect of it, the way he had said it, sent shivers of fire running up and down her spine.

"How do you know my name? I don't think I ever told it to you."

"Who here at the fort does not know it? Is it not on the tip of every man's tongue?" he countered. "I may be Indian, but I do understand and speak English. Tell me," he continued, "does giving yourself to me include marriage?"

She shook her head.

And he said, "It is as I had thought." He looked, if anything, briefly disappointed before he continued, "Then you are prepared to act the part of a woman of little virtue?"

"I have just said that I am, haven't I?" She still could not look at him.

"Then I suggest you do it now."

"What?" That had her casting a quick glance at him.

But he looked calm, as if he were in the habit of being propositioned in this manner every day of his life. He said, "If this is the thing you intend to do, then I should know if your heart speaks true. You should give me a sample of that which I can expect from you . . . at least a look at what I might have."

"But—but . . . I—I—. *Now? Here?*"

He nodded.

"I—I . . . No, not now. Besides you have already seen me naked once tonight."

Oddly, he seemed to be appeased, although he said, "If you will not do it, then how do I know you are sincere?"

"Because I tell you that I am, that's how."

He grinned. "And am I to take the word of a thief?"

"How dare you!" she uttered.

He simply shrugged and looked away from her, saying, "I would know that which I am getting, I think."

She frowned at him. She even placed her hands on the belt holding her night coat together. But she found she could not do it; she could not budge; could not even untie a simple coat. In defeat, she gazed down at the floor.

And he came up onto his feet, moving away from her so swiftly and so silently, she had no choice but to call out, "Wait!"

He hesitated, his figure at her window.

"Wait, Lone Arrow. Please, I—I . . . can do this, if you insist. Please, give me a little more time."

He made a negative hand motion. "No, do not do it," he said, "for it would do you no good. I am afraid that I am guilty of teasing you, when perhaps I should not.

Know that I cannot be enticed into doing this for you, for I cannot take you to the cave. Go home, Carolyn."

He turned to leave.

"Wait!" she clamored. "Give me another chance. Please, I can do this."

Where before her fingers had been like knots, they became now fluid with motion, and without further thought, she drew off the coat, the warm material of it falling to her feet. Next her grip came to the buttons of her nightdress; first one undone, and then another.

Carolyn felt mortified at what she was doing, but with a quick glance up at him, she knew she could not stop. At least she had his attention.

Too soon, she had no more buttons to undo, and with a shrug of her shoulders, she let the nightdress fall to the floor, her nakedness clearly illuminated before him.

She did not flinch beneath his gaze, and it was at some length before Lone Arrow at last spoke. In truth, so quiet did he become, he might have turned to stone.

Suddenly, and without beckoning them to do so, incidents from their past came back to swamp her, a similar happening between them coming clearly to mind. Surely he would not push her away . . . not again.

She was older now; she had more to offer him. Couldn't he see that?

Still, he said nothing, and into that silence, Carolyn offered, "Please, Lone Arrow, I would marry you, too."

She did not hear him tread toward her. She did not even know he was right upon her until she felt his fingers graze over the smoothness of her cheek.

She groaned and in truth, she barely heard his words, "So beautiful. So very, very beautiful," before he silently strode away from her side.

Carolyn opened her eyes, and saw that he was beside the window again, ready to climb through it. Desperate, she said, "Why, Lone Arrow? Why don't you like me?" She took an unsteady step forward.

She did not hear his moan, or maybe she did. Had it been him, or the wind making a sound?

He did not answer her question, either. Alas, she hardly registered his words as he said, "I cannot stay here any longer. There will be trouble if we are discovered together."

She felt like crying. She had come all this way for what? She had humiliated herself for what? Absolutely nothing?

Taking another small pace toward him, she said, "Then you're going to leave just like that? You're not even going to try to help me?"

He did not answer. He simply turned around to stare at her.

One moment passed. Another. And Carolyn, under his intense scrutiny, dared not move.

He trod a few steps forward. "Know that my reasons for not helping you are not because I do not wish to do it. Know that it is that I must not do it."

"Why?"

"Because I am sworn to protect that land and that cave, even from someone as pretty as you."

She gulped, her eyes glued to his, as she closed the distance between them. She said, "But I must go there. Please, you took me there once before."

"There was no other way to save you."

"There is no other way to save me now, either. I would give you all that I have . . ."

He made some low sound, deep in his throat, before he added, "And had I the means, know that I would take it. But I cannot." His glance seemed to sear into her body and with some effort, he added, "I must go."

Still, he made not a single move to do so.

"Very well," she said and, turning her back on him, stepped as quickly as possible to her clothes, which lay on the floor, as though they had been put there to attest to her shame. Quickly she donned the nightdress.

And he said, sounding as if it had taken the strength of ten horses to whip it from him, "Know that I have always liked you, The-girl-who-runs-with-bears. Perhaps," he continued, more to himself than to her, "I have liked you a little too much."

And with nothing more said, Lone Arrow made his escape through the window, leaving Carolyn alone to determine what to make of that statement, and what to do next.

Chapter 8

Having knelt down in the dirt and grasses, there beneath his old friend's window, Lone Arrow paused to admonish himself. *Ho,* what had he done? He had hurt her, he knew, and it was not something he had meant to do.

But what else could he have done? No honorable man would have taken what she offered, regardless of his desire to do so. She was not that kind of woman; he was not that kind of man.

What was it about The-girl-who-runs-with-bears that made him want to act in inappropriate ways? For, he acknowledged to himself, he had more than desired to take her in his arms. He had wanted to kiss her, had wanted to lie with her. He had physically ached with the need . . .

Glancing up toward her window, he knew he owed her yet another apology. He should have explained things to her; told her about his life, impressed upon her the importance of that cave, of keeping it sacred. Maybe if he had mentioned his duty in regard to those mountains, she might have understood.

Yet seeing her in all her natural beauty here tonight had given him pause. In truth, he had barely been able to think.

Beautiful. There was no other word to describe her, he thought. She was beautiful. And given any other circumstance, he would not have walked away from her.

But he'd had little choice. He could not do the thing that she asked. His honor, his very standing within his clan and his tribe, depended upon him acting in a responsible manner. He had made a mistake once in leading her into that place; he would not repeat it.

Originally, when he had come to her this night, he had intended to render her an apology, an explanation, perhaps, for his past acts. Yet the words had not formed upon his lips.

Instead he had come away from his meeting with her with doubts . . . about her. What was she doing here? Why had she returned?

She was lying. He must not lose sight of this.

As the wise ones have often said, it is in the eyes of a living being that one can know the truth, or not, of his words. And so it was that Lone Arrow knew that The-girl-who-runs-with-bears had spoken to him with a tongue that is forked.

But what did she hide from him? And why was she really here? To replace something of little worth, as she said?

It was unlikely. More feasible was the notion that she was here to take something else.

He wondered, what was this thing she had taken? He did not believe for a moment that this thing that had brought her back here was "nothing." It had caused her to return, hadn't it?

Even as Lone Arrow struggled with his thoughts, he crouched, stealing silently through the shadows of the fort with care, knowing that if he were caught in this place after dark, there would be trouble. Questions would be asked that he was not prepared to answer.

Stooping, he rolled into a nearby thicket of bushes, trying to keep as little sound as possible from the night wind. Nonetheless, the breezes whisked at his back, seeming to whisper at him, *"She is beautiful."*

And though he made no argument, it was also upon his tongue to mention that she was also a nuisance. But then, he thought, she had always been both of these things to him.

Even as a youngster, she had been trouble, yet comely—although at the time he would have dared the wrath of three enemy tribes rather than admit it. Truth was, even then he had appreciated her. From her hair, which reminded him of the color of a fawn; to the earth-toned hue of her eyes, he had always looked upon her with "pleasant eyes."

And although she was a slight little thing—she stood no higher than chin level to him—she more than compensated for her lack of stature with a determined disposition. Her face shape was distinct, too. Not round, as was common amongst his own people; not straight up and down, like so many of the whites he had known. Hers appeared to resemble the shape of a heart.

A heart? Lone Arrow shook his head. If he did not know himself better, he would have thought his ideas sounded love-struck.

But he did not think of her in that way.

Or did he? Certainly, he could not deny that he found her attractive, now, then . . .

At that thought, incidents from eight and a half years ago filled his consciousness. Certainly, he thought, back then he had been more than a little aware of her prettiness. He had simply been too young, and much too annoyed with her at the time to value it.

Still, all those years ago, he could have handled her with less hostility.

She had been innocent, and so very pretty . . . And as he recalled again her shy advances toward him, and in particular his reaction to them, he remembered that she had embarrassed him . . .

Fort C.F. Smith looked like a stronghold, but to Lone Arrow it represented a sort of haven. At last he would be able to dismiss the girl, allowing him to return to his mountain and to his people.

He paused at the top of a butte, waited for her to advance to a position beside him, and caught her hand as a means of stopping her progress. He was aware of the exact moment when she came to stand beside him, and looking out from their hilltop, he pointed out the fort to her.

"Íkee, look," he said to her, even though he knew that she did not understand his language. "We will be there before the sun finds its way into the sky this day."

He glanced down at her, his look catching her in the act of smiling up at him. And that was when it happened.

His stomach dropped. She was so pretty, so innocent, so sweet.

In the distance, he heard the white man's music—its refrains being sent up to them on the wind.

She leaned in toward him.

She said, "Dance with me," but he did not understand her words.

He turned away from her, only to have her race after him, stop him and pull him around toward her.

She touched him, and shock filled his system; and not only because she had put her arms around his shoulders. She was even now carrying his arms to her, placing them around her waist.

He stood still, not knowing what to do. For although she was too young to know, far too young to understand what could happen between them, he was not. He was sixteen, a man in many ways.

He knew that he should move away from her, do something to stop this. Still, he could not take his gaze from her, and he moved his body as she dictated.

They danced; his steps fitting hers as if the two of them might have rehearsed these movements a hundred times.

For a moment, he wanted nothing more in this world than to kiss her. But he did not do it. Instead, remembering who he was and who she was, he made a move to turn away. He should have. But she reached up to him, there to place a sweet kiss on his cheek.

And Lone Arrow became lost in it. But not so lost that he did not recall that she was no more than a child.

And so he did nothing to return the embrace, for he knew that he must not show her what he felt. Alas, he had to get away from her.

Shrugging off her hold on him, he pointed her in the direction of the fort and gave her a small push toward it.

He was pleased to note that she took a step away

from him, but she went no farther than a few paces before she turned back to him, confusion in her eyes.

"Délaah! Go!" he said, using gestures and signs that he knew she would understand.

He watched as the hurt came over her face; watched as she so obviously read other meanings into his actions.

And how he wanted to go to her, to ease that look from her eyes. But he could not do it.

Again, he signaled her to go away.

And at last she did as he demanded. But not before she had swung around and rushed to him, throwing herself into his arms.

And when her body came into contact with his, he lost a little bit of himself to her; she, a mere child.

He must not, he could not, let her know what was in his heart. Wrenching her arms from around his neck, he accidentally pulled off the silver locket she had given him. It was broken. He had broken it.

It was as though the locket mirrored what must take place between them. But perhaps it was for the best, he reasoned. After all, in his experience, the white man demanded payment for all things given. Perhaps this jewelry would buy the things she would need to survive.

Forcing himself to let the chain drop into his hand, he offered the locket back to her. And then he did what he had to do. He signed to her to go away. And this time she would not misunderstand him.

Without any further communication, he turned his back on her and trod off in the opposite direction.

He knew his actions hurt her; knew she did not understand that he did what he had to do. But there was nothing else he could do if he were to be true to his honor.

In the end, he watched her all the way to the fort, only leaving the vicinity himself when someone from the stockade rushed out to escort her inside those gates.

And when that gate closed, Lone Arrow felt as though a part of his life had been shut out from him . . .

It was all so long ago.

And despite it all, he knew he owed her an apology. At a time when she had needed him, when he had been her lifeline within a sea of confusion, he had treated her as though she meant nothing to him.

If only she had known the truth.

But the truth was something he could not share with her. Now, or ever.

"She is beautiful," came the refrain in the wind.

And Lone Arrow made a sound low in his throat. He had best rid himself of such thoughts. He must keep reminding himself that, though she might be lovely to look at, this woman had secrets. Secrets, he suspected, that she believed would make him think less of her . . . or she would not be withholding them from him.

Slinking soundlessly through the fort, he made his way to a spot outside the main stockade, all without incident. Once outside the fort's walls, he found the cache where he had hidden his weapons, as well as some food and, picking up a knife, he sat down to put his weapons into order.

Still, he could not keep his musings from focusing on one thing: he had not been completely immune to her when they were children. If he had to spend more time with her, how would he restrain himself now?

Ho! There was only one thing he could do: he must ensure she left to go home on the morrow.

*   *   *

Sleep came in fits and spurts. It was impossible. But what had she expected? How could she sleep when every fiber of her being cringed in embarrassment?

What had made her think that because she was a grown woman Lone Arrow's attitude toward her would have changed? Would she never learn?

Apparently not.

Well, what was she to do now? She supposed she could seek out Lone Arrow tomorrow and give him the cross. Surely, she realized, she could trust him with the treasure.

In truth, it was probably the best solution . . . or was it?

She frowned, reckoning that she could dog Lone Arrow's steps until he would have no choice but to take her there. But would that work?

He was Indian. He probably knew more ways to avoid her than she could possibly envision. Although, could he? If she did not leave his presence ever?

But such a feat would be an impossibility. After all, a girl had certain needs that she must attend to now and again. She simply could not be with him every moment of every day.

What, then, was she to do?

She could go to the mountain by herself. Carolyn paused as the thought struck her.

She could do this, couldn't she? After all, hadn't Lone Arrow taught her how to survive in the wilderness? Hadn't she done it before she had met up with him eight and a half years ago?

And she had survived. Barely, she reminded herself, but she *had* weathered the experience.

Turning over in bed and staring up at the ceiling, Carolyn mulled over her choices. There certainly weren't many of them.

Truth to tell, as cockeyed as it might be, the more and more she thought about it, the more and more she liked the idea. For one, striking out on her own would make her less dependent on him and less reliant on his good will. For another, it placed her destiny into her own hands.

But there were problems. For instance, would she recognize that same mountain, even once she was within its vicinity? She might, she answered her own question. Chances were particularly good, if she could locate that circle of stones.

And then there was the question of finance. Where was she going to obtain the money to buy the necessities she would need for such a trip?

She had little in the way of funds. Alas, she had made her financial calculations based on obtaining Lone Arrow's cooperation. And since Indians traveled with nothing but the shirt upon their backs, she had estimated that the entire trip would cost her little. At the time, such an idea had been a godsend, and had helped her to confirm her travel arrangements.

But if she were to do this thing on her own, she would need supplies, and in the very least, a horse. How was she to accomplish this, she wondered, with no money, no collateral; with nothing of worth to sell or trade?

Her fingers came up to nervously twiddle with the locket around her neck. And several moments passed before another idea struck her. Wide-eyed, she held the necklace up before her face, doing nothing more than looking at it, really looking at it.

By itself, it was worthless. But the Indian maid, Pretty Moon, had wanted this trinket, had been willing to trade most anything for it.

Could or would Pretty Moon help her? Would this locket buy Carolyn an ally? Or at the very least a horse?

Clutching the pendant into her hand, Carolyn came to a decision. True, her plan might only be a dim possibility at the moment, but just wait. She was going to make it become a reality, or die trying. . . .

Much farther south, at Fort Laramie on the North Platte River, two men sat in a dark corner, huddled around a bottle of whiskey.

To all outward appearances, they could have been mountain men, or perhaps scouts, clad as they were in wide-brimmed hats, buckskin coats and high-topped moccasins. But there the illusion ended, for the slow drawl in their voices left no doubt as to the Southern origin of their birthplace.

Dixon, the one with darker coloring, looked sullen; while Jordan shuddered.

"It's imprinted in me head, ah tell ya," said Jordan.

The bushy, dark brows of his companion, however, drew together in a frown. He said, "Now, you know ah wouldn't wanna call you a liar or nothin'," Dixon's voice was low, though distinctly harsh. "But I'll be hog-tied to a whore afore I'll trust that noggin of yourns. Ah reckon ah didn't wait any part of those two-bit years in a Yankee prison, waitin' to come back here, only t' be told there ain't no map."

Jordan shrugged. "You could'a made one yerself."

"Why ya yaller-bellied coward."

A chair squealed against the floor in accompaniment to the words; the table wobbled for a moment as though it might tip over, and Dixon burst to his feet. In the aftermath, a blaze of furniture crashed to the floor, the noise only adding to the already tense atmosphere.

Dixon made a grab for his companion, clutching at Jordan's lapels until he had nearly pulled him clean off his feet.

He roared, "What was that ya said?"

"N-nothin', Dixon. Nothin' at all."

"Now, ya listen up real good like," Dixon hissed, though he kept his voice low. "Ah said it before, 'n' I'll say it again. Ah want that map, and ah want it now. Get it fer me tonight, or else." He shook the smaller gentleman. "Do ya understand?"

Without waiting for an answer, Dixon pushed Jordan up against the wall.

Jordan nodded and said, "Sure thing, Dixon. Sure thing. Ah'll have it fer ya first thing . . . tomorrow, ah promise."

"Ya better." Dixon's brows narrowed. "Ah know what yer thinkin'. But don't ja believe for a minute that ah wouldn't be able ta find ya, if'n ya was ta run out on me. And don't think ah would take kindly ta' yer double-crossin' me. We're partners, after all. Got that? Partners."

Jordan swallowed. "That's right, Dixon. Partners." He nodded pathetically. "Ah'll have it fer ya. First thing tomorrow."

Dixon grunted. "We leave at first light. Ah expect ya here with supplies and with the map. Got that?"

"Y-yeh. First light."

With another snarl, Dixon let his "partner" go, slapping the bottle of whiskey, already toppling dangerously on the table, to the floor.

"No more fer ya tonight," said Dixon. ". . . And pay

the trader on yer way ta' bed . . . if'n yer fixin' ta sleep tonight."

With an ugly sneer, the big oaf swung around and stomped from the trading post, the Indians and a few others in the crowd making room for him.

Meanwhile, Jordan pulled out a dirty piece of cloth, clutching it in his hand before he ran it across his face, unaware that this action made a mess of the dirt and sweat which had accumulated there.

What was he going to do? He had no map. He'd never made one.

Nor had Dixon, he reminded himself. Dad-blame it, anyway. It wasn't *his* fault. Eight and a half years ago, Dixon had been as scared as he. Yet you didn't see Dixon making no map.

"*Do this, Jordan, do that,*" he mimicked under his breath. "Well, Ah'm tired of it," he continued. "Tired, ah tell ya. Ah won't do it. Let Dixon make up his own map. Ah'll jest leave here 'n' . . ."

Remnants of a bad memory stirred Jordan's features, and he brought a hand up to run over his neck. It was as though the recollection itself brought pain.

Well, he thought, best to put pen to paper, and produce something for Dixon. He didn't like it, but he'd do it. It was better than the alternative.

Chapter 9

A recent squall had flooded the Montana region with hot air, causing Carolyn to feel as though her simple chambray skirt and white bodice more resembled a suit of sweltering wool rather than that of washed cotton. Luckily, her wide-brimmed bonnet was made of white muslin and trimmed in eyelet so that it reflected the sun. At least her head and neck were spared the direct light, if not the heat. Even her paisley shawl, which she had let fall to her elbows, had, only moments ago, felt like lead around her shoulders.

Still, as she made her way to the fort's main gate on this bright day in June, her steps felt light upon this earth; lighter than they had been in days.

And why not? She had a plan.

As Carolyn paced through the gate's wooden pillars, moving on into the Indian camp, she brought back to mind an image of Lone Arrow as he had appeared to her last night. Her breath caught.

Darn the man. No doubt about it; he was handsome, perhaps a little too handsome. And it was very probable that women surrounded him night and day. Maybe this would account for his rejection of her.

Perhaps.

But as though the thought itself had power, embarrassment consumed her, and she wondered if she might ever have the nerve to look Lone Arrow in the eye again. Drat the man. Why wouldn't he help her?

She knew the answer to that, of course. She realized that he considered the cave sacred; probably thought that hers was an impure cause. And of course there was the most obvious reason for his lack of cooperation: he did not trust her.

Not that she had given him any reason to do so. *What would he do, what would he think of her, when he discovered that she had actually stolen an artifact from the cave?*

Well, hopefully, he would never know.

Carolyn squared her shoulders, determined to set these considerations aside, at least for the time being. It was a beautiful, bright day—and she had hope.

Having browsed about the Indian encampment these past few days, Carolyn knew where she would find Pretty Moon's lodge, and she made her way there now, traversing the Crow encampment, the smell of campfires heavy upon her nostrils. How colorful were these Indian dwellings, Carolyn thought, as she sped past them.

It wasn't long before Carolyn found the young woman whom she sought. There she was, on hands and knees, at work outside her tepee. Good.

Briefly, Carolyn studied the scene before her. Funny, how the young woman looked small in comparison to the lodge. Who would have thought an Indian dwelling would be so large? standing perhaps twenty feet tall?

But the attraction of Pretty Moon's lodge was more than its size, Carolyn realized. The skins on it had been bleached until it looked as white as linen. It had been painted with designs of bright blue, red, and yellow; and pictographs of war scenes, animals, and row after row of multicolored porcupine quills adorned it.

In truth, the scene before her was so peaceful, so full of harmony, that for a moment Carolyn's most urgent purpose faded beneath its beauty. Of course, adding to that inducement were the delightful sounds of children playing, as well as the quiet talk of the women and low hum of the old men, who were perhaps regaling the young with stories of their past.

But too soon, Carolyn remembered who she was, where she was and why she had come. She smiled.

"Ka-hee." Carolyn said the Crow word, which when translated, meant hello.

Pretty Moon glanced up, and seeing her visitor, broke into a wide smile. She responded to Carolyn with her own, *"Ka-hee."* Then she sat back on her haunches, while Carolyn squatted down beside her.

Resolutely, Carolyn took a deep breath and came directly to the point. Grasping hold of her locket, she undid its clasp, letting the jewelry slide into her hand. Next, so that there would be no misunderstanding, she offered it to Pretty Moon.

It was only when this was done that Carolyn said, with words and with signs, "I have changed my mind about this necklace, Pretty Moon, and have decided that I would like to trade. Very much," she added.

Pretty Moon's first reaction seemed to be one of shock, although that look was quickly replaced with a gaze of fascination. Shyly, she glanced first at Carolyn, and then at the necklace.

Carolyn sensed the other woman's pleasure, watched as the young lady struggled to contain her enthrallment. At last, Pretty Moon said and signed, "Have . . . many things . . . trade." Her eyes sparkled with warmth. Then, advancing another timid look up at Carolyn, Pretty Moon added, "Would . . . white woman . . . like . . . see what . . . this one . . . has?"

Carolyn was more than prepared for this inquiry, but instead of answering Pretty Moon's question directly, she asked one of her own, "Do you have any horses that you could trade?"

Pretty Moon nodded.

"Would you trade a horse, and perhaps a mule for the locket?"

Pretty Moon frowned. Without speaking, she signed, "Why do you want the horse? And a mule?"

As it had been the previous evening with Lone Arrow, Carolyn found that she was without adequate means to express herself. So great had been Pretty Moon's captivation, that Carolyn had not anticipated the need to explain her intentions.

For a moment Carolyn looked away from the locket, and from Pretty Moon. At length, however, gaining her thoughts, she said, with words and with sign, "I need to travel east, into the Bighorn Mountains. There is something there that awaits my return. I have no horse of my own, and do not think I can make it there afoot."

Pretty Moon bobbed her head, then still without speaking, she signed, "My people live there, and I know it well."

Carolyn nodded.

To which Pretty Moon made another series of gestures, "Will the soldiers accompany you there?"

Carolyn shook her head.

"Then my husband and I will go with you," signed Pretty Moon.

"No," the word was out of Carolyn's mouth before she could stop it, and she watched as a frown crossed Pretty Moon's countenance. Carolyn added, "How kind of you to offer, but you needn't go out of your way. The horse and the mule will be enough."

In truth, Carolyn did not want the company. Not from her would these people learn of the cave, if they didn't already know of it. So she had promised Lone Arrow.

Pretty Moon, however, seemed to have other ideas and persisted, asking with signs, "Do you know the way?"

Carolyn hesitated. Should she tell the truth?

Carefully, she shook her head.

"Then you will need us," affirmed Pretty Moon. "The white people in the fort, the soldiers, would never excuse us if we were to trade a horse to you and let you go that way alone. We would be blamed if anything happened to you."

"But I would ensure that the soldiers understood," Carolyn signed.

Pretty Moon merely smiled, signing, "No, it is no trouble, and my heart would be happy to accompany you." She pointed to herself. "Pretty Moon and her husband are good friends to the white man. We will not let you become lost."

"But . . ."

"It is good that we go with you," continued Pretty Moon. "You deserve more than a horse and a mule for a necklace like this. Besides, my husband and I would be honored to accompany you. Good friends, are Pretty Moon and her husband, to the white man."

Carolyn cast the girl an uncertain look. This was not going well. She said, as firmly as possible, "No, I could not possibly put you to the trouble. I will find the way myself."

Pretty Moon merely shrugged, and signed once more, "It is no trouble. We have been anxious to be away from the white man's fort for many passages of the sun, but our chief has kept us here in order that we show our friendship to the white man. But now we have reason to go. When do you want to leave?"

Carolyn sighed, then brightened as an idea crossed her mind. She signed, "I wish to leave here without delay, this afternoon." Perhaps the speed with which she meant to travel would put the other woman off. As if to instill this fact upon the Indian woman, Carolyn pressed the locket into Pretty Moon's hands. "So of course I will understand if that is too soon—"

"It-chik," said Pretty Moon with a firm hand motion out and away from her chest—the sign for the word "good." She continued in sign: "Pretty Moon can be ready to go before the sun is high in the sky. It is always a good time to be on the move."

"But—"

Pretty Moon laughed. "I will tell my mother at once. She will be excited that we are being given the chance to leave."

Luckily, another thought occurred to Carolyn, and she signed, "Won't you need to ask your husband if he wishes to go?"

Pretty Moon laughed, making a gesture which said, "It is nothing. He will do as I ask. Have you not yet learned how to manage a man?"

Carolyn gave Pretty Moon a blank stare, as though to say, *Is there such a thing?*

To which Pretty Moon added with gestures, "You are not yet married, are you?"

"*Baa-lee-táa*, no," Carolyn answered in the Crow tongue, using one of the few words that she knew.

To which Pretty Moon giggled, and signed, "Watch me carefully when I am with my husband, and you shall see how it is done."

Carolyn found herself unable to keep from gawking at the young girl, wondering if she had missed something in their exchange. However, she found that she was barely able to keep herself from smiling. *Now, that would be a valuable piece of information.*

Nonetheless, as though to keep their conversation on firm footing, Carolyn asked, "Will you show me the horse and the mule?"

"Certainly," signed Pretty Moon, adding, "I will also come with you to help you pack."

"Oh, that's not necessary."

Pretty Moon sent Carolyn a surprised glance, before saying, "White woman . . . does not like . . . Pretty Moon?"

"Of course I like you."

"Yet," the young lady signed, "I would be scolded by my mother and others if I did not help the white woman to pack."

"You would?"

The young lady nodded. "I would be called lazy and unworthy to be your friend."

Carolyn sighed. She did not want to do this; she did not want the company.

Or did she? In some ways, the idea did have merit.

Pretty Moon and her husband would add companionship on a trek that was already difficult. Their presence would also make Carolyn's task so much easier, and so much more pleasant, their company ensuring that at the very least, she would not get lost. Also, with Pretty Moon's husband along, the two women would be ensured a constant supply of food.

There would be only one problem, Carolyn figured. Once they arrived at the mountains, she would have to invent a reason which would demand her departure from these two; some reason why Pretty Moon and her husband would feel obligated to leave her there, alone.

Was there such a cause?

Well, she would have many weeks in which to ponder it, she decided. For Carolyn had given her word, and she would never—not ever willingly—betray Lone Arrow's confidence.

Never.

And so upon this hopeful note, Carolyn and Pretty Moon made their plans.

"Where is the white woman going?"

The question had been made by a masculine voice, one that Carolyn recognized only too well. The inquiry had also been addressed to her, in all likelihood—not to Pretty Moon—since the words had been spoken in English.

Lone Arrow had to be standing directly behind her, Carolyn decided. With a grimace, she finished tying a blanket onto the mule in front of her, and even as she did so, she straightened her back, as though preparing herself for battle.

Because Lone Arrow would not be pleased.

She sighed. Could he stop her?

She supposed that he might try. But she knew she would fight him.

Before she turned to confront him, however, Carolyn gazed at Pretty Moon, the woman standing directly in her line of vision; there, next to the pony, her back to Carolyn. Both she and Pretty Moon had led the pony and the mule to Carolyn's quarters, tying them in front of her building, that they might load them.

Perhaps that had been a mistake.

Nevertheless, Carolyn could not help but wonder: when it came down to it, would Pretty Moon side with Lone Arrow? Or would she take Carolyn's part, helping Carolyn to persuade this man to their way of thinking?

Carolyn gazed up briefly toward the heavens, as though seeking divine intervention. But when inspiration failed to strike, she nervously cast a glance over her shoulder.

Oh, dear, there he was. And as she espied him, a short gasp escaped from her throat. Goodness!

If she had thought this man handsome last night, she had been deceived; deceived by that blanket Lone Arrow had worn. This man was magnificent, purely and truly.

At present, the trade blanket had been discarded. All the man wore now were breechcloth, leggings, moccasins, plus, she admitted, a great deal of jewelry.

But if one might have considered that the adornments would add a touch of femininity to this man's demeanor, he would have been greatly mistaken. The finery did not detract from Lone Arrow's masculinity—not in the least. Somehow, the jewelry added to it.

Nonetheless, she took a minute to appreciate the sight of him. His shoulders were broad, she noted, well formed and practically boasting of their ability to hold her.

She scowled at that thought.

Around his neck he wore a beautiful, if common, Crow ornament: a loop necklace, made with strings of shells and beads. The embellishment hung down the front of Lone Arrow's chest with row after row of quarter circles, one tier falling down after the other—the full effect of it not completely covering his ample, and *naked*, male breast.

Also, she observed, at the side of his waist were six to eight feathered ends of arrows, which he must surely be carrying in a bow and quiver case stretched across his back. Over one shoulder he had suspended his bow, while in his hand, he wielded a gun. In truth, these weapons did a great deal to affirm her conviction that this man was dangerous.

But the most distinguishable thing about this man, Carolyn was quick to notice once again, was his hair. As with most Crow men, his dark mane usually hung long in length well below his hips. He had at this moment, however, tied two braids at each side of his face, each braid strung with "Crow bows," a type of shell ornament which resembled an hourglass. And on one side of his face, nestled there along with the Crow bows, was a single eagle feather, which was at present fluttering in the wind.

As she turned slowly toward him, she brought her gaze up to stare into his eyes, noticing that his hair had been cropped short in front; the hair there pulled up and away from his forehead.

Truly, she admitted to herself, he looked splendid, and Carolyn was certain that her heart skipped a beat or two. Perhaps that explained her breathlessness.

He did not say a word to her, however. It was as though he merely awaited her answer to his question.

Well, he would have a long wait, she decided, for she had no intention of telling him anything.

Hoping to disconcert him, she mumbled in a voice barely audible, "I thought you left last night."

He raised an eyebrow. Obviously, he had heard her, and he asked, "And what would make you think that?"

No sooner had the question been asked than a soldier passed by them. The young man raised his hat to Carolyn, adding a softly spoken, "Mornin' Miss," to the greeting.

To Lone Arrow, however, the soldier sent a frown, while he ignored Pretty Moon completely.

"Good morning, soldier," Carolyn responded calmly enough, even though another uncertainty embraced her. Should she explain Lone Arrow's presence to the man? Hadn't Lone Arrow intimated that, as far as the Indians were concerned, only a fool would speak to a white woman?

"Pretty Moon," she called over her shoulder, and with signs, she asked, "Could you come here to my side for a moment?"

The other woman was quick to respond, and as soon as Pretty Moon had planted herself beside her, Carolyn said and signed, "Would you be so kind as to explain to this man"—she pointed to Lone Arrow—"that we are going on a trip." It was no question.

Before answering, however, Pretty Moon, seeming confused, contemplated first Lone Arrow and then Carolyn. And it was several moments before Pretty Moon at last spoke a few words in the Crow language, to which Lone Arrow muttered a mere, "Humph!"

A long discussion between the two followed thereafter, but Carolyn was only able to keep up with it in brief, since both were using very few precious signs.

"So." Carolyn heard the English word and glanced up to catch Lone Arrow frowning at her. "The white woman has decided to go into the mountains on her own."

Carolyn lifted her chin. It would appear that the attack had taken a more personal turn. She said, injecting what she hoped was a note of boredom into her voice, "I told you it was important."

But if he noticed her attempt at bravado, it did her little good. His stare at her seared into her own, and Carolyn had difficulty simply training her gaze to meet his.

At last, however, he uttered, "We will see."

"Yes," she said just as certainly, "we will see."

"If . . ."

"If?"

He nodded. "If Pretty Moon will be so eager to help you when her husband disapproves."

Carolyn winced, and despite the impression that she should not try to persuade him to explain, she found herself inquiring, "Why would her husband disapprove?"

"Because he is my friend, that is why. And because I will tell him what you intend to do."

"Oh," her lips rounded on the word, and Carolyn wondered if her face fell. Drat, the man. He held the upper hand.

Still, straightening her shoulders, she shook her head at him. "Fine," she responded, "tell her husband what you want. I am going to the mountains with or without you—or Pretty Moon." Darn him. She turned her back on him.

"And do you know your way to the mountains?"

His voice came from a distance much too close to

her. Carolyn fretted, not so much for herself but for him. Would there be trouble because he was speaking to her?

And why should she care?

"Do you?" he prodded. "Do you know your way there?" His voice was closer even still.

"You know that I don't."

"Then the white woman should go home, as I told her to do last night."

Carolyn gritted her teeth. She was fast becoming tired of hearing this from him. She said simply, "No."

She could perceive the heat of his glance, there along the nerve endings on her back. She said no more to him, however, nor did he utter a word.

Instead, he turned away. She wasn't sure how she knew he had done so, since she did not hear a single sound to indicate motion. But she knew he had left. Perhaps she should say that she felt it; felt the release of pressure, there upon her being.

Carolyn sighed in resignation. Swiftly, she glanced toward Pretty Moon, espying on the other woman's countenance what must have been determination.

Too bad, Carolyn thought. She would have enjoyed the other woman's company on this trek.

Well, enough. That was that.

As Carolyn smiled at Pretty Moon, she tried to disguise her own disturbing thoughts, and she signed, "Your help has been appreciated. You have taken pity on me, and I'm sorry that in the end, you had to stay behind."

Pretty Moon's eyes grew round. And she uttered, "This one," she pointed to herself, "stay . . . behind?"

Carolyn shook her head. "Yes, you'll need to remain

here now, since your husband will most likely object to your going with me."

Pretty Moon frowned. She signed, "It is true that my husband's friend Lone Arrow will tell him about us. It is true that my husband's friend Lone Arrow will try to persuade my husband against what we do. Because of this, my husband will try to sway the opinion of his wife against the white woman. And all this, because of the words of his friend Lone Arrow."

Carolyn nodded. "I'm so sorry."

But Pretty Moon grinned. "Still," the young woman signed, "does the white woman think that these things would make a difference to Pretty Moon?"

At the question, Carolyn was taken slightly aback, and she asked, "Doesn't it?" only remembering belatedly to add the signs.

Pretty Moon's eyes twinkled. "If Pretty Moon stopped doing the things that bring her pleasure simply because her husband disapproved," she signed, "she would have no pride. You must learn that it is the woman who determines the happiness of her home, and it is Pretty Moon who is master of her lodge, not slave to her husband."

Really? Carolyn was at once fascinated. How many of Carolyn's contemporaries could say such a thing?

Pretty Moon, however, was not finished, and she asked, "Do you not know this?"

Carolyn shook her head.

"It is as the old ones say. The white women are slaves to their men. But not you. You watch Pretty Moon. I will show you how to manage a man." She completed the signs and then said in English, "You . . . watch."

Carolyn could not help but smile at the young woman. "Then . . . are you telling me . . . that you will still go with me?"

Pretty Moon nodded, saying only, "Humph!"

"And we'll leave as we planned?"

Pretty Moon made a rather distinct, and perhaps indecent, gesture in the direction where Lone Arrow had retreated. She signed, "If our men object, they can try to find us, but by then, we should be well on our way."

Our men? It was in Carolyn's mind to correct Pretty Moon's impression about Carolyn's own relationship with Lone Arrow. But she thought better of it. After all, might she not have misread those signs?

Still, as Carolyn gazed at the young woman before her—with an expression that might have been part inquiry, part awe—she began to realize that she had made a friend. And she was pleased to note that the knowledge gave her great comfort.

Pretty Moon signed, "We leave tonight, as soon as our men sleep. When I send you the signal, you are to come to me in the Indian camp. Do you understand?"

"I do," Carolyn confirmed, and as she observed Pretty Moon's expression, she could not help it. Carolyn grinned, the gesture turning easily and swiftly into a deep, spontaneous laugh.

Chapter 10

Standing on firm, high ground, Carolyn gazed out over the grayish-green bog before them. A few buffalo were grazing on the low land, the animals munching on the lush grasses which grew so abundantly around the swamp.

In the distance Carolyn's eyes fastened on a huge mountain of ashen-brown rocks jutting up into the morning brilliance of a blue, cloudless sky. Those rocks appeared to Carolyn as though they might have once been a majestic cathedral or a gigantic castle worn down over time to mere rock and grit.

Closer at hand, the ground rose up on a gradual incline toward those rocks. It was here that she was mesmerized by the sight of a buffalo herd so vast it looked like a blanket tossed over a spot of grass. And right in front of her a part of that herd—fifteen or perhaps twenty buffalo—grazed. The animals were probably not more than thirty feet away. Brushing a fly from her face, Carolyn thought she would never again mistake the scent of buffalo.

Funny how that one sense, the one of smell, could bring back memories of eight and a half years ago. Funny, too, how she had forgotten.

But then, why should she remember these things from her past? As life had gone on, and when she had thought of the past at all, she had overlooked many things: like her reaction to Lone Arrow.

Would it have made a difference if she had remembered? Would it have changed her decision to come here?

Of course not.

She sighed, and as she did so, she inhaled the sweet fragrance of the grasses and flowers which littered the bog. Their scent, all mixed up with the grimy odor of dirt and marsh, stimulated her, bringing back wave upon wave of memories. Ones she hadn't even known she had.

Odd, she thought. This was probably the closest she had ever been to the buffalo; even eight and a half years ago, she had never come so near to them. Usually the animals moved away as soon as they caught the human scent.

Which brought to mind another question: why didn't these buffalo run?

Carolyn turned to Pretty Moon, thinking to put the question to words, but as though the other woman knew her thoughts, Pretty Moon said, by way of signs, "It is the wind."

"The wind?" Carolyn signed the question.

Pretty Moon nodded.

Ah, so that was it; Carolyn at last understood. She and Pretty Moon stood downwind from the buffalo; and because of this, the pack could not pick up the human scent. These buffalo literally had no idea that they were being watched by human eyes.

Inhaling another earth-fragrant breath, Carolyn continued to watch the scene before her with fascination. Meanwhile, Pretty Moon silently slipped off their pony's back. The young Indian woman came to stand by Carolyn, and together, both of them stared out upon the land before them as though it were the most beautiful thing under God's creation.

And perhaps it was.

Carolyn relaxed. She felt good; moreover, she was experiencing more than a slight feeling of kinship with this woman who stood beside her.

It was an entirely new experience for Carolyn. Never having had any siblings or close friends her own age, Carolyn began to wonder what she had missed by not having sisters.

Had it been only this morning that she and Pretty Moon had made a pact? It seemed so long ago.

Having only the one pony to ride, they had agreed that they would alternately ride or walk, each one taking their turn atop the animal while the other led the pack mule. It was a perfect arrangement; absolutely perfect, for friends.

Pretty Moon touched her shoulder, and gaining Carolyn's attention, she pointed out something. Carolyn stared off in the direction shown her. Ah, there it was—there, to her right. A coyote was crouching behind some bushes, he, too, watching the buffalo herd; only this wiley animal did so with hungry eyes.

Carolyn smiled. Alas, this was, indeed, a glorious moment, and she felt as though a part of her were expanding—at least that part of her which had nothing to do with the physical body. Leisurely, as though she had all the time in the world, she let her vision travel to the far corners of the surrounding countryside.

Interrupting her thoughts, a bee flew before her eyes, perhaps showering her with little bits of pollen, for Carolyn all at once sneezed, then sniffled.

Fishing in her pocket for a handkerchief, she let her thoughts drift back to the early hours of the morning, to the fort. Strangely enough, the two women had escaped Fort Ellis and the Indian encampment, as well, without incident. Carolyn had simply explained to the fort's guards that she had hired Pretty Moon to lead her to her parents' graves, which were located somewhere in the Bighorn Mountains.

It was a factual enough statement, since it was something Carolyn meant to do . . . if she had time. She really hadn't lied.

Had she?

So why should the half-truth bother her?

No, she thought as she ran the idea around in her mind, she had done what she had to do. The trouble was, and this was what was difficult to understand, leaving the fort had been so easy to do.

Too easy. Perhaps that's what bothered her.

Would their men follow them?

Their men?

Carolyn instinctively shied away from that thought, as well as any reason as to why she might have had it.

Of course Lone Arrow and his friend would follow them. And they would be angry.

At least Lone Arrow could not stop her, could he? Not now anyway, now that she had left.

After all, what could he do?

She groaned. A great deal, she feared. He could ensure she never found the cave.

Carolyn was not aware that she was frowning until
Pretty Moon reached out toward her, cutting into Carolyn's contemplations. In her hand Pretty Moon extended a piece of jerky.

Ah, breakfast. A smile came easily to Carolyn's face
as she accepted the food readily, tearing off a section of
it with her teeth.

Reaching into her own bag, Carolyn replaced her
handkerchief and took out a couple of honeycombs that
she had brought with her from the fort, offering one of
them to Pretty Moon, who accepted it.

Presently, Pretty Moon indicated that the two of
them should keep moving, and Carolyn nodded.

"Make no sharp movements," Pretty Moon signed as
Carolyn, finishing her meal, licked her fingers and
threw her bag over the pony's back.

Positioning herself as she had watched Pretty Moon
do, Carolyn jumped up onto the pony.

Although it took her three or four attempts to accomplish it, at last, Carolyn sat atop the pony. She nodded,
and the two women headed out of their shrub-bush
cover, out into the midst of the buffalo herd.

Hopefully, they would be halfway to those imposing, rocklike mountains before the men caught up to
them. That she would have to explain herself went
without question. That she and Pretty Moon might be
required to turn around and go back to the fort didn't
bear consideration.

In the meantime, Carolyn decided, she would enjoy
herself and the little bit of freedom she had left.

*   *   *

It started harmlessly enough. A bee buzzed around Carolyn's face and fingers, most likely because honey still clung to her in those places.

Darn. She hated these little bees. She swished at the insect, but the little bugger wouldn't leave her alone.

She could stick a few of her fingers in her mouth to wash off the honey, she supposed, but she hated to do that. What with petting the horse, keeping hold of the reins and pushing aside bushes in their way, Carolyn's fingers were filthy, covered with bits of dirt and dust . . . and they were sticky.

Wait, she had put her handkerchief into her bag only a few moments ago, and it was within her reach. It would take her only a second to get it.

Hating to bother Pretty Moon, Carolyn leaned down to open her bag. Unfortunately, she brought up her leg sightly as she turned, not realizing until too late that the movement hit the bee, which had already landed on the horse.

The bee stung the horse, who then reared, and Carolyn, already twisted in her seat, could not hold on. She flew off the horse's back, sailed through the air and came down with a plop, landing in a boggy mire of dirty water.

"Ouch!" Lifting a mud-soaked hand out in front of her face, she wiggled her fingers and toes; at least everything still seemed to work.

And perhaps the entire incident would not have been so bad if it hadn't been for Pretty Moon. The other woman stood beside her, laughing.

Carolyn smoothed a lock of hair from her face and grimaced as she watched a rivulet of muddy water slide down its length.

"Go ahead and laugh," Carolyn called to her. "I know I would, too, if someone looked as silly as I must. Although, don't you think that one of us should go after the horse? He's carrying all our supplies, and the mule's following him."

Pretty Moon nodded, although she made no move to go after the animal.

Carolyn came slowly to her feet, her bonnet flopping down over her forehead. She tried to push it back from her face, but it kept collapsing forward, splattering even more mud and gunk on her.

Her antics caused Pretty Moon to giggle even more furiously than before, one hand thrown up over her mouth.

Drat, Carolyn thought, she was wet from her neck clear down to the tips of her toes; her skirt and petticoats, now muddy and slimy, clung to her legs like oily rags, and her boots gushed murky water with each step she took. Even her bodice was drooping.

"Oh, no," she said. "Look at me. I'm going to have to change into another skirt."

Pretty Moon nodded, trying her best to keep from smiling. "Pretty Moon," she pointed to herself, "will take mule . . . and catch . . . horse. Does . . . white friend have . . . other dress?"

"One," Carolyn said. "I didn't bring many of them, since I figured we'd do some laundry along the way."

But she hadn't thought she'd need to do it so soon.

"If you'll go and fetch the pony," continued Carolyn, "I'll slip out of these clothes. Maybe there is some clear water here where I can wash the skirt."

"There . . ." Pretty Moon pointed in the direction of a small stream. "Pretty Moon . . . go . . . get horse."

"Yes," Carolyn agreed. "Please."

In answer, Pretty Moon turned around and took off, chasing after their single mode of transportation.

Carolyn took a step forward, only to trip over her own skirt.

Goodness, it was one thing after another. Maybe she should step out of the skirt so she didn't keep tangling herself up in it.

Reaching down, she began to undo each of the buttons which held the skirt in place. So intent was she upon her task that she was unaware for the moment of the things going on around her. Perhaps that was why she didn't see it.

Something poked her in the backside.

Turning around, she saw the reason at once. A buffalo calf had come up behind her. Curious, she reached out a hand toward it.

"You're a cute little fellow," she said with a smile. "Where's your mother?"

As if in answer, the little guy switched its tail.

"Well," she said, pulling the skirt down around her feet. "It's been nice talking to you, and you're a sweet little thing, but I really have to be going. I'd like this skirt to be washed before Pretty Moon comes back."

Carolyn took a step. With one foot precariously raised, she lost her balance and fell backward . . . right into the calf.

It cried, and as Carolyn pitched to the ground, the calf collapsed over her.

Goodness, but the little guy was acting like a baby. It whined and cried as though she had done it bodily harm.

Carolyn tried to extricate herself from underneath

the calf. Praise be, but it sure did weigh a great deal. She shoved against him, but she could not budge him.

"Would you move off me?" Exasperated, the question came out as more complaint than question.

The calf merely let out another moan. Goodness gracious!

Unfortunately, another buffalo, perhaps the calf's mother, was making its way toward them, a little too quickly.

But Carolyn barely noticed. She had her own problems. The calf could not get up, and she could not move it, either. Its feet had become entangled, and the more it struggled, the more ensnared it became.

Carolyn sent a helpless glance up toward the heavens. What was she to do?

As she tried once more to move and could not, she realized that she was going to have to help the little buffalo get to its feet. Leaning over, she touched its hairy legs and began to set its feet out, one over another.

There, now. She almost had it. In another moment, she would have the calf back on its feet, and gain her own legs out from underneath it.

Miserably, she noted as she glanced around her, she had drawn a crowd. Four buffalo had come to stand over her, looking down at her as though she were the latest in Wild West entertainment.

In little time, however, the calf was back on its own legs, and Carolyn was able to struggle to her feet. Taking a deep breath and stepping completely out of her skirt and petticoats, she paced around the other buffalo that had come to watch her.

They reminded her of cows somehow. Big, dangerous, wild cows, yes, but cows nevertheless.

The stream that Pretty Moon had pointed out was only a short distance away, and Carolyn paced quickly toward it, unaware that the calf followed her. And so it was that Carolyn had little knowledge that the calf's mother followed it, and that the other buffalo began to follow the mother, keeping to its quickened pace.

Soon a few buffalo tramped by her. Then several more.

Carolyn did notice that the animals appeared to be moving a little too fast. But she didn't think much about it; certainly it was no reason to glance behind her.

Unaware of what was beginning to take place, Carolyn picked up her pace. In truth, she began to run toward the stream. She had almost made it, too, when it happened.

The buffalo, which had begun to surround her, were beginning to pass by quickly, their speed perhaps matching her own. And at last, Carolyn thought to glance over her shoulder.

Dear Lord, she thought as she took it all in. How had this happened? The entire herd was beginning to follow her and the calf. Worse, unless she did something soon, she might likely be trampled to death.

But if they were following her, would they also stop if she did?

The little guy behind her let out another whimper as the bigger animals pushed past them. Carolyn turned around, her gaze falling onto the baby. At least he wasn't running away from her. Carolyn fell to her knees before him, throwing her arms around the animal. Could he possibly be her lifeline?

Would the other buffalo be aware of them, perhaps even watch out for him, making a path around him?

As the thunder of pounding hoofs began to drown out even this disturbing thought, Carolyn could only pray that it would be so.

Chapter 11

Lone Arrow was not happy. It was an understatement.

How could the white woman have left the fort as she had? After he had forbidden it?

And Pretty Moon; what did she have to do with the white woman's escape? Did the two of them think it a mere game to defy their men?

Their men?

Raising up from the ground where he had been squatting over the women's trail, Lone Arrow snorted at the thought. He was not her man; she was not his woman.

Staring off in the direction the women had taken, he tried to speculate on what was in the white woman's mind. From her tracks, here in the sand, he could tell that she was agitated. What he did not understand was why the women were not bothering to cover their trail, nor the direction of their path.

Did they think no one would come after them?

Perhaps the white men at the fort might be content to let them go. But he . . .

That was another thing. How had Carolyn convinced the soldiers not to follow them? She must have done something, for the bluecoats were making no moves to send out a rescue party.

Lone Arrow looked off into the distance, and he figured that from the freshness of the tracks, he and his friend were only a half day behind them. In the meantime, his pony snorted and shoved her nose under Lone Arrow's hand.

"Easy, girl," he said, whereupon, without thinking, he began to pat the animal.

Why weren't the women traveling more quickly?

Obviously they wanted to be found.

Why?

Lone Arrow scowled. Who knew the workings of a woman's mind. As the old ones had often said, "Do not try to understand them. Simply love and protect them."

Shrugging, he signaled to his friend, telling him to move on ahead. And Lone Arrow, jumping up to regain his seat atop his pony, refused to try to make sense of these clues he found.

At least the women were not far ahead of them. If he and his friend rode hard, they should catch up to the women by the time the sun was highest in the sky.

Hopefully, The-girl-who-runs-with-bears and Pretty Moon had met with no trouble, although that seemed unlikely. This was, after all, The-girl-who-runs-with-bears. She seemed to be involved in more accidents than any single person he had ever known.

He could only hope that Pretty Moon would be alert

enough to rescue her, since Lone Arrow was certain that his white woman would need it.

His white woman?

Lone Arrow pulled his brows together, frowning, as an abrupt realization came over him. He was worried about her . . . really worried about her. . . .

Lone Arrow heard the thunder of buffalo hooves in the distance. It meant that the herd was in the throes of a running stampede.

His stomach turned over at the sound. Why? There was nothing to fear there; nothing unusual.

Or was there?

He stared down at the imprints in the ground, which told him a story. He did not like this. He did not understand it, either. Why would the women's path lead them in the direction of a stampeding herd? Pretty Moon would have avoided contact with the buffalo, if at all possible.

It had to be the inexperience of The-girl-who-runs-with-bears. She did not know the ways of the plains well enough to discern danger. He had observed this in her too many times in the past not to be aware of it now.

Pulling back on his buckskin reins, Lone Arrow stared straight ahead of him. What was wrong? Why did he feel as though he were on the verge of toppling over the precipice of some high cliff.

Glancing over his shoulder at his friend Big Elk, Lone Arrow gave him to understand that they needed to hurry.

Why this was so, he did not know. It was only that he had a bad feeling about this.

* * *

He saw her at once, heard her scream, even over the beating of buffalo hooves.

How she had managed to situate herself in the midst of a stampeding buffalo herd, he might never know. But it was of little value to ponder it.

This time, he thought, The-girl-who-runs-with-bears had gone too far. This time her antics had gotten her into more than a simple stumble over herself.

This was serious. She could be killed.

The sudden realization brought on a sense of panic within him, and alarm swept through him like a tide of black fear.

He had to do something.

For she must live. For herself; for him.

Ho! There it was. In this moment of stark unreality, one thing stood out clearly. He had feelings for this woman; raw, carnal yearnings.

And so it was with no sense of surprise that, perhaps for the first time, Lone Arrow admitted the truth. His own happiness, his own future, was irrefutably wound up with that of The-girl-who-runs-with-bears.

Turning toward Big Elk, who was watching him, Lone Arrow signed that the rescue of the white woman was to be *his* concern alone. Big Elk should go and find his own wife.

And while Big Elk spun about, Lone Arrow pressed his war pony forward, into the herd of buffalo.

"A-la-pee," he called the Appaloosa by her name, which meant in the Crow language "Grass Fire." "We will have to rescue her, do you understand?" The pony whinnied and shook her head, and Lone Arrow continued, saying, "Step sure of foot, my friend."

The animal snorted, as though it understood every

word he had said, and Lone Arrow thanked his medicine, as well as his spirit protector, that he'd had the foresight at the start of this journey to ride out on his best mount.

At least, thought Lone Arrow, the herd was not in a full run . . . yet. But if the animals caught the human scent or had the least inducement, they might stampede . . . and then there would be no hope . . . for her . . . for him.

He had to get to her quickly.

"*Délaah*! Go!" Lone Arrow shouted to his pony over the noise of the herd. But the encouragement was hardly needed. A-la-pee sensed the excitement and began to squeeze her way into the herd, avoiding oncoming buffalo, and heading toward the girl.

Had The-girl-who-runs-with-bears seen them? Did she know that help was on the way? No, she could not, he answered his own question. Her head was down.

And what was that she was holding? A calf?

Lone Arrow silently congratulated her on her wisdom. Even the mean-tempered, old bulls would skirt around the calf, protecting it.

"Carolyn!" he shouted over the noise of striking hooves.

He had been right. She had not noticed him, for she stared up at him quickly, sending him a startled glance, and as she did so, he added, "Take my hand."

Her eyes looked big and white in her face as she swung around to glance up at him, and he heard her mutter, "Lone Arrow," as though she did not believe she was seeing correctly. "You've come after me."

He nodded. "I come. Now, give me your hand."

She did so at once, and he pulled her up behind him.

"Hold on to me," he instructed, although he might

not have bothered. She grabbed hold of him instinctively. "Do not let go of me no matter what happens. Do you understand?"

She nodded. And he began to ease A-la-pee out of the herd.

Trained to respond to knee pressure alone, and sensing her master's intention, the Appaloosa needed little direction. She sidestepped her way out of the buffalo herd, pressing toward the edge of it, dodging one buffalo after another, avoiding the horns of an ill-tempered bull moving ever closer to safety.

In truth, she had almost cleared the herd completely when a particular buffalo bull spun about toward them.

Lone Arrow saw the animal at once, witnessed its turn and, at the sight, felt his heart jump up into his throat. Recognition of the animal made his spirits sink. This was not good; not at all.

This was not the sort of bull who bluffed a charge at the enemy, attempting only to make his foe go away. This buffalo was a special type of animal. Lean and skinny, its mangy mane hung down over its eyes bluntly, as though its coarse hair had been cut that way. This alone made the animal easy to identify.

This was the type of buffalo that never charged unless it meant to kill you; it never gave up. And it had put its sights of *them*.

A-la-pee must have seen the animal at the same time as Lone Arrow, for she had made a series of moves, away from its charge. Lone Arrow could feel her desire to run, and he struggled to hold her back.

Lone Arrow's muscles bulged under his exertion, and it was with little more than personal willpower that he forced A-la-pee to retreat, while ever so gradually winding her way to the side of the herd.

Still, the buffalo charged.

Another turn by his mount kept them out of the bull's reach. Unfortunately, the pony and riders faced the oncoming charge of the rest of the herd as well. There was a moment of confusion, as the entire world seemed to be coming down around them, and Lone Arrow could feel A-la-pee's panic.

Had he saved The-girl-who-runs-with-bears only to be killed together?

"*Ap-xi-sshe.*" He used an endearment to calm the animal. "We will survive this. You are the best war pony a man ever had."

A-la-pee raised her head as the buffalo made yet another rush at them.

The Appaloosa dodged at the perfect moment, swinging around to confront the bull. Another step, another pace or two, another dodge from the oncoming bull, and they were free at last.

But the buffalo followed them, making another charge. It was at this moment that Lone Arrow let A-la-pee have her rein, and so quickly did she spin away from the herd, to run across the prairie, that one might have thought a demon were after her.

And perhaps it was true.

Lone Arrow glanced over his shoulder, noting that the buffalo was giving them chase. And though Lone Arrow knew the huge animal's speed was no match for his pony, he still experienced a moment of concern.

Soon, however, A-la-pee put more distance between them and danger, and Lone Arrow watched—again over his shoulder—as the bull stopped, the huge beast pawing the ground in frustration. And then, as though realizing it had done all it could do, it turned tail and headed back toward the herd.

Seeing this, Lone Arrow drew a deep breath. It was only then that he allowed himself a moment of relief.

A very short moment, for he would not let himself rest. He could not. Guiding his mount up onto higher ground, he wasn't satisfied until they had put more than a few hills and gullies between themselves and that buffalo.

At last, Lone Arrow drew back on the reins, bringing A-la-pee to a halt.

Jumping down from his seat, Lone Arrow threw the buckskin reins onto the ground, expressing his foul mood. Never, not ever, could he remember being so upset with another human being. Never had a woman given him reason to lose his temper like this.

Striding back and forth in front of Carolyn, who was still atop the Appaloosa, Lone Arrow quipped, "You— you were supposed to go home! This land, my country"—he extended his arms in a circle—"is a dangerous place for people who do not know the ways of it. Do you realize what would have happened to you, soon . . . very soon, if I had not come for you?"

She did not answer, which only incited him further, for she looked innocent, much too innocent. And it was this, her attitude, that was more than he could stand.

Did she not understand that she had almost lost her life?

He continued, "How did you manage to get into the middle of that herd?"

He watched her gulp, as though she attempted to answer, but no words formed on her lips. Narrowing his eyes at her, he beheld her fear, watched as she seemed to choke on mere syllables, but he was not inclined to spare her the tiniest bit of sympathy. Instead, he carried on, saying, "Where is Pretty Moon?"

The white woman pointed, although again she said nothing; it was as though fear had taken hold of her voice.

But not so for Lone Arrow. "What were you thinking?" he said. "You will never find that cave and help your family if you get yourself killed. Do you not know this?"

She nodded.

"Then why did you leave without me?"

That question, more than anything, seemed to stir a spark of life in her, for she narrowed her eyes at him, raised a well-arched brow and spat, "Without—you?"

He crossed his arms over his chest, muttering only, "Humph! *Éeh,* yes. Without me."

"You, you—you . . ."

He jerked his head slightly to the left, while she tipped her chin defiantly toward the sky.

And then, as though she had at last found her tongue, she began, "You, Lone Arrow, made it abundantly clear that you would *not* take me where I need to go." As though she gained inspiration by speaking, she jumped down from the Appaloosa, her feet hitting solid ground with a dull thud. She even took a step toward him before she continued: "Is it my fault that you chose to ignore me? Is it my fault that you are bullheaded and stubborn? Is it my fault that you can't seem to trust me?

"No, it's not," she answered her own questions. "And it's certainly not a sign of weakness on my part that I seek a way to get to the mountains without you. And don't think you can talk me out of going there, or Pretty Moon, either, for that matter. I'm determined to get there. And she is, too . . . I think," Carolyn added, although Lone Arrow had to strain to hear this last.

However, all he uttered in response to her was,

"Humph!" before he said, "Where are the rest of your clothes?"

A look of shock passed over her features as she gazed down at herself. Mayhap she had forgotten that she stood before him in no more than calf-length drawers and corset.

Ignoring her red-faced countenance, he went on to say, "Pretty Moon knows not this cave that you seek or where it is."

Carolyn appeared to recover quickly enough, and placing her hands on her hips, she said, "But I do. I'll recognize it again when I see it."

He squinted his eyes at her. "Will you?" he asked.

A glimmer of doubt crossed over her features, but he said nothing. At last, bringing his arms down to his sides, hands clenched in fists, he took one step toward her, saying, "You are not to defy me again, do you understand?"

She did not appear to take orders well, he observed, for she stood straighter and countered, "I will do as I please. You are not my lord and master."

"Am I not?"

She shook her head.

"Ho," he said, "and what happened to your marriage proposal? Have you forgotten it so soon?"

That simple statement seemed to startle her. Her glance dropped to the ground. And Lone Arrow was silently congratulating himself on his cleverness, when she said, "You have already told me what you think of me."

Again Lone Arrow experienced a moment of anxiety, though of a different sort and, for a moment, his stomach knotted up. *Had he told this woman of his concern for her? How could he, when he had only just become cognizant of it himself?*

"Please," she said, "don't rub my nose in it. I understand perfectly that you do not wish to have anything to do with me. Do me a favor, please. Truth be known, I would consider it an act of kindness if you would simply go away and . . ."

Go away? Strangely enough, relief flooded his system. He had not revealed himself to her after all.

". . . And leave me and Pretty Moon alone."

Leave her alone? After that hair-raising rescue?

It was with some revelation that Lone Arrow realized he could no more leave this woman alone than he could stop the wind from blowing. But he had no intention of telling her that. And with good reason.

And so, he uttered, "Pretty Moon's husband might have something to say about what she does, as well he should."

Carolyn tilted her head, sending him a glare. "Perhaps," she said. "But I think she is running away from him."

Lone Arrow uttered a grunt beneath his breath, while aloud, he commented, "He is here with her now. He will take her back with him, and you will follow me."

"I will not."

"You have not the choice."

"I have every choice."

Lone Arrow set his feet together in a stance as natural to him as the act of breathing: feet not too close together or too far apart; weight on one foot while the other was thrust slightly forward. One hand at his side, the other holding his bow, which had previously been hanging from his shoulder. It was a way of holding himself, a position and a manner which said, "Do not tamper with me." As if to complete the image, he commanded, "You and Pretty Moon are not to go anywhere alone. It is obvious that you will only get into trouble. I forbid it."

Lone Arrow was happy with himself, though he carefully hid such satisfaction from her. And why should he not feel some elation? He had done well so far; curbing his anger toward her. He was even instilling caution within her with his well-chosen words.

Yet his self-appreciation died a quick, silent death. For when she spoke, despite the fact that she should have shown him deference, she seemed completely unaffected by him. She even went so far as to utter, "You, Lone Arrow, have no right to forbid me anything."

Why that statement should bother him, he did not know. Yet it did all the same.

He narrowed his eyes at her but did not reply at once. And it was with some feeling of surprise that he realized he itched to shake some sense into her. But of course he would not do it. As the elders always said, only a coward or a man of little character would use physical force on a woman or on anyone who could not fight back.

Yet, for all his good intentions, Lone Arrow could not curb his tongue, not quite. And though he knew he should think the thought through, perhaps a little more thoroughly, he found himself uttering, as though in challenge, "Then I accept."

Color slowly drained from her face, and she stared at him as though he had gone mad. She asked, "You what?"

He did not move a muscle; he merely stated again as calmly as possible, "I have decided that I will accept your proposal."

"M-my . . . what?"

He gritted his teeth. "I will marry you."

He watched as her throat worked against itself, as though she did not know whether to swallow or to speak. At some length, she said, "You . . . you wish to . . . marry me?" She raised her eyes to his. "Really?"

He nodded.

"Then . . . you . . . have some . . . feelings for me?"

He did not budge. He did not even blink, and he said, "And as your husband, I will forbid you to go any further in search of this cave."

"Oh," she uttered. He watched as darkness fell over her features. "I see," she continued. "Well, then I guess I will not marry you, after all, because there is nothing— not a single thing that you can do that will make me stop my search."

He stepped forward. "I could tie you up," he stated, though he made no move to do it. Instead, he reached out to push a lock of her hair away from her face.

She knocked his hand away. "And I will only get loose and come out here again. The only thing you would gain is time. But because I have so little of that, by doing such a thing, you could cause the ruin of my family."

"*I?* I have not caused their ruin now, nor will I cause it in the future, no matter what I do. Others cannot live your life for you."

"And yet, you rescued *me* today."

He shrugged, seeing no harm in admitting the obvious.

"Yet, you would keep me from rescuing my family?"

"That is different." He watched as the wind blew that same lock of her hair forward, and once more he reached out to tuck it behind her ear.

This time, however, she did not whack his hand away, though she did say, "How is it different? A rescue is a rescue, whether it be from bears or buffalo or a land-hungry banker. You would deny me the right to help another? The same right that you take for granted?"

He sighed. Why was it so hard to win an argument with this woman?

"Lone Arrow"—she reached up and grabbed his fingers with her own—"I once offered you the only gift I have to give to a man. Now you accept my proposal, but only in exchange for my obedience to you. Somewhere in between, there must be a compromise we could make. Marry me, but take me to the cave."

One touch.

That was all it had taken. One touch of her hand and his body came to instant alert. He supposed he could remove his fingers from her own, but the will to do so was not there within him.

He said, "That is no compromise at all, and well you know it. It would be more like my surrender. Besides, I could make you marry me."

She shook back her hair. "I think not."

"I can prove it to you." He took a step forward.

She shook her head.

And that's when it happened. He kissed her.

Chapter 12

Oh, what a kiss.

As his lips captured hers, his hands came up to cup her face, holding her gently, as though even his fingers adored her. Slowly he trailed a forefinger down over her cheek, to her neck.

And while raw hunger swept through her like a living inferno, Carolyn, closing her eyes, went limp. She simply could not control it. Despite what she had said, despite what she had tried to make him—and perhaps herself, too—believe, she had yearned for this moment.

And as his tongue swept into her mouth, shutting off whatever protest she might have made, Carolyn could barely conjure up a single thought.

Not when the soft texture of his mouth, the musky scent of his skin, the utter thrill of his lips on hers made her wish that this moment might never end. She leaned in closer to him, and instinctively, she knew she needed more, so much more.

She felt herself sway in toward him, and he took a step forward, as though in welcome, the action bringing his body into full contact with hers. Of their own accord, her arms wound around his neck, and she held on like she might never let go.

Hard contours pressed up against her soft ones and Carolyn became aware of him, of the rugged imprint of his masculinity which thrust against her.

Lord help her, their positions, her awareness of him, created such an ecstasy within her, she felt it impossible to catch her breath. And without willing herself to do so, she pushed herself even further into his arms, merging her body with his in silent invitation.

His voice was strained when he asked, "Do you understand, Carolyn?" He relinquished her lips for a moment, giving her time to come up for breath. And nuzzling her ear, he whispered, "Do you see? Do you accept that I could make you mine?"

She shook her head slightly, resting her face against the crook of his neck, listening to the harsh sound of his breathing, glorying in the solid feel of his chest as it rose and fell.

Had *she* done this to him?

She said, "Then marry me, Lone Arrow, marry me and be done with it. Only Lone Arrow," she threw her head back slightly so that she could look up at him, "don't think that you will be able to control what I do because of it."

He groaned. "A woman should obey her man."

"I will, when I marry," she said, "as long as I agree with him."

"And if you do not agree?"

"Then we will have to speak to one another about it, because I would never do something that I thought might be wrong, and I will not stop searching for the cave."

Lone Arrow sighed, and even the simple movement of his chest beneath her fingertips seduced her, creating a yearning that gnawed at her.

And as raw excitement filled her soul, she realized that, right or wrong, she wanted this man. He might be from an entirely foreign culture, he might be her nemesis at this moment, yet she craved his arms around her. Craved his presence in her life. In truth, she wanted all of him, mind, body and soul.

"Such a stubborn, stubborn woman, you are," he observed as he stroked her lips with his tongue.

And at the magic of that caress, a tremor stormed through her. She shivered.

Nonetheless, she found it within herself to return his criticism, saying, "Such an obstinate man, you are."

He paused. Then, "I will not show you the caves because of it."

It? What was *it?*

She became lost. Was he talking about love or caves or marriage . . . or was it sex? This last notion sent dizzying eagerness bolting through her. And oh, how she ached to have his lips back on hers.

Why were they talking?

But he seemed intent on the matter at hand, and he went on to elaborate. "I do not accept your challenge, no matter what you might think."

Was she supposed to be thinking? She asked, "My challenge?"

"I will not show you the cave, no matter if I make you my wife."

Oh, yes, of course, marriage. They had been speaking of marriage.

She opened her mouth to state again what she must, but at that very same moment, he raised one of his hands and ran the backs of his fingers down her cheek. And, heaven help her, her mind went blank.

Reaching out with both his hands, he cupped her face in his palms and gazed down at her. And there was such a look of intensity upon his face that it made her insides somersault. Truly, she felt as helpless as if she were a rag, fluttering in a summer storm. And then he kissed her again, fully, completely, absolutely.

Carolyn forgot all the reasons why she was supposed to resist him. In truth, she could not even recall why she was here, let alone understand the topic at hand. All she could think of was him, his lips, his embrace. And dear Lord, she wanted more. Always more.

But as if destined, it did not last. Just as she'd been about to surrender her heart to him, he dropped his arms from around her and took a single step backward.

Carolyn swayed. She felt bereft. And she might have thrown herself back into his arms, if she hadn't made the mistake of looking up at him at that exact moment.

His look caused her to frown. What was wrong? Why did he appear suddenly forbidding? All she wanted was another kiss.

He said, "I would have you understand."

She must have looked confused, or maybe she simply continued to frown at him, for he went on to explain, "I would have you understand, without the lure of passion filling your soul, that if I make you my wife, I will not be coerced into taking you to the cave. We will go back to my people."

Oh. So that was it.

Well, fine. She understood; of course she understood. What he did not seem to know was that at this moment in time, it mattered not at all. Alas, nothing seemed to concern her.

Something was happening to her. And try though she might to look straight at him, she seemed to be gazing down upon them both, from a viewpoint far above them. And at present, she felt carefree.

It was an odd feeling; strange, really. For the world suddenly seemed a bright, sunny place. And there was nothing wrong. In truth, there seemed to be nothing of worth happening in the world at all, except her, him, the passion they shared, her family.

Her family?

Like an arrow shooting straight to its target, Carolyn remembered; why she was here, who she was, who he was and why she needed him. And like a hunter's target, she felt herself plummet to the earth.

She teetered on her feet unsteadily for a second as a heaviness descended upon her. And clearing her throat, she found she could barely speak, although she knew she must. Finally, mustering together what she could, she was able to utter, "I—I do understand. Y-you want to marry me so I will have to obey you. But my conditions remain. I will marry you only if you promise to take me to the cave. I'm sorry, Lone Arrow, but I am desperate."

So, there it was. They had reached the same impasse that they had encountered the previous evening. They both knew it and yet, he said, "It is wrong. I know it is not a thing I should do, still . . ."

Still what? She wanted to ask, but she was afraid. So she remained silent instead, daring nothing.

And at last he said, "I would have you."

It appeared that he had settled some point of argument within himself, for at once, without waiting for her to answer, he fell to his knees before her, drawing her down to the ground as well.

It was a highly erotic position. Knee to knee, chest to chest, his arms swept around her, holding her.

"Say it," she said, as he pulled down her drawers, his fingers going unerringly to the softness of her core.

"Say what?"

Was he so dense that he didn't know? Or was he merely unaware that she needed to hear it from his lips?

On a sigh she uttered, "Tell me you care for me."

"I care." He complied to her request at once, although he went on to mutter, "Against my better judgment, I care."

But this last didn't matter. Now now. Not when raw passion filled her heart.

And oh, how she wanted his touch there, even though she felt a twinge of embarrassment. But as a drop of moisture does to the heat of day, even her shyness fled as he moved against her. Heaven help her, she found herself twisting against him, also, in a most erotic way, shocking herself . . . almost . . .

Desire filled her soul, and as she stared up at him, he pushed back her hair, his touch sending liquid fire streaming along her nerves.

And with a huskiness in his voice, he said, "You are ready for me."

Was she? Did she even know what that meant?

She gazed into his midnight eyes and asked, "Is this what it means to make love?"

"Yes," he replied.

"Are we going to make love?"

He did not answer her right away; indeed, he stared at her with such fervor, it made her feel as though he looked straight to her soul. And perhaps he did, for she felt as though they had been as one, if only for a moment.

He nodded. "We will make love."

She gulped.

And he said, "I would make you my wife."

"I see," she said. "Is this how it is done, then?"

Another nod from him.

"It is not the way of things in my culture," she said softly. "In my world, I would be branded a loose woman if we were to seal this lovers' act."

Lone Arrow did not miss a beat as he said, "The white men have many strange customs. Know that in my world, this is how a man and woman secure their vows." And then, with his gaze trained so very, very softly onto hers, he asked, "Do you become my wife?"

There was a lump in her throat that she could not quite swallow, as she tried to find her voice. At last she was able to state, "I . . . yes, Lone Arrow, I do."

He nodded, satisfied, and with barely a pause, he proceeded to remove those drawers. But she brushed his hands away. She, too, would be certain of him. And she asked, "Do you also promise to be my husband?"

Lone Arrow breathed in deeply and brought a finger up to caress her cheek, before he placed a light kiss on her lips. He said, "I will."

Carolyn shut her eyes, as though in defense against an emotional tempest. Her lips quivered, and no matter that in her world, theirs would be no real marriage, together, beneath the bright blue heavens and within the sight of God, they had made their vows.

She said, "Then I suppose we are married . . . in a way."

He caressed her face with a delicate touch, smiling

down at her as he replied, "There is no suppose about it or at least there will not be in a very short time."

And so it was upon that final note, he drew her to the ground.

Was this love?
It felt as though it might be.
Carolyn gazed up at Lone Arrow as he lay over and above her. She was no fool. Carolyn was aware that there was a difference between a schoolgirl crush and a lifelong love. Was this it? And if it were the same, when had it started?

Just now? Or had it been at the age of eleven?

Had she actually fallen in love with this man all those years ago? The notion was perhaps a little far-fetched, yet for all that, it could be true.

She glanced up at him as she drew her fingers through his dark, coarse hair, loosening his braids, hearing him groan in reaction to her. At the same time, a shimmer of excitement swept through her.

She repeated the action, satisfied when she felt him tremble beneath her fingertips. Then, without taking his gaze from her, he broke away to sit up and remove his quiver from around his shoulders, his motions quick, exact. In less time than such an action would seem to take, he was finished and he threw himself back into her arms.

Smiling up at him, with a gentle touch she let her fingers trail down the hard plane of his chest.

He shivered, moaning in her ear and Carolyn wondered, did he melt at her touch, as she did with him? Did he yearn for her?

She murmured, "Do you feel it too?"

His eyes met hers as though the two of them were co-conspirators in a sea of swirling motion. And he asked softly, "Do you mean the fire?"

Fire. It was a perfect word for a perfect feeling.

She smiled and nodded, while her fingers caressed the toughened edges of his face.

He groaned as though in appreciation, then said, "It has always been this way with us, I think. It has been there, simmering."

Was he admitting that he had liked her, had maybe even desired her, all those years ago? It was hard to believe. And she observed, "But you barely paid any attention to me when we were younger."

"You were eleven years old."

"So?"

"You were a child."

"You were, too."

He shook his head. "I was a man of sixteen winters."

Carolyn had to smile at that, he sounded so proud. But she made no comment. Instead, she said, "I see. And now I am no longer eleven. Is that it?"

In answer, he bent down to kiss the words from her lips.

And, in response, Carolyn forgot to question him further.

However, changing the subject, he asked, "Have you ever known a man in this way?"

"In this way?" she asked in a whisper, momentarily confused. "You mean have I ever made love to a man?"

He nodded.

Shaking her head, she said, "No."

He stiffened. She felt it at once, and she wondered at the cause.

At length, he asked, "Never?"

"No, why?"

He rolled away from her, casually, as though nothing were wrong. And though he kept her in his embrace, Carolyn witnessed such a stern look of determination on his face, she felt disconcerted.

She opened her mouth to say something, but before she could voice a single word, he withdrew from her. Why?

She reached out to touch him. But he drew back.

And she asked, "What's wrong?"

Dropping his arms from around her, he turned his back on her. Worse, he picked up his quiver case and bow, positioning them back around his shoulders, a sure sign that something was wrong.

"What have I done?" she tried again, stretching out a hand to him, but not touching him. She dared not, for even the space around him vibrated.

He did not answer her right away. Indeed, he drew in his breath so deeply and let it out so swiftly, she wondered if he were ill. Finally, he said, still without glancing at her, "Look around you."

She scanned the horizon. "All right," she said, "I did."

"What do you see?"

"A flat prairie. Mountains in the distance, some hills; a very blue sky."

"And where is the sun?"

She glanced up. "Hmmm . . . almost overhead."

"Humph!" he said. "And now you know why."

"Why what? What am I supposed to know?"

He made another one of those animal sounds, deep in his throat before he spoke, at last saying, "We cannot make love . . . here . . . now."

She frowned. "We can't?"

He nodded, still without turning around to confront her. Then, casually, as though he might have undergone this conversation every day of his life, he said, "Ho! It should have occurred to me, but it did not. Or maybe I did think about it, but did not want to admit it."

He had lost her. "Admit what?" she asked.

"It did not occur to me," he said, "that you would not have known a man by now. Since you presented yourself to me in the flesh last night, I assumed that you had been married, or at least had some experience."

He must have heard her slight gasp behind him, for he went on to explain, "It is not so unusual for me to think this. Girls in our tribe are usually married by your age. Some are already widows. Though you told me you are not now married, I thought perhaps you might mourn a husband."

"I see," she said, but did she? What did this have to do with what was happening between them, here and now?

But she did not have long to wonder, for he went on to say, "Your innocence should not be taken here, at this time, and in a place where others could find us. A woman's first experience should be special for her. We will wait, I think."

"Oh." So that was it. She might have said more. Maybe she should have. However, she was at this moment, a little too embarrassed about the subject at hand, too flustered to speak up. Plus, if she were to be honest, she would have to admit to being extraordinarily stimulated. Indeed, at this moment, *she* simply did not care about the time of day.

She was not so uninhibited that she could tell him that, however.

But he was continuing to explain, extinguishing her need for a reply, and he said, "My friend and his wife,

Pretty Moon, will find us soon, and perhaps we should not be caught in a lover's embrace. In due time, our friends will come to know what is happening between us, but we do not need to show them so plainly. We will wait to marry, I think."

When he turned around to face her, she thought she espied a look of sympathy, illuminated there within the depths of his gaze.

Sympathy? Why? She needed no one's sympathy.

And while a momentary surge of protest welled up within her, and she opened her mouth to voice it, the words never materialized. For he had extended a hand toward her, letting a single fingertip smooth down over her cheek.

She bent her head toward that touch, while a flood of unadulterated desire raced along her nerve endings. She even reached out to touch his chest.

But he would not be swayed from his decision, it would appear, no matter what she did. He came up onto his feet, casting one last glance at her before he trod away. And so quickly did he go, Carolyn felt as though she had been left midair.

Worse, she had the strangest feeling. As if she had held the world in her hands and had let it slip away from her.

It was then she realized that she knew nothing about what was going on between herself and this man. In truth, she knew little about Lone Arrow, about love, or about men in general, for that matter. Let alone what might be expected from her in his, or even her culture.

She wondered: What did men want from women? What did women want from men? What did she need? And he? Should she have done something differently?

Would Pretty Moon know?

Briefly Carolyn recalled the other woman's words in sign: *Watch me with my husband tonight and you will see how to manage a man.*

Well, good enough, Carolyn thought. It required little effort to sit and observe. Perhaps she might learn something useful.

In the meanwhile, she had better busy herself with preparations for tonight. Surely Lone Arrow would approach her then.

And so it was that on this note Carolyn arose to follow her man.

Chapter 13

"Watch," signed Pretty Moon, touching her eyes and then pointing with her first and second index finger toward Big Elk. "You will learn how to handle your man."

Snapping down the index finger of her right hand, Carolyn gave Pretty Moon the sign for agreement. She added a nod for good measure.

It was about time. Big Elk and Lone Arrow had been deep in conversation for what was probably several hours, and although both women were becoming anxious to be alone with their men, neither Big Elk nor Lone Arrow seemed to be inclined to do much more than sit and converse with one another. Curious, Carolyn lent Pretty Moon her undivided attention, for whatever this technique was, Carolyn wanted to ensure she witnessed it all.

Waiting, Carolyn tried to recall how her adoptive mother had managed to gain her husband's attention.

Had the woman even developed a system? Hmmm . . . if she had, whatever it was had completely escaped young Carolyn's observation.

And then it began.

Without even seeming to catch his eye, Pretty Moon cast down her lashes and batted them. She repeated the procedure twice.

Had Big Elk seen?

Carolyn wasn't convinced Big Elk had shown his wife enough interest this evening to catch such a display.

Another few moments passed. Carolyn watched Big Elk closely. Well, what do you know? Something had changed. Big Elk sent his wife several short glances. However, neither he nor Lone Arrow ended their conversation.

Undiscouraged, Pretty Moon shifted position, wiggling slightly and flicking a braid over her shoulder.

Within a matter of seconds, Big Elk stood, his body language indicating he was bringing his conversation with Lone Arrow to a close.

Carolyn's mouth popped open.

"Watch," came the sign once again from Pretty Moon.

And Carolyn did exactly that. Truth was, at this moment she could not have taken her glance away from the couple had she tried.

Within a few moments, Pretty Moon raised her arms over her head and stretched, adding a vocal, feminine sigh to the movement. It was an obvious ploy.

Carolyn carefully noted the interplay between the couple, amazed when, within a few minutes, Big Elk had taken the necessary few steps toward his wife and sat down next to her.

Before Pretty Moon gave her entire attention over to her man, she turned to smile at Carolyn. And Carolyn grinned back.

Wow! Pretty Moon's maneuvers could not have been more effective had the other woman tied a rope around her man's neck and pulled on it.

And Carolyn really did not need Pretty Moon's signs, "Now you try it," to compel her to do the same.

Nonetheless, Carolyn found it difficult to initiate a single flirtatious gesture, so great was her reticence . . . at least at first. But when Lone Arrow seemed uninclined to acknowledge her presence, despite the fact that he now sat alone, Carolyn quickly overcame her hesitation.

What was the first thing Pretty Moon had done? Oh, yes.

Sitting up straight, Carolyn batted her eyes at Lone Arrow. Twice.

Tentatively, she glanced up at Lone Arrow. Had he noticed?

Carolyn frowned. Perhaps not. In Carolyn's estimation, the man appeared as immoveable now as he had a few moments ago.

Well, fine. Maybe the action had been too subtle for Lone Arrow. Perhaps she should go on to step two. What was it that had Pretty Moon done next?

Oh, yes. Shifting position, ensuring that she wiggled her hips a little in the process, Carolyn flicked a section of her long hair behind her shoulder.

Casting a quick glance at Lone Arrow, she tried to determine if there had been a change in him at all . . . anything?

Carolyn's spirits took a plunge. There he sat, whittling away with his knife over some stick . . . utterly ignoring her.

All right, fine. She would advance to step three, and if that didn't work . . .

Casually, as though she had done this sort of thing as a matter of course, Carolyn stretched her arms over her head and sighed. She even added another wiggle to the gesture for good measure. Then studiously, feeling as though she were perched on pins and needles, she watched Lone Arrow for any sign of a response.

Had it made a difference? . . .

It was still early in the evening and Lone Arrow sat with his friend, Big Elk, before their small campfire. So far the two men had been engrossed in conversation, trying to reach an agreement as to their next course of action.

At present they sat mute. Finally it was Big Elk who spoke first, saying, "My friend, you talk of backtracking, but I fear that we may not return to the white man's fort for many a moon."

Lone Arrow nodded, yet queried all the same, "Why do you say this?"

"Your wife," said Big Elk, pointing toward Carolyn, "appears to be headstrong."

Lone Arrow shrugged, restraining himself from either agreeing with his friend or from correcting the man's impression. Certainly, she was headstrong, but she was not his woman. Not yet. And in truth, he should not make her his wife, even though he had said that he would.

He chided himself. What had he done this day? Had he set into motion something he could not take back?

Moodily, he tried to stare straight ahead, though

from the corner of his eyes, he couldn't help but scrutinize her. In the distance, a night hawk squawked and a screech owl hooted above a wind that never seemed to tire of howling. That this same breeze was responsible for whipping strands of Lone Arrow's long unbraided hair into his eyes was only a mild irritant at present.

Though he gave the impression of speaking with Big Elk, Lone Arrow watched her; watched as she conversed with Pretty Moon, watched as the evening breeze blew a curl of her chestnut hair back from her face.

Without willing it, he suddenly wished to coil his fingers through that silky tress; yearned to feel its velvety texture within his grasp. In truth, he could barely control the urge to spread his fingers over her skin, her face, her cheeks, if only to satisfy himself that her responses this afternoon had not been more than a warrior's mere dream.

"How did you rescue her from the buffalo herd?" asked Big Elk. "When last I saw you, you were edging your way into the midst of them. I feared, my friend, that I might never see you again."

Again Lone Arrow shrugged, as though the rescue had been nothing. He said, "I have A-la-pee, a very smart pony."

"*Éeh,* yes," said Big Elk. "But even smart ponies sometimes stumble. Your medicine was with you today, my friend."

Lone Arrow nodded and had he been alone, he might have cursed, for Big Elk's words caused Lone Arrow to remember . . . remember his fear . . . for her . . .

He had died a little today, he realized, witnessing the danger to The-girl-who-runs-with-bears. And that moment had changed him. For he could no longer deny his feelings.

He cared for her. Ho! It was that simple.

But there were problems.

"She looks to be a good woman," commented Big Elk, "and when I look at her, I see that her heart speaks true. Yet . . ."

Lone Arrow glanced up.

"Yet," continued Big Elk, "what will you tell your clan mothers when they ask you why you have taken a white woman as your first wife?"

"I have not yet married her," replied Lone Arrow.

"But you will, my friend. You will."

Would he? he wondered. What would happen if he did not marry the white woman?

That there would be no commitment from either of them was clear. However, that he would also, perhaps, be only half alive, was a truth that he could not entirely discount.

Fact was, The-girl-who-runs-with-bears did not understand his dilemma. How could he tell her that the cave she sought was sacred to his people? That those things she had seen there were to remain as they were, undisturbed? How could he do this without giving away its secret?

"Your mother's people and your father's, too, will want to know why you have chosen this woman instead of a bride from amongst the people," Big Elk was continuing. "For all my life I have known you as my friend. For all my life I have acknowledged that yours is a sacred way of life, for you alone speak to the mountain god. It is a hard way to live, my friend, because the people expect more from you than from another who does not, perhaps, have your power."

Lone Arrow remained silent.

"Do not misunderstand," Big Elk went on to explain. "I do not say you should not marry her. If she were mine, I would do as you are. My only word of caution is that you should commit a few words to memory to explain this thing to your clan."

Lone Arrow inclined his head. Big Elk's word was good. However, difficult though it might be, dealing with his clan was not the shattering obstacle that Big Elk believed it to be. The truth was that his people would eventually be happy that Lone Arrow had at last found someone to marry.

Ho! His relatives, his clan, and their reaction to his choice in a wife, although filled with uncertainty, was not the problem that Lone Arrow feared.

No, it was something else that worried him. Something that went deeper than the color of one's skin.

He did not trust her.

Why should he?

And he found himself wondering why a white woman would commit herself to an Indian husband. True, the two of them had a history together, which in itself was unusual. But in Lone Arrow's opinion, her easy acquiescence was an oddity.

Perhaps his mistrust was ill-founded. Maybe her heart was sincere, as Big Elk believed it to be. But from Lone Arrow's experience, he knew he had to be cautious.

After all, no matter the friendship his people had shown to the white man, such people as Nate Stormy and his ilk rarely regarded the Indian as being on the same footing as their white counterparts, in trade or even in treaty.

Why should she be different from the rest?

And yet, she was. Instinct told him this was so.

Lone Arrow frowned as he wondered if his intuition regarding her was clouded by desire.

It could be, he acknowledged, for he could not deny that he coveted her. Indeed, he was only too well aware that he physically ached with the need to be with her, to breathe in her earthy fragrance.

In truth, he craved her body beneath his, longed to watch the stirrings of passion take hold upon her countenance. And the image of her body, moving against his in the time-honored dance of love, as it had briefly done this afternoon, was practically more than he could stand.

Lone Arrow uttered a low, masculine sound, wishing he could curb his thoughts as well as he could master the yearnings of his body. But alas, he seemed to be as incapable of ruling his mind as he might be were he trying to change day to night.

"Will you tell her of your duty?"

Lone Arrow lifted his shoulders. "She will come to know of it soon enough," he said.

"I have never understood," Big Elk said, "why you have not yet married one from amongst us. You have many coups, though you are young. You are well respected. The right is there for you to do so."

As was fitting, Lone Arrow thought for a moment before he replied. At last, he said, "I have known The-girl-who-runs-with-bears since I was sixteen winters old. She had been lost from her people and I found her in *Ba-sa-wa-xaa-wúua,* Our Mountains, The Big Horn. I led her to her people, and then went home to my own. Perhaps my spirit has been entwined with hers ever since then. Perhaps," he said, "I have been waiting for her to return."

Lone Arrow glanced at his friend, catching the fleeting look of surprise in Big Elk's eyes. And then, as though in afterthought, he said, "Although perhaps not."

And while Big Elk accepted this, Lone Arrow sighed. Truth was, he faced a major problem. One he had no means of solving.

For thousands of years, the Absarokee, or Crow people, had lived, hunted and subsided on this land. For thousands of years, Lone Arrow's family had been granted the duty of guarding the treasure cave and all the riches within it.

That cave, the cache there, was not his own, nor anyone else's, to do with as he pleased. Another people had once lived on this land—a very large people, and a small people, if the skulls of these ancient races were indicative of their size.

But no one touched their things. Not their stone arrowheads, not their gold, nor even their remains. To do so would be to court disaster, or at the very least bad luck.

Perhaps the god who lived in the Bighorn Mountains had once been the long ago peoples' god. Unfortunately, there was precious little tradition amongst his own tribe that explained the god of the mountains, this old race or the things which they had left behind. No tradition, that is, except as had been passed down through Lone Arrow's lineage.

In truth, he understood little more than this: the Bighorn Mountains and all within it were the realm of the mountain god. And as Lone Arrow's father had done, and as his father had done before him, it was Lone Arrow's duty to protect these mountains and the treasure cave.

That also meant defending them from *her*.

Yet, how could he do that when The-girl-who-runs-with-bears was so determined?

Once again, the thought occurred to him: if only he could trust her.

But he could not. The best thing to do would be to extricate himself from her and this situation, if only he could think of a way to do so.

Unfortunately, The-girl-who-runs-with-bears had secrets and designs that demanded Lone Arrow's attention, even if he did not actively help her. And this alone, would bring him into constant contact with her.

Alas, the thought of this brought on the awareness of another dilemma.

However, at this moment, Big Elk rose to his feet and stretched. "It is that part of the day when one should seek his sleeping robes with the one he loves," he said.

Lone Arrow nodded and waved his friend away, wishing at the same time that he hadn't been reminded of their individual sleeping arrangements. It made him think of her . . . in that way . . . again . . .

Uttering a low guttural noise in his throat, Lone Arrow glanced up toward The-girl-who-runs-with-bears, sending her what was probably his most irritated look. Little did he anticipate, however, that at that very same moment, she would gaze back at him, catching the expression in his eye. He grimaced. For, as they stared at one another, she batted her lashes at him, twice.

Ho! What was this? His body responded to hers, in a most natural way . . . natural, that is, if they were husband and wife.

Lone Arrow stirred restlessly. Impossible. How could a single glance from her cause his pulse to race?

Worse, The-girl-who-runs-with-bears flicked her hair over her shoulder and wiggled, casually stretching her arms over her head, the action drawing attention to her breasts. Moreover, she sighed, her voice no more than a feminine whisper.

All at once, his blood pumped furiously.

Was she flirting with him? Openly?

Big Elk unexpectedly laughed, interrupting Lone Arrow's train of thought. It also caused him to switch his attention toward the other couple. Big Elk had placed his robe around Pretty Moon's shoulders, the effect blanketing the two lovers completely. Such was an Indian's way of pronouncing to others that he wished privacy.

Soon Lone Arrow knew that these two would seek a more secluded place, leaving him alone with *her*.

What was he to do then?

Logic and an unswerving sense of duty urged him to wait, to put her at a distance. After all, as the old ones had often counseled, one must think before one acts.

Ho! That was it. He needed some time alone, to reflect upon his choices. Especially at a time when it appeared he had only two paths before him, both of them laden with problems.

Ho! Glancing above him at the star-studded heavens, Lone Arrow made a decision.

Thus resolved, he rose, and without so much as a single glance at The-girl-who-runs-with-bears, he strode out into the night.

So much for Pretty Moon's lesson.

Carolyn watched Lone Arrow leave. As he disappeared, a flood of contrary emotions filled her. She wanted him to stay with her, pay attention to her, yet at the same time, she knew that something bothered Lone Arrow; she could sense it.

But what was it? And what could she do about it? That is, if she wanted to do something about it.

A series of giggles drifted to her from across the fire.

Oh, dear. Pretty Moon's husband had thrown a blanket over the two of them. Was this an attempt at privacy?

Carolyn debated what she should do. But then, with little to no warning, the two figures moved beneath that blanket, until it looked as though Big Elk had positioned Pretty Moon on the ground.

Dear Lord, was the couple going to make love right here, right now?

Embarrassment consumed Carolyn. She could not stay here.

There was nothing for it. She would have to follow Lone Arrow, no matter that he seemed moody and uncommunicative; no matter that he had ignored her rather obvious invitation.

But it was dark, much too dark away from the fire. It had been a long time since Carolyn had been required to face the dark wilderness on her own. At the thought, a shiver of fear washed through her.

There would be animals out there—perhaps snakes.

At that thought, a feeling of revulsion swept over her. Carolyn had always hated snakes.

What if she were to stumble over a rattlesnake?

More giggles issued from the couple beneath the blanket, and with them came the sound of clothing being removed.

That, more than anything else, decided her.

Coming to her feet, Carolyn left the camp, heading

out in the general direction where Lone Arrow had gone.

Perhaps, despite the darkness, she might meet up with him. She could only hope, for her own sake, that it would be so.

Chapter 14

The rustling of a leaf, the snap of a stick beneath her footfalls, made her jumpy. She could not see a thing. In truth, the dark reminded her of another time in a very similar place as this. A very hard time that had been for her, too, with fear her constant companion.

"Remember, do not fear the darkness. If you travel in it long enough, there will be sufficient light for you to see where you go."

She heard Lone Arrow's wisdom speaking to her through the language of sign from all those years ago. It was as though he stood beside her now.

"When you walk in the dark, you must overcome your natural fear. Only then can you develop an understanding of the living things around you."

She was trying to do what he had taught her to do, but it was not easy. In her mind's eye, danger lurked behind every rise in the land, behind every bush. What if she ran into a wild cat?

No sooner had the thought occurred to her than something materialized in her path. She froze.

"You must remain perfectly motionless if danger suddenly presents itself to you. And while the body pauses, you must think quickly, for you must devise an escape."

The thing was right in front of her. It did not move. And Carolyn called upon every ounce of her strength to remain still. A cloud passed overhead, uncovering the moon.

As the light illuminated her enemy, she drew a deep breath. It was no more than a shrub bush.

Releasing her breath to calm her racing pulse, Carolyn stepped around the bush and tripped down a small ravine. She let out an involuntary shriek.

Drat! She should not have uttered a sound. As she knew from past experience, the night had "ears."

She sat up and, getting to her feet, climbed out of the ravine. Alas, she had no more than found her footing, than she was hit by a force coming at her from the opposite direction. It was alive, and it grabbed her.

She screamed, only this time it was not a mere shriek. Nonetheless, it seemed to make no difference. Together, she and whatever it was fell back down into the chasm.

They rolled over and over, and Carolyn was too stunned even to cry out, though it might have been her last utterance . . .

He tumbled with her down the ravine, trying as best he could to shield her from the bumps and scrapings from the rocks and bushes. However, he was sad to note, as she toppled over him, he could not protect her completely.

Why had she screamed? Had she not seen him approach her? Certainly, he had not expected her to fall backward, nor had he anticipated this plunge into a chasm.

There seemed nothing he could do to stop their sliding, either, and as they shot straight to the bottom of the gorge, the best he could do was keep her on top of him. In some ways, the fall seemed to go on forever until, suddenly, it was over.

For a few brief moments, Lone Arrow lay stunned, trying to catch his breath.

It did not take long. Not when, coming to his senses, he found himself lying beneath her, with all her soft curves and her gentle peaks imprinted upon the hard length of him.

Ho! What was this? Like a drop of dew in the warmth of the morning sun, his resolve, so recently made regarding her, evaporated.

His blood rushed to the center of his body, making him more than aware of what it wanted.

He, however, knew he must keep his wits about him. He was aware of how this woman affected him, and he reminded himself that ethically he should not have anything to do with her.

But how was that possible when she lay against him, her position—with her legs straddling him—impossible to ignore?

Clearing his throat, he said in English, "Are you hurt?" To his credit, he refused to lift his arms to his sides, realizing that to touch her would be to undermine his determination.

She did not answer him at once. However, as she nodded, he felt the motion of her head, there against his shoulder. Then she was sitting up, trapping him beneath her. And despite himself, despite his conviction not to, Lone Arrow felt any antagonism he might have assumed toward this woman fade.

He groaned.

At that same moment, as if to tempt him more, moonlight crept out from behind a midnight cloud, its heavenly radiance washing over her in shades of gray and silver. He muttered a deep, low sound in his throat. Was he being tested by the Maker?

How, he wondered, was he supposed to resist her when The-girl-who-runs-with-bears looked more beautiful at this moment than any person, thing, or object he had ever seen?

Worse, she sat above him; her face was mere inches from his own.

This was possibly more than he could stand. Did she know what she was doing to him?

Without warning, she brought up a hand to smooth back her hair from her eyes. At once, his attention drifted down to the imprint of her breasts against her dress.

Again, he moaned. Again, he felt the frantic beating of his heart, as well as the answering rise in his groin.

She said, "I'm sorry, Lone Arrow. I couldn't stay in the camp."

And he found it impossible to answer her intelligently. In truth, his voice seemed not to work at all. And so he remained silent.

She continued, "I . . . I'm sorry. I tripped."

When he continued his silence, she at last glanced down at him, looking as though she might like to study him as well. What she saw there, however, he might never know. All he was aware of at this moment was that she had moved, wiggling as though she attempted to rise to her feet.

It was, perhaps, more than he could take.

"Humph," he grunted. He could not keep himself from uttering something. And he certainly hoped she would manage to get to her feet without his help, for he knew if he so much as lifted a finger to help her . . .

He shifted, but all he accomplished was arousal, as certain parts of his bare body came into further contact with certain parts of hers.

He froze. It had been a mistake to move so much as a muscle, for in doing so, a shock, much like that of a streak of lightning, bolted through him. And Lone Arrow found he had nothing on his mind—literally nothing else—except her.

He wanted her. He lusted for her. He needed her. Right now.

Yet he would not, he could not take her. Had this not been the very reason he had left camp?

Still, despite himself, he found his arms coming around her. And he thought, *just once*. Just once he would touch her, and then he would let her go.

He reached up to smooth back a lock of her hair, and in that instant, as he did so, he knew pure panic. Worse, as though his tongue belonged to another, he found himself uttering, "Your position does much to remind me that we have not committed the act that will wed us."

She did not answer, not in so many words. However, she drew in her breath and let it go in a soft, high-pitched sigh, as though she agreed with him perfectly. At last, she said, "Yes."

And Lone Arrow felt as though he might likely die.

Such a simple word from her; such a bizarre reaction from him. And try as he might, he could think of no good reason that he should not have her, should not take her right here, right now.

Perhaps as a last defense, he whispered, "This is not the time or place to come to know one another." Contrarily, however, he brought her head down toward him as he lifted up, meeting her halfway.

Even when he knew it was wrong, he found his lips touching hers, softly, gently at first. A mere peck.

He should leave it at that.

But again, she sighed, and Lone Arrow found himself lost to the thrill of her touch. And as pure sexual excitement raced through his veins, he muttered a quickly spoken prayer to the Maker.

For good or for bad, he realized, he was committed to this; he was committed to her. For his own sake, and for hers, he had better make it good.

He kissed her lightly, softly, the caress doing much to tease her, when he whispered, "You must be prepared to feel hurt the first time."

Her only answer had been a moan, and then he was leaning up toward her, taking her lips once more into his own.

Excitement swam through her veins and Carolyn squirmed against him, barely able to contain herself. What was this pleasure she kept reaching toward whenever he touched her?

She heard Lone Arrow's low groan before he brought up a hand to grope beneath her skirts. That he was also brushing aside his breechcloth had the effect of exciting her, yet scaring her, all at the same time. And although she could not see that part of him, she did feel the expanse of him against her soft thighs, as she sat above him.

Dear Lord, he was big, and she found herself murmuring, "I am afraid."

He barely answered her, uttering only a rasping sound from his throat. At length, however, he whispered against her lips, "I think that you compliment me, but do not worry. Your body is meant for this. It will hurt, but only the first time."

She nodded and gazed down into his dark, dark eyes.

Carolyn wondered if her gaze mirrored the affection she felt. Could he see it? Could he sense it?

Or more importantly, would he even care?

If not love, he must feel something for her, she thought. After all, he was making her his wife. It was not something he would do if he did not like her . . . at least a little.

He shifted his weight against her, and Carolyn held her breath. While she was not unaware of the facts of life, to be presented with its reality close-up was another matter.

He must have perceived her concern, for he lifted himself up to kiss her again. He said, "I cannot keep from hurting you at first. Be assured that the next time we do this, it will bring you more pleasure."

She gazed down at him. "Then we will do this again?"

She witnessed his instantaneous grin before he murmured, "Many, many times, I think."

"Oh."

"Come here," he said, as he took hold of her waist and shifted her position until she lay beneath him. That he grabbed hold of a part of his clothing, pushing and fluffing it until it lay like a pillow beneath her head, did much to attest to his care. That he also centered his robe upon the ground so that she could lie down on it, confirmed her opinion that Lone Arrow was, indeed, a gentleman. He said, "You should be on the bottom the first time. It will hurt less."

She simply nodded.

Having so agreed, she thought that he might make love to her right then and there. But he did not.

Instead, he reclined to the side of her, one arm bent so that he cradled his head in his hand, while with his other . . . she shuddered with delight.

He touched her everywhere, trailing gentle fingers down her face, over her jawbone to her neck. Down farther still to one breast, the other. And where his fingers touched, his lips soon followed, even if that meant that he had to kiss her through her clothing.

Tenderly, though with a sure hand, he undid each button of her chemise, one by one, his eyes bright as he gazed at her. And then, perhaps too quickly, it was done.

Timidly, she glanced up at him. But such shyness had no chance to fester within her, for it fled beneath the surety of his touch. And when she witnessed the fervor blazing in his eyes, she lost herself to the wonder of him.

Gradually, he peeled away her cotton chemise.

"Beautiful," she heard him mutter as her body became exposed to his gaze.

She might have said a word, or perhaps a cute phrase back to him. It was in her mind to do so, but before she could so much as utter a single syllable, his lips were there upon her bosom, creating havoc within her.

And as he took each tender nipple into the hot recess of his mouth, she arched herself against him. She could not help herself. The pleasure he gave her was fierce, and in response she breathed out the deepest of sighs.

He dallied over her as though she were a feast, and in response to his ministration, she squirmed in his arms. She wanted more.

But he was not about to satiate her, it would appear. At least, not at this moment. Instead, he traced a series of kisses down the length of her body. Down over her stomach, lower still, to her very core, past even that to the length of each leg.

Carolyn quivered with pleasure. She felt as though every inch of her had been loved, explored and worshiped.

Scooting back up toward her, he let his fingers feel their way to the privacy of her femininity, and he murmured, "You are ready for me."

Was she? Most likely, she was. In reality, she supposed she had been ready for him for eight and a half long years.

And then his fingers were doing things to her down there that she had only imagined possible. Pleasure erupted within her, making her feel as though she were a living volcano.

Once more, his kisses trailed down over her body.

And as his caress came closer and closer to that most exquisite of pleasure sources, she brought her hips up to meet him, never dreaming that he would kiss her there.

Yet he did. And she thought she might surely die from the pleasure of it.

Oh, how she cared for this man. And a thought occurred to her: Was this the reason she had never looked at, nor been interested in another man for these past eight and a half years?

She might have explored that thought in more detail, but she was given little resource to do so.

His tongue had found her, stealing her attention away completely. And with her body entwined within his arms, he slowly brought her up to a height of stimulation she hadn't known was possible.

Then it happened. The intensity; the trauma. In truth, her body convulsed with so much energy, she wondered at its source. Over and over, the pleasure came to her; over and over she thrashed under Lone Arrow's expertise.

And as her body went weak, she felt as though she were expanding as a spiritual being, gaining more space. Truly, she felt as though she looked down upon herself and upon him from a viewpoint far above them.

And in that instant, she knew the truth for what it was.

She loved this man; had always done so. There was no doubt about it; none whatsoever.

Oddly, the realization gave her peace. And as her breathing resumed a more normal pace, she slowly drifted back to earth. He, however, had lifted up until he came to rest upon a forearm. He watched her, his gaze tender. Yet it was also all mixed up with a fiery light of yearning, as well as some other emotion she could not quite identify—admiration?

He smiled at her, and Carolyn found herself returning the gesture wholeheartedly.

Once more, he said, "You are ready. It is time."

There was more?

Without further delay, he reached up to kiss her, his tongue sweeping into her mouth to mate with hers. Mouths slashed across mouths, as if a kiss, all by itself, were the act of love.

What was this? Once more, liquid fire swept through her veins. And even the taste of her own scent upon his breath did not diminish her pleasure. In truth, so caught up was she in the simple act of what they were doing, she did not feel him rising above her.

"It will hurt but a moment," he whispered into her ear.

She knew what he meant and waited for the worst. But it did not happen.

Instead, she felt the evidence of his fingers playing with her, creating another series of reactions rebounding through her.

And then, as casually as if they had done this all their lives, he substituted himself for those fingers.

Gradually, so as not to disturb her, he became as one with her, and all the while his dark eyes were trained on her. She thought that it was as if he might register her every reaction.

And oh, how she loved that care.

Coming up onto his forearms, he smiled down at her, while he swept up a wayward lock of her hair into his fingers. And dear Lord, he gazed at her as if she were the most precious thing on earth.

Inadvertently, she shifted position, observing that her action caused him to close his eyes as though he were in agony. But she knew it was good, and when she heard his deep groan, which was so obviously one of pleasure, she rejoiced. Had she done that to him? With a simple wiggle?

He whispered, "I try to go slowly for you. It is not easy for me, for I want you in a very bad way. When you stir like that, I can hardly hold myself back."

She gulped. She did not want him holding back. She wanted all of him—now; moreover, she desired that he experience the same sort of pleasure that she had known. As he had imparted to her, so, too, she wanted to give back to him.

She said, "Don't go slowly. I would have all of you, all that you can give me."

He groaned, as though he could barely stand to hear these words. And he shook his head, saying, "I think that you do not know what it is that you say."

"Perhaps, but I think you are wrong, Lone Arrow. I am not unaware of the way in which people mate."

He gave her a grim sort of smile. "Still," he said, "we will take it my way."

She nodded, then watched as fine beads of perspiration broke out on his forehead; watched as he swallowed, obviously fighting for self-control.

And slowly, as he had predicted, little by little, she took in the whole of him until he fit her perfectly. They both froze.

One slow beat of time followed upon another. And then, all at once, his lips came down over hers, his tongue sweeping into her mouth. Someone made a high-pitched sound. Was it her?

It might have been so, for the noise, quiet though it was, seemed to be his undoing. He broke off the kiss, placed his forearms at each side of her head, and positioned his cheek by her cheek, as though he could afford to do no more than this. Into her ear, he whispered, "I have needed this, wanted this from the moment I saw you in your room two nights ago."

Joy filled her heart. Did this mean that he loved her?

She sought out his lips, moving her head to the side until she could touch her lips to his. She said, "Kiss me again, Lone Arrow. For I, too, need you."

He growled, as though he were as wild as this land over which they roamed, and he granted her request without pause, as though he, too, could not help himself. He swept his tongue into her mouth, and this time, she rejoiced, relishing the taste of his musky scent.

Tentatively, she twisted against him, causing him to whimper a low-sounding groan. Oh, what a wonderful sound.

Rising up slightly to glance down at her, he asked, "Do you know what you do to me?"

She did not answer. It seemed unnecessary. Instead, she whispered, "I want you, Lone Arrow. All of you. Please make love to me. Please."

He gave her that guttural noise again, which seemed to be half animal, half human, before he murmured, "I will. I promise."

And without another word, he began to move within her, oh, so very slowly.

At first his thrusts and plunges hurt. Then, as she became more and more accustomed to him, it was with some shock that she began to experience again, that same pleasurable feeling, down there, deep within her.

What was this? Could she attain that same plateau of passion once more? So soon?

Seeking it, while at the same time, wanting to give back to him, she gyrated her hips against him, instinctively knowing what to do. And always, she wanted more; more of him, more of this. Gazing up at him, she became aware that she had somehow surprised him.

She found him watching her, even while he moved

against her. And his look was intense. Still, he grinned down at her, and she found herself smiling back up at him.

Did he feel it? Did he acknowledge what was between them? It was a kind of power. Power, she thought, because there was so much beauty between them. A beauty in being this close to each other; a beauty in sharing.

He murmured, "It is good for you?"

She nodded. "It is good. But Lone Arrow, I would have more of you. I think that you are still holding back."

Her words seemed to drive him a little crazy, for as soon as the statement was uttered, he thrust against her, once, again, over and over, so quickly and so enthusiastically, that it left her feeling as though she were spinning.

But it was good, so very good, and she met his gyrations, one for one. In truth, she could not have stopped had she wanted.

No, in essence, she found herself fidgeting right along with him, pushing herself toward that same bliss that she had experienced only a little while earlier.

The change came suddenly, like the dawning of a new day, and she felt the joy of release bursting within her.

This time the magnitude of the pleasure startled her. She hadn't expected that, not again, not so soon. And she must have surprised him, too, for she could not keep her feelings to herself.

High-pitched whimpers, low-resounding sighs escaped from her throat, leaving Carolyn hoping that the wind itself would commingle with the clamor, making her own noise part of the nature all around her.

In response, he beamed down upon her. And in his look was so much affection, Carolyn thought she might purr. Resting his weight on a forearm, he mumbled, "It was good for you, even this, your first time?"

She nodded, whispering, "It was wonderful."

But it was not over. Carolyn knew inherently that he had not met the same release as she, and so, as though to aid him, she began her gyrations all over again. Over and over she strained, until he all at once took over their rhythm. Coming up onto his knees, he placed her legs over his shoulders, and with his gaze softly staring down into her own, he bore against her, once, again and again.

She knew the exact moment he spilled his seed within her, watched as he shut his eyes against what must be an overpowering sensation for him. And she sighed.

It was like heaven to her. She listened to his raucous release; gloried in the feel of him, in the sound of him, in the scent of their lovemaking. Truly, she had never felt closer to another being in her life. And she thought that there, for a moment, it was as though— perhaps for a moment only—they shared the same space.

In the aftermath, as he gradually sank down upon her, she felt herself become one with him, not only in body, but in spirit. And as the two of them drifted off into the surroundings above them, she found herself sharing a part of her with the one she loved.

So this was lovemaking. It was an awakening of life such that she had never before experienced.

And so it was that she fell into a pure, relaxing sleep,

with the arms of her Indian lover firmly holding her, protecting her.

Truly, as she snuggled deeper into his embrace, she felt as though she had come home.

Chapter 15

Ho! Despite many good reasons why he should not, he had done it. Lone Arrow let out a low grunt, while at the same time, he silently admonished himself.

What a predicament he had made for himself. He had consummated their vows. And in doing so, he might as well have promised to take The-girl-who-runs-with-bears to the treasure cave. He knew it. She knew it.

And truth be known, it was not that he could not take her there; it was that he must not.

"Ho!" he muttered to himself once more, grimacing.

To say that Lone Arrow was not pleased with himself would have been an understatement. He knew he should have exercised more control, more restraint where The-girl-who-runs-with-bears was concerned. He knew it; he had ignored his own wisdom.

Still, as Lone Arrow rested beside her, here in the

coulee, beneath the beams of a midnight moon, he felt as a man, divided. Logic and an unswerving loyalty to his clan demanded from him certain actions: preserving secrecy; observing particular rites and ceremonies; protecting the treasure cave.

On the other hand—and this was what was startling to him—his sense of duty, alas, his very being, directed him toward trust, toward placing his belief in a woman whom he knew to be lying.

It should not be a problem. Yet it was.

Looking down upon the beauty of her, as the faint beams of moonlight washed over her skin, he knew that he had been defeated in this, the first battle of their wills. Oh, he was not mistaken, she had won.

Truthfully, it was not that he desired to fight with her—he could think of better ways to spend their time alone. No, it was more a case of dissention.

If he helped her, and her intentions were not pure, then by befriending her, he would have betrayed his people. On the other hand, if she spoke true, if her family's welfare depended upon her, then, by the same reasoning, if he did not help her, would he not have betrayed her?

It was hard to know what to do. If only he could trust her as easily as he desired her. He shut his eyes and frowned. Desire . . .

Alas, even now, he fought a constant struggle simply to keep his hands to himself. So soft, she was, so perfect. So feminine.

It would be easy to touch her, much too easy . . . Pulling a face, he reached out a hand toward her but jerked it back at once. He should keep to himself, he decided. After all, how could he make important decisions about her, about himself, if he were constantly tempted by the flesh?

But no sooner had that thought materialized, than she stretched, causing him to reevaluate. And he found himself reaching out once more toward her, only this time he met with success, and he found himself running the tips of his fingers down the length of her.

She shivered, and despite himself, he responded in kind.

What was this bond between them? he wondered. Was it no more than mere lust, as he suspected? Certainly, passion was a part of it, but was there more to it than that?

More, he wondered, of *what?* Respect?

He snorted. *Baa-lee-táa,* no. He answered his own question. How could he respect a person he did not trust?

At that thought, Lone Arrow stiffened his spine. Was that not what this was all about?

Still . . . Would he admire a woman, no matter the beauty of her body, if she were as treacherous in spirit as he suspected this woman to be? And upon this thought followed another: Would he honestly feel a bond with her if she were so dishonorable?

Lone Arrow knew his own mind. Always, he had been taught to rely on himself and to respect his own judgment. Ho! Then in view of his feelings toward this woman, should he not be more inclined to give her quarter?

Lone Arrow's mind stilled with this thought. Perhaps he should reconsider. Maybe he should sit his woman down and keep her talking until he discovered the extent of her problem.

Then again, if he were wrong . . . if she were dishonest . . .

He grimaced. What was wrong with him that he was allowing a woman to rule his mind?

Frustrated with himself and with this circular line of thinking, it was perhaps with more antagonism than might be fitting, that Lone Arrow spat out, "So you will now expect me to take you to the cave?"

She opened a single eye, to peep up at him, answering him sleepily, "Must we talk about that so soon?"

He nodded. "We will talk about it now, I think."

"Naked?"

He heard the humor in her voice, he acknowledged it, and truth be known, he responded to it, to her. But he could not allow himself to be swayed by her, not even by her wit; at least not until he was certain as to whether he could place his faith in her or not. And so he said, keeping as much emotion from his tone as possible, "To speak to one another without clothing is, I think, the best way to settle an argument . . . that is, if those two people are husband and wife."

She sniffled. "I'm not so certain," she said. Then, "Of course I expect you to take me to the cave. And with all possible speed."

"Humph!" he answered. "I have not agreed to accompany you there."

She stiffened. "And yet," she said, "I have sealed my end of the bargain."

"I made no such bargain with you."

She sighed, and he watched, enchanted, as the valleys and peaks of her chest rose and fell. She said, "Please, Lone Arrow. Please, I don't know how to persuade you to my cause, other than with what I have al-

ready done. Please, will you take me? It is very important to me."

Lone Arrow rolled away from her, onto his back.
The feel and solidity of the earth beneath him com-
forted him, if only because it was something which was
familiar. In contrast, she seemed suddenly alien.

Ho! He had not expected her to plead.

She continued, "I know that you don't wish to lead
me to the cave, but remember that these were my conditions. In a way, you are obligated."

He cut a glance toward the heavens. But he did not
refute her. If he were to be truthful, he knew that the
words she spoke were true.

Ho! What a mess he had made of this. For despite
what he had told her of his intentions, he had certainly
been aware of her own.

He sighed, then muttered, "And so it is this reason
why you have lain with me? To elicit my cooperation in
showing you the cave?"

She hesitated, he noted it at once. And turning his
head, he watched her closely, for it was in this way, as
the wise men had always counseled, that a man can
know what is in the heart of another.

But whatever it was that she felt, she kept it hidden.
For he could detect nothing in her countenance, except,
perhaps the aftermath of lust.

Inhaling a deep sigh, he at last proffered, "I have
been thinking."

She sent him a piqued glance.

He ignored it. "I have decided . . ." he said, speaking
so deliberately that she was forced to lean forward. "I
have decided that you are right."

Halfway toward him, she went rigid, he felt her do

so. Ah, he thought, so this last statement had gained him her attention.

He continued, "I knew the consequences of this act with you, even though, before I committed myself, I told you I would not lead you to the treasure cave."

"But—"

"And so I will take you there."

Stunned, surprised, perhaps even dazed. It was the only way to describe her expression. And it was several moments before she uttered, "In truth? You . . . will . . . take me there?"

He shrugged.

"Tell it to me once more, Lone Arrow, so I can be sure that I understand you perfectly."

He kept his silence. He had said it once, he would not repeat it. And so he voiced instead, "You are now my woman. It is your obligation to obey me."

She hesitated. "That is not the answer that I seek, and you know it."

He uttered nothing more, however, but merely stared at her.

And she appeared to study him for a moment, until at last she asked, "Why this change? Why are you suddenly accepting my conditions?"

Lone Arrow sent her a brief scowl. How was he to answer that? He could not very well explain that seeing her there amongst the buffalo this afternoon had changed his view of her. Ho! It had changed him.

He frowned. It was a truth even he was reluctant to admit to himself, let alone entertain the idea of telling her. And so, in an effort to maintain his dignity on the subject, he jerked his head to the left, a self-conscious gesture.

At some length, he uttered, "Perhaps I changed my mind because it is the only way I can think of to keep you safe."

"Oh," was all she uttered, her voice sounding as though the breath had been knocked from her. And despite all the reasons why he should not, despite his unwavering stoicism, he sensed her loss, observed her crestfallen expression. But it was not within him to give her comfort . . . not at this moment, especially when he did not understand why she even needed comfort. At last she continued, "Then you are only marrying me to protect me . . . not for any other reason?"

He nodded.

"You once said you cared for me. Is there nothing more? A feeling of . . . of affection . . . of love?"

At her question, he hesitated. It was within the realm of possibility that he might deny it. It was also with some revelation that he realized he could not do so. Thinking quickly, he said, "I have made no such statement."

She sighed. "No, you haven't."

She turned her head away from him. And even though her body was pressed up against his own, he felt her withdrawal. He was quick to note, as well, that her retraction from him stung.

At length, without looking at him, she continued, "You wish to keep me safe—like you did when we were children. Is that the only thing that is important to you?"

He sat back, putting a tiny bit of distance between them. Meanwhile, he searched within himself for an answer. What could he say, he wondered, without revealing too much about himself?

She, however, did not wait for his answer, and she

said, "Couldn't you like me just a little bit more? If, for no other reason than the fact that you simply like me?"

Ah, so that was it. Lone Arrow sighed and found he could not meet the look in her eyes.

He had made love to her. He was aware that she would desire reassurance of his devotion to her. Did not most women?

Yet he could not acquiesce and give her what she needed. Not when he did not know what was in *her* heart.

After some moments, he said, "Are you certain that I do not already like you? I desire you; I have made you my wife. Is that not enough?"

She gave him a curious look, one he could not interpret.

And he continued, "As the wise ones have often said, 'the heart that is critical hides its own deeds.' And so I would ask you a similar question, I think. Is your interest in me the fact that only I can take you to the cave? Did you play me wrong when you married me, or do you have feeling for me?"

She drew in her breath rapidly, the action creating a slight hiss. But it was all she did before she, too, fell into silence. Although, after a moment, she uttered, "I asked you first."

He breathed out silently, deciding that the truth might not hurt, at least this once. He said, "I have some feeling for you. I always have."

She made an odd noise in her throat, sounding as though she choked, but she said, "*Always* have?"

He ignored the question. "I will take you to the treasure cave. It will be my gift to your family. But I will not take you there directly. Nor will you go to it with open eyes."

"Fine."

"There is one more thing."

She raised an eyebrow.

"You must wear no clothing when I take you there. No dress, no jewelry, not even *huupé*."

"What is *huupé*?"

"Shoes."

She frowned. "No clothing?"

He shrugged. "It is my condition."

"But it's rocky there. Rocky and cold, and, if I remember correctly, we have to crawl into it to reach the chamber. Don't you think I could scrape myself too easily, or step on a sharp rock, or something similar?"

He did not answer. For he had come to a decision. And indeed, having done so, he would not bend.

After a while, she asked, "And you? Will you also go there naked?"

He did not so much as blink. "I will remain clothed."

"But—"

"My honor is not in question."

"And mine is?"

He drew his arms up over his chest. "Must you ask?"

She sighed. "I'm assuming I can remain clothed until we reach the cave?"

He nodded.

She lay back. "This last request is a rather extreme condition, don't you think?"

"Perhaps," he said. "I know only that it is my requirement."

"Hmmm," she said. "Will Pretty Moon and her husband accompany us?"

Lone Arrow nodded. "Most of the way. It is always better protection to travel with more than two people.

Although we are in Absarokee country, one never knows when one might encounter an enemy."

"Then her husband would witness me—"

Lone Arrow came up onto an elbow, glaring down at her. "Do you think I would parade you in front of him?"

"I—I wasn't sure, I—"

"You will be with me, alone. But my eyes will be eyes enough."

Silence. Stiff, uncomfortable silence.

In truth she became silent for so long that, after a time, Lone Arrow wondered if she had fallen asleep. However, at last she said, "Then, Lone Arrow, I believe that my answer will be, yes." She sighed, then, "When do we start?"

He rose above her. "You are certain that you will do this?"

"I am certain."

"Even knowing that, seeing you that way, might slow our progress?"

It was a suggestive comment he made, and he leered down into her eyes so that she could, by gazing up at him, understand the truth of what he suggested.

And stare back at him, she did, straight into his eyes, until at last, she said, "I am certain."

"Then so be it," he said. "We leave tomorrow, before the sun rises to meet the sky."

She acknowledged him with a nod. "All right. But Lone Arrow?" she asked.

He turned his head toward her.

"I find it difficult to sleep when I am cold."

"Are you cold?"

"Very."

He sat up, bringing her with him so that he could

grab hold of his buffalo robe beneath her and unfold it. Laying it out flat, he put her back upon it while he proceeded to wrap her up in it. He said, "I know of other cures that will keep you very warm, much more pleasurable cures."

But it seemed she was to have nothing more to do with him this night. Turning her back on him, she fell to sleep almost at once.

And while she rested, he tossed about for most of the night.

Perhaps in a way, it served him right.

"His eyes . . . not . . . leave you." This statement was made to the accompaniment of a series of hand motions.

Carolyn shook back her hair, placing the few strands of the chestnut mane behind her ears. Feigning disinterest, she glanced up from where she and Pretty Moon were sitting, looking in the direction where her friend pointed.

Carolyn muttered, beneath her breath, "His eyes don't leave me?" It certainly did not look that way to her. Lone Arrow was deep in conversation with Big Elk, and, as far as Carolyn could determine, she might as well have been a tree stump for all the notice he took of her.

But Pretty Moon was continuing, "The friend of Pretty Moon's husband . . . do . . . much to . . . not let you see. But . . . he watches." It was as though Pretty Moon had read Carolyn's thoughts. "This one," Pretty Moon pointed to herself. ". . . has gift . . . of . . . how to see to heart . . . beneath."

Carolyn nodded and gave her friend a reassuring smile. "I'm sure you do," she agreed as she sat back on her haunches. She sighed. Fact was, what use was it, even if he *were* watching her?

It wasn't as though the man had any great feeling for her. Oh, yes he felt responsible for her; of this she was certain. Perhaps he was even a little fond of her. But that seemed to be as far as it went.

For almost a week now, their party had been traveling over Absarokee terrain, traversing their way from one butte to another, tramping over hills and valleys, picking their way across rolling prairies and mountainous grades. And during that entire time, Lone Arrow had barely acknowledged her existence.

Undoubtedly, there were a multitude of reasons why he avoided her. After all, during the day, one of the men was required to lead their party, while the other pulled up the rear. And at night the two men were obligated to stand guard. But even during moments when Lone Arrow might have rested, he kept well clear of her.

True, Carolyn could have approached him. But she'd be darned if she'd do that.

Carolyn gazed skyward and blinked. The sun had finally ascended to midpoint in the sky, she observed, the time of day when the men usually called a break. Carolyn hoped that they would make camp here, if only so that she could catch her breath. *They* might be able to press on; she, however, was tired.

Carolyn ran her hand over her brow, which appeared to prompt Pretty Moon to observe, "Mountain . . . air . . . weak. Take heart. Soon . . . your body . . . breathe . . . easy."

Carolyn nodded.

While Pretty Moon continued, "You . . . ride . . . pony. This one," she pointed to herself, "will walk when we . . . begin our . . . march again."

Carolyn smiled but shook her head. "No, you go ahead and ride. The higher we go into these mountains, the colder it gets. To tell you the truth, if it's a matter of riding and freezing or walking and being tired, I'll take being tired."

Pretty Moon nodded, but said, "Runs-with-bears could ask . . . husband for . . . robe. Runs-with-bears's husband . . . not wear it."

Carolyn met this statement with silence, as she gazed around her, surveying the lay of the land. Several wildflowers and different tufts of grass grew here in this higher elevation. And despite herself, she could not help but admire their wild beauty.

For instance, at her feet was a wandlike species of flower whose petals were lavender mixed with white. And about four feet away spread numerous patches of a pinkish-violet flower that looked much like the phlox. Their sweet perfume merged with the more earthy scent of the short grasses and pine trees. Inhaling, Carolyn decided that a more inexperienced person might have been left with the illusion that all about them was peace and harmony, so great was its enchantment.

But alas, such an impression would have been no more than a mere illusion, and more than a little dangerous. Carolyn knew better than most that this country was as rugged as these peaks and ridges over which they traveled. That the danger from an enemy always lurked over the next ridge, beyond the next pass. Truth be known, it required the utmost skill simply to survive.

Pretty Moon, however, had not quite given up in her attempt to persuade Carolyn to ride, and the Indian woman said, "Runs-with-bears's husband . . . should . . . give her . . . robe. Runs-with-bears should . . . ask."

Carolyn shook her head. "No," she said. "I'd still be cold, I'm certain. After all, do you feel this wind?" Carolyn pulled her woolen shawl more closely around her shoulders. "It seems to blow here incessantly."

"What . . . this word, in-cess-aunt-lee."

"It means that the wind blows all the time."

"Ah!" Pretty Moon repeated, "In-cess-aunt-lee . . . all time?"

"That's right. Besides, I'm not so sure that my husband's robe would do me any good. It's simply too cold here. In fact, it feels to me as though, if I'm not standing in direct sunlight, I'm very chilled."

Pretty Moon paused. Then, "White woman is . . . afraid . . . of husband." It was no question.

"Of course I'm not afraid of him. It's simply that my shawl is enough." As if to emphasize the point, she fussed with the article of clothing until it covered not only her shoulders but her arms, too.

Pretty Moon shook her head. "If not . . . afraid . . . then ask . . . for robe."

"I don't need the robe. As I said, I have my shawl, and—"

"Runs-with-bears . . . ah . . . ," she gazed about her, "needs robe . . . very much. She all time . . . ah . . . *alóochiak* . . . stopped on trail . . . very much. Pretty Moon see it . . . hard . . . for Runs-with-bears to . . . catch breath. She need . . . ride. Others not . . . wait . . . for her. Runs-with-bears always . . . running. Not good."

All right. So what if Pretty Moon was making a fairly good point. Under no circumstances was Carolyn going to approach Lone Arrow and ask him for anything. Not after that silly condition that he had imposed upon her.

How could he have asked such a thing? To go to the cave blindfolded *and* naked; no shoes, no jewelry, nothing?

More importantly, how was she to carry the cross?

"Go now. Ask . . . husband for . . . robe."

Carolyn shrugged. "Truly, I am fine."

But Pretty Moon would not be put off. "You . . . wait. This one," she said, "go . . . ask."

"No!"

But it was useless. Pretty Moon had already sprung to her feet, was already approaching the men.

And had there been a convenient hole that Carolyn could have crawled into, she would have gladly done so.

Carolyn watched the exchange between the petite young woman and the men. And Carolyn was dismayed to see Pretty Moon scolding not only Lone Arrow but Big Elk as well.

Neither gentleman, thank goodness, looked over to where Carolyn still waited on the ground, however. *Thank you for that, dear Lord,* Carolyn uttered a silent prayer.

True to her word, Pretty Moon returned within a matter of minutes. And slung over her arm was Lone Arrow's robe. It was a beautiful article of clothing, Carolyn admitted, even though personally, it awoke memories of the first time she had made contact with the item. Hadn't Lone Arrow wrapped her up in it?

Bleached white, the robe was painted in a design that prompted Carolyn to think of arrows; vivid red, blue, green and brown arrows, their placement on the robe forming four different concentric circles. Worn fur side in for warmth, it seemed too stunning to be a mere piece of clothing.

"It's beautiful," said Carolyn. No matter that she would have died rather than ask Lone Arrow for assistance, she could not resist admiring such a lovely article.

Pretty Moon grinned, giving the robe to Carolyn. "*Éeh,* it is pretty. It . . . made . . . by . . . she who was . . . ah . . . *búua-lí-ché* . . . like a wife."

Like a wife? Carolyn grew very still.

Was Lone Arrow already married? Dear Lord, married? It was a scenario that Carolyn had not even considered.

And why hadn't she? Wasn't she well aware that Indian men generally married more than one woman? It was a commonly accepted practice.

Carolyn shut her eyes as if to ward off the realization. Funny how she had not even contemplated such a thing. Funny, too, how the feeling of hurt swept through her. And it was as instantaneous as it was consuming.

Inhaling a deep breath, Carolyn barely gave the robe another glance, despite the fact that Pretty Moon held it out to her. And to Pretty Moon's sparkling words, "You . . . ride now," Carolyn shook her head.

No matter that Pretty Moon might be staring at her as though she had suddenly turned green and grown horns, Carolyn said, "I could never wear something made by another woman."

Carolyn did not so much as touch it. Turning her back on Lone Arrow, as well as Pretty Moon and her husband, Carolyn arose and ambled toward a particularly lonely stretch of meadow. She needed to be alone.

Never in her life had Carolyn felt more alien than she did to these people, to this part of the country, than she did at this moment. Let them think what they wanted.

Carolyn only knew that she could not be with them. Alas, all she wanted at present was to get this entire ordeal over with and go home.

Quickly . . .

Chapter 16

"**H**as something happened?"

Carolyn glanced over her shoulder, noting that Lone Arrow had come to squat beside her, the reins of his pony, A-la-pee, held in his hand, while the pony grazed off to the side.

Carolyn looked away from the sight of him and that pony, her gaze fixed ahead of her. Odd, how her eye caught onto the little things in the environment: how the aspens grew aplenty in this part of the country; how few were the deciduous cottonwoods or ashes which dotted an otherwise monopoly of pines and evergreens.

Lone Arrow came closer, however, and no matter that she tried to ignore him, Carolyn could feel the strength of his presence, there at her back. She ignored him as best she could, but he would not be overlooked, not for long, and he repeated, "Has something happened?"

She swallowed noiselessly. Of course something had

happened, was happening to her. But she could not tell him that. No, to Lone Arrow, Carolyn shook her head, turning her face away from him to stare straight ahead of her.

"My friend's wife said that you refused the offer of my robe."

Carolyn fidgeted.

"And yet she says that you are cold."

Carolyn did not say a word, did not shrug, did not move. Nothing.

"If you are cold, there is no reason why you cannot wear it. I am not chilled." He placed the robe around her shoulders.

But Carolyn shifted, letting the robe fall to the ground. Rising, she took a few steps away from him. She could not look at him, and she wished he would go away and leave her alone.

With time, she thought, she might be able to talk to him again. With time, she might be all right. But not now. Now, she needed a few guarded moments to herself. Could he not understand that?

"Did Pretty Moon say something wrong?"

Carolyn shook her head.

"Is it me?"

Carolyn didn't utter a single word.

But it did not seem to matter. Lone Arrow said, "What have I done?"

Carolyn sighed. She did not want to communicate, she did not want to say a word to him. But on the other hand, he did not seem to be leaving, either.

Taking a deep breath, she uttered, "You could have told me. You have been with the white people long enough to learn English. You know how I would have felt."

"Tell you what?"

She groaned. She could not say it.

But he insisted, "What should I have known? What should I have told you?"

"It's nothing."

"If it is nothing, you would not be over here, in a spot that is not easy to defend if some enemy should come upon us."

She took another step away from him.

And he repeated, "What is it that I should have told you?"

She turned on him. "I can't believe that you would do it. That you would actually suggest . . . That you would actually . . . Oh!" She made to go around him, but he leaped in front of her, blocking her way. Exasperated, she gave him a slight shove, but when he did not budge, she accused, "How could you?"

He could not have looked more confused had she unexpectedly changed form and become a buffalo bull. However, he seemed to have enough wit to ask, "That I would have actually suggested . . . ? What?"

"You know."

It was his turn to send an exasperated glance to the heavens, and he said, "If I knew, I would not be asking."

"What does it matter? It would mean nothing to you. Only to me."

He arched a brow. "Appease me," he said. "Pretend for a moment that I am no more than a child and need these things explained to me."

She stiffened her spine and raised her chin at the same time. She said, "All right, I'll tell you what's wrong, if you really want to know, but only this once."

He nodded, arms over his chest, waiting. Gently, his pony came up to him and nudged him forward.

"*Kó-cháseh,* stop that," he told the animal. And dutifully, the animal went back to its munching.

Carolyn took a step away, and she said, "You could have told me that you were . . . that you were . . ." she broke off.

"Were what?"

She stomped her foot. "That you were married, all right? I know it means nothing to you, but it does to me. It's something you could have told me before . . . before . . . before—"

"You know very well that I am married."

"Now," she said. "Now, I know. But I didn't then."

"Then?"

She tilted her head. "You know, before . . ."

"Before what?"

"Oh! How can you be so stubborn?"

It was his turn to inhale deeply. "I do not know what I am being stubborn about. You know that we are married. I was very exact about that."

"I don't mean us."

He frowned, although it took barely a moment for realization to strike. And like a cloud dissipating before the blaze of a summer sun, he smiled.

"Oh!" she said. "How can you grin about such a thing?"

"You are jealous," he observed. "You are jealous that I might already be married."

"I am not," she said, although, in truth, the fight seemed to go out of her. However, attempting to muster it, she said, "It's not that I am jealous. I am just . . . disappointed in you."

"Disappointed?" He frowned. "I did not please you?"

Now it was Carolyn's turn to be confused. "Please me?" she squinted her eyes. "About what?"

He sighed. "I believe that we made love. Have these past six days been so long that you do not remember?"

"Oh," she replied, "that." Carolyn gazed toward the ground, looking for all the world as if the grass beneath her feet was of the utmost interest.

He prompted, "You are disappointed in me as a lover?"

"I—"

"It will be better next time."

Carolyn sighed. "It's not that."

"Is it not?"

She glanced up to catch his quizzical look at her. His brow was furrowed and it appeared as though he might be trying to see straight to her heart. But when this appeared to fail him, he asked, "Then what is it?"

Carolyn remained silent.

In truth, she was contemplating how to respond, when he said, "Pretty Moon thinks she might have spoken when perhaps she should have remained silent. She believes that she might have caused you to think bad things. Is this true? Or are you simply disappointed in me?"

Carolyn pulled a face, but still she said nothing.

"How did you come to think I am married?" he mumbled the question more to himself than to Carolyn. He picked up his robe, confusion marring his brow, until all at once he appeared to understand something. He asked, "Did Pretty Moon say anything about this buffalo robe?"

Carolyn did not articulate a single word. It was in her mind to shake her head, but that would have been a lie, and all she accomplished doing was to send her chin reaching to the sky.

He narrowed his eyes. "Did she tell you about my *búua-lí-ché*, my almost wife?"

Carolyn spun around, presenting him with her back. She'd be darned if she was going to let him see that those few words stung.

He asked, "What is wrong with my having a woman who was my *búua-lí-ché*?"

"I think there is a great deal wrong with it."

He hesitated for an instant, but then persisted, "Have you never had a boyfriend?"

"Of course I have, but—"

He must have been taking tiny steps toward her, for she could feel his breath on the top of her head when he asked, "Do you expect me to be jealous of your boyfriends?"

Blast the man. He simply did not understand. Turning her head a slight degree, she said, "There is nothing to be jealous about."

"Humph!" he made the sound low in his throat. Then, "And there is nothing for you to be jealous about."

It was her turn to utter a grunt, before she retorted, "Forgive me if I disagree."

He blew out his breath. "I cannot help that she made this robe for me."

"And you couldn't help marrying her, either, I suppose?"

He hesitated. And she thought that it sounded as though he were picking his words carefully. However, in a trice, he said, "I did not marry her. I am not married to her. She was a girlfriend, no more."

Carolyn went still.

Lone Arrow continued, "Perhaps it is right that you should know that there has been much opportunity for me to marry, but until you asked me, I have not done so."

"You . . . you haven't?" she asked, her back still held stiffly, though she leaned forward slightly. Then, in afterthought, she threw over her shoulder, "And I did not ask you to marry me."

"You did ask, and *baa-lee-táa*, no, I am not married to anyone but you." He waited barely a moment before he added, "Though I could have been a husband many times."

Carolyn shut her eyes, letting the feeling of relief sweep through her. *He was not married to another.*

The knowledge made her feel, oh, so much better, but she still could not quite give quarter. Not yet, anyway. Truth be known, this whole episode had brought on a few more questions. And spinning around to face him, she asked, "But that doesn't bar you from wanting to marry another in the future, does it? No matter that you are tied to me, you could still take another wife into your home, couldn't you?"

He said, nodding, "Custom allows me this."

This was not good; not good at all. Biting her lip, Carolyn crossed her arms over her chest, as though the position might give her protection against what she was afraid she'd say next. But no matter his answer, she had to know. She asked, "And does custom also give you the right to cheat on your wife?"

"What is this cheat?"

She raised her head. "You know very well what it means."

Lone Arrow sighed. Indeed, he took a step away from her.

She witnessed the withdrawal and surmised that perhaps he was feeling as stymied as she. But she could not allow him the chance to avoid the topic. This was too important a matter, and she would have this out with him, here, now, before another minute passed between them.

It did not take him long to respond. Placing his hands gently upon her arms, he brought her a pace closer to him until she had no choice but to confront him, face-to-face. Only then did he say, "Know that it is a man's privilege to have as many wives as he can afford. This is not a bad thing, for a wife's duties are many, and help with the work is usually appreciated."

Carolyn snorted.

"Know, too," he continued, as though she had not reacted, "that it is a man's right to mate with whomever he pleases, whenever he pleases. To have only one woman is, to my people, either a thing of shame or a thing of great beauty."

Carolyn bit her lip. *Shame?*

"It is a shame to vow yourself to one woman and to remain faithful and loyal to her?"

And when he responded in the positive, she said, "That's a terrible thing to say."

"Is it? Then I would ask you to think on this, too," he continued. "For the Absarokee, a woman is as free to love another man as her husband is. Know that if you ever tire of me, if I do not treat you as you think best, you can throw me away and find another husband who suits you better."

Carolyn took a step backward, out of his grasp. But, as though she were cold, she promptly brought up her hands to chafe her arms.

This concept was, perhaps, more than she could easily assimilate. What was this? A woman could break her marriage vows as easily as a man . . . without consequence to her standing within the tribe? Had he really told her that?

Well, if that comment was supposed to make her feel better, Carolyn decided that it had missed its mark completely. Although this "eye for an eye" philosophy might seem fair to some, for Carolyn, two wrongs would not make a right.

At least not for her. And she said, "But I could not do that. I could not watch my husband with another woman, even knowing that I could do the same thing back to him. It would cause me anguish, I fear. Nor," she continued when he might have spoken, "could I throw you away, divorce you, and keep my self-respect. Besides, I think we're speaking of different things. I'm talking about the possibility of your taking another wife, as well as keeping me. You're telling me about Crow wives being able to take lovers. It's not quite the same thing, is it? Unless . . . Do the Crow allow a woman to have more than one husband at the same time, like a man does?"

"Of course not." Lone Arrow shook his head. "What woman would want another one? Someone else demanding that she cook and sew for him? That she have his children?" He snorted. "I know of no woman who would desire this."

Carolyn shot up her chin. "Then it's not the same thing at all, is it? And to tell you the truth, it doesn't really matter if a woman is allowed to divorce her husband or not, for she still doesn't have the same rights as a man."

He looked askance at her. "And," he said, "in your world, women are allowed this?"

"No, but—"

"Then the Absarokee way is better," he said. "For the women from my tribe could have a lover as well as a husband." He pointed to her. "You could, if you wanted one."

Carolyn chanced a quick look up toward him, and caught his frown. She asked, "While I am married to you?"

He nodded.

She grew quiet at that, until at last she asked, "If I were to do that, what would you do?"

Lone Arrow's frown deepened until the two furrows between his eyes looked as though they might never disappear. He said, "It is a great man who will endure a hurt, such as having his wife take another lover. It is a great man who would suffer this without seeking revenge. Know that I would not like this to happen," he said, "but I would tolerate it. I would only hope that you would not love this other man."

"But you would let me do it?"

"*Éeh*. It is not my choice. You are as free to love another as I am."

Carolyn swung her gaze up toward the heavens, as though only from there could she find solace, or perhaps a place away from where such unconventional customs were understood. And she asked, "Then why get married at all?"

Lone Arrow glowered at her. However, he also appeared to be deep in thought, and it took him some moments before he said, "A man and a woman get married because it is within the heart of every person, be they man or woman, to love one another for their whole life. While my people may encourage a man to stray, and will not condemn a woman who does—for the flesh can be weak—it is still within the hearts of all men and women to marry and love each other . . . forever."

Ah, she thought, how agreeable did these words sound; very pretty. However, there was still something missing in this scenario; something that did not sit well with her. And she said, "But this makes no sense. You tell me that you can have a lover anytime you desire. Then you tell me that it is within the hearts of all men and women to fall in love, to marry and to remain married for all their lives. My question is: how can a woman love a man who constantly takes another to his bed, perhaps even into his heart?"

When Lone Arrow did not answer at once, she continued, "No, I am afraid you speak in riddles. It cannot be both ways."

He shrugged. "And yet it is. I have known many a husband and wife who have been married all their lives . . . some as many as fifty years. Perhaps when a man loves a woman enough, he does not wish to have another wife."

"Perhaps," she conceded. "Although," she asked after a slight pause, "what is to be my fate, when you do not even know if you love me?"

He remained silent.

After a moment, she asked, "So why did you?"

"Why did I what? Marry you?"

She nodded.

"Because . . ." he hesitated. "Because . . ." he began again . . .

"You don't even know, do you? Did you marry me only to bed me?"

He drew in a ragged breath, as though he were shaken. But whether from shock that she would voice the words aloud, or from an inability to find the right thing to say, she did not know. Ultimately, however, he let out his breath, giving her an odd look before he began, "I know why I married you, and *éeh,* yes, taking you to my bed was part of it."

"Oh!" She turned her back on him, not wanting him to witness the hurt that this admission caused her.

She had sensed this, of course. In truth, she had counted on his carnal desires; had made her plans to encourage whatever of his lust she could muster, hoping that she would be able to enlist his aid because of it.

And in doing so, a small voice within her asked, had she been any better than he?

Perhaps not, she answered to herself. But at this particular moment, she could not even consider her own misdoings. Truth be known, she had all but forgotten her part in this.

She heard him come up behind her, could feel the heat of his presence, there at her back, but she refused to turn to face him. After a moment, he placed a hand on her shoulder and said, "There is more."

She tossed her head, but otherwise remained silent.

And he continued, "You are a part of me." He had said it softly, into her ear. "I do not understand it, myself. Perhaps it is because you once disturbed me when I was seeking a vision. Maybe it is something else. I can only tell you that somehow, in some way, I am not complete without you."

Carolyn caught her breath. "Truly?" she uttered.

"Have you known me to lie about such things?"

Slowly, she turned until she was able to stare up into his eyes. Heartened by the look of sincerity she saw there, she asked, "Does that mean that you like me well enough that you would not marry another, if the opportunity ever presented itself?"

She watched as he drew his brows together; watched

as the joy went out of features, watched as he withdrew from her in spirit. And at length, when he said, "While it would aid my cause if I could tell you that"—Carolyn knew she had asked more than he could give. And she did not need his—"but I cannot"—to confirm her loss . . .

Chapter 17

Lone Arrow, however, had not finished speaking, and he continued, saying, "Understand me well. It is also for your sake that I tell you this."

For her sake? Had she truly heard that? How could a man say such a stupid thing? How could he say it and expect a woman to believe it? Resentment flared within her.

Truth be told, none of this was for her. It was an "all for me, none for thee" philosophy. And quite readily, Carolyn flung back at him, "For me? Forgive me, but I don't think any of this has been said for my benefit."

While his stare might have thrown daggers at her had he been able, all he said was, "Our women do much work. What if you discovered the tasks to be too much for you? Would you not ask me to marry again?"

"I would rather perish first."

He shook his head. "I think that you might."

"Might what? Perish?"

He snorted. "Ask me to take another wife."

"Never," Carolyn uttered. "I would never do that."

She should say something else, something damaging about all this extra wife nonsense. But what? It wasn't that she was afraid to speak up to him, or to tell him what was in her mind. It was rather that she did not know what to say that would make any difference.

To tell him that polygamy was bad would have gained her nothing. *He* had grown up with it; it was a common factor in his life. Not only that: *he* understood and agreed with it.

In truth, this entire conversation confused Carolyn.

True, though she might have known that the Indian male held fast to the idea of polygamy, the concept that it might affect her had not been readily apparent. At least it hadn't been back there in Virginia City, when she had first made her plans, and where the heart of Indian country had seemed miles away. Of course back then, she had not even considered the idea of marriage.

Problem was, Carolyn was not prepared for the reality of such a mindset—now or any time in the future. And she really did not require him to repeat himself.

Nevertheless, as though he were duty-bound to reiterate it, he said, "I could not promise you a marriage without other wives."

At a loss for words, Carolyn gulped, taking a quick step away from him. After some moments, she said, "I see. Then, I must confess that our marriage is doomed—"

"It is not doomed."

She looked away from him. "I'm afraid," she said, "that I would have to disagree."

"Why? There is no other woman in my life."

She glanced at him out of the corner of her eye, as she said, "But there is a good chance that there might be one in our future."

"There is always that chance, no matter if you are Indian or white."

"I don't think so," Carolyn countered. "A white man is not allowed more than one wife. Before his God, he pledges himself to one, alone."

But her words seemed to have no effect on Lone Arrow, for he observed, rather smugly, "And the white man just as easily forgets those vows."

Carolyn shook her head. "Not if he be an honest man."

Lone Arrow snickered, saying, "If there is such a thing, bring this person here and let me meet him." Lone Arrow held up his hand when she would have interrupted. He continued, "Do not be deceived. Though the Crow are friendly to the whites, do not think that we have not found this man difficult to understand. As the wise ones in my tribe counsel, the white man keeps his laws and his god always behind him."

"Behind him?"

"*Éeh,* there for use when dealing with strangers, and that is all. We long ago learned that although the white man may speak loudly about his law and how it is made for the good of all, we soon realized that although he expects the Indian to obey this law, the white man, himself, will break his own principles without a second thought."

Carolyn remained silent. In essence, she was once

more at a loss for words. Unfortunately, what Lone Arrow said was too close to the truth.

But her reply was unnecessary, for he went on to say, "This is not the Indian way. We do not make a decree and then break it when it suits us to do so. We expect to keep our laws like we keep our word, once pledged."

Carolyn threw back her head, tilting it up at an angle as she said, "If that is true, then you should keep your vow of marriage."

"I am," he countered. "I said I would take you for my wife. I have."

"But when I married you," she pointed out, "I thought that we were pledging our fidelity to one another, alone. I had no cause to think otherwise, for this is what marriage means to the white man."

He sighed. "This is not the Absarokee way."

"But it should be."

Lone Arrow did not speak for some moments, neither to agree, nor to refute her.

And Carolyn went on to say, "I am sorry, Lone Arrow, for I realize that you might need an Indian wife, if only to help with the work or to make our marriage more acceptable. However, know that I cannot be part of such a scenario. Perhaps it is best if I tell you that *if* you take another woman as a wife, I cannot stay with you."

He nodded, as though the concept of her loss meant nothing to him. He said, "That is your right."

Darn the man!

She said, "Let me take it a step further."

He nodded again.

"As I've already said, when I married you, it was with the belief that we were vowing our loyalty and devotion to one another. If what you say is true, and you cannot give me your pledge of fidelity, here, now and in this place, I will have no choice but to end our marriage."

Carolyn bit her lip. Had she really been reduced to delivering ultimatums?

She watched as he frowned; stared at him as he jerked his head to the left, as though he were fighting a battle within himself. And at some length, he said, "Isn't that . . . taking too large of a leap?"

"Perhaps," she said. "But I think it is fitting for the occasion."

He clenched his jaw, throwing his chin up at an angle, as he said, "Then do you throw me away?"

"I . . ."

He took a step forward and, placing a finger under her chin, raised her face to his so she would have no choice but to look into his eyes. He said, "You should know what you do."

"I . . . I . . ."

"You should know that a man would be made the butt of jokes, that his honor would be gone, never to be repaired, if he were to ever take back a wife who had thrown him away."

Never?

She said, "You don't understand. Even if I didn't want to divorce you, I must."

"Must?"

She nodded, continuing, "I had thought that perhaps, because you have spent time with the white man, you would have known this. But maybe I was wrong."

"I have not had very much to do with the white man's laws of marriage."

"I see."

He paused, then added, "You said nothing of these things when you proposed to me. And you had much opportunity to do so before you went into the union with me."

"That may be so, but I'm saying it now."

She stared at him as a muscle flicked in his cheek. But all he said was, "I would never presume to pass judgment on another's beliefs or his country's laws, but I do not understand why your people would demand vows that are too easily broken. It is not that your men and women are any different than ours."

"Perhaps they are."

He arched a brow. "Are they?"

She took a step back.

And he went on to say, "I have seen married men come amongst my people and take our women to their sleeping robes. I have seen a white man marry more than one woman. I have even witnessed a white man take to his bed another white woman who was not his wife."

Carolyn cleared her throat. "Yes, I am aware that there are men of little character who might do these things, but—"

"And tell me true, in your culture, is a woman allowed the same rights as a man?"

Carolyn groped for words. "Some women are."

"And are they well thought of afterward?"

Of course they weren't. Such women were regarded as ladies of the night—to whom no God-fearing woman would even speak.

But Carolyn was not about to tell Lone Arrow that.

He took one more step forward, she another hasty one back. He said, "The white woman is not well thought of if she strays. I have seen that she is not. At least the Absarokee do not have one standard of character for a man and another for a woman."

Score one for Lone Arrow, Carolyn thought.

Nonetheless, she took another pace away from him, and said, "That is not the point."

He sucked in his breath slowly, and he took his time before he said, "Is it so wrong that I am honest? Is it so bad that my people are honorable? That they do not punish a moment of weakness? In either their men or their women?

"Hear me now," he continued. "I cannot tell you true that I will never have another woman. For I do not know what the future holds. I can only tell you that I would keep you as my wife. I would grant you more honor than I have ever given to another woman. And I would do all within my power to make our lives a happy one. He who would promise more is a fool."

"And you are certainly no fool," she said.

She might have uttered a few other thoughts on the subject, but she had no more than opened her mouth when he said, "Think well on all we have said before you throw me away. When we married, we did not know what was in each other's hearts. Now we do."

"But I could—"

He held up his hand. "Think on it," he said. "As the wise ones counsel, a thing once said cannot be taken back."

"I—"

He placed his fingers over his lips.

One long moment followed upon another, neither of them making a move to leave; neither speaking. And truth be known, they might have stood as such for the entire day had Big Elk not called to Lone Arrow, seeking assistance.

Even so, it took Lone Arrow a lengthy time before he straightened up, and then he said to her, "You should go back to camp and help Pretty Moon. We leave from this place at once."

This said, he made to leave.

But Carolyn caught his arm when he would have walked away. And though her touch was light upon him, she felt him tremble.

It gave her pause. Was he as upset as she?

And this brought on another worry. She said, albeit a little sheepishly, "Do we still go to the cave?"

He pulled his lips into a line before finally gazing down at her. Shortly, he said, "What would you do if I said no? That we make camp and wait until you make your decision?"

Would he do that?

She must have appeared flabbergasted, for he continued, "Do not worry. Though the white man might be allowed to change his mind to suit only himself, I am a man of honor. I said I would take you there. I will."

"Truly?"

"*Éeh*. Why would I hesitate?" he asked, leering at her. He continued, "There is no reason why I should not take you there. Especially since, once we arrive near the cave, I will be able to see you, as nature intended me to see you, as I have often witnessed you in my dreams. And for that moment," he added, "it will be worth the journey."

And upon this rather carnal suggestion, and with a half-cocked rakish grin, he spun away from her to trod off in the opposite direction, leaving Carolyn alone with her own thoughts.

And they were considerable.

Chapter 18

Carolyn and Pretty Moon sat together in a meadow beside a pine-covered mountain and watched Lone Arrow and Big Elk disappear into the forest.

Glancing toward the place where she had last seen them, Carolyn wondered what the two men were doing. She hated to ask, particularly since Pretty Moon did not volunteer the information. However, after a time, Carolyn questioned, "Do you have an idea what's going on? Why we have stopped here?"

Pretty Moon contemplated her seriously for a moment, causing Carolyn to wonder if she had committed some Indian faux pas with her simple question. But soon, Pretty Moon grinned. She said, "Our men . . . find . . . war lodge."

Our men? Carolyn grimaced. Was he still *her* man? Aloud she asked, "War lodge?"

Pretty Moon inclined her head. "In . . . forest." She pointed, then using sign language and speaking in

Crow at the same time, she said, "We must be close to a war trail, for this is where our tribe, and even our enemies, build these kinds of lodges."

Carolyn, while she did not understand the foreign words, certainly grasped the meaning of the signs. In response, she gestured, while she spoke in English, "Are we in danger?"

"Our men go . . . see. You . . . not . . . worry. If . . . enemy here in . . . Absarokee country, they . . . find," Pretty Moon signed, as she spoke the English words. "Your husband . . . good . . . wolf."

"Wolf?"

"*Éeh,* yes. White man . . . call it . . . scout, I think."

A good scout. Was he? Carolyn frowned. There was so much about Lone Arrow that she did not know.

She should also correct Pretty Moon, Carolyn thought. She should tell her that neither she nor Lone Arrow were married, at least not to each other at this present moment.

No, that was not right.

Perhaps she should simply say that she and Lone Arrow were uncertain as to the exact nature of their relationship. There, that was a little truer.

But, as these things sometimes do, the moment when she might have confessed, passed. Carolyn remained silent.

After a while, she asked, "What is a war lodge?"

"It is lodge," said Pretty Moon in English, "warriors build . . . when . . . on warpath."

"Really?"

Pretty Moon nodded.

"Will we be able to see it today?"

"If . . . there is . . . no enemy." Then, in sign, "Because we are in the mountains, these war lodges stand in the deep forest. It hides them better."

"I see," Carolyn said.

Pretty Moon inclined her head, then continued in sign, "War lodges are built close to a war trail, also, and this is not good. We are not prepared to meet an enemy."

Carolyn pushed back a lock of hair that had fallen into her eyes, before she ventured, "We aren't?" Hadn't she seen both men carrying weapons? Very deadly looking weapons?

"*Baa-lee-táa*, no," said Pretty Moon, switching to gestures. "There are only four of us, and, as you know, two of us, women. If an enemy war party were too big, we would be overpowered."

"Oh," said Carolyn.

"That is why," continued Pretty Moon in sign, "our men are being cautious, why we are traveling so slowly."

Perhaps it was foolish to mention it, but Carolyn could not resist saying, "We are going slowly?"

Pretty Moon grinned, then nodded. "For . . . Indians."

"Oh!" said Carolyn, and she might have stated even more, but at that moment, Lone Arrow and Big Elk returned.

Speaking in Crow, and ignoring Carolyn completely, the men addressed Pretty Moon. Carolyn, meantime, glared at *him*.

All right, so they'd had an argument. That did not give him the right to ignore her, did it?

Perhaps it did.

Carolyn looked away from the three of them, but her

eye kept being drawn back to *him*. And secretly, she studied him.

Drat! Why did he have to look so attractive?

His hair was once more caught in a braid at each side of his face. Each plait was tied with rawhide, she noted, to keep it in place, while an eagle feather dangled from one of those braids. And at the back of his head, Lone Arrow had positioned two more feathers, which stuck straight up. It was a stunning effect, particularly since Carolyn knew the feathers meant that he had counted coup, and at such a young age.

Look away, she scolded herself. She should take no undue notice of him.

Still, she could not resist the opportunity to study him unobserved, to compare him to Big Elk.

While both men were tall and slim, Big Elk's face looked perhaps a little more foreign. Rounder or broader, maybe. Of course it was only her opinion, but Big Elk was not nearly as handsome as her own man.

Her own?

Carolyn sighed. It never ceased to amaze her how, no matter her frustration with the man, she was drawn to him.

Dark, midnight black eyes; long, aquiline nose; high cheekbones, full lips. His features were striking, but in her opinion, his good looks were threatened by his intense pride.

How, she wondered, had Lone Arrow become so self-assured? And at such a young age? If he had been no more than sixteen when she had first known him, then he was only twenty-four or twenty-five now.

She shook her head. While Lone Arrow might look that young, he certainly did not act it. No, by the way he held himself, by his attitude and the wisdom with which he spoke, one might have thought he had lived an entire century.

She sighed, and while her gaze skimmed lower, to his chest, she wondered why he hadn't married—that is, until she had proposed it. He would have certainly made a good prospect for some young woman.

That thought was anything but pleasant, for Carolyn was not so naive that she believed there had been no women in his life. In truth, both he and Pretty Moon had intimated as much.

Carolyn glanced away from him, but within moments, without consciously deciding to do so, she found her awareness drifting back to him. His chest wasn't overly large, she decided, but even beneath his shirt, she could see that he was solid, strong and muscular.

He would have to be, she realized. To have counted coup on an enemy at such a youthful age would have required great physical strength.

She fidgeted and looked down, pretending interest in her hands, yet all the while, continuing to observe him. Around his neck he wore a beaded choker, as well as a large pink shell-necklace, held there with a piece of buckskin. Ever present, too, was a series of shell beads, strung in half circles, each strand longer than previous.

Shirt, leggings, breechcloth and moccasins completed Lone Arrow's dress. Across the top of one of his arms was his bow, while in his hand he held a .52 caliber Sharps Carbine. And around his waist was his ever present bullet belt.

He looked to be exactly what he was: a warrior, dangerous and threatening.

He shifted position and her gaze was caught and held by the edge of his shirt where it met his leggings. Good Lord, his shirt did not completely cover his thigh. Rocking back onto her knees, Carolyn was treated to the seductive sight of the rounded image of bare buttock. Unwillingly, a rush of awareness raced across her nerves.

Darn him! How dare he look so good.

Worse, as though he were aware of the effect he was having upon her, he glanced at her. But he did not smile. Instead he approached her and, without pause, came down to his haunches beside her. However, she scooted slightly away.

"We need to replenish our food stores," he said. "It is what we are telling Pretty Moon. To the north of us, is a good buffalo range. But it will take us many days out of our way to reach it."

Many days? Did she have that much time to waste?

She asked, "Do we go there now?"

"*Baa-lee-táa*, no," said Lone Arrow. "Big Elk has killed a deer. It is not the meat of choice, but it will get us through these next few days. But this meat, though it is not buffalo, will need to be smoked and made into *iaxshe*."

"*Iaxshe?* What's that?"

"Pemmican, I think the whites call it. Pretty Moon will show you what to do."

"But—"

"Your help is needed to do this quickly," he went on to say. "My friend and I have found a war lodge we can use. If we smoke the meat inside it, it will not alert any enemies that there is someone in the vicinity."

"But—"

"We cannot stay long at this place. To do so is to

court disaster. War lodges are built on the trails of our enemies. Therefore, you must work quickly."

"But—"

"Remember that I told you that a woman's work is often hard and long? Your help is needed."

"But—" Carolyn stopped herself, thinking she might be interrupted again. When Lone Arrow remained silent, however, she said, "But I have no knife with which to work."

"Ho!" he said, as he untied a buckskin sheath from around his waist and offered it to her. Tentatively, she reached up to take it, but he held it back from her.

He said, "This, too, was made by my *búua-lí-ché.*"

Carolyn pulled back her hand, while she inspected the sheath gingerly, noting for the first time that the bead work on it matched the paintings on Lone Arrow's robe.

Realizing this, a multitude of emotions converged upon her—jealousy, fear, hostility. She was more than aware of these. However, there was also within her, if she were to be truthful, a bit of thankfulness. Particularly since she realized that she might at last have a weapon.

Lone Arrow reached out for her hand, taking it into his own. And in truth, so caught up had she been in her thoughts, she was momentarily startled by the contact.

It lasted but a moment, however, for Lone Arrow did not simply hold her hand. Taking her fingers, he placed them one by one on the sheath as he said to her, "Know that my *búua-lí-ché* is no longer my girlfriend. I tell you true that she is now married to someone else. But these things she gave me are mine—and I give them to you now for your use."

Spreading his fingers over her own, he said, "Do not

fear these things. They are but objects of beauty. They do not, and have never represented what is in my heart. If it will help to heal the wound between us, know that when I return home, I will burn these things if it pleases you."

"You would?" She swallowed, hard.

"*Éeh*," he said. Then dropping the volume of his voice to a whisper, he said, "When we came together in marriage, you did not know our customs. I did not know yours. Perhaps we should start again. Maybe I should have done as you first suggested and merely sought out the use of your body."

With these words, Carolyn sat as though stunned to silence. But he was continuing, "No one from my tribe would have thought less of you for this thing. If you wish it, we could take back our vows of marriage, as though they never happened, and say that we have had only a romance—that is all. This thing that I suggest to you is allowed by my people. Maybe," he said as he brought his face closer to her, "if we are lucky, we could still have that romance."

She stared at him for some moments, feeling as though she were being slowly mesmerized by his nearness. However, after a time, she said, "Lone Arrow, I—"

"Do not give me your answer now. Think on it. As the wise men say, and as I have said to you, 'ponder over these things before you act.'"

Carolyn nodded, but otherwise remained silent.

And Lone Arrow stared at her for several more moments, as though with a look alone, he might instill her with courage. But at last he treated her to a brief nod, and rose up onto his feet. Before he left, however, he said, "Pretty Moon will show you what to do."

And with that, he and Big Elk left forthwith, abandoning the two women to themselves.

A fire had been built in the middle of the war lodge. Over it the women had constructed frames of willow branches, bent so that they curved directly over the fire. On this framework hung many slices of meat.

At present, Carolyn dug her knife into the last few pieces of venison, cutting them into strips. Soon, she would place these, too, atop the wooden structure.

Though she had been working for many hours without rest, Carolyn felt perfectly happy. It was not as if the work was difficult, and no one pressed her. In truth, both Pretty Moon and the men seemed glad for anything she was able to contribute. Plus, she had taken a position next to the fire, which meant she was able to keep warm. And this, because of their high altitude, was a blessing.

A war lodge was an odd structure, Carolyn thought, as she bent over her task. Made from windfalls of timber, the framework of the structure was composed of perhaps four sturdy tree trunks locked together, though these were not tied at the top. Added to this, heavier pieces of timber—about twelve feet in length—were propped up against the four main trunks. It made for a very sturdy structure.

The outside of the lodge was then covered with bark, long pieces of it fitted so closely together that there was not even a crack that would let in rain or snow.

However the structure had a lighting problem, Carolyn was quick to discern. With the single exception of the very top of the lodge—the spot where the poles met—there was no light, except for the fire, of course.

But Carolyn had to admit that even the dimness of the war lodge had caused little problem. Eventually she had discovered that one's eyes adjusted.

On the inside of the lodge, and strewn throughout it, were boughs of dry pine, a reminder that the lodge had once housed other occupants. Although in this particular lodge, someone had left a bearskin.

Pretty Moon seemed disinterested in it, but Carolyn had taken to using it as a rug.

The other strange thing about the lodge was the entryway, Carolyn observed. Constructed as it was, there was only one entrance, which was a triangular opening in the lodge itself. Extended out from this opening, for perhaps ten feet, were several smaller pieces of timber, placed in such a way as to form a crawl space, which was about four feet high. Built of smaller but heavier timber, it required a person to stoop or crawl into the lodge.

While Carolyn understood that these lodges were constructed in this way as a point of safety, it was, nonetheless, a hindrance. Getting into it and out of it could be quite a nuisance.

Carolyn was nudged from her thoughts when Pretty Moon caught her gaze and said, "Fire . . . need . . . more wood . . . soon."

Carolyn sent a grin to her friend. "Yes," she said, "I can see that. I'll get it. You stay here."

Pretty Moon smiled and nodded.

Standing—for the lodge was tall enough that one could do so easily—Carolyn stepped to the entrance where she came down onto her haunches.

"Is there anything else you need before I leave to get the wood?" Carolyn called over her shoulder.

Pretty Moon wrinkled her brow for a moment, then said, "Pine branches . . . for bed."

Carolyn knew exactly what Pretty Moon wanted and why. Ever since their party had come into fir-tree country, they made their bed each night upon pine boughs, sometimes softened and made even more fragrant with sweet sage. It made for a comfortable bed.

But these boughs which had been left inside this lodge were dry and old. She and Pretty Moon needed new ones. Fresh ones.

"Will we be sleeping here tonight?" Carolyn asked.

"*Éeh,*" Pretty Moon nodded. "We," she pointed to herself and Carolyn, "will. Our men . . . stand guard . . . through night . . . we . . . make *iaxshe.*"

This was news, and Carolyn asked, "Lone Arrow and Big Elk will be on watch the entire night?"

Pretty Moon nodded. "We . . . in country . . . dangerous. On war trail . . . not safe to . . . sleep."

"Then why do we stay here?"

"We need . . . ah, *oo-ssha* . . . food. Not safe to make *iaxshe* . . . in open."

"Oh, I see," said Carolyn. "Then I will get as much wood as I can. Enough to see us through the night."

Pretty Moon nodded once more. "Not . . . *baachiia* . . . ah, pine. No good . . . fire . . . makes . . . sparks."

"But that's about the only kind of wood that there is here."

Pretty Moon shook her head. "Find other."

Find other?

"I'll try," Carolyn said, realizing that her task might be a little more difficult than she had at first anticipated.

Then she crawled through the entrance, which was really no more than a very long passageway.

As she moved past row after row of slanted logs, Carolyn discovered that she was glad to be taking her leave from the lodge, if only for a few moments. Particularly since, for the past several hours she and Pretty Moon had been doing nothing but preparing the venison.

At last, she came to the end of the entrance, stood up, and, raising her hands over her head, stretched. *Ah, that felt good.* She sighed.

Smiling and placing her hands on her hips, Carolyn gazed with awe toward the western sky, which was throwing multitudes of pinks and reds, oranges and golds over an otherwise green and brown landscape. It was a dazzling sight, especially after being confined to the dark lodge.

Funny how the browns and beiges were so easily transformed into pinkish, reddish, even gold colors. Every tree trunk, every blade of dry grass, even the earth itself had converted in color. It was as though nature herself were an artist.

Enough, she cautioned herself as she inhaled deeply. She had come here with a purpose.

"Wood for the fire," Carolyn mumbled to herself as she stared at the ground.

Gee, but this was not going to be easy. There was nothing here but pine and fir branches. Where was she to get another type of wood? Where, she wondered, had the men found those willow branches?

Perhaps, she thought, she needed to find the men first, then the wood. Where would Lone Arrow and Big Elk be?

She considered reentering the lodge and asking

Pretty Moon about it, assuming that the young woman would know. But Carolyn decided against it. It was simply too difficult crawling into and out of that thing.

Maybe if she ventured a little farther afield, the men might find her. Carolyn cast her gaze upward and sniffed at the fragrant, pine-scented air. It was incredible here. Beautiful. Who would guess, she wondered, that there might be danger in the air?

And so it was upon this last thought that Carolyn ventured forth, seeking out the men.

Chapter 19

"**A**h don't rightly know what it is."

Like a playful imp, the wind pulled at the two men's broad-brimmed hats, forcing each gent to clamp a hand down onto his head. It was either that, or lose the dang things altogether. Meanwhile, the cold, bracing air nipped at every exposed place on their bodies, while the sun contrarily teased those same spots with flickerings of warmth.

Here before them was a tribute to nature. Here was a place of mystery, a place of strange beauty—all in one seemingly simple spot.

Alas, had either man but noticed.

But they did not. Together, the men stood staring out at the centuries old stones, which had been fashioned into a circle. A buffalo head had been placed by some unknown person at the center of the circle, while spokes, each formed with stone, extended out and intersected the rim of the ring.

Standing as they were, nearly ten thousand feet above sea level, one might have thought these two men would have been impressed. Especially since, had another person been the one looking, he would have been accorded a treasured view of the earth; one that a more timid, citified person might never see. In truth, panoramic views, mountain peaks and the immensity of the rolling prairie stood ready to greet these two men on every side of them, had they but looked.

But neither man did.

Shame.

"Looks like some wheel spokes, don't it, Dixon? Don't suppose settlers have been up this way, do ya?"

"Ya gual-derned idiot! On top of a mountain? Think next time afore ya speak."

Jordan clamped his lips together. He was getting a little tired of Dixon's constant harping at him; telling him to do this or that—and how to do it, too. Why, if it weren't for the debt he owed the brute . . .

"Don't rightly 'member comin' this here way," Dixon scratched his beard, interrupting Jordan's thoughts. "Give that map here."

Jordan handed over the worthless thing, the same map he had scribbled together in the wee hours of a morning several weeks ago. He said, "And was ya lookin' at where we was all them years ago, Dixon? Ya was as scared as me."

"Bah! Was nothin' ta be scared of. Yer memory's gone daft." The big man laid the map out over one of the six large clusters of stones, not even noticing that each one of these assemblies pointed in a particular direction.

"Was too scared . . . as a rabbit." Jordan quirked an odd smile.

"Was not."

"Was too."

The wind howled, appearing to rise up from nothing. With seeming intention, the gust slammed into Jordan's face. And with it came the dawning of recognition.

"Dixon?" Jordan's eyes grew round, bulging; and the hair on the back of his neck stood up on end. "Did ja feel that?"

"Feel what?" Dixon was pouring over the map.

"That wind?"

"Yea, what 'bout it?"

Jordan stepped back a pace. "Ah don't like this place."

Dixon did not even look up. "What's ta like?"

Before Jordan could utter another word, the wind kicked up speed, bellowing around the bend in the mountain pass. Indeed, so intense was the blast that it appeared to be spinning.

Jordan had heard tell 'bout this kind of wind. Devil winds the folks out here called 'em. Some folks even told stories about Indian spirits that had come back to life within these whirlwinds; heard tell that those spirits hung around places like this, only waiting to haunt and curse any white man. Some other kinder folks had been known to believe that the winds were nothin' but simple ghosts.

Interestingly enough, not one theory held the notion that the winds were simply that: wind, all mixed together with dirt and gusts.

At present, as though it had been granted life, this one approached the two men.

"Dixon? . . ."

"Yeah?"

"Look up. Ah have nary seen sich a—"

"What?"

The bigger man finally raised his head. None too soon.

"God, Almighty," he was heard saying.

Fear finally struck. Both men crossed themselves. One wide-eyed glance met the other.

Someone screamed, or was it two screams? Perhaps there was no one to keep count.

Without another word uttered between them, the two men jumped up from their task, allowing their legs full stride as they shot back down the lonely mountain trail, the same one which had brought them here. In fact, so quick was their departure that one might have thought they had miraculously sprouted wings.

Curious. The two men were behaving as though some imaginary monster were after them.

Perhaps it was.

Long after the men had gone, the winds continued to sweep over the landscape, as though they might erase all traces of the ill-timed visit. The draught blew at a piece of paper half stuck to the ground. And it was not long before the vast gale had dislodged even this worthless bit of human artifice, sending it scurrying after the men.

At length, Carolyn found some deciduous trees in the river's bend, and she found them long before she located the men. Odd that, although the war lodge had been constructed no more than several hundred yards from the stream, she had not known that she'd been so close to it. Perhaps that was because it had been Pretty Moon who had collected the fresh water earlier in the day. That, and the fact that the war lodge filtered out the sounds of the babbling water.

Carolyn cut a glance upward, noticing that the wind, which was stirring the branches of the trees, was a cold wind. Involuntarily, she wrapped her shawl more tightly around her shoulders.

In the shadow of the trees, she recognized a cotton-wood, and over there, a willow. But looking around her, she decided that there were more ash trees in evidence than any other species. They weren't extremely tall trees, she noted, probably standing no more than fifteen to twenty feet high.

Glancing back toward the ground, Carolyn remembered her purpose. And the sooner she accomplished that mission, the sooner she would be back in the lodge, sitting around the warmth of the fire.

Goodness, she thought, there weren't many branches on the ground. Had Pretty Moon or perhaps the men already collected whatever timber was available in this spot?

Carolyn was tempted to keep winding her way down river, but not knowing the lay of the land in this high mountain place, or what danger might threaten her if she were to venture too far from the lodge, she decided that idea was unwise. She would make do with what she had.

Bending, she began to gather up what was left of the branches, one by one. This wood seemed awfully green, however. What was needed for the lodge was dry timber; it burnt better, was easier to manage.

By the time she had accumulated an armful of the right kind of timber, the sun had almost left the sky. Best to make her way back to the lodge. She turned to retrace her steps when she heard them . . . voices. *Voices?*

Every sense within Carolyn sharpened, and she

paused, listening. Definitely low, masculine voices.

Taking a few deep breaths, Carolyn tried to still the rapid beating of her heart. Perhaps it was nothing, she tried to assure herself. It was probably Lone Arrow or Big Elk returning to the lodge.

After all, an enemy would not be speaking aloud, for fear of announcing their presence . . . or would they? This was not a Crow war lodge, after all.

She must take precaution; she must hide, and quickly. Bending, she set the sticks on the ground, and without a second thought, she clambered up one of the trees, a willow. It was probably the easiest of the trees to climb, plus it was also the closest one to hand.

"*Óole!*" came the deep call.

Immediately, Carolyn breathed in a sigh of relief. She recognized the voice of her husband. Glancing down, she noted that he was near enough that she could see him, there, through a cluster of trees. She made a quick movement, thinking to jump down from the tree, but without warning she stopped.

The two men, who had been speaking Crow to one another, abruptly froze, midstride. Carolyn also went completely still.

What was wrong?

Was there danger?

Slowly, silently, Carolyn let out her breath, daring nothing more, lest she draw the attention of an unseen foe.

At last, Lone Arrow made a series of sign motions, and he said, "I sense the presence of someone. There has been movement here—recently."

Lone Arrow's companion, a man Carolyn did not recognize, made the gesture for agreement, but signed, as well, "Perhaps it was an elk."

With his right hand next to his heart, two fingers extended, Lone Arrow made the back and forth sign for maybe. But then he motioned, "The birds no longer sing, I see no squirrels on the ground and all is too quiet. There is someone here, I think."

Perhaps it had been her own motions that Lone Arrow sensed. She had better show herself, least they mistake her for an enemy. She lifted her foot that she might begin her climb to the ground.

Meanwhile, Lone Arrow's companion signed, "You are too nervous. There is nothing here but maybe a scared rabbit. I see nothing. I feel nothing. Perhaps your senses are overworked because you have recently taken a white woman into your home, and have no good Absarokee women to comfort you."

Stunned, Carolyn soundlessly replaced her foot. *Had she read those gestures correctly?* Easing herself into a position where she might see the two men better, she peeped down upon them.

Lone Arrow, she noted, did not say a word or make a single sign in response to this. Not even in his own defense. In fact, he grinned at his friend.

And after a slight pause, he gestured, "Running Coyote, you have yet to meet my wife. Once you see her, you will understand why she is the one I have married."

Wife? Hadn't Lone Arrow only today suggested that the two of them could start again, perhaps have no more than a romance? Hadn't he given her the choice as to whether they were to remain married or not?

Lone Arrow's companion, however, barely stopped to read his friend's gestures, and Carolyn found she had to abandon her own thoughts and give these two men her undivided attention.

Running Coyote gestured in sign: "But what will

your mothers and fathers say when they see she is white? And you, the speaker for and protector of these mountains? Have the white men had such influence over you that you now wish your skin to be white? Do you seek this by way of marriage?"

How rude.

But again, Lone Arrow merely smiled. And once more, he made no move to defend himself. Not even to deny the accusation.

The friend continued, however, signing, "The others in your clan will begin to say, 'there goes Lone Arrow, a wanna-be white man. Next we will have to bargain with him instead of with the Indian agent.'"

To this, he laughed. Then he signed, "It would be an improvement. I would not cheat my people, as the agent does."

After a moment, when Running Coyote appeared to have no more to say on the matter, Lone Arrow signed, "Come, let us go to the war lodge and you will see my wife. And I think you are right. It must have been the motion of an elk which I sensed."

Carolyn's foot slipped on a branch. Barely a sound resulted.

Yet while Running Coyote took a few steps toward the war lodge, Lone Arrow did not budge. Not a single bit. Alas, he seemed to become vigilant once more.

Carolyn stopped dead.

After a moment, however, Lone Arrow relaxed, and taking a step forward, addressed his companion, saying in English, "Maybe you are right, my father. Maybe I should find a good Crow woman to keep me warm at night. A woman who knows how to please her man. After all, when a wife neglects her duties to her husband as mine has done . . ." The rest was lost to the wind.

And off he went, following on the footfalls of whomever was this man, Running Coyote.

Crouching in the tree, it was some moments before Carolyn was able at last to stir herself.

A good Crow woman? Duties to her husband? Pleasing her man?

Humph! Carolyn did not know what to think, what to do. On one hand, she would have liked nothing better than to jump down from this tree and haunt Lone Arrow's steps until she could shake some sense into him. On the other hand . . .

Could he even have sense shaken into him? And from whose viewpoint would this sense arise?

Again she reminded herself that *she* was the one who objected to him taking more than one lover. *He* seemed to be perfectly happy about the arrangement— he even appeared unperturbed at the idea of her suddenly up and having an affair.

However, Carolyn remembered that it was also true that the Crow ideal for marriage was one of fidelity, love, and respect; one that lasted an entire lifetime. And weren't these the very attributes that she admired? Didn't this ideal more closely approach her own notions of what a good marriage should be?

And if this were so, could Lone Arrow not, then, be brought into understanding her point of view? And not simply to tolerate her perspective, but to understand it and to abide by it?

Perhaps.

It was strange, though, she thought. Strange that he should suddenly switch from sign language to English, particularly if he thought there might be an enemy in the vicinity.

Carolyn blinked, twice. *English? . . .*

Had he known she was in this tree? He hadn't looked up to see; he hadn't even turned his head so much as an inch. Still, why would he have switched to English? Was it possible that he had said those words for *her* benefit?

Impossible.

She shook her head. Enough. She was certainly going to accomplish nothing while perched in this tree like a bird. Perhaps, she thought, it would be to her advantage to climb down and dog this man's steps until she either brought him around to her way of thinking, or . . .

She did not finish the thought.

Looking down, she realized she had another problem. It was too far to jump. She was going to have to shimmy down this tree much like a snake. So, sliding down a foot, she found her first foothold and put her weight on it . . .

Oops!

She slipped on that branch. Worse, she heard a snap. And it was with a sinking feeling of the inevitable that she looked down, acknowledging that her instincts had been correct; it was *her* limb that had broken. The limb supporting her weight . . . it was cracked.

Oh, dear. More to the point, the branch was splitting, even as she watched.

Grimacing, she tried to swing up to another limb, but she could not find anything substantial to hold on to, at least not fast enough.

She heard a loud pop, and that was it. Down she came, tree limb and all.

Plop! Oomph! She landed on her fanny, right on the ground. Luckily the earth was sandy in this place, and she did not appear to be hurt. At least, not physically. But she had landed with all the dignity of a cat in heat.

She tried to move. "Oooo!" She rubbed her backside. Would she be able to sit these next few nights?

Anger stirred within her, but whether such ire was roused because of the tree limb or because of Lone Arrow's ill-spoken words, she did not know. Still, she thought as she broke the branch into pieces, the least she would get out of it was firewood.

By the time Carolyn was able to stalk back to their camp, it was dark.

Drat! She had forgotten something—those pine boughs for Pretty Moon. Giving her surroundings a swift once over, she espied several pine shoots littering the ground.

Without looking closely at the offshoots, she gathered up what she could, along with her load of sticks and wood.

It was a large burden to carry, and coming up close to the war lodge, Carolyn sighed. She knew the Indians had made these entrances so that a man could not easily go into or out of them. But this was ridiculous.

How was she to get all this wood plus the boughs into the lodge? And at one time?

There was nothing for it but to place the wood in front of her and scoot it along the passageway, as she dragged the boughs behind her.

She tried it, but it was too difficult. In truth, she had gone no more than a single foot when she realized this would not work, not at all. And so, backing out of the entrance on hands and knees, she sank down upon the ground. There had to be another way.

That was it. It would take her longer to accomplish it, but there was no other means to get all of this into the lodge. She was simply going to have to divide the chore into halves. First, she would scoot the wood into the lodge.

This proved to be easy enough, and she did it quickly, considering that one did have to, after all, traverse a long passageway on one's hands and knees. And if the men were in the lodge—which she assumed they were—she did not see them. But then, she hadn't bothered to look, either.

Retreating, she crawled back through the entrance and collected up the boughs, pulling them into her arms and then dragging them behind her into the lodge.

At last, the chore was finished and she was able to crawl through the entrance. It was with some feeling of accomplishment that she stood up, but when she sent her gaze around the lodge, she was greeted by the sight of Pretty Moon alone.

Darn! All the while she had been crawling into and out of this space, she had been practicing what she might say to Lone Arrow. In truth, she had stirred herself up, and was ready for a good argument.

But all her preparation was for naught. Instead, she found herself speaking to Pretty Moon, and she was able to say, brightly enough, "Look, I've not only gathered some wood, I've brought us a couple of nice, green boughs to sleep on tonight."

Pretty Moon glanced up to smile at Carolyn.

Carolyn returned the grin and, bending, collected the boughs into her arms. She took a step toward Pretty Moon. But something moved in those boughs. Something long and slimy.

Carolyn looked down.

Oh, my God, a snake!

Carolyn dropped the pine boughs, snake and all. Unfortunately, she also released the whole of it into the fire.

Not only that. That same slimy something that had moved in those shoots now curled at her feet.

Carolyn screamed. And though Pretty Moon jumped up, Carolyn realized the other woman would not be able to help her quickly enough. Practically in hysterics, she groped around her, looking for a weapon.

She found it in the bear rug. Without so much as another thought, Carolyn leaned forward to grab hold of the rug, and clutching it tightly in her hand, she beat it over the ground, at her feet, all around her, unaware that in doing so, she also fanned the fire.

Soon, as might have been expected, the fire began to emit not only mere puffs but big bellows of black, sooty smoke. Surely, clouds of the blackened smut filled the lodge with seeming speed.

Pretty Moon coughed, then shouted. "Leave . . . lodge."

Carolyn nodded, but her feet felt paralyzed. She could not move. She cried back, "I can't. There's a rattlesnake at my feet."

"Rattlesnake?" Pretty Moon's words trailed away. After a moment she said, "This one . . . not . . . hear . . . rattle."

"It's crawling at my feet, I tell you."

Wap, wap, wap, Carolyn beat at the ground with the bear rug.

Pretty Moon, at least, appeared to be slightly calmer

than Carolyn, and the young Indian woman ordered, "Jump . . . back."

"I can't," Carolyn shouted. "I'm afraid it'll bite me."

Wap, wap, wap.

As luck would have it, the rug caught fire, smoldering slowly, large blusters of smoke beginning to rise from it, too.

"Don't . . . beat . . . fire!" said Pretty Moon.

"I'm not," cried Carolyn. "I'm trying to get rid of the snake."

"Snake not go . . . if . . . beat it. White woman stay. Pretty Moon . . . get . . . her. Stand . . . still."

Still? Was Pretty Moon serious? How could a body stand still when there was a deadly snake at your feet? Still, squealing and squeaking like a chicken turned mouse, Carolyn did as asked, and she encouraged, "Do hurry!"

"White woman . . ." Pretty Moon tried to speak, but ended up coughing instead. Finally, she managed, "Need . . . leave lodge . . . hard to . . . breathe. This one . . . cannot see."

"I know. You go ahead," said Carolyn. "Save yourself."

A note of humor might have crept into the other woman's tone as she said, "Pretty Moon help . . . not leave . . . friend." And with this declaration, Pretty Moon came down on her hands and knees and crawled toward Carolyn. But she did not reach her. "Smoke . . . heap . . . bad now. Cannot find white woman."

"I'm over here," called Carolyn. "Watch out, there's a rattlesnake at my feet. I can feel it."

"Snake only bite . . . when . . . coiled. Here . . . take hand. We crawl out . . . like one."

Carolyn could see Pretty Moon's hand extended toward her. And reaching out, she made a grab for it.

Never, thought Carolyn, had a grip felt so good.

"Follow . . . Pretty Moon."

"I will. I promise."

"Crawl."

"Yes, but I'm afraid to."

"Must do it . . . before snake coil."

Carolyn dropped to the ground, and with her hand still clasped within her friend's, she followed Pretty Moon toward the entrance, dragging the bear rug with her. It was the only weapon she possessed, the only thing that stood between herself and the snake.

"The snake's following me," Carolyn said. "I'm sure of it. I can feel it."

"It . . . afraid, too. Keep . . . going."

"I will."

Why had the Indians built the lodge so that one could not easily get into and out of it?

"Keep hold of . . . hand . . ."

"I am."

"Pretty Moon almost there."

"It's following us."

"Snake scared, too. Keep hold . . . of hand."

Carolyn did as she was instructed.

Finally, Pretty Moon managed to crawl out of the lodge; she stood up. And without letting go of Carolyn's hand, the young Indian woman tugged and pulled.

But the way out was still several paces ahead of her, and it was too dark to see.

Letting out a cry, Carolyn said, "Pretty Moon, I think the snake is around my leg. What am I to do?"

"Crawl out."

Carolyn did as ordered. And heavens be praised, she made it.

Never had the black of night looked so inviting. Never, thought Carolyn, had she been more happy to leave a place.

She came up onto her feet at once, finally gaining the chance to look down at her leg. Moonlight illuminated the shape of the snake as it coiled around her leg. And upon seeing it poised just so, Carolyn screamed, and screamed, and kept screaming.

Where fear rules, logic fails. So it would follow that without any rational thought whatsoever, Carolyn grabbed hold of the bear rug, and with it firmly in hand, she beat at herself with all her might.

Not once did she stop her howling, and she shrieked as though the devil himself were after her.

Then the worst thing that could have possibly happened did. It bit her.

The odd thing of it was that Pretty Moon stood beside her, laughing; laughing so hard the other woman could not even talk.

Lone Arrow was the first to spy the telltale evidence of smoke. Silently, he poked his companion in the ribs, and pointed.

Lone Arrow frowned. Now, while it was true that the women were supposed to be smoking the meat, it was not something that one should be able to smell, let alone see. He signed, "I had better investigate. You stay here. Watch. I go."

His companion nodded.

As swiftly and as silently as he could, Lone Arrow

approached the war lodge. Had an enemy attacked? Did they have The-girl-who-runs-with-bears?

He heard a scream. Another, followed by another series of them.

Baa-lee-táa! No! His heart turned over.

He ran.

But it was odd. He heard no war whoops. No cries. Not even the swish of an arrow. Nothing to suggest an enemy.

What was wrong?

At last the war lodge came into view. And there he saw a sight he thought he would never forget so long as he lived. There stood The-girl-who-runs-with-bears in the clearing of the lodge, stomping her leg up and down, beating at herself with a . . . bear? While Pretty Moon stood to the side . . . laughing?

"How can you laugh?" he heard his wife ask.

But Pretty Moon could not answer. In truth, Lone Arrow could see that the other woman could barely breathe, so hysterical was she. Though, in all fairness, Pretty Moon tried to hide it.

"Oh!" It was his wife's cry.

Lone Arrow ran toward the two women. "What is wrong here?"

Pretty Moon, still unable to speak, pointed toward his wife's leg.

At first he thought his wife's action merely unusual. But then he, too, grasped the situation. And though he would have liked to have remained neutral, perhaps stoic even, he could not help himself.

He, too, broke out into a fit of laughter.

"Well, I'm glad to see that the two of you find my death amusing."

He grinned. His wife had barely been able to say the words. How could she when her actions were consumed with stamping up and down, as well as beating at herself with that rug. She said, "I hope you'll laugh all the way to the burial grounds."

"Perhaps that time may yet come, my wife," said Lone Arrow. "But I think that the time is not now."

She almost cried. He could see it in her features, and she asked, "How can you say such a thing? I've just been bitten by a—"

"Vine."

"A . . . rattle—A vine?"

He nodded, pointing to her leg. He said, "While I am sure it has a bad bite, the white woman will live, I think."

He witnessed his wife's bewildered look before she uttered again, "A vine?"

Once more, Lone Arrow nodded, while Pretty Moon turned away, her hand still covering her mouth, her shoulders still shaking, and her giggles still loud enough to be heard.

But all his wife said was, "Oh."

He crossed his arms over his chest, his glance motioning toward the bear rug, which was still smoking. And though he knew he should leave well enough alone, he could not help but observe, "Is it your intention to eat . . . bear?"

"Eat bear?"

"When my friend and I asked our women to smoke the meat, we did not mean the bear rug, too."

She gave him a weak sort of grin. "Ha . . . ha."

But Lone Arrow merely beamed at her. He said, "I think because of this great occasion, that I will have to give you new name."

"What? Because of this?"

"Yes, because of this." He thought for a moment. "I think," he said, "that from this day forward I will have to call you . . . Smoking-the-bear."

And while he grinned at the brilliance of his own wit, his wife gave him the shortest of looks, uttering once again, "Ha . . . Ha . . ."

Chapter 20

They spent the rest of the evening outside the lodge—and a good distance from it.

In truth, they'd had to move out of it, since hours later, the smoke still hadn't cleared. Plus—and this was perhaps more important—the smoke could have alerted any wandering war party of their presence.

And of course it rained. What should she have expected?

The men had set up a temporary lean-to as protection. However, it was far from adequate, and as Carolyn lay upon her back, looking up at the arrangement of timber and sticks, she shivered.

Not that she would have slept inside the war lodge either, Carolyn reasoned. With a snake in there?

Luckily, the men had retrieved the meat that the women had dried and was now thoroughly smoked. Lone Arrow had reported, too, that the snake was doing well and that it was a bull snake, not a rattler.

To this, Carolyn had turned a deaf ear, especially when both Pretty Moon and Lone Arrow had, in turn, laughed.

Returning from scouting, even stoic Big Elk, who hardly ever uttered a word in her presence, could barely keep a straight face around her.

Well, what did it matter, after all? People make mistakes all the time. And she certainly wasn't an exception.

The only person who had not laughed outright at her was Lone Arrow's friend Running Coyote. Some day, Carolyn thought, she would have to thank the man for that.

But not tonight. Tonight she had other things on her mind.

At present the three men were sitting guard; not in shifts, but at the same time. Did they never sleep? It seemed to Carolyn as if all this protection was unnecessary. Wouldn't one sentry be enough? It was not as if she and Pretty Moon were sleeping in the lodge.

Problem was, Carolyn was wide awake. She could not stop thinking. But whether this was because she was too overwrought or too excited from all the tumult, she was uncertain.

She only knew that hours ago she had spread her blanket upon the ground, and here she lay, tossing and turning. Plus, she hadn't yet been able to speak with Lone Arrow.

Biting down on her lip, she stirred uneasily. She needed to talk to Lone Arrow, particularly since she feared that, until she did so, her thoughts would not let her be.

It was puzzling. First she and Lone Arrow were married, then they weren't. Then, according to him, they were again. In truth, it was getting so that she did not know what to expect from him.

Actually that was not true. She knew exactly what to expect from him. *That* was the problem.

She sighed. There was nothing else for it; she was going to have to seek out Lone Arrow and talk to him. And she was going to have to do so this night if she wanted to get some rest.

No sooner had the thought materialized than she threw off her blanket and sat up, peering out into the night. Although she could not see where the men were, she knew they were there.

Carolyn crawled from beneath the lean-to, which, she thought, might be more accurately dubbed a double lean-to, since four poles, two sets each, had been set up against a long, yet strong overhanging willow limb. The whole thing had been covered in bark, which, truth be known, had done a fairly decent job at keeping out the rain.

But not the cold.

Pulling her shawl more closely around her shoulders, Carolyn stood up. Wet grass, along with a good portion of mud, seeped into her shoes as she took a step forward.

Squish, came the noise of a single footfall. Odd, how that sound carried on the night air, even over the wind. Odd, too, how cold a body could feel when one's feet were wet.

She shivered, her teeth rattling in her head. However, she did her best to ignore it. After all, she could not allow her discomfort to keep her from her purpose.

Carolyn inhaled, and the rain-soaked air, freshly perfumed with the scent of pine, filled her lungs. It smelled good, this high-mountain atmosphere; it felt good on the body, too, when it was not so cold, and closing her eyes, Carolyn took another few sniffs.

Enough. She had to find Lone Arrow. Opening her eyes, she tread forward yet another step.

"Why do you not sleep?"

Startled, Carolyn jumped. She had not heard Lone Arrow come up behind her.

She pivoted, and was at once met with an image that was as intoxicating as it was gorgeous. She caught her breath. Goodness, but this man was handsome.

The lighting was perfect: shimmery, misty, ethereal; the moon's radiance outlining Lone Arrow in reflections of softness and dark. All at once, her insides tingled and her stomach fluttered as though a thousand butterflies had been let loose within it.

Beautiful. It was the only word that came to her to describe him. This man was absolutely beautiful.

Funny how his onyx-colored hair looked brown in this light; odd, too, how the ephemeral moonbeams highlighted a single one of his cheekbones, leaving the other to be outlined in shadows of grey and black. The rest of his image remained hidden to her, however, beneath the blanket of darkness, although his silhouette stood out majestically, proudly against the moonlit sky.

Looking at him made her feel as though the breath had been knocked from her. But heaven forbid if she could afford to ever let him know that.

Sniffling, she tossed back her head, hoping beyond hope that her nonchalance would hide any lingering reaction to him. Even so, it occurred to her that it was a shame that she had to take such precautions.

Shame, because she could not have him. Shame, because, if she were to be completely honest with herself, she would admit that she wanted him.

Why not have him? urged a little voice inside her. All it would require is that Carolyn bend a little . . .

Mesmerized, perhaps by the man's arousing image, Carolyn briefly considered letting go of a moral or two. Could she make love to this man and walk away? Did men not do that to women?

But her spirits sank at the mere thought of it, and she exhaled slowly. No, she could not do that. Her own sense of worth, her own conception of virtue, would not allow it.

Then what about marriage? He had not thrown her away, nor had she done so to him, at least not yet.

But could she honestly marry a man who declared his right to take another wife? A man who openly admitted that either he or she could bring another lover into their lives?

Silly questions, Carolyn decided. Religious beliefs aside, there was no man alive, no matter how beautifully put together, that was worth the expense that this scenario might cost a feminine heart. And as surely as the sun rises each day, there would come a time when she would hate him, hate herself.

Barely daring to breathe out and rocking back on her heels, Carolyn realized there was little point in further contemplation of the matter. And before she had time to change her mind, it would be best to confront the man with what must be her final word on the subject.

So decided, she swept back her hair from her face and, stiffening her resolve, she stated, "I left the lean-to in order that I might talk to you yet this night. I have something important to say. But you . . . you startled me."

Lone Arrow did not answer all at once, although at length, he said, "I detected movement, and, not knowing what it was, I needed to investigate."

"I see."

"It was not my intention to startle you."

"Wasn't it?" she began, gazing away from him, as though she did not expect him to answer. And when he remained silent, she stated simply, "I could not sleep."

He nodded. "It is to be expected. You are still frightened of the vine?"

"No," she denied, grinning slightly at her own expense. "And remember that I was frightened of a snake."

The wind caught at her, whipping her shawl from around her shoulders. And though she managed to keep the shawl in place, she shivered.

He said at once, "Are you cold?"

Carolyn tilted her head. "Not very."

"Does 'not very' mean 'yes' or does it mean 'no'?" he asked, although he did not wait for an answer. Drawing off his buffalo robe and taking a step toward her, he placed the whole of it around her shoulders, fur side down for warmth. Briefly his fingers stole over the length of her arms.

And in return Carolyn gasped. *Heaven.* Dear Lord, his touch felt like a breath of heaven. Unbidden, shivers of anticipation stole over her arms. Oh, how she wanted to draw in closer to him; oh, how she craved his arms around her.

But she could not do it; she must not do it.

Indecisive, she did nothing; said nothing for several

moments. Neither did he. It was as though each waited for the other to speak first.

After some moments, however, Lone Arrow took the initiative and said, "You should keep this on while we are in the mountains. I am more accustomed to the cold than you are."

So saying, he let go of the robe and took a step away from her.

Carolyn bobbed her head in agreement, and this time she graciously accepted, too cold to consider doing otherwise. Especially when his warmth, plus the scent of his skin, remained within the folds of the robe.

"*It-chik,*" said Lone Arrow, making the sign for "good." "Looks good on you." And Carolyn felt herself blush at the compliment.

They sat in silence for a short while longer. In the far distance a storm cloud thundered, and Carolyn stared out to where the sky was awash with light and dark clouds. And although above them a bright moon shown, in many ways, this night reminded her of another time, another place; a period eight and one-half years ago.

He asked, "Does something bother you?"

Carolyn exhaled without saying a word. This was it. Now was the time to put words to what was on her mind. But what exactly to say, and how to begin?

She hugged her arms around her while she scrambled for the right words. Meanwhile, he waited, and after a moment, his silence seemed to invite her to say, "Yes, something is disturbing me. It is why I am not sleeping, why I am walking around our camp, despite the late hour."

A low grunt was his crisp acknowledgment.

And she continued, "The truth is, Lone Arrow, that there is much to be said between us, and I fear the time has come for us to speak frankly to one another. Otherwise, I may never find sleep this night."

He inclined his head once and, crossing his arms over his chest, leaned back against a tree.

One more breath for courage, and she began, "I have something personal to ask you."

Again, he nodded, though he said not a word.

"Do you mind?"

Briefly he looked puzzled. "Mind?" He shrugged. "You are my wife. I would hope that you would be personal with me . . . very personal."

She chanced a quick glance at him. Had there been a glimmer of humor in his voice? Was he laughing at her? Somehow the idea that he might be was more discouraging than it was humorous, for she could not laugh with him.

And so, with more than a little trepidation, she asked, "Would you . . . would you really rather be married to a Crow woman?"

At first he appeared puzzled by the question. Then, as he so obviously mulled over her words, he grinned. Darn him! He *actually* grinned.

It made her want to turn her back on him; it also caused her some bit of anguish. Goodness! How she wanted to walk away from him; how she desired to pretend that she did not need him, so much as an inch.

The trouble was, she reminded herself, she did need him. Needed him, not so much for herself, but for those she loved; those she had left behind in Virginia City.

Tightening her mouth, she gritted her teeth as she stewed. And it was not long before she observed,

"Just because I am dependent on you while we are on the trail does not give you the right to take advantage of me."

Her words caused Lone Arrow to frown, and whatever good humor he might have been feeling, faded. He said, "And how do I take advantage of you?"

She lifted her shoulders. "By laughing at me," she said, "and by . . . by . . ."

He waited.

She cleared her throat. "By . . . wanting to be with other women, when you are supposed to be with me."

Lone Arrow's frown deepened, and he said, "Who has told you that I do this?"

"You have."

"I? . . ."

"This afternoon," she said, coaxing his memory.

Her statement appeared to make his hesitation more pronounced, and the scowl on his face deepened, looking as though it might become a permanent fixture. At last, he said, "You are right to feel as you do, if I gave you that impression. Know, that I do not want other women."

She snorted. "That's not what I heard back there next to the stream."

Once again puzzlement gave way to enlightenment, all within the heightened breath of a moment. After a time, he even chuckled.

"Oh! Stop that."

"What?" he asked innocently.

"That. Don't do that," she uttered. "How can you laugh at me?"

"I am not laughing at you," he said.

"It appears that way to me."

"I am sorry. I am not laughing at you, I give you my word. It is only that—"

"Oh!" Carolyn turned away.

Indeed, she would have left posthaste, if he hadn't placed a hand on her shoulder, and if he hadn't said, "I knew you were in the tree."

That stopped her, but she was not ready to give him quarter. Not yet. She stuck out her chin. "You couldn't have known I was there."

"Could I not?" he asked. "Have I not said so?"

"But—"

"My father does not speak English."

"Your father?"

"*Éeh*, the one who was with me."

Father? she thought. The same fellow who had so recently joined them? The one who was, himself, no more than a youth? How could this be?

And she observed, "How could a man who looks hardly older than you be your father?"

Lone Arrow slanted her a frown. "Why would that be unusual?"

"Because he could not have fathered you."

"Ah," said Lone Arrow, "I think I understand why you are confused, and if you will bear with me, I will explain. Know that my companion today is not he who fathered me. But he is, nonetheless, my father."

Carolyn's head spun a little as she tried to make sense of this line of thought, and she wondered if she looked as baffled as she felt. She said, "Well that's still not very understandable, is it? He is your father? He isn't your father?"

Lone Arrow grinned, and, clearing his throat, he said, "Let me explain. The one that you saw me with today is a male relative from my father's clan. All the male members of my father's clan are called father."

She paused. "Oh," she said at last. "I see."

"But we leave the point," Lone Arrow went on to say, "which is that I knew you were in the tree. Why else would I have said those words in your language, if not for trying to tease you?"

"Tease me?" She took a moment to compose herself. "Tease me? It didn't seem like teasing to me. And if that is the manner in which you jest, you should think again, for all you gained by doing so was to worry me."

"I am sorry."

Was he? she wondered. He did not look very contrite. And she said, "If you want my opinion, I think it was a cruel, bad-mannered thing to do, to say."

He shrugged. "It might have been bad manners," he conceded, "but it was not meant to be cruel. And you must admit that I spoke truth. I have not had the warmth of my wife beside me for many a night."

Despite herself, that statement had the effect of sending waves of pure excitement running up and down her spine. Just the remembrance of the one night they had spent together . . .

Did he want to repeat it?

The thought was naughty beyond comparison. Naughty, yet stimulating. And in reaction, she quivered.

Clutching her hands together, as though the gesture might still their trembling, she observed, "If you have been alone these past few nights, it's your own fault. You have not approached me. Plus, you are always with your friends."

"And I would be welcome if I did come to you?"

She raised her shoulders.

He let out his breath. "It has been in my heart," he said, "to let you decide what you want to do with our marriage."

"I know," she replied. "And I thank you for that, but . . ."

He remained silent, scrutinizing her while she hesitated.

And she continued, ". . . You will abide with whatever decision I make?"

He nodded.

And Carolyn looked away. What had happened to her earlier resolve to "let him go"? And she wondered, why was it so much easier to decide to end an affiliation like this when one was not confronted by the person?

He asked, "Do you know yet what your decision will be?"

But she could not speak up, and when it seemed there might be no forthcoming answer, he asked further, "What is it that you want?"

She groaned inwardly, while she grasped for words. What *did* she want? That was easy. *Him,* she answered her own question readily.

But was that true? How could she desire this man, be in love with him, when she aspired to change him?

Perhaps, she thought, this was why she kept coaxing herself to walk away from him. Because she loved him, because she wanted only the best for him, she would *not* try to change him, would *not* press him into being something that he was not.

That did not mean, however, that she could live in polygamy. No, she had to live her life as she knew it to be right for her.

The truth was, she admitted, she had promised Lone Arrow either marriage or the use of her body. And she had honored their agreement with her innocence. There was little more to consider.

Except that she loved this man. And the very essence of that emotion made her *want* to be close to him . . .

To his credit, Lone Arrow did not prompt her as she stood before him, emersed in thought.

At last, she said, "I would stay married to you," she began, "if I could put aside my ideals of what is a good marriage."

He did not utter a word, and his gaze did not falter from her.

She, on the other hand, could barely spare him a quick glance as she continued, "But, I cannot do that. I cannot put aside all that I have ever held dear about the holy state of matrimony. It would destroy me to do so."

Looking to him for a reaction, she noted that a muscle flicked in his cheek. But he did no more than nod at her, although eventually, he muttered, "I have no wish to destroy you."

"I know," she said. "It is why I think that we should—"

She did not get the words from her mouth, for he had placed a finger over her lips.

He said, "Do not say it."

She acknowledged him with a nod.

He gazed away from her, his breathing ragged.

Observing him thusly, she wondered, *Did it mean so much to him?* Dare she hope?

How long they sat there, not uttering a single word, she didn't know. But, with other things still on her mind, she broke the silence. "Lone Arrow, there is something else I must know."

He nodded, an encouraging signal for her to continue.

And she said, "You did not defend your reasons for marrying me very well to your, ah . . . father . . . I'm sorry, Lone Arrow. I can't think of that young man as your father."

"I understand," said Lone Arrow.

But she barely heard him. "Truth be known," she went on to say, "you didn't defend yourself to your . . . your friend, either."

Lone Arrow acknowledged her with a quick head motion, and then, mumbling to himself, he uttered, "I forgot that you can read our signs."

"Well, yes, I can."

He nodded and said, "There is something I should tell you, something that you should know. It might help you to understand my conversation with *biilápxe* a little."

"*Biilápxe?*"

"It means 'my father' from my father's clan. You might think of him as a male relative."

"Fine," she said.

"Come," he said. "Come sit with me and I will tell you about this."

"About? . . ."

"*Éeh,* yes, about *it.* Come," he motioned to her. "Come with me. There is yet a more secluded place where we can talk without the ears of the night listening to us."

The ears of the night? What did that mean? Were there other people listening to them?

An image of Lone Arrow's clan "father" swam before her eyes. But surely not. He was off in some other part of the forest, wasn't he?

As though she might clear her mind, Carolyn shook her head. She would ask Lone Arrow about it later. For now, it was enough that she follow Lone Arrow's footsteps as he led her to yet another place.

Chapter 21

The screech of a night hawk, along with the constant howling of the wind, added an eerie quality to the night. Carolyn pulled the buffalo robe more tightly around her and stared off to her left, where she had heard a branch break . . . and tripped over a tree limb, falling face forward.

Darn! She should have been watching where she was going. Luckily, the robe cushioned her fall, and she was able to hold back her cry. But not the wetness on the ground. Rain-soaked earth met every exposed inch of her body.

And Lone Arrow, who had swung back around, crept toward her. He said, "I have never known anyone to have more accidents than you."

Was there humor in his voice? Yes, there was, but this time Carolyn did not object.

Indeed, grabbing a handful of mud and twig-filled

dirt, she waited until he was close enough to her. Then she let him have it.

In reaction, he chuckled. And picking up a twig or two himself, he came down onto his haunches beside her, where he proceeded to drizzle them into her hair.

"Oh! Not the hair," she said, reaching up to comb her fingers through her tresses. But it was useless. One by one, Lone Arrow kept dropping twigs and bits of dirt upon her.

"All right, all right," she said. "I give up."

"Give up what?" he asked, grinning at her. Then pulling his features into a straight face, he asked, "Do you give yourself up to me?"

"Hardly."

"Does 'hardly' mean yes or no?"

"It means a very hardy no."

"*Éeh*, I see. Then perhaps I should continue to shower you with sticks, maybe even some dirt until you do decide to become one with me."

These were heady words, and staring up at him, she asked, "Do you really want that?"

He did not answer. Instead, he grabbed hold of her under the elbow and, helping her to her feet, he said, "Come, we will get too wet sitting here on the ground. There is a better place where we can say what we must to one another."

Carolyn made no objection as he helped her to her feet, although she did notice that he appeared to take pains to keep from touching her.

"Come," he said, releasing his hold on her, and with that, he turned away.

He guided her only a little way into the forest and soon they came upon a small clearing, where several large timbered pieces of wood littered the ground. In the distance were the familiar shapes of their horses, hobbled and munching the wild, mountain grasses. Closer were several large logs.

Upon reaching a particularly bulky one, he said, "*Dihchisshih,* rest here on this tree trunk."

And she sat. As she settled herself into a comfortable position, he perched himself upon the log as well, placing his legs over each side of it so that he was sitting facing her. Without further ceremony, he began, "There is much that we should say to one another. Let me begin by telling you a little about my people."

She acknowledged him with a quick motion of her head.

And he paused. "The Absarokee are a tribe of clans. Did you know that?"

She shook her head.

"Ho! Now, *biilápxe,* the one who joined us this day," he said, "as I have mentioned, is from my father's clan. He is my father's brother's child."

"I see," she said. "Then he's a cousin."

"He is my father, or *biilápxe,*" he emphasized. "I think that the white man has a hard time understanding this kind of relationship. Some white people I have known have called these men by the name of clan uncles, and maybe we should call him this, so that you will be able to understand it better. Will that be easier for you?"

"I don't know." Carolyn frowned, trying to follow this line of thinking. But no matter how much easier he tried to make it for her, it was still difficult to grasp. She said, "We could try that. Perhaps calling your . . . ah . . . friend by the name of an uncle would be simpler for me."

He nodded. "There is more that you should know

about this, also. In the Absarokee tribe, a child always belongs to his mother's clan. And to his mother's clan a child must give nothing but respect to his fathers and mothers, or as you might think of them, clan uncles and aunts. It is believed that by doing this, by showing respect and fidelity in this way to his uncles and aunts, a person will be in better harmony with the rest of the tribe. And if a person is in harmony with his tribe, he will be better able to control his environment, and from that, all of life."

Carolyn tilted her head to the side. "I see," she said. "That's interesting."

He nodded. "But this is only how one treats a member of his mother's clan. To his father's clan, a child is expected to tease and to be teased by any member of it. And no matter what is said or done, a child is taught to endure it; to laugh, along with the others."

"Goodness!" she said. "But what if the teasing is rough or crude? Like it was today?"

Lone Arrow raised his shoulders casually. "Our cultures—yours and mine—have some differences, I think, but try to understand. It is believed that it is a good thing to be able to brave anything. If a man can do this, he can live a life that is free. If he cannot or is unwilling to face anything, he will be haunted by shadows. And so it is in this way that a man, or a woman is expected to abide the jokes and the teasing of his father's clan, no matter what is said, no matter what is done."

"But—"

He held up his hand. "It is assumed that such teasing makes a person think, which makes him strong. It is also how a wayward child is taught the difference between what he should and should not do."

"Oh," was all she said.

"So you see," he went on to say, "this joking relative is a very important part of Absarokee life."

"All right," she agreed. "I think I understand this. But let me be certain. Your father . . . ah, your uncle—or the one you call, *biilápxe*—is from your father's clan?"

Lone Arrow flicked the index finger of his right hand down, twisting his hand at the same time, the sign for "yes."

"My father, or *biilápxe*, was also making me think."

"Making you think of me, is that it?"

"Perhaps."

She bristled at the thought and said, "Not that we are truly married or anything, but was he trying to make you question why you would *want* to marry me?"

Lone Arrow shook his head. "Perhaps, but do not feel slighted. It is his way of ensuring that I consider consequences. He was making a point; trying to induce me to ponder, to think about whether I was marrying you only because you are white. And if this were true, he was trying to coax me into reflecting upon this a little more."

"And were you only interested in marrying me because I am white?"

Lone Arrow did not hesitate so much as a second before he answered, "*Baa-lee-táa,* no."

She let out her breath, unaware until she did so that she had been holding it. She asked, "What did your uncle mean when he said that you would have to explain yourself to your fathers and mothers? I'm assuming that means your aunts and uncles?"

Lone Arrow nodded.

"Will they be upset because you have married me?"

Lone Arrow faltered for a moment, as though he might be deliberating over something. Then, as though he had come to a decision, he said, "They might be angry at first, for they will not understand what I have done. But they will not keep anger in their hearts, not after they meet you."

Carolyn bit her lip, glancing obliquely at him. She said, "I wouldn't be so certain."

"I am."

She held her peace, but only for a moment before she observed, "This means, however, that you are expected to take a Crow wife?"

"Maybe several years ago, this might have been true," said Lone Arrow, "but when I failed to find anyone I wished to marry, my aunts and uncles stopped asking me about it, stopped teasing me about it."

"I see," she said, then added, "But might they still expect you to marry someone from within the tribe?"

He nodded. "It is possible."

"Hmmm . . ." she mumbled, resigned. "Then this is another reason why we should not—"

He held a finger to her lips, and dutifully, she let the rest of the sentence trail away.

But she did feel obliged to point out, "There would be disappointment." It was no question.

"No, my aunts and uncles would come to understand, and they would be happy that I am happy."

"Would they?" she asked, not really expecting an answer to the question. She crossed her arms over her chest, much as Lone Arrow was doing as he sat before her, and she went on to say, "There is one more thing."

After a brief bob of his head, she continued, "What did your . . . ah, clan uncle mean when he said, 'because of who you are, you will be expected to marry as determined'?"

Lone Arrow shrugged, but did not answer.

And she waited . . . in vain. At last, she asked, "Who are you?"

That made him smile. "You know who I am."

She shook her head slowly, saying, "I do and I don't."

His face appeared unusually somber, and after a brief pause, he said, "I am the one who led you to the treasure cave once before; I am the same one who is doing so again. I am also the one who has been your husband."

"I . . . I—"

"And I am also a man who misses the warmth of she who has been his wife. It has been my desire to hold this woman in my arms, at least one last time."

These words, the intention behind them, sent a shudder racing over her. Did Lone Arrow have any idea what this sort of talk did to her?

However, the only response she made was to give him a look that she hoped appeared unconcerned. After a moment, she said, "Why did you tell your clan uncle that we were married?"

He hesitated. "Because," he said, "at the time, it was true."

"But it wasn't," she denied. "Hadn't you told me that we could start again, perhaps have only a romance?"

He inclined his head.

"Well, if that were true, then why did you tell your clan uncle that I am your wife?"

"Because," he answered, "until you give me your answer, that is exactly what you are."

"Oh," she said. She hadn't thought of it in that way. "But I am not—"

"And I would like you to be that to me again."

Whatever protest she had been about to utter, died on her lips.

What was happening to her? With those few simple words, her insides twisted, and she realized that her mouth was gaping open.

She took a deep breath and closed her mouth. Had Lone Arrow had a change of heart? Is this what he meant?

She hesitated to ask, half afraid of the answer. Yet she wanted to know, and inwardly she debated over what to do. Finally, however, she questioned, "Lone Arrow, do . . . do you mean that you have changed your ideas about marriage? That you want only one wife?"

When he did not reply at once, she swallowed the knot in her throat. And just as easily as it had come, her optimism began to fade. Still, she waited.

And, after a time, he uttered, "Let me say this. I do not know why the First Maker has brought us together, for our ideas on life are too different, one to the other to be compatible. Still, we are connected in a manner that I do not understand. At first, I thought this was all there was to it . . . to whatever it is between us. Know that I have come to realize that there is more to what I feel for you than even this."

Did he love her? Was this what he was saying?

But he was continuing to speak, and he said, "Know that I am no more than a man. And although I cannot tell you exactly what is in our future, I can promise you that I desire you at this moment. There is even more to it than this, for I wish you great happiness. Know also that it is I who aspires to be the one to provide this for you."

"Do you?"

He inclined his head, adding, "Are these not the things that should draw two people together? Are these not the principles upon which a strong union is forged? We are lucky in many ways, I think, for some people never have even this."

Carolyn paused, not moving so much as an inch. These were fine concepts, fine words he spouted, yes, and she had no quarrel with them. But, at the same time, she realized that he had skirted around the question most dear to her heart. Ultimately, she started to say, "But—"

"Ho!" He cut her off. "Regardless of what we think of each other's notions of marriage, is this not enough for us to build a life together?"

She opened her mouth to respond, but no words came to her.

Looking up, she cast him a quick glance as he sat before her. It wasn't fair. The moon was painting him in shadows of grey and silver, and he looked too desirable, seemed too magnanimous. What was more, her convictions were becoming too bendable. It was as though the very forces of nature were conspiring against her.

Inhaling, she caught the aroma of his musky fragrance, which only added to the cacophony of her thoughts. And beneath her, the log upon which she sat felt more solid than it had only a few moments ago, and she realized that her senses had become acutely attuned to the world around her.

Was it because of him? Was it because of the heightened affinity between them? Whatever it was, Carolyn's resolve thawed a little.

But maybe it was for the best. In the last few minutes, there were two things that had become clearer to her. One was the raw strength of the love she felt for this man; the other was an intense awareness that he, too, had feelings for her.

Was that enough to overcome the barriers between them? Not quite, she told herself.

And yet in the last eight and one-half years, while she might not have been aware of her feelings for Lone Arrow, there had never been another man in her life. Why not?

Carolyn glanced skyward, noticing without really seeing that the storm which had threatened in the distance had moved on; that the multitude of stars and the moon, which shone straight above her, had effectively taken over the midnight sky. She inhaled deeply, more than aware of the humidity in the air which filled her lungs. Hoping against hope, she thought that the breath she took might give her a few moments in which to think.

But it was not to be.

Gazing up at him, she took note that he sat silently, watching her. And although his arms were folded over his chest, although he did not touch her, he might as well have been holding her in his arms. For she was more than aware of him . . . in a sexual way.

Clearing her throat, she began, "Lone Arrow, you compliment me, I think."

He remained silent, not making so much as a single movement.

And she went on to say, "For many people, what we have would be reason enough for marriage."

He nodded.

"But not for you and me, I think," she said. "As you say, there are too many differences between us. And I don't simply mean that you are Indian and I am not. There is a great divergence in the way we think. There is one thing that I could not forgive, and you know what that is."

"But you might think differently," he argued, "when you become aware of the amount of work that would be expected of you."

"I don't think so."

Yet as though he hadn't heard her, he said, "You are good friends with Pretty Moon. What if she were one of my wives? You would still like her, would you not?"

"I . . . no. Besides, there is more to it than this, and you know it."

He did not say a word.

And she uttered, "Understand me well. As you desire to change me, so, too, would I desire to change you. And you must admit that this is not the way in which to enter into a marriage. Perhaps it is because I do love you that I feel we must not take that step. In truth, I have no desire to change you. Not really. I love you as you are. But because I do love you does not mean that I could *live* with you."

He did not utter a word for several moments. Alas, all he did was reach out a hand to touch her, his fingers softly caressing her cheek.

When at last he did speak, he said, "You are so wise, so beautiful, in spirit as well as in body. Know that I would not seek to change you in any way."

He would not? Truly? Despite herself, she melted.

But he was continuing to speak, and he said, "Know that I would do all I could to remain with you and only you all of my life. But I cannot promise you this."

It was the last sentence that broke the spell. And all she could think of to say was, "I know."

After a time, she started to add, "It is why I think that we should—"

Again he brought that finger to her lips, and he said, "Do not speak it. To say the words might make it so."

Bending toward her, he brought his forehead next to hers, and he said, "To say the words would be as to take away all hope."

She groaned. "Never," she whispered, "never would I want to do that."

"I know," he said, and then softly, so very softly, he murmured, "If we must part, as you say we must, then I think that we should do so with a kiss."

A kiss?

Dear Lord, no, she thought. Not a kiss. A kiss might strengthen his cause, might weaken hers.

But as though the forces of nature were, after all, conspiring to seduce her, the moon lit Lone Arrow's countenance in silky, gossamer-like beams. He looked so good, so masculine, so virile, and she was so very much in love with him.

Her defenses crumbled. Why did she keep up this fight? After all, it seemed so pointless, especially when his face was close to hers—so very, very close. And the wind kept whispering at her, seeming to tell her that it would take nothing on her part, nothing at all, to bridge the distance between them.

But there were reasons—good reasons, she reminded herself—why she had to stand firm, and at the last minute, when he would have kissed her, she turned her head away from him. His lips met the hollow of her cheek.

It should have been nothing. It should have done nothing to her. She would have been a fool, however, if she believed that.

With his touch, cascades of longing swept through her, and she shut her eyes as overwhelming waves of passion overtook her. Still, she swallowed, trying to count off the reasons why she should hold herself back from this man. But like a frightened shadow in the night, her well-thought out justification fled beneath the brightened aura of Lone Arrow's nearness.

His face swam closer to her, so close that when she breathed, she inhaled his intoxicating, musky scent.

And then he ran his lips over her cheek, her chin, her ear, his tongue nuzzling her there. In a heartbeat, raw hunger filled her soul, and her body turned to putty. Alas, like a sun-starved flower, she tilted up her face toward him in silent invitation.

Raising up slightly, he glanced down at her, and as he did so, she espied the yearning which burned there within the depths of his eyes. And with that recognition, her stomach dropped and exhilaration filled her being.

Slowly, his head descended toward her. Slowly, as though each moment dragged by, she awaited the touch of his lips upon hers.

Truly, she barely dared to breathe, so that when at last, his lips touched hers, she shivered with need. In the next instant, his breath mingled with hers, and with it, she became lost to the power of him.

It was a simple enough kiss, and yet not. The reality of it said that it should have been no more than lips touching, caressing, loving. And yet, it was so much more. More, because surges of pure joy swept over her being.

He shifted position so that he became a little separated from her, and though the movement was infinitesimal, she felt immediately bereft.

So it was that when he lifted his head to stare down at her, she collapsed against him. She let out a brief sob, realizing the futility of it all. One kiss was not enough. It was simply not enough.

Kiss me again, she pleaded silently as she gazed up at him.

And as surely as one day follows upon another, Lone Arrow reached out for her, bringing his head down to hers, repeating the caress.

She sighed against him, scooting forward and entwining her arms around his neck. It was as though she had been awaiting this moment all her life. And although something within her demanded that she protest, "We shouldn't be doing this," she kissed him back, giving him everything that was in her to give.

And he accepted it all. In truth, he accepted her.

At some point, she mumbled, "I love you," against his lips.

She felt the quiver which ran through his body. Felt his hard muscles against her as he took her in his arms, and she heard him say, "I know."

Nothing more; nothing less. And yet, those two words had the effect of telling her all she wanted to hear.

She surrendered . . .

Chapter 22

Lone Arrow closed his eyes and sighed.

It was within him to tell her that he loved her also. But he could not do it.

He might care about her more than he had ever cared for another human being. It might even be true that he loved her. It certainly appeared that this was so. Yet he could not say the words.

Alas, he felt pulled in two different directions. As a lover, as a man, he bestowed upon this woman a trust that was implicit, that was complete. Yet as the protector of his people, of the sacred mountain and the treasure cave, he knew he had no right to pass this responsibility to her.

Yet he wanted to trust her. Truth was, he desired her in many different ways that were not at once understandable to him. It was as though he wished to merge his being with hers, and to do it so thoroughly that neither of them would be able to see where one of them ceased to be and the other began.

But, he reminded himself, he could not do this. He might admire her, yes. He might even love her, but duty to his people, to his clan and to the god of the mountain would not allow him the freedom to put words to his feelings.

Yet how beautiful she looked. How wise and how lovely she was. And he was here. She was here, and above them was a moon that demanded he take her into his arms, that he love her . . .

And so it was that he brought his lips to hers again. As he did so, his head spun. He could not get enough of her. Not when she tasted of sweetness and spice. Not when the womanly scent of her upon his lips drove him half mad.

She murmured, "We must stop this."

He nodded, knowing she was right, but he could not quite let her go. Not yet.

She turned her face away from him, and he sighed.

"Dance with me," she said.

Dance? Now? Lone Arrow groaned. It was not that he was unaware of the white man's mode of dancing. He had witnessed it often enough at the white man's forts. No, it was more that he was ready for her, ready and aching for her.

He clenched his jaw. It would be sweet agony for him, to be so close to her, and yet hold himself back from her. With some desperation, he tried to remember why he should keep himself from her. But at the moment, all his well thought-out reasons escaped him.

He said, "I do not know the white man's steps."

She turned her head toward him and exhaled, her breath creating a mist in front of her face. She said, bringing a finger to her lips, "Shhh. Do you hear it?"

He frowned, yet he listened.

And she continued, "It is as though the wind were singing a song. Can you hear it?"

He paused, giving his full attention to his sense of hearing. After a time, he said, "I do."

But he wondered; he wondered about her, about how she knew. Was it by instinct that she should come to realize this? Was she aware that his people believed that the wind *did* sing?

All at once, he felt closer to her. Not physically, but rather spiritually.

"Please," she said. "Please dance with me."

He groaned. Could he do it? It would be an exquisite torture for him—to hold her so close, yet to be so far from her. Still, the opportunity to feel her body's imprint against his own was practically more than he could resist. After all, who knew what might happen in these next few days?

And they had the night before them.

He said, "I do not know the steps."

"You need no steps to dance the white man's dance," she responded. "And the music of the night is calling to me. All you need to do is hold me."

Lone Arrow knew when he was lost, and nodding, he stood. Holding out his hand to her so that she might willingly come into his arms, he said, "I will try."

She took his proffered hand, and as she did so, she murmured, "Do you remember dancing with me once before?"

"I do," he responded, pulling her up and into his arms. Greedily, he enfolded her into his embrace.

As he did so, he heard her moan, the sound of it high-pitched and suggestive. Unwittingly, he heard himself echo her need; heard himself groan.

For the moment, she was his; he was hers. In truth,

her soft curves fit him so well that she might have been created for him alone. And when she seemed to melt into him, he knew he was in trouble. Ho! Why did he fight her so much?

If the truth were known, he was becoming tired of resisting her; tired of telling himself why he should stay away from her. Certainly, he was tired of pondering the reasons why he could not put his faith in her.

But she was speaking, interrupting his thoughts, and she said, "We danced so long ago. Do you remember? It was that time when you brought me to Fort C.F. Smith."

"I remember," he murmured against her ear.

"But you walked away from me afterward."

He did not move. It was true. He had done exactly that.

And she said, as though she pleaded, "Don't walk away from me tonight."

He took a deep breath. "I will not," he said. It was a promise, too.

Until this woman said the words to sweep him out of her life, she was his wife. At least she was for tonight.

These next few days would be telling for them both. Not only did she have major decisions to make, he, too, had need to decide what he was going to do about her.

And he wondered, when all was unfolded, would she prove to be innocent of the doubts he leveled at her, or would she turn out to be as treacherous as he feared? Trouble was, either way, he was committed to her.

There it was, he thought. *He was committed to her.* And it did not matter her crime. In ways he did not understand, he *did* trust her.

Lone Arrow paused as the fullness of recognition

came to him. This woman was important to him; important in ways he did not fully grasp.

Yes, he realized that without her, he felt only half alive; half of a completed whole. This was not a new thought for him. But in the past, whenever he had considered this, he had struggled against the idea, thinking it to be no more than a weakness.

But was it weakness . . . or strength?

Perhaps he thought, he had been wrong. Maybe he had been fighting against the wrong thing.

It was a powerful revelation. Powerful because of its simplicity. Powerful because of its beauty.

Why had he not understood this before?

She was as much a part of him as he was of her. And because this was so, he would know her heart as well as he knew his own.

Ho! He *did* trust her. He *did* believe in her.

The realization had the effect of calming him, and placing his head against hers, a feeling of peace stole over him, as well as another sort of understanding.

She was in trouble; trouble, which up till now, he had chosen to ignore. Yet whatever had caused her to come here must be intense, if she could not confide it to him.

Maybe, he thought, it was time to be a little honest with her. Perhaps if he had been more so in the past . . .

And so he said, "Do you know why I left you all those years ago?"

She grinned. He could feel it, there as she rested her face against his shoulder. She said, "Because I annoyed you?"

He shook his head.

She took another guess, saying, "You were happy to be rid of me?"

Again he made a negative response. And though he could already feel the softness of her curves against him, he enfolded his arms around her even more tightly, drawing her closer into his clasp. And when in response, she twined hers around him, he thought he might die a little.

He said without thinking, "I want you."

"What?" she asked.

"I wanted you," he corrected. "At that time, eight and a half years ago, I was shocked by what I felt for you. You were a mere child of eleven winters. And I was a man; a man with no coups to his name. Had I a coup, I might have taken you back to my people and married you at once. I would have then watched you grow into the beautiful woman that you are now. But a man without a coup is a sad creature. He is not even allowed to marry until he is twenty-five winters old, and I was a mere sixteen."

"You . . . you were thinking of marrying me?" Her tone was a whisper. "Back then?"

He nodded.

"I . . . I didn't know," she said.

"I know that you did not. I did not want you to have this knowledge."

At these words, she went limp in his arms and he took her weight upon himself. She said, "There is something you might not have realized."

"Ho, is there?"

She inclined her head slightly against his shoulder, and she said, "I had so hoped, so desired that you would take me back with you to your tribe."

He held her slightly away from him, that he might stare down at her.

But she went on to explain, "I had no one in the world. No one but you. I would have been proud to go with you to your people. The truth is that I was hoping that you would take me there."

He drew her back into his arms, hugging her. He said, "Perhaps we both made unwise decisions back then. But we were young, and I could not help feeling that your people were the white people. They still are your people."

She sighed. "Yes, they are. And they, my people, are in trouble."

There it was again, the reason why he might distrust her, why he had done so in the past. But these reasons were no more than shadows now; that doubt gone from within him. In truth, at this moment he felt only the urgency of her need, and he said, "Soon we will be at the cave and your troubles will be no more. But before we go there, let us settle what has been between us. The night is yet before us, and there are many things we should say to one another, many things we could do."

"Yes," she followed his lead as he took a single step upon their dance floor of pine needles and wet earth, the crunching of the needles a welcome sound. After a moment, she asked, "We are that close to the cave?"

"We are."

"But didn't you say that the others will not be going to the cave with us?"

He inclined his head. "They will be leaving us within the next few days."

"They will?"

Again he nodded.

He felt her displeasure. It was almost a physical thing. But why? What had he said to cause it?

He was not left long to wonder, however, for she soon remarked, "Then I won't be seeing Pretty Moon again?"

"You will come to know her again if it is your decision to remain married to me."

He felt her breath on his shoulder; heard her say, "Yes," but she did not elaborate. She continued, "I must give her something so that she will remember me."

"You have already given her something of value."

"I have?" she asked. "What is that?"

"Does she not have your necklace?" he asked. "The one that you once gave to me?"

"You know about that?"

He nodded. "She is very proud of it."

"Perhaps I should have told you something about that before now," she said. "I traded it to Pretty Moon for the pony that she and I ride. At the time, I never expected her to volunteer to come here with me. But she did, and I am happy that she did. She has been a good friend."

He nodded.

"I am sorry about the necklace. But, you did give it back to me, all those years ago."

He shrugged. "At the time, I thought that you might use it. You could have bargained with it for something that you needed at the white man's post."

"That's why you gave it back to me?"

Again he inclined his head.

She said, "I thought you were simply irritated with me and wanted no remembrance of me."

He pulled her, if it were possible, even closer into his embrace, and he said, "It is true that you irritated me all those years ago, but it is also true that I was aware of you as a female. Perhaps my crossness had more than a little to do with that."

He took another step, his wife following him with ease. She said, "All this time, I have thought that you were simply too proud to have much to do with me."

He shrugged. "It is perhaps the impression that I wished to give you, for at that time, it was not in my nature to tell you what was in my heart."

"Then you liked me?"

He grinned before he answered, bringing his lips to her ear. "Have I not said as much?"

She did not reply. Instead, she began to hum. And it was interesting to note that the tune also had a definite rhythm.

Without willing it, his steps began to keep time to the beat of the song she sang. And with every step he took, she followed.

He shut his eyes, the sound of her voice mixing with the throb of the wind, and he began to sway.

She said, "I love you. I think you should know."

Lone Arrow found himself wanting to respond to her in kind. But instead, all he did was moan.

Carolyn continued speaking, and she said, "I think I have loved you since that first moment I tripped over you on the mountaintop."

Lone Arrow swallowed hard. He knew that she desired him to say those same words back to her; he literally anticipated her need. And truth be known, his first inclination was to hold back from her. But then it came to him . . . why?

Why should he not give to her all that was in him to give? He might never have another chance.

With this decision came a feeling of freedom, and clearing his throat, he began, "When I was a little boy, there was a girl that I loved. I could not see her face, yet I loved her. When I grew up a little, she was always there beside me. I think that she has been with me in thought all through my life."

She remained silent, standing still in his arms.

And he continued, "That girl was you," he said. "Though I have little understood it, you have been with me always. And always, have I loved you."

She made a sound against him, much like a cry, and in response to her, he said, "Let us have this night together."

"Yes," she said. "Oh, yes."

He stared down at her, his mood awash with a mixture of desire and worry, for he had not anticipated such an easy capitulation. And he asked, "You are certain?"

She glanced back up at him. "I am," she said.

That was all he needed to bring him to his knees. And as he knelt down in front of her, he guided her down to him.

His arms encircled her, and in the next instant, he kissed her. And he kissed her, once more, again and again . . .

He loved her. Dear Lord, he loved her.

Carolyn rejoiced, and with every ounce of hope within her, she returned Lone Arrow's ardor. Yes, there were still problems between them. Yes, there were things they must discuss; important things.

But they loved one another, and with that, all things were possible.

She reached up to touch her fingers to his cheek, running them lazily along his jawline. That he shivered beneath her caress filled her with joy. That he returned the embrace set her afire. She mumbled, "You are so handsome."

"I have to be," he responded, "for you are so beautiful."

She grinned. From another man, similar words might have been spoken for no other reason than to create an effect. But not Lone Arrow. Alas, it was his very honesty which made the compliment all the more powerful.

Looking up at him, she said, "Love me."

"I intend to."

He stared down at her tenderly, yet his glance smoldered with intimacy. And Carolyn felt herself sway against him.

"They say," she confided, sending him a shy glance, "that a woman's interests are best carried out under a moonlit sky."

He grinned, his smile a lopsided sort of affair. And staring up at him, at the fine picture that he made, her heart leapt into her throat.

Reaching beneath the buffalo robe, his fingers found their way unerringly to the softened mounds of her breasts. Oh, the thrill of it.

He said, "Do you like that?"

She inclined her head. At the moment, it was the most she could do.

He smiled. "I am a lucky man, I think."

Another compliment; one which she knew was honestly meant. She shut her eyes, as though only in this way could she savor the delight.

Outwardly, a breeze rushed by her, blowing her hair back from her face, but tossing tendrils of *his mane* around her, as though even this part of him would make love to her.

"You are so beautiful," he said. He brought up a finger to run over her cheek.

With that touch, her knees buckled, making her a little afraid that she might swoon.

His fingers trailed down the delicate curve of her neck, each touch sending shivers of ecstasy racing along her nerves, and she curved her body in toward his. She whispered, "I like that."

He groaned.

"Perhaps," she said, "it was a good thing that I took what I did all those years ago. For it has brought me back to you."

He nodded.

However, her eyes popped open. What had she said?

Gasping, she brought her gaze up to meet the look in his eyes. But if he noticed anything out of the ordinary, he made no mention of it.

Instead, he said, simply, "*Éeh,* it was a good thing."

He did not hate her? He did not think she was no more than a petty criminal? This was to be his only reaction?

Perhaps he simply had no idea what she had done, what she had taken.

But he was continuing to speak, and Carolyn listened as he said, "Do not look so startled. You have already told me that you took something . . . small. It has been a difficult thing for me to understand, and it has been hard for me to trust you. But know that I do not give my love away freely. Whatever it was that you took, I am grateful. It has brought you back to me."

Carolyn stared at him as though she had never seen this man until this moment. "Do you mean that?" she asked.

He nodded. "I do."

"Oh, Lone Arrow," she sobbed, "I love you so much."

"As I love you."

"Say it," she said. "Say it in your language."

He swallowed, as though a lump had arisen in his throat. However, after a few moments, he said, *"Dé-awa-chi-shik."*

"Dé-awa-chi-shik," she repeated.

He grinned at her. "That is right. It is good to hear Absarokee words upon your lips."

"Really?" she asked. "Then I will learn your language as quickly as I can."

This seemed to please him. It was not so much that he said so, or even that he acknowledged her desire to do so. It was more a feeling. *He was pleased that she would want to learn more about him.*

But she had no chance to follow this thought further, for he had taken his robe from around her shoulders, and was placing it beneath her. Gently, as he settled her on top of it, he said, "It has occurred to me that the first time we lay together, we had too much doubt between us. I suspected your intentions, and you would seal a bargain with me."

"But that's not the reason I—"

"Let there be no more uncertainty between us. I would make you my wife, once again, if you will only but agree to it. Not because of our bargain, but because we love."

Carolyn shut her eyes as a warmth swept over her body. It was perfect, *almost* perfect, and she could think of no reason why they should not love. Except one . . .

"Let us not speak of marriage, but of love," she said. Then with her gaze softly locked with his, she pleaded, "And please do love me."

"Éeh," he said. "I will. I do."

He took her in his arms, her head nestled gently against his. Leisurely, he brought a hand up to run it down her torso. He did not undress her. At least not right away. Instead, he touched her body through the material of her clothing, his hands running over the length of her, up and down.

But it was not enough, not for her. Reaching toward him, she pressed her hands beneath his shirt, the warmth of his skin a heady inducement beneath her fingers.

Oh, how she gloried in the hard contours of his chest. Oh, how she loved his reaction to her.

He had drawn in his breath, and had fallen to the ground beside her. And though he tried to take her in his arms and position her beneath him, she soon squirmed free to sit up next to him, then atop him.

For whatever reason, she needed to have the upper hand. At least this once. Why this was, she did not know, except that she had followed this man halfway across the country, always in his shadow. Tonight she needed to come into her own. Tonight it was she who would control the pace of their lovemaking, if she only knew how to do it.

Slowly, she wound her hands up to his chest, massaging the solid outline that she found there, not satisfied until she witnessed his moan of sweet agony.

"Do you like that?" she leaned down to whisper the words.

"Too much," he answered. "So much do I like it that I fear that if you want this night to last a little longer for us, you should let me be the one to—"

"No," she uttered. "You are in my power tonight."

Sighing, he relaxed back against the ground in a pose of complete surrender. He said, "I am yours."

Now it was her turn to smile, and she said, "I know."

Easing off of him, she began to undress him. His shirt was the first thing to go. In truth, he slipped out of it quickly. With admiration she once again explored the hard contours of that naked flesh.

She said, "You are a handsome man," and with these few, simple words, as if to prove her point, she trailed her hands over his taut muscles. In response, he withered beneath her ministrations like a babe.

But she wanted more.

And she could not resist taking it. Unbuttoning her dress, she slid the clothing down to her waist, finding that Lone Arrow's eyes watched every movement she made.

When she had finished, he grinned up at her, saying, "I think that I like it when you are chief."

She gave him a tender look. "That is my intention."

He did not utter a word in response; merely smiled at her.

And she came up over him, settling herself into a position so that she was able to press her chest to his. At the contact, both of them gasped.

"That is good," he said.

Carolyn had to agree. She felt on fire. Yes, the wind continued to blow; yes, the air had not changed its bitter temperature, not in the least.

It was she who had changed.

Groaning, he took her by the waist, rolling over with her until she, at last, lay beneath him. The grasses and vines were wet beneath her, but she barely noticed them.

Pulling up her skirt, his fingers went unmistakably to the core of her femininity. But she was not yet ready for that.

"No," she said, "not yet." And twisting, she managed to rotate their positions until, once again, she sat atop him.

She said, "You are wearing too many clothes."

To which he sent her a rakish smirk. "I agree." Immediately he sprang up to help her, and he removed his leggings and breechcloth, even his moccasins.

Finished, he lay back, with all his masculine magnificence laid out to view. With some feeling of homage, Carolyn gazed down upon him. And she could not help but notice that he was more than a little ready for her. She said, "I am hoping that you know more about these things than I do."

With another wayward grin from him, he said, "It is possible that I do."

Her skirts were already in disarray around her legs, and it took him little effort to position her to receive his loving.

He said, "You are not very accustomed to this, I fear, and so it may still hurt at first."

She nodded.

"Do not be in a hurry."

Again she acquiesced.

Then, slowly, so very slowly she came down upon him. And she was more than a little relieved to discover that her body appeared to be built for this. Smoothly, they became as one.

Still, she paused, uncertain of herself. Such shyness, however, was hard to be maintained, and it literally stood no chance against the onslaught of his lovemaking. She felt as though she were opening up for him, much as a morning glory might do to the light of day. Pleasure ebbed and flowed within her, and as she gyrated against him, she found herself laboring for breath. Looking up, she caught his glance, and seeing it, she swooned. There, within his gaze, was such adoration . . . and for her, she thought she might likely explode.

Shutting her eyes, the fire within her blazed, encompassing her completely. One moment, another, and pleasure shot throughout her system.

It was a wicked, wonderful sensation, made intense by the knowledge that she had felt his gratification as well as her own.

Contentedly, she sighed. Yes, there were some things still unsaid between them, some agreements they needed to make. However, for the moment, she could conceive of nothing more important than being held in her lover's arms.

It was not long before Lone Arrow reached out beside him for his robe, and without disturbing her, he pulled it to him, and around her. He murmured, "I think that we left this behind us as we rolled over and over upon this earth."

She was too limp to do more than smile at him, and within moments she was asleep.

Chapter 23

"Do not . . . speak . . . to . . . husband's, ah, . . . clan father, Running Coyote," said Pretty Moon in broken English, her hands forming the gestures needed to help her communicate fully.

As Carolyn and Pretty Moon sat upon the ground on this grand morning, they might have epitomized the image of domestic tranquility. Both the women were busy preparing the dried meat, putting it into parfleches, in preparation to leave camp.

"Why?" asked Carolyn of her friend. "It's not that I feel like I have to talk to him or even that I want to, but why shouldn't I be able to at least thank him for not laughing at me last night. After all, he is a relative of Lone Arrow, and they are 'fathers' to each other. Should I not be friendly?"

"*Baa-lee-táa*, no. Reasons . . . there are . . . many . . . heap, big reasons . . . you . . . must not. Him a . . . ah, Lumpwood, your husband . . . a . . . Fox."

"What?"

"Him from War Club . . . Lumpwood Society. Your husband from Foxes."

"And?" Carolyn encouraged, reaching down toward her leg, as if she might scratch the red welts there, the same sort of welts that were appearing as a rash all over her body.

But no sooner had Carolyn reached down a hand, than Pretty Moon knocked that hand away. "Not . . . scratch. Rash . . . spread if . . . you do."

"But it itches so bad."

"It . . . be worse . . . if . . . you scratch," said Pretty Moon, covering Carolyn's leg with yet another poultice of herbs. "Your . . . husband . . . has same . . . rash."

"Yes, I'm afraid he does," said Carolyn, glancing up at Pretty Moon. Carolyn paused. Was there a light of mischief simmering there within Pretty Moon's gaze?

She was not long in wondering, for Pretty Moon went on to say, "Does, ah . . . *ii-waa-ih-chaap-ku-lu-tta-tuua*, ah . . . you call it poison ivy?"

Carolyn nodded.

"Does *ii-waa-ih-chaap-ku-lu-tta-tuua*, poison ivy . . . make . . . good . . . ah, *ba-le-a-la-xa-pé* . . . good bed . . . for you . . . and husband?"

Pretty Moon giggled, but Carolyn, mortified, stared wide-eyed at her friend. She could not believe that Pretty Moon had asked such a thing.

Was she blushing? Carolyn could only hope that she was not. Nevertheless, responding first with what she hoped was a humorous sort of smile, as though she, too, took part in the joke, Carolyn said, glancing down toward the ground, "We did not see the danger."

Perhaps if her skin did not prickle so bad or if she, herself, weren't quite so embarrassed, she, too, might see the comedy in this. Perhaps she might even be able to poke fun at herself. Especially since her own rash was mirrored upon Lone Arrow's body as well.

Ultimately, however, she could only wonder: How could she and Lone Arrow have been so unaware of their environment last night? It seemed impossible. Yet the reality of the rash could not be denied.

She and Lone Arrow had made love atop a clump of poison ivy, rolling over and over upon it. Alas, they had both awakened this morning, itching.

Carolyn stirred uneasily. It was maddening to think that these things always happen to her. Certainly, it was an easy enough mistake for anyone to make. After all, it had been dark. She and Lone Arrow had clearly had their attention on pursuits more enjoyable than that of checking the ground.

Had Lone Arrow not been so caught up in a passionate embrace with her, he would have seen the danger from the plants. What was irritating was that Pretty Moon, also, was well aware of this fact.

Carolyn chanced another glance up at Pretty Moon, catching her friend's grin. Shaking her head, Carolyn groaned.

"White friend," said Pretty Moon, "should not be . . . *baa-wah-te* . . . ah, sensitive to this. It is . . . good thing . . . when . . . husband forgets . . . everything else . . . but wife . . ." Pretty Moon said, still grinning.

Carolyn tried to respond in kind. But, try as she might, she couldn't quite muster an adequate smile.

The point was moot though, for within moments Pretty Moon became serious. Leaning forward, she went on to caution once again, "White friend . . . should not . . . talk to . . . Running Coyote . . . alone." She shook her head.

Carolyn raised a brow. "Is there some other reason besides their different societies?"

The question appeared to agitate Pretty Moon, for she began a series of difficult and confusing gestures, and so quick and erratic were they that Carolyn could not follow them. Finally, grabbing hold of the other woman's hands, Carolyn shook her head. "Not so fast."

Pretty Moon gave a nod of agreement, and switching to English, she said, "Him . . . Running Coyote . . . have . . . bad . . . reputation. Him . . . belong to . . . War Club, ah . . . Lumpwood Society. Your husband . . . belong . . . Foxes."

"Yes," said Carolyn. "So you have said. But I don't understand what difference any of that makes."

"Much difference," said Pretty Moon. "Lumpwoods and . . . Foxes make war . . . with . . . each other's . . . women . . . their wives."

"Women? Wives? Make war?"

Pretty Moon nodded.

"I don't understand. How do they do this?"

"They . . . steal . . . wives."

Steal wives?

"Custom . . . demands . . . a wife be . . . former . . . *ak-hiik-she*, lover, if she . . . be stolen. But . . . Running Coyote has . . . bad name. Him might . . . pretend . . . and try . . . steal you . . . anyway."

"But that's silly. I simply wouldn't go with him."

"Him . . . stronger. Could use . . . force. And if Running Coyote . . ." Pretty Moon continued, "steals you, can . . . never go back . . . to . . . Lone Arrow. Would . . . bring Lone Arrow . . . shame . . . take you . . . back."

"But—"

"That why white friend . . . must stay . . . away . . . from Running Coyote."

"Yes, I understand that. But, what I don't completely grasp is the threat," said Carolyn. "Let's go over this again, shall we?"

Petty Moon nodded.

"Now, the Lumpwoods are a society, is that right? As are the Foxes?"

Another nod.

"All right. They are rivals?"

"What . . . this . . . rii-vel?"

"Enemies, like opponents in a game?"

"Ah," said Pretty Moon. "*Éeh*, yes."

"And they steal each other's wives, but only if that woman had once been a lover?"

"*Éeh*, yes."

"And she must have been a lover to the man doing the stealing?"

"That . . . right."

"But Lone Arrow knows that I have never been with another man, and it could easily be proven that the abduction was done by force, if it were to be done at all. So if that is the case, what is the danger?"

"It . . . not . . . matter if . . . Lone Arrow . . . prove . . . you not . . . lovers. Running Coyote . . . could lie."

"But my husband would know that he's lying."

"Rest of . . . tribe . . . not know. One man's . . . word . . . against another. Lone Arrow . . . be disgraced. It . . . custom. An . . . honorable . . . and a good man . . . must not . . . take back . . . stolen wife. Would be . . . shamed."

"Even if—"

Pretty Moon gave a quick incline of her head. "Even if . . ."

"Oh," said Carolyn. "That's not good. Tell me, does this wife stealing happen often?"

Pretty Moon nodded. "In . . . *a-wa-siia*, moon when . . . earth is . . . visible . . . ah . . . spring, it happen. But could . . . happen . . . *hin-né baa-pé*, this day. White friend . . . should have . . . care."

"Then you are right," said Carolyn. "I should take every precaution to stay away from Running Coyote, and keep him at a distance, so long as he remains with us."

Pretty Moon inclined her head. "*It-chi-kaa-she*, very good. You remember . . . this one's," she pointed to herself, "words."

"I will."

Oh, dear. Her back itched again; itched to the point where she could not tolerate it, and reaching up behind her, she attempted to scratch it. However, as had happened before, Pretty Moon brushed Carolyn's hand away.

Pretty Moon said, "You tell . . . this one . . . when . . . you . . . itch. This one . . . rub in . . . medicine."

"All right," agreed Carolyn. "What herbs are these that you are using? I should like to remember them."

"Them called . . . ah . . . root of . . . yellow dock. When we go in . . . woods, this one . . . show you." And with this said, Pretty Moon applied a little more of the herbal poultice to the area, as she said, "Your husband . . . ah, *baa-éh-chek* . . . him wise."

Carolyn could only agree.

"Him also . . . *ah-pa-láax-iax-paa-liia* . . . man-who-talks-with-god."

"He does what?"

"Him . . . talk to god . . . of mountain. I tell you . . . this . . . for no man of . . . honor . . . ever speak of . . . own . . . deeds. Him . . . your husband . . . have . . . many good deeds."

This last, Carolyn could well understand. After all, hadn't Lone Arrow played her hero eight and a half years ago? Wasn't he even doing so now? But to speak to a god . . .

"Do you mean that he prays?"

"Like . . . all good Absarokee . . . people, him . . . pray to . . . First Maker. *Heh-taá,* but . . . that not . . . the god."

Carolyn was confused, and she said, as encouragingly as possible, "That's not the god that he? . . ."

"Speaks to."

"I see," said Carolyn. "And do others talk to this god, also?"

"*Baa-lee-táa,* no."

No? Carolyn frowned.

"Like his . . . *ak-saa-wa-cheé* . . . his father, only he . . . talks to . . . god . . . of mountains."

The god of the mountains. Funny, both she and Lone Arrow had spoken of this being previously, but up until now, Carolyn had not thought to question him about it. Why hadn't Lone Arrow told her that it was he, and he alone, who could communicate to a god?

As though Pretty Moon read her thoughts, she repeated, "Honorable men . . . never speak . . . of own . . . deeds. Clan aunts and . . . uncles . . . be proud . . . of him . . . of you."

"Me?"

Pretty Moon nodded.

"Are you sure? I overheard Running Coyote say that my husband would have to explain himself to his people. That he would have to justify why he had chosen a white wife."

Pretty Moon snorted. "Do not . . . be . . . *ii-waa-chí-sseek* . . . anxious . . . about it. Anyone with . . .

eyes . . . see you . . . bring Lone Arrow . . . *baa-it-che* . . . good things. They will . . . love you."

Carolyn smiled at her friend, and she could think of nothing else to say, except, "Thank you, but I think your faith in me might be misplaced."

Pretty Moon frowned. "What . . . this mean . . . misplaced?"

"It means mistaken," said Carolyn, but when Pretty Moon still appeared confused, Carolyn went on to say, "I should probably tell you that there is actually little danger of the clan aunts and uncles liking or disliking me. For you see, Lone Arrow and I are not really m-m . . ." Carolyn broke off on the last word, hesitant, as Lone Arrow had once cautioned, even to speak it.

Meanwhile, Pretty Moon glanced at her expectantly.

"Actually what I'm trying to say is that . . . well, it's . . . it's complicated."

"What means . . . com-pla-ca-ted?"

Carolyn sighed. "Pretty Moon," she said. "May I confide something in you?"

"Con-fide? You mean . . . tell . . . ah, *baa-aah-xua* . . . secret?"

"Yes," said Carolyn. "A secret."

Pretty Moon gave a quick bob of her head.

"The truth is . . . well, the truth is that Lone Arrow and I have talked about our marriage, and we are uncertain that it is going to work out between us."

"Work out?"

"Our . . . our ideas about marriage are too different to make a marriage between us an easy thing."

Pretty Moon furrowed her brow. "The white woman . . . thinks of . . . leaving Lone Arrow?"

"I . . . I . . ."

"What . . . are . . . differences . . . between you?"

"Mostly his attitude about other women," said Carolyn.

"Add-i-tude?"

"It means the way someone thinks about something. Truly, it is because Lone Arrow cannot promise me that he will remain faithful to me and only me that causes a problem."

"Lone Arrow wishes . . . other wife . . . so soon?"

"No," said Carolyn. "Not now. It's only that he cannot promise me that he won't take another wife in the future."

"It . . . his . . . right."

"But it is not his right in my society. I could never remain married to a man who might insist on having another wife . . . no matter how far off that might be in the future."

"But there . . . heap big work . . . so much . . . work for . . . woman. You . . . need help."

"I know, but it doesn't matter. There are other reasons why I feel this way, good reasons. But I won't bore you with them. Just know that I cannot make a marriage with a man who might take future wives."

"Hmmmm," said Pretty Moon, appearing as though she were lost in thought. After a moment, she said, "There . . . some . . . Absarokee men . . . never take . . . more than . . . one wife."

"Yes," said Carolyn, "I'm sure that there are. However, I could not risk that Lone Arrow might be one of them. Know that it would be a sacrilege to all I believe to remain married to a man who did this."

Again Pretty Moon nodded. "This one," she said, pointing to herself, "need to . . . think. You . . . go pick . . . berries. Come, will show . . . you where are . . . berry bushes. Give this one . . . time . . . think."

"But—"

"Come. Will show . . . you."

And Carolyn, realizing the futility of trying to argue, once Pretty Moon had set her mind to something, did as she was bid. But it was a hard thing to do. Particularly since she could think of little else but the things that she and Pretty Moon had discussed this day.

And she wondered if it be true that Lone Arrow and Lone Arrow alone could speak to the god in the mountains, then he must be a person of some standing within his tribe, his clan.

Moreover, because of who she was, would she be a hindrance to him? And if she were an encumbrance and he knew it, why did he keep insisting on marriage?

Also, and perhaps most importantly, was there anything she could do to ease Lone Arrow's burden?

These were difficult things to comprehend, and shaking her head, as if to clear it, she made her path to the berry patch.

Chapter 24

"Did you manage to steal a pair of Running Coyote's moccasins?" Speaking in Crow, Pretty Moon asked this of her husband.

"They are here," Big Elk said, reaching into a parfleche to draw out the buckskins. He handed them over to his wife, and said, "But I am not certain that I agree with what you are thinking of doing."

Pretty Moon, although obviously listening to her husband's concern, did not share his viewpoint. Alas, she simply shook her head as she said, "Sometimes love needs a boost. His people are not here. Her people are not here. Is it not good to be that boost?"

Big Elk did not reply. In truth, so much did he love his wife, he would have granted her most anything, even if he did not understand it. And so, to her unarguable wit, he merely gazed skyward and grimaced.

* * *

Lone Arrow was glad to see the last of Running Coyote. He wanted no trouble from his clan father, particularly since he was well aware of Running Coyote's reputation as a troublemaker.

Luckily, Running Coyote had left their camp without need for persuasion, and as Lone Arrow trod back toward the lean-to, he experienced a feeling not unlike relief. Plus, he had another reason to feel merriment: he would soon see his wife again.

The mere thought of this brought last night more vividly to mind, and it elicited a smile from him. Ah, the utter pleasure of it, the utter delight. For although the night had been filled with the culmination of the act of love, over and over again, there had been more. More love, more talk, more admiration.

True, they had both awakened with red welts all over their bodies, but that was a small thing in comparison to what they had shared. And no amount of itching, due to the poison ivy bushes, could dull that which they had found together: each other.

And so it was, that confidently, Lone Arrow strode into camp, immediately espying Pretty Moon and Big Elk. And he asked, "Where is my wife?"

Sweetly, almost angelically, Pretty Moon answered, "My husband, would you tell your friend that his wife is picking berries next to the river."

Dutifully, Big Elk repeated, "She is picking berries next to—"

"I heard," he said. And without so much as a backward glance at his friends, Lone Arrow turned away from camp and headed toward the river. He had seen those berry bushes. He knew exactly where they were.

Meanwhile, a pair of feminine eyes watched Lone Arrow disappear. Mischievously, she grinned.

However, Big Elk observed, "My wife, you should have let me tell him what to expect."

"No, my husband. It is better this way."

Big Elk did not respond. Instead, he silently shook his head.

Where was she?

Lone Arrow examined the tracks left here, for evidence of what might have taken place. Had Carolyn encountered some wild animal? A bear? A mountain lion?

There was no evidence of this. Here were her tracks, here were Pretty Moon's.

He followed their footprints in and out of the bushes.

But wait! What was this?

Here was another set of prints, although those tracks had been partially covered over with grass—as though someone tried to hide them.

Running Coyote had been here.

Lone Arrow's gut twisted, the sensation anything but pleasant. Surely, Running Coyote would not attempt an abduction . . .

Not here, not now. Running Coyote had left a short while ago. Lone Arrow had watched him go.

But he must have circled back, Lone Arrow finished to himself.

If it were possible to perish, due to surprise, he felt certain he might have done so at this moment.

"*Baa-lee-táa*, no!"

Except for the fact that Running Coyote was a Lumpwood and Lone Arrow a Fox, his clan father had no cause to attempt a wife snatching. Forget for the moment that The-girl-who-runs-with-bears had never been the sweetheart of Running Coyote. Forget also that she was undecided as to the state of their marriage.

Would this stop Running Coyote? Not likely, he answered his own question. If only because Running Coyote might be able to get away with it.

For one thing, only Lone Arrow would know the truth of his wife's innocence. If put to the test, it would be one man's word against the other. And although his relatives understood Running Coyote to be little more than a cheat and a scoundrel, an argument between the two of them—and over a woman—would create a spectacle, something from which neither man would recover.

Forever, would his reputation be in tatters. Forever, would he be known as *bian-ish-dat-tuua*, a man dominated by a woman, a man of little honor, since custom, and a man's own sense of dignity, demanded that if a wife were stolen, a gentleman would be civilized enough to let her go.

But in his heart . . .

No! He had only come to know his wife. He could not lose her now.

Perhaps, he thought, if he were to follow them, in this single instance, he might be allowed to have her back without censure.

Never. While there were many who might readily understand his plight, Lone Arrow would never be looked to again by the young, by the elders, or by anyone else in the tribe in a respectful way.

Lone Arrow sank down upon the ground, examining the evidence of what was left behind. There had been no struggle. From these tracks, it would appear that his wife had left with Running Coyote of her own free will.

Shutting his eyes, he felt the pain of his loss, and for a moment, he experienced a moment of indecision. All his life, he had been taught to bear the sufferings of life with charity, with no animosity or hatred. But as he stood here alone, within this grandiose mountain forest, Lone Arrow knew hatred.

Never once, in his entire life had Lone Arrow been given cause to question the why of things, especially those aspects of life which dealt with matters of the heart. They simply were as they were.

Yet he did so now.

She was his. His.

Damn the rules, Lone Arrow thought, using the English word, even to himself. And damn other people's opinions. Running Coyote was not within his rights.

Lone Arrow would go after his wife. He would retrieve her, right or wrong, custom or no custom. Those who mattered most would understand, and those who did not . . . he could not live his life in the shadow of other people's opinions. Such was certain slavery. And, make no mistake, Lone Arrow was no slave.

Ho! He would steal her back, and this time, no matter the consequences, he would ensure that she would never be given cause to leave him, or to wonder as to the state of their marriage, even if that meant that he would take no other wives.

She had objected to the practice of polygamy, and in his ignorance Lone Arrow had failed to listen to her. Alas, so focused had he been on imposing his own will over her, he had failed to realize the importance of her perspective. *Éeh*, as she had once accused, he had been intent on changing her.

Well, no more. He loved her, and that meant accepting her as she was, for who she was. And if that required that he marry only once in his lifetime, then so be it.

Whatever the difficulties that might come, he would face them with her. For of one thing he was certain: Without Carolyn, his life would be no more than a dull shell of existence.

Ho! Why had it taken a catastrophe to bring him to this understanding?

Perhaps, he thought, because he had been so convinced of his own opinion in the matter. He cringed, shutting his eyes as full recognition came to him.

He had always loved her, had never stopped loving her. It was a bond which, once forged, had never been broken. Not in eight and a half years.

Sitting upon a large log, which had fallen across the stream, Carolyn pulled up her skirt so that she could dangle her feet in the frosty water and wash them.

Oh! It was cold!

Uttering a soft, yet delightful squeal, she pulled her feet up out of the water and tucked them beneath the folds of her skirt. She supposed that was enough to clean them.

And they had been quite dirty. Rain had muddied the ground around the berry bushes, and as a result, both her feet and her shoes were filthy.

Taking hold of her slippers and bending down toward the stream, Carolyn let the gushing water clean her shoes, as well, and hoped they would dry quickly.

She really should get up, she thought, and gather her bag full of berries, which she had left on the shoreline. The others might be looking for her. Even so, she could not resist a final look at the scene before her. As she sat upon the log, she had a bird's-eye view of the stream which babbled and rushed away from her.

It inspired within her a feeling of peace and tranquility, perhaps even a feeling of loving and being loved.

Ah! She smiled as memories of the previous night flooded her mind. What a night she and Lone Arrow had shared. And although she'd had little more than a few hours sleep, due to the heat of the moment, she felt refreshed.

With anticipation, yet dread, she wondered—Was there hope for them? Would he ever understand her? Or perhaps more importantly, would he ever accept her?

Wasn't that all that stood between them and a lifetime together? It would be a shame if they could not settle this matter between them.

However, Carolyn was not blind to the fact that for another woman, there might have been other, bigger obstacles. Alas, for another person, the fact that Lone Arrow was Indian and she, white, would have been a barrier of insurmountable odds. But not so for Carolyn.

She had no qualms about becoming part of Lone Arrow's life, or in joining his tribe. In truth, it was what she had hoped for when she had been eleven years old. And now?

If she were honest, she would admit that ever since his daring rescue, all those years ago, Lone Arrow had never been far out of her mind. And as hard as she'd tried to start her life without him, she had always come back to this one conclusion: she was connected to Lone Arrow.

Call it spiritual, call it whatever one pleased, it was an inescapable fact. He was a part of her life.

And if they could not overcome this hurdle?

Carolyn shook her head. She dare not even contemplate the possibility. Somehow, the two of them would resolve it. They must.

A noise caught her attention. Had something shuffled in the bushes? Casting a quick glance back in the direction she had come, Carolyn was surprised to see Lone Arrow.

What was he doing here? Squatting down upon the ground, his attention appeared to be centered upon something there, and it was obvious that he was unaware of her presence here.

She should call out to him, she thought. And she would do so . . . eventually. But it was a rare occasion when she had the opportunity to study this man unobserved.

Lone Arrow was worried, that much was evident. She could see it, there, in the tilt of his head, the stiffness with which he held himself.

What was he doing? He looked to be examining something, perhaps some tracks? Yes, she could see the imprints from here.

She watched him carefully, watched as he placed a hand upon one of those tracks. And then, gently, with so very much care, he stroked the ground there, as though it were a living being. And then, before her eyes, she saw him bring those same fingers to his lips.

They were her tracks.

Watching him, knowing what he did, Carolyn felt as though something inside her burst to life. And without another moment's pause, she called out, "They are but mere tracks. If you will turn your head, you will see the real thing."

Lone Arrow glanced up, his gaze catching hers. And there, within the heightened beat of a moment, they became aware of one another.

Carolyn rose to her feet.

He did not say a word. Instead, he stared at her as though he might be scrutinizing a ghost. At length, however, he muttered, "You are here."

"I am here."

She watched as Lone Arrow swallowed hard, watched as he paced a step toward her. He said, "I thought he had stolen you away from me."

"He?"

"My clan father, Running Coyote."

"Hasn't he left our camp?"

Lone Arrow tread another pace toward her. "I thought that he had, but here I see his footprints—next to yours."

"But"—Carolyn placed a careful step upon the log, balancing herself precariously. Cautiously, she scooted forward a pace—"but Running Coyote has not been here."

"Yet I see his tracks."

Carolyn shrugged. "I cannot help that. I can only tell you that he is not here. He was never here."

Lone Arrow shrugged. "It does not matter. It is only important that you are here, unharmed. Careful," he said, when she almost lost her balance. "Here, let me help you from that log." He hurried toward her.

But it was too late.

The log had moved, it must have jolted, for it threw her off balance. And caught in the act of swinging her arms, she knew she was going to fall a second before the fact of it. And true to her instinct, she plunged butt first in the icy stream.

"Oh!" She came up shivering. The stream was only knee-deep and she was quite unhurt, and in absolutely no danger of drowning, but the Good Lord be blessed, falling in this water was like dipping into ice. She was freezing.

Lone Arrow waded out to her. "Come," he placed an arm around her shoulders. "My robe is on the side of this stream. I will wrap you in it."

She tried to nod, but her teeth were chattering so furiously, she could not even respond.

"Come."

And Carolyn did as he bade, practically throwing herself into the warmth of that robe.

As he sat her up, wiping the water from her and fixing the robe around her shoulders, he chuckled. "I have never known a person to have so many misadventures," he said. "When we reach my people, I will have to ensure that I never leave your side for very long, so that I will know you are safe."

"Perhaps one of your wives could have that responsibility," said Carolyn, mayhap with a touch of sarcasm in her voice.

"Humph!" Lone Arrow replied. Then, as though the words were each one gilded in gold, he said, "I have decided that you are right."

"Right?" Carolyn asked. "About what?"

"It has come to me that I have been foolish."

"Foolish?"

He nodded. "I have been thinking only of myself, and not listening to you and what was important to you."

Carolyn gave him what must have been a strange look, and she said, "You have?"

"*Éeh*, I have. Know that I have realized that for us to make a happy marriage, I must be willing to change my mind sometimes. At least about things that are important to you. It did not occur to me until a short while ago that my foolishness could have lost you to me forever."

"And that would make a difference to you?" she asked, barely daring to hear his answer.

He nodded. "You must know that this would make much difference to me."

"Would it?"

Inclining his head, he acknowledged her, and said, "You were right. I have been trying to change you. It is strange because I have always loved you exactly as you are. Why I desired you to be different, I do not know, except that perhaps, unwisely, I thought it would make me more of a man."

Wide-eyed, Carolyn stared at him.

And he continued, "I have come to see that our life together, its strength and happiness, is not dependent upon whether you can fit into the image I have envisioned, but whether I can make you as content as you make me."

Carolyn shut her eyes, taking a deep breath.

He said, "And so I will take no other wife. I vow this to you."

She opened her eyes, staring at him. And though she would have liked to say something, her voice did not work.

But it did not matter. Lone Arrow was continuing, and he said, "If it is important to you, then it is important to me."

At last she found her voice, but all she was able to utter was, "Lone Arrow, I . . . I . . ." She dropped the robe and threw her arms around him.

And he pulled her into his embrace as though he might not ever let her go. "Know that from this day forward, what happens to us will be met by the two of us, together. It is a new start for us."

"A new start," she reiterated. "Yes, I like the sound of that. And I promise you," she added, "I will make you a good wife."

He grinned. And as he gathered his robe from around her, and as he placed it over the ground, he said, "There is no cause for you to promise this, for I know that you will."

And with nothing else to be said for the moment, he positioned her onto that robe, where he began to show her how utterly certain he was of this . . .

Chapter 25

Amazingly enough, the mountain over which they traversed was familiar to Carolyn. In the distance was a rock formation; over there were a few trees surrounding a green meadow. They were all known to her.

This was good. It had to mean that she and Lone Arrow were close to the cave.

Of course, there were other things that would indicate this, the most pronounced of them being that it was only the two of them traveling together. Earlier in the day, she and Lone Arrow had said their farewells to Big Elk and Pretty Moon.

Parting had been a difficult thing for both of the women. And only the knowledge that they would soon see one another again had allowed them to part.

Still, it had not been a completely sorrowful occasion, since their separation meant that Carolyn was that much closer to her destination.

She fidgeted uneasily, contemplating that thought. This was the end of the journey. And while this was a happy occasion, for it meant the beginning of a new life—for her, for her parents, for Lone Arrow—it came with caution.

How was she going to get the cross, which still remained in her pocket, into the cave? That is, how was she going to do it if she were to go to the cave blindfolded, as well as naked?

Perhaps she should ask Lone Arrow about that. So many things had changed between them. Maybe he had altered his way of thinking about that, too.

Should she ask? She should, of course. She was, however, more than a little leery of doing that.

But why not? If it were true that he trusted her, did that not also mean that he might allow her to go to the cave dressed as she was? Or, perhaps a more important question was, did she deserve that trust?

Despite Lone Arrow's confession to her, she had not confided in him. The truth was, that she had almost forgotten the real reason she had begun this excursion. Sad, but true.

She had fallen in love on this journey, and that circumstance had outshone all else, even her worries about her parents' affairs. But that did not mean that their plight was forgotten.

Not in the least.

Still, he had been honest with her. Should she be as open with him?

And what if she were honest and he decided to take the burden of the cross upon himself? He might try to do it. However, Carolyn was uncertain that Lone Arrow could make restitution for her.

Then why do it? They were almost there. Surely she

could wait a few more hours before unleashing the burden of her soul.

It would be best; best then, if she simply kept the knowledge to herself. However, she had better discover *his* intent.

And so she called out, "Lone Arrow."

He was leading his black and white-spotted Appaloosa, A-la-pee, behind him, up through the mountain trail. It was an entirely typical yet, at the same time, strange sight to witness. Strange, for master and pony seemed to move as one, together.

Carolyn knew that Lone Arrow showered affection upon this mare. A war pony, A-la-pee was never hobbled or tied far away from her master. Often painted, as though Lone Arrow anticipated battle at any time, A-la-pee seemed to wear those marks much like a badge.

Lone Arrow had once told Carolyn that the circle around A-la-pee's eye granted her good vision; the hail marks on her behind were to empower her with the vigor of a hailstorm. And the eagle feather, braided into her tail, afforded her swiftness of foot.

Lone Arrow had also once confided that A-la-pee was probably his best friend. Observing them together, Carolyn could understand why.

"Lone Arrow," she called again.

He paused, looking at her from over his shoulder.

And she began, "Might I ask you a question?"

He nodded.

And she said, "I wondered if you still intend to blindfold me when we go to the cave."

"I must," he said with a shrug. "It is a place that is sacred to our people, and I cannot let you see the way there."

"But I have already been there; I saw it once before. What difference would it make now?"

"A great difference," he explained. "When you were young, there was no other way to save you. I did what I had to do. But that does not mean that now, when I have the choice, I should not follow the teachings of my father. Except for my father and myself, as well as his fathers before him, you are the only other person who has gone to that cave. And so, you will go there blindfolded, I think."

"Fair enough," she said. "But will I also have to go there without any clothes?"

Lone Arrow did not answer at once. Instead, he began picking his way downhill.

And Carolyn waited, following his lead, guiding her own pony by its reins.

At last, they came to a grassy knoll, and Lone Arrow turned toward her. He said, "It would be worthwhile to see you naked upon your pony, and for that reason alone I might make you do it." These words were accompanied by a cheeky sort of grin.

In response, Carolyn felt herself grow warm.

"But," he continued, "I must think on this last, for my mind is crowded on it. When I made this condition, there were reasons for it. Some of those reasons no longer exist. I will ponder it, and when I reach a decision, I will tell you."

"All right," said Carolyn, and having no other choice in the matter, at least not at this moment, she let the subject drop.

By that evening, Carolyn had reached her own conclusion. She was going to plant the cross upon Lone Arrow's person. She simply had no choice.

He had still not given her his determination, and she could not wait a moment longer. Especially when there was every possibility that they would reach the cave on the morrow.

But where to put it? Where could she plant it, so that she would be assured that, even if she were naked, the cross would be carried into the cave? It would have to be a place out of view, so that Lone Arrow would not realize that he had the thing upon him.

She studied him. She could not very well tie it to his shirt. He would find it. Neither could she attach it to his robe.

Watching him from across their campfire, she tried to envision him as he might dress for this occasion. What did he always wear?

Moccasins, leggings, breechcloth, shirt and robe. Feathers, hair ornaments. Could she tie it to one of those—perhaps in back of his head?

No, when he went to sleep he removed these things. He might find it.

Then where? What else did he always have upon his person?

A knife, his bow, his lance, his quiver and bow case. His quiver? . . .

It was perfect. What could be simpler? She would not even have to worry about attaching it. She could simply drop it into the case.

It was wonderful.

Tonight, she would wait until he was asleep.

In the end, her worry had been for nothing. Lone Arrow had decided that he trusted her . . . she remained clothed.

It was good. It was an affirmation of his faith in her;

yet she could not help but feel annoyed. All that wasted effort, and *he* had the cross, not she.

At present, she rode her pony, while Lone Arrow led it, plus his own mount.

And though the sun beat down its rays upon the top of her head, it was not enough to warm her. It did, however, serve to remind her that she and Lone Arrow were traveling in the light of day. While a seemingly mild observation, it was significant.

It meant that they must have entered into an area where Lone Arrow felt secure against the threat of a war party. Plus, due to the lack of shade, Carolyn was able to discern that they were traveling at a very high altitude, above the tree line. It was either that, or they were in a very large meadow.

Earlier this morning, before the sun had yet made its way into the sky, Lone Arrow had tied a piece of soft deerskin over her eyes. And though she had thought she might protest its presence upon her, he had left her hands entirely free.

In such a way, he had made it known to her that she was on her honor. And she swore she would not disappoint him.

Soon after covering her eyes, he had lifted her upon her pony, and they had left camp.

So far, the way had been uphill, stony and steep. That is, it must have been uphill if the movement and the position of the pony beneath her was any indication. Plus, she could feel her pony picking its way carefully.

She called out to Lone Arrow, "Are we almost there?"

"Soon," he replied. "Soon."

Carolyn bit her lip in consternation. She had been

asking the same question throughout most of the morning, and had been receiving the same reply in return. Meanwhile, frigid, cold air kept blasting her, whisking her hair back from her face, and seeming to find its way into every pore of her skin.

Finally, Lone Arrow stopped. Carolyn waited.

She sensed that he had come to stand before her. Not because she had heard him move, and she certainly could not see him. No, it was more a matter of simply knowing he was there.

He said, reaching up to take the deerskin blindfold from her eyes, "I have brought you to a sacred place, that you might see it, and that I might pray. This I would do before we go to the cave."

As soon as he removed the blindfold, she blinked her eyes rapidly, bringing up a hand to shield her sight from the bright rays of the sun. Where were they?

Gazing around her, she was awestruck, not only by the beauty of the place but by Lone Arrow's words as well.

She asked, "This is a sacred place?"

"*Éeh,*" he nodded. "It is a very sacred place. My people call this place the Medicine Wheel." Lone Arrow had turned to her pony, was taking out a small bag from his belongings.

And Carolyn watched. However, after a short time, she said, "I have been here before."

That statement appeared to surprise him. "You have?"

"Yes," she replied. "Eight and a half years ago. I stumbled upon these stones."

"*It-chik,* good," he said. "Did you pray?"

She shook her head. "I did not know this was a holy place."

"Ho," he said. "It is good that I have brought you here, then, for now you can pray."

Carolyn nodded. But she wondered, should she tell him the rest of what had taken place here? Would he think her demented?

One deep breath for courage, and she said, "It is here that I discovered the whirlwind."

For some reason this statement stopped Lone Arrow in his tracks.

Turning to her, he asked, "A whirlwind?"

"Yes," she said. "It came to me after I had fallen over one of these stones. The odd thing was that the whirlwind acted like a living creature. In truth, it brought me to you."

"To me?"

Carolyn nodded. "I had asked it to lead me to Fort C.F. Smith, and after several attempts at trying to get me to follow it, it brought me to you."

For the space of a moment, Lone Arrow stared at her, his mouth open and disbelief clearly etched upon his face.

However, shrugging, and extending a hand out to her, he did no more than say, "Come, let me show you the wheel. There are legends connected with this place."

"There are?"

He nodded. "Many. Would you like to hear them?"

Carolyn bobbed her head, and placing her hand into his, they took a few paces toward the stones.

"Here," he said, indicating a place on the ground. "Sit here, next to me, and I will tell you my story."

Carolyn sat.

"It is said," Lone Arrow began, "by some of my people that this is the place where the sun comes to visit and to camp. Some say that these stones are evidence of the sun's camp. Others claim that the wheel was made by Burnt Face, a man of some legend amongst my people. But whether it is the sun or Burnt Face, many of my people come here to fast and to say prayers. It is here where a person can best commune with the One Above."

As the wind whisked into her face, Carolyn felt a shudder, which could be part awe, part fear, run through her body. Trembling, she placed her hand within Lone Arrow's own.

He continued, "Do you see that there is a large circle here?"

She nodded.

"And do you see that there are spokes, like those in a wheel, leading from the center to the outer circle?"

Again she nodded.

"Some say," continued Lone Arrow, gesturing toward the circle, "that this was once a gigantic tepee that was built by Burnt Face. Now, as I said, Burnt Face is a legend amongst my people. He was a man who accomplished many great things, even though his face was scarred when he was a child, and he was made the object of some ridicule.

"Now, there are many," he continued, "who tell of the eagle who took pity upon Burnt Face here, in this very spot. And do you know how it first appeared to him?"

Carolyn shook her head.

"It came to him first as a whirlwind."

"A whirlwind? Here?"

Lone Arrow nodded. "There is more. Did you know that eight and one half years ago, as I lay upon a nearby mountain, I was having a vision of the whirlwind?"

Again Carolyn shook her head.

"It has been my helper all through my life," he said.

"And it assisted me, too," said Carolyn.

Once more, Lone Arrow treated her to a searching glance. He said, "And now I will tell you another story. One that you may have wondered about . . . the story of the cave."

"The cave?"

He nodded. "Have you not puzzled over the riches that you saw there? Where did they come from? Who put them there and why?"

"Yes," said Carolyn, "but I was afraid to ask."

"As you should be. Now," he said, "this is the story that was told to me by my father, and his father before him, as was passed down from grandfather to grandfather. It is a story that is sacred to my family, and it is one that is repeated save only to those who are to become the protector of the cave."

"And you are telling me?"

He nodded. "I have reason," he said, "to believe that this is the right thing to do."

Carolyn gulped.

"Long ago," Lone Arrow began, "before the world was as we know it, there lived a different people here upon this earth. Some were giants. Some were little people, no taller than my knee. The little people still live here, in caves and in the underground. Sometimes you can see them in the mountain range that the white man calls the Pryor Mountains.

"Now, these people, though small, are yet very strong. They have been seen carrying a full-grown antelope upon their backs."

"Huh."

"*Éeh,* but I leave my story. The little people and the

336   KAREN KAY

giants went often to war. You have seen the evidence of
this in their stone arrowheads which can still be found
upon this land. Now, while the little people lived in
caves, the giants built strong forts. Here they kept many
beautiful things that they made from gold. But gold is
not always an easy thing to find, and in order to obtain
the gold they needed, the giants disturbed the dwellings
of the little people.

"Thus," he went on to say, "the giants and the little
people went to war. Now, in this war, the giants, though
a larger people, kept losing. One day, they knew that all
they had would be lost. In an effort to save their king-
dom, they gathered their things together and hid them
in the cave, which you saw eight and a half years ago."

"Then the gold belongs to the giants?"

He nodded. "As they predicted," continued Lone Arrow with the story, "the little people overwhelmed the
giants and killed them to a man. And so great was the
loss, that you do not see nor find the remains of these
giants, even to this day.

"Now as the legend goes, before the last giant was
killed, as revenge to the little people, he placed a curse
over the treasure, so that misfortune would befall anyone who dared to take something that was not his own.
And so it is that many times have the little people found
that cave; many times have they taken something; many
is also the time they have suffered for doing it."

As she had, thought Carolyn.

"But there was someone else here, though not of
physical form. Someone else who watched what was
happening. Someone who guarded the mountain and
all within it, be they little people or large. My people
call him the mountain god. And this being, seeing his
children suffer, called upon my people to help.

"Now, the message went out throughout the land," Lone Arrow continued. "There would be tests. Tests of skill, tests of honor and of endurance. The god of the mountain called upon all the valiant warriors of my tribe to participate in these trials. Many took part, but in the end, only one was chosen to become the protector of the treasure and of the sacred mountain. That person was my ancestor. And so it began. It has never stopped. The responsibility for the cave and for the mountain has been handed down father to son in every generation. It is now mine to assume."

He paused, and Carolyn sat in silence, not knowing what to say, what to do.

"There is more," he said. "The spiritual helper for all those in my family who are chosen is always the whirl-wind. As it has been my father's helper, it is now mine . . . and yours . . ."

"Mine?"

He nodded. "It is perhaps fitting, for I have always felt a special connection to you. Even before we were married, before you returned to this, your home, you were a part of me. And now, it is clear to me why this has been."

And Carolyn, gazing up at him, asked, "Why?"

"Do you truly not know?"

Although she suspected what was to come, she shook her head.

And he explained, "You are as much a protector of that cave as I am. It is now your responsibility, too. You share it with me. Come," said Lone Arrow, taking her hand in his. "My people journey here to pray. Before we go to the cave, let us say our prayers."

Coming up onto his feet, Lone Arrow looked upon her with open admiration. After a few moments, he reached out a hand toward her, where he twirled his fingers into her chestnut-colored curls. He said, "You are so beautiful. It is a good thing that I have brought you here, for it has caused us to become even closer. We will pray, each in our own way, I think."

Carolyn nodded and bowed her head, while Lone Arrow produced the bag he had taken from the horse. In it was an herb.

She asked, "What is that?"

Lone Arrow looked at his hand. "This is a plant the white man calls sage. I am offering it to the four directions, to the four winds and to the One Above."

Carolyn nodded, and quietly, with the wind whipping around them, they prayed, and as Lone Arrow had suggested, each in their own way.

Chapter 26

Both Carolyn and Lone Arrow were quiet as they left the site of the Medicine Wheel, each lost in thought.

It was true, Carolyn had felt closer to her Maker at that spot, but she had also been disturbed. Whatever the cause of such uneasiness, however, she could not guess.

She did sense that it was as though the spirit who lived here was agitated about something. But what?

Was it her? Should she not have gone there? Had she committed some faux pas by praying there, when she was white, not Indian?

As she and Lone Arrow had descended the mountaintop, Lone Arrow had taken pause to ceremoniously give her the soft deerskin, which had covered her eyes. It was no longer needed, he said.

Wasn't it? If it were not truly needed, then why did she feel that the spirit that lived there was angry? And possibly at her? She had, after all, taken something from that cave.

Glancing back the way they had come, Carolyn searched out that high spot in the mountains, wondering if she could still see the circle from here. Perhaps wondering, too, if the whirlwind might not make itself known to her once again. For a moment, she was unaware of her surroundings.

She felt a jerk on her buckskin reins, followed by the sound of sliding rocks nearby. Another jerk, another pull, then the horrible din of rocks crashing together.

Spinning around in her seat, she called out, "Lone Arrow."

No answer.

Dear Lord, what was happening? She did not see him. His pony, yes, but where was he?

Carolyn stared around her.

She and her horse, as well as A-la-pee, were situated on a narrow ridge. Dismounting, Carolyn dropped to her feet and peeked over the ledge.

She gasped. There was nothing below her but a steep drop.

Pure panic filled her soul. Had he fallen down there?

"Lone Arrow?" she called, paying no attention to the fact that if there might be danger of landslide, one should speak softly. In truth, she could barely think.

"Lone Arrow?" she cried once again.

What might have first been panic became horror. *Dear God*, she prayed, *please let him be alive.*

What had happened? Just a few moments before, he had been leading their horses. Carolyn had to think. She'd seen nothing, of course; she had been gazing off in the opposite direction. But she had felt the pull on the reins, heard the crash of rocks.

He must have slipped.

Lone Arrow slip? How could that be? He knew these mountains better than anyone else.

But he now carried the cross upon his person.

Groaning Carolyn sat back upon her haunches. How could she have done it? So involved had she been in the story he had weaved around her, she had forgotten to tell him about the cross. And especially that she had planted it on him.

The fault was hers. Hers.

Stunned, Carolyn froze. Why, oh why, she admonished herself, had she not told Lone Arrow about the cross?

Please let him be alive.

Situating herself on her stomach, she once more peered over the ledge. He had to be alive; he just had to be.

But she could see very little, and the wind kept whipping her hair into her eyes. Reaching up, she tried to push that hair behind her ears, but it was useless.

She had to do something. But what? There was no hero here to save the day. There was no one here but her.

What could she do?

She glanced up toward his horse. Was there a rope upon A-la-pee? One that she might be able to use to climb down the face of this mountain?

That was when she saw it.

The whirlwind.

Grass and rocks scattered as it came twisting toward her. On it came, closer and closer, until Carolyn felt certain it might encompass her. But it did not.

Skirting around her, it slid down the mountainside. And following its progress with her gaze, Carolyn came down full length upon the ridge, peeking over the edge to sneak a look below her.

The thing had alit onto another rocky edge of the mountain, one that might have been wide enough to break the fall of a man.

Hope sprang up within her. Carolyn had not seen that projection.

There the thing stopped, and beside it was . . . what? The figure of . . . a man?

Was it Lone Arrow? Was he alive?

Quickly but steadily Carolyn stood, and with care, she edged her way toward A-la-pee. Did the pony have a rope tied to her?

No, only the buckskin reins.

Glancing around her, Carolyn despaired. She had nothing, nothing that would get her to him, if it was him.

Could she climb down there? Peering over the ledge, once more on hands and knees, Carolyn thought she might attempt it, but when her first footfall caused a minor landslide, she knew she would have to find another way.

Glancing down, she called, "Lone Arrow, is it you down there? Can you hear me?"

No answer.

"Oh, please wake up."

Oddly enough the whirlwind twisted around the body there, as though it protected it.

And she said, "Are you the god who lives in the mountain? The same god who protects this place?"

No answer came from it.

"If you are that god, I know that you mean no harm.

You once saved me by leading me to Lone Arrow. I am now going to do the same for him, for I think it is Lone Arrow down there on that ledge. But I have to leave here to get a rope."

She started to rise, thought better of it, and sprawled back out onto the ledge. Glancing over the rocks, she addressed the whirlwind once more, saying, "If that is Lone Arrow, he has the cross upon his person. But he does not know it. I placed it there last night. I meant no harm. I only did it to ensure that the cross was returned to the cave. Please understand," she cried, when she detected no change, "I am here not to take anything else from the cave, but to return that which I stole from it a little over eight years ago."

Still, no answer came to her, nor did the whirlwind turn into an eagle like it had in the story of Burnt Face. But it did do another thing.

It centered itself upon the body there, darting from head to feet. And as Carolyn watched, it repeated the maneuver, this time shooting from feet back to head.

And in the next instant, the person awoke. Bringing a hand to his head, he tried to sit up. It *was* Lone Arrow.

"Don't move!" Carolyn sobbed, calling down to him from the ledge. "You fell and are on a very thin ridge on the mountain."

Dazedly, Lone Arrow glanced up at her. "What happened?"

"I don't know," she said. "I only heard the crashing of rocks, and then I couldn't find you."

Lone Arrow nodded. "I remember."

"If not for the whirlwind, I would still not know what had happened."

"Whirlwind?"

"Look to your right."

Lone Arrow did, but it was of no use. The thing had vanished.

"It was there. I saw it. It found you and brought you back to life."

Lone Arrow took this knowledge in stride, acknowledging her with a nod. He said, "I think I can climb out of here."

"No, do not try it," said Carolyn. "Lone Arrow, I should have told you before now, and I am sorry that I could not muster up courage enough to say it sooner."

Looking up at her, he asked, "What?"

"The thing that I took . . ."

Lone Arrow remained silent.

"That thing that I told you was of no value . . . remember?"

Again Lone Arrow did not speak.

"Well," she said, "it was a small, golden cross, and it has brought me and my family nothing but bad luck. Know that I have told the truth about my intentions. I have wanted to do nothing more than return the cross to where it belongs, but I have been afraid to tell you. Afraid that you might think badly of me or refuse me aid; afraid that you might insist on taking the cross from me; afraid that if I, and I alone, did not return the cross, that the curse could not be broken."

Staring up at her, Lone Arrow said, "I am glad that you have decided to tell me, but—"

"You now have the cross."

"I?"

"Well, I was afraid that you might make me go to the cave naked, after all, and then I would have had no hiding place for it. And so I hid it on you. It is in your quiver and bow case."

Quickly, Lone Arrow removed his quiver, and taking his arrows from it, reached down into it. Within moments, he brought out the cross, holding it up to her.

He said, "This one?"

"Yes," she said, "but put it back. Holding it can bring on the worst of luck."

"It will bring me no bad luck, now that I know I have it." He tried to stand to his feet, but no sooner had he put weight upon his feet, than he fell over. Rocks scattered everywhere.

"Lone Arrow?" She practically screamed his name.

"I am here."

Carolyn breathed out heavily.

He said, "I think that I have broken my foot. You are going to have to go and get a rope and pull me up."

"A rope? Where will I find a rope? There is none on your pony or mine. And I am afraid that we are alone, completely alone."

"Then you are going to have to retrace your steps and find Pretty Moon and Big Elk. They will know what to do."

Carolyn cried. "I don't want to leave you."

"You must. And you must go as quickly as you can."

Why? she wondered. Why did they have to be here alone? She was no master trail woman. She could barely find her way on a well-traveled path, let alone within the wilderness. A wilderness filled with bears, wolves and mountain lions.

She said, more to herself, "I am no trailblazer."

"You do not have to be," said Lone Arrow. "Call upon your helper, the whirlwind. It will come to you, and it will lead you to a place where there is help."

"But—"

"Do not fear. Be strong of heart, for it will come to

you. Follow it," he urged again. "And hurry."

"Yes," said Carolyn. "Do you have weapons so that you can defend yourself?"

"I have my bow and arrows, and my knife. My shotgun is gone. These are enough. Now go!"

Getting to her feet as quickly, yet as carefully as possible, Carolyn edged her way back toward solid ground.

As Lone Arrow had predicted, her helper, the whirlwind, came to her. Urging her to follow, it led her through the high mountain forest. Strangely, while watching the thing, there were moments when Carolyn caught an odd glimpse of it. And in those moments, she could have sworn that she espied a big, black bear.

But, at these times, she would rub her eyes, and the image would quickly fade.

Carolyn rode A-la-pee instead of her own mount. A-la-pee, it seemed, was aware of the danger to her master, and she, too, hurried to help him.

Besides, Lone Arrow had often boasted as to the intelligence of the animal. And Carolyn needed all the assistance she could get.

Meanwhile, they followed the trail of the whirlwind.

Never again, she thought, would she doubt that there was a being who lived in and protected this mountain. Never again would she fear a spirit, for without this one to guide her, she would be lost.

It was early evening when she spotted the fire. Sighing with relief, and dismounting, she approached the camp steadily, not bothering to hide her advance. If what she knew about Big Elk were true, he probably already sensed her presence.

Anticipation at the pleasure of seeing Pretty Moon

had Carolyn stumbling, when she should have been watching where she was going.

"Who goes there?"

The words had been in English.

Startled, Carolyn paused. And in her confusion, a shot rang out in front of her, barely missing her.

"Don't shoot," she shouted, placing her hands over her ears. "I'm unarmed."

"A woman? Here?" The words had been said by another voice—those words in English, too.

Where had the whirlwind led her?

"Please don't shoot," she said, "I need your help." And with this said, she stepped into the camp of two men whose appearance brought to mind that of two mangy grizzlies. With fur coats, beards and long hair, they looked more animal than human.

"Ah wouldna belief it iffn I hadn't seen it with me own eyes. Looky, Dixon, it's a woman."

"Ah can see that fer myself. What's ja doin' here in these parts, ma'am?"

Carolyn paused to catch her breath. "My . . . my husband and I have been traveling in these mountains," she said, "and he has slipped and fallen onto a ledge. I need a rope so I can pull him up. Do you have one?"

"We have a rope, little lady, but yer goin' to be needin' our help."

Carolyn gave the men a weak sort of smile. "I'd be beholden to you if you would help me. Please," she said, "there's not much time left before nightfall."

"Now, see here, ma'am," said the big, darker one of the two men. "We've been trackin' from one holler to tother and we're plumb tuckered out. Sit yerself down a spell and have some supper. We'll git to it soon enough—tomorrow."

Carolyn sighed. Why, oh why had the guardian spirit led her here. If it had been Big Elk and Pretty Moon, they would already be on their way.

She said, "You don't understand. The situation is desperate, and we need to leave now. Please, if you would just lend me your rope, I'll be on my way."

"Dixon," said the smaller of the two gents, "why don't we help the little lady?"

"Because ah'm tired, that's why."

"Do you have a rope that I might borrow?" Carolyn asked.

"Borrow?" asked the big, dark man. "Borrow? More'n likely steal it. Naw, ah ain't given yourn no rope."

Well, there was nothing else to do. Clearing her throat, Carolyn said, "I have a gold cross I could give you if you will come with me yet this night."

"A gold what?"

The bigger of the two men was already on his feet.

"A gold cross."

He said, "Let's see it."

"I don't have it here. It is upon my husband's person. But I promise that as soon as he is rescued, we can give it to you."

The big man rubbed his chin. "Now, how big would ya say this cross is?"

Carolyn held up her fingers, exaggerating the cross's height by perhaps an inch or two . . . maybe three.

"That big is it? And how fer away is it that he fell?"

"No more than a few hours." Shifting her weight from one foot to the other, Carolyn anxiously awaited their answer.

However, even she was not ready when, without

warning, the big man jumped to his feet and shuffled dirt into their fire.

"Now, why didn't ja say so in the first place? But I'll be warnin' ya. Iffn thar ain't no cross, we'll be obliged to have ta kill ya."

Carolyn did not answer. There was no point. She merely nodded.

Turning around, she quickly jumped onto A-la-pee, and away they went, back the same way she had come.

"Is that Injun thar yourn's husband, ma'am?" asked the tall man, waving a torch down the steep incline.

"He is," replied Carolyn, "and he has the cross upon him."

"Injun," called out the skinnier, shorter of the two men. "We're a goin' ta need ta see that cross afore we git ja up here all nice like. Yourn had best throw it up here."

"Are ya loony?" the bigger man asked, taking a swat at the shorter one. "What if he misses?"

"Wait!" said Carolyn. "Why not have him show you the cross? That way you'll at least be able to see that I'm telling you the truth."

"Good idee there, ma'am. Did ja hear that, Injun?"

However, Lone Arrow was not being very cooperative. Crossing his arms over his chest, he asked, "Why should I?"

It was Carolyn who answered, Carolyn who said, "Because I have promised these men that they may have it, if they will only help you up."

"And have they eyes with which to see it in the dark?" came Lone Arrow's cocky reply.

"Now don't go being smart, Injun. Jest hold it up."

With great ceremony, Lone Arrow complied.

As the two men once more swung the torch down the cliff's incline, Carolyn watched their eyes alight with greed.

Barely daring to breathe, she said, "It is solid gold, and very old."

"Jest what we need," said the bigger man, the one who more closely resembled a bear.

But Lone Arrow practically ruined the rescue when he called up to them, "This cross, though it is well made, and as my wife has said, is solid gold, is cursed. You should know this."

The bigger man laughed. "Oh, ah'm so afraid. Does ya belief in curses, Jordie?"

"Naw," said the skinnier fellow, though he appeared slightly anxious. "Does you?"

The bigger man did not answer. Instead, he said, "Ah think it's time we hauled this Injun up here with us folks. We'll do it real easy like."

No sooner had the words been spoken, than he produced a rope. One end was tied to his horse's saddle, the other was thrown down to Lone Arrow.

"Grab hold, Injun, and we'll bear ya up."

But the big, reddish horse would not move, and no amount of cursing at the animal did any good.

Finally, Carolyn could stand it no longer, and she said, grabbing the reins out of the shorter man's hands, "Here, A-la-pee." She placed the reins within A-la-pee's teeth. "You know what to do, don't you, girl? You need to lead this other horse. He's pulling Lone Arrow up from that ledge down there. You can do that, can't you, girl?"

A-la-pee whinnied, bobbing her head up and down. And she did exactly as she had been bade.

The sorrel followed her without question, and Carolyn held her breath as steadily, inch by very slow inch, Lone Arrow was hauled up toward them. Finally, he was close enough that the two men were able to pull him up onto the ledge.

First she could see his head, then his torso, then his legs. Finally, gaining purchase on the ledge himself, he rolled to safety. Meanwhile Carolyn, bending down, threw her arms around him.

But Lone Arrow had other things on his mind, and sitting up, he held the cross out to the two white men, saying, "Here is the cross that you were promised. Know, that if you take it, you will be cursed, for that which belongs to the mountain god must remain with the mountain god."

The big, dark man yanked the cross out of Lone Arrow's hands. "We ain't superstitious, Injun."

"Naw," said the skinnier gentleman. "Thank ya, ma'am, but we'll be goin' on our way now."

"But it's dark and—"

"Ah don't know if we'll be goin' right away, Jordan," said the darker of the two men. "Ah've an idee tha' this here woman'd make a fine widder."

"Naw, Dixon," said the smaller gent. "We's helped the lady, let's git."

"He's only an Injun. Wouldna make a difference iffn we was ta take a little more. Besides, it'd be easy. He's plumb broke his foot."

Carolyn gasped. Had Lone Arrow retained his weapons? Were they in a position where he could use them?

But she needn't have worried.

With a grin, Lone Arrow said, "I think this here Injun might have a thing or two to say about it." And with a whistle, A-la-pee came running toward him.

"*A-wa-ssaa-hii*!" he called, whereupon A-la-pee began to rear. Up and down, twice. One of the men fell to the ground beneath her.

"No!" cried the man.

"Call her off! We'll leave!"

Another whistle from Lone Arrow, and A-la-pee stood still.

That, however, was all the two men appeared to need. Without another word, or so much as a backward glance, they stumbled toward firmer ground, running away so quickly, they might have resembled two scared jackrabbits.

Lone Arrow laughed, and coming up onto his knees, he brought A-la-pee's head down to him. "Good girl," he said, as he breathed into her nose. "Good girl."

But Carolyn was not quite so demure and she stared after the men until they were no more than mere specks. After a moment, she said, "Thank goodness they've gone. Let's get off this ledge and make camp. Then I had better see to your injury."

"*Éeh*," said Lone Arrow, "we will, but before we do that, there is something that you should see."

"Oh?" she asked. "What is that?"

Digging into his quiver, Lone Arrow produced a handful of gold coins.

"Wh-what? Where did you get these?"

Lone Arrow grinned at her. "On the rocks below us. There was a sign there like this." Picking up a stick, he scratched into the dirt<<<<<<>>>>>. He said, "I became curious and began digging, and I found the white man's gold. There is more there, but I thought this might be enough for you."

"For me?" she asked. "You mean for my family?"

He nodded. "Did you not say that they need the white man's riches?"

Flipping one coin after another through her palm, she said, "I think this will be more than enough. But is it safe? Is it cursed?"

"It is not part of the treasure from the sacred cave," he said. "I have no knowledge where this came from, only that, while you were gone, it was shown to me by the god who lives in the mountain."

"Then I could keep it?"

"I think there is no one else who could find better use for it."

While Carolyn laughed. "My goodness," she said. "Who would have thought that *I* could have good luck? You know what? I think the miners are right. This Montana Territory certainly is a 'treasure state.' In more ways than one."

And sitting precariously upon the mountain's rocky projection, the two lovers embraced.

Chapter 27

❧❦

Carolyn relaxed down into the sudsy warmth of the perfumed bath, lost in thought.

She smiled. Alas, she had many things to smile about.

Things had gone well for her in Virginia City. Not only had the gold paid her parents' debt, there had been enough left over so that her mother and father could make a fresh start. But best of all, her father had miraculously healed while she had been gone. He still limped, but he could certainly walk.

The only problem had been that Lone Arrow had not accompanied her back there. Instead, he had escorted her to Fort Ellis, telling her that when the time was good, she would return to him.

He had given her a horse, saying, "It is for your parents."

"But," she countered, "I already have the gold."

"A white man's gift," he said. "This pony is a red

man's gift. It is said by our wise men, that when a man gives a horse for a woman, that marriage has great promise. I think it could be true."

Carolyn had smiled, and had accepted the offering.

Even her parents had been joyous with the endowment, and although they had at first been upset with her decision to return to Fort Ellis, they had eventually yielded to her. It had been Carolyn's own happiness that had been the deciding factor.

"But you must come and visit from time to time," her mother had coaxed.

"Of course I will," Carolyn had told her in return. "I will even bring Lone Arrow, if he will come."

"You do that," her mother had said.

"It's not good-bye," said Carolyn. "I promise you that."

And embracing, both mother and daughter had cried.

But Carolyn's tears were those of joy. How could she feel anything else but happiness? For within only a few days she had returned to Fort Ellis, here to await her husband. And it was here that she would remain. She and Lone Arrow would make their lives beneath the shadow and within the protection of the Bighorn Mountains.

After all, the sacred treasure cave was now as much her responsibility as it was Lone Arrow's. An obligation she would cherish so long as she existed.

She raised up an arm, to wash it, and as she did so, a breeze stirred the hairs on her delicate skin.

At last, she thought, and inwardly she smiled. Outwardly, however, Carolyn pretended that she hadn't felt so much as a stirring of a single hair.

Indeed, she proceeded with her bath, humming. First

she washed one arm, then the other. One leg raised, then the other.

And it was not long before she heard the words, "I think that my wife teases me."

Grinning, Carolyn swung her head around until she was able to cast her gaze upon Lone Arrow. She sighed contentedly. Never, had she seen a more wonderful sight. And the only thing she could think to say was, "What took you so long to get here?"

She heard his chuckle, watched as he approached her, watched as he knelt next to her.

"I had things to attend to."

"Did you?" she asked.

"I did," he replied. "First I had to check the infirmary to see if there were any soldiers who had fallen or had some mishap while helping you."

"And were there?"

"There were none," he stated. "Nor have there been reports of unusual accidents."

She grinned. "Not a one."

He sighed. "Then it is my belief that you are no longer cursed."

"I know," she said, with a slight giggle, while he raised a finger to her cheek, there to caress it gently.

She closed her eyes and moaned.

And then, without a word passing between them, she felt him place something around her neck.

Gazing down, she saw her necklace.

"Lone Arrow!"

"It is another present. Your friend did not at first understand why I needed to purchase it from her. But when I told her that this should remain with us because it is the emblem of the first vow between us, she gave it to me gladly."

"Oh, Lone Arrow. I—I—"

"There is more," he said. Bending, he extracted something from a parfleche bag, and standing up, held a dress out for her inspection. It was a very beautiful dress, too. He said, "It is an elk-tooth dress. It is a special kind of garment, and highly prized amongst my people. When one's family gives a bride this gift, it is their way of saying that she is welcome to their family and to their clan. They would have you know that they are happy for me, for you, and that you are now a part of us. They welcome you."

"Oh, Lone Arrow. It . . . it's perfect. I . . . thank you. Please you will tell them thank you for me."

Coming down onto his knees beside the tub, he said, "Soon we will be at my home, and you can tell them yourself."

Carolyn grinned. "Yes, I will. Now, come, help me out of here," she said.

"It will be my pleasure."

She placed her water-wrinkled hand in his own. And, seeing his questioning look, she said, "Remember, when I left here a few short weeks ago, I told you that I would wait for you to find me, just as I once had?"

He nodded.

"Well," she said, "I think I am water soaked. I have been waiting for you in this tub for hours."

He chuckled, and lifting her out of the water, he took her into his arms. "Look at these little fingers," he murmured, taking each one into his hands. "You are right. They are much too waterlogged, I fear. But do not fret, for I have many ways of making them, making you, feel better."

"Do you?"

Bending his head toward her, coming ever closer and closer, he said, "I promise."

And in truth, it is said that Lone Arrow was a man who kept every one of his pledges.

Epilogue

Two men, one big and dark, the other small and scrawny, hurried away from the Bighorn Mountains. But it was not easy.

Not only wind and weather, but time itself seemed to be against them.

No sooner had Dixon fallen down into a large gopher hole, requiring rescue, than Jordan stepped the wrong way and had twisted his ankle.

"Ah'm beginning to believe that Injun, Dixon," said the smaller man.

"Now that sounds jest like you. Ya don't know what yer sayin'. Ain't no such thing as curses."

Perhaps not, yet neither man could deny that a whirlwind chased them. In truth it never seemed to falter in its unfailing pursuit of them.

But perhaps all these things were the price one pays for glory and riches.

At least, in this one case, it would appear that it was so.

Note to the Reader

I thought it might be interesting to share with you some of the inspiration for this story, since it is considerable. What I am about to tell you, by the way, is a true tale, or perhaps we should call it a legend.

In Arizona, there is a mountain range called the Superstitious Mountains, just outside of Phoenix. Some of you might be familiar with the legend of the Lost Dutchman's gold mine. Some may not. Bear with me.

There are many, many miners who go into the Superstitious Mountains today, hunting for the Lost Dutchman gold mine. Many years ago stones were found, upon which was written some hieroglyphics, thought to be part of a map. Many of these stones were discovered all over the Superstitious Mountains and all of them were thought to be part of a map that would lead others to the Lost Dutchman's gold mine. Today, those stones are on display in a bank where all can see them and try to discern where the gold mine is.

What is not generally known is that many hundreds of years previous, there were Jesuit priests in these mountains. They befriended the Indians and managed to get the Indians to bring them gold from these mountains, whereupon the Jesuit priests made artifacts out of the gold. Many, many artifacts.

These priests were recalled to Spain. Most of them refused to go and so Spain sent an army into the Southwest to drive the priests home. The priests got word of the oncoming army and, deciding not to let the army get their gold, nor take the gold back to Spain where it would most likely be claimed by the king, they hid their treasure. It is the Jesuit priests who etched the map on the stones in hieroglyphics and left these stones in fairly inconspicuous places, thinking to come back and collect the gold at a later date.

Recently miners have found, after using the stones on display, and digging about twenty-two feet deep in these mountains, two crosses with more hieroglyphics on them.

To date, neither the Lost Dutchman's mine, nor the stash of gold from the Jesuit priests has been found. Added to this is the fact that the Indians believed that the Thunder God lived in the Superstitious Mountains and in fact, up until the late nineteenth century, no one was able to go into the mountains and mine the gold without great risk to their lives. Any white person found in the mountains was at once killed.

Another interesting fact is that earlier on, two brothers got word of the mines in those mountains and were mining one that they had found. They made two successful trips into the mountains and obtained a great deal of gold. On the third trip they were discovered by the Indians. And so the brothers loaded up all of their gold and put it into bags, which they tied onto their mules.

Of course, these two brothers were found and killed by the Indians, but the mules were let go, still carrying the bags of gold. The last bag of gold to be found was in the 1920s or 30s (I forget which), and contained gold to the amount of approximately $12,000 at that time—today the find would have been close to half a million dollars.

So the question is: Has anyone ever found the Lost Dutchman's Mine? Not to my knowledge.

Has anyone discovered the gold that was hidden by the Jesuit priests? Not that we know of. But I would have to ask you this question. If you were there and you found it, would you tell anyone?

Glossary

Some of the words and ideas in this book need further explanation. Hopefully this glossary will help to improve your understanding.

Absarokee—this is the name by which the Crow call themselves. The name actually means "Children of the Long Beaked Bird."

Clan—a division of society that believes it is descended from a common ancestry. The word for clan in the Crow language means, literally, Driftwood Lodges. For the Crow, a child belongs to his mother's clan. From his father's clan comes the "joking" relative. By using jokes, this relative is supposed to make a person better by making him think.

Dreams/visions—for the Crow Indians, this was the way in which one communicated with the One Above. It was also used by some to try to foresee the future.

Helper—given in a vision, a helper was usually an animal, which would help and protect the person all through his life.

Medicine Wheel—located high on a mountaintop in the Bighorn Mountains, about 10,000 feet above sea level, this is a wheel of stones. It is thousands of years old. The place where it is situated is a place of great beauty. But if you go there, be advised that there are high winds. While no one knows the origin of the wheel, there are many legends about it. Two of them, I told in my story. An interesting thing is that this summer, my husband and I visited the Medicine Wheel. And I must confess that it was a spiritual experience.

River and Mountain Crow—these are two main divisions of the Crow tribe. An interesting point is that it was the River Crow who scouted for the U.S. Army with Custer. The Mountain Crow never did. They remained neutral.

Societies—all Indian tribes that I have studied have societies. Some were secret. But all men in the tribe belonged to a society. Some of these societies were mystic. Each had their own special dances, as well as individual kinds of clothing, which were often worn for special occasions. Some societies were rivals, like the Lumpwoods and the Foxes in the Crow tribe.

War Lodge—in the northwest war lodges were built much as I have described them in this story. War lodges operated as strategic outposts, allowing the war party to assemble in order to make food—like the women did in this story—to sleep, or to use the lodge as a place of defense if the need arose.